A Time to Gather

A Time to Gather

A Safe Harbor Novel

SALLY JOHN WITH
GARY SMALLEY

THOMAS NELSON
Since 1798

NASHVILLE   DALLAS   MEXICO CITY   RIO DE JANEIRO

Published in Nashville, Tennessee, by Thomas Nelson. Thomas Nelson is a registered trademark of Thomas Nelson, Inc.

Published in association with the literary agency of Alive Communications, Inc., 7680 Goddard Street, Suite 200, Colorado Springs, CO 80920.

Thomas Nelson, Inc., books may be purchased in bulk for educational, business, fund-raising, or sales promotional use. For information, please e-mail SpecialMarkets@ThomasNelson.com.

Scripture taken from the HOLY BIBLE, NEW INTERNATIONAL VERSION®. © 1973, 1978, 1984 by International Bible Society. Used by permission of Zondervan Publishing House. All rights reserved.

Publisher's Note: This novel is a work of fiction. Names, characters, places, and incidents are either products of the author's imagination or used fictitiously. All characters are fictional, and any similarity to people living or dead is purely coincidental.

Library of Congress Cataloging-in-Publication Data

John, Sally, 1951–
 A time to gather / Sally John and Gary Smalley.
  p. cm. — (Safe harbors ; bk. 2)
 ISBN 978-1-59554-429-2 (pbk.)
 I. Smalley, Gary. II. Title.
 PS3560.O323T55 2008
 813'.54—dc22

2008022898

Printed in the United States of America

10 11 12 13 14 EPAC 13 12 11 10 9 8

For my neighbors on Aguamiel Road

"A man reaps what he sows."

—Galatians 6:7

The Beaumont family

Max—Married to Claire. Founder and owner of Beaumont Staffing, a nationwide staffing firm.

Claire—Married to Max. Volunteer for community organizations and violinist.

Ben and Indio—Max's parents. Their grandchildren call them *Papa* and *Nana*. Their home, the Hacienda Hideaway, is a retreat center located in the hills above San Diego, California.

Max and Claire's four grown children

Erik—News anchor for a local San Diego television station.

Jenna—High school English teacher. Married to Kevin Mason.

Danny—Lexi's twin. Software guru and surfer.

Lexi (Alexis)—Danny's twin. Gardener. Artist.

Others

Felicia Matthews—Erik's coanchor and girlfriend.

Rosie Delgado—San Diego police officer.

Bobby Grey—Rosie's partner.

One

Lexi Beaumont trotted as best she could along the narrow, uneven path, her camera bouncing against her hip. The guy ahead of her—that would be the one with the long legs sprinting gazelle-like over the rough terrain—set their pace. As usual, keeping up with Zak Emeterio was a challenge and a half.

Not that she was complaining. Hanging out with him was the major highlight of any week. Or month, for that matter. Her achy quads over the next few days would remind her of their time together.

Oh, stuff it. She sounded like a bubblehead. The moony teenager phase had to stop.

Her big toe slammed the edge of a half-buried rock. "Yow!"

Zak spun around and caught hold of her flailing arms. "You okay?"

"Yeah." She smiled through a wince. "But ouch! That hurt."

"I'll slow down."

"Don't you dare."

"Way to hang in there, Short Stuff."

Lexi groaned like a drama queen, although she didn't really mind his nickname. He'd dubbed her "Short Stuff" the night they met, his voice hushed and full of gratitude. *"You are amazing,"* he had said with a small smile, the whiteness of his teeth in stark contrast to his soot-covered face.

I can just imagine the headlines: Alexis Beaumont, aka Short Stuff, leads three big, highly trained, half-wit firefighters to safety.

Grinning now, Zak let go of her arms, tugged the brim of his cap, and took off again. "We're almost there!" he yelled over his shoulder.

Their destination lay in sight just a short distance below at the end of a steep descent to the lake. Lexi followed more slowly, placing her feet carefully on the packed dirt and embedded rock. She squinted against the sunlight, harsh in spite of her ball cap and shaded glasses, and took in the vista of the wilderness preserve through which they'd hiked.

Talk about amazing, she thought. There they were, within walking distance of densely populated San Diego communities as well as a freeway, and yet total wilderness surrounded them. No sign of human life marred a 360-degree view of rock-strewn mountains and a tranquil lake. March wildflowers, a few trees, and native bushes grew on the hillsides. Hawks and turkey vultures soared lazily above. Egrets stood serenely along the water's edge. Ducks and grebes paddled, squawking intermittently.

"Can you paint it?" Zak called to her.

She lifted her camera and shrugged. "It won't fit."

He laughed.

Painting wildlife was her favorite pastime. Well, second favorite, right after hanging out with Zak. She photographed subjects and worked from the prints. He didn't know the first thing about art and wasn't interested in it one bit. Sometimes, though, he connected the dots: *Lexi plus camera plus wildlife equals painting.* His efforts to enter her world zinged her every time—turned her to slush.

She stepped onto the outcropping where he sat. It was a fairly level stretch of rock that jutted out from the shore a few feet above the water, just large enough for the two of them. Adjusting the shoulder strap, she shifted the camera to her lap and sank cross-legged beside him.

"It's coming." He grinned like a kid in a toy store. "Hear it?"

"No."

"Listen. It's really faint."

She waited in silence. Try as she might, no way could she tune into anything beyond her own booming, erratic heartbeat. Its cause had little to do with the two-mile hike up and down a craggy, sun-drenched trail.

On the surface Zak Emeterio met, in her opinion, every classic requirement for eye candy: tall, sculpted muscles, strong jaw, wavy black hair, eyes the color of Wedgwood—a winter-sky blue muted by the sheerest of clouds. Hands-down beautiful.

Beneath the surface he was a hero: kind, funny, smart, and a brave firefighter who saved lives. Hands-down knight material.

And he sat beside her, Lexi Beaumont, she of the mousy attributes from straight brown hair to khaki cargo pants to personality. Hands-down fumble queen of relationships.

Zak looked at her. "You okay?"

"Sure. A little out of breath. That hike was not exactly a breeze—"

"I mean this . . ." He waved an arm as if to encompass the two thousand acres before them. "This preserve reminds me of your grandparents' estate."

That would be the one the wildfire had ripped through the previous fall, the night she met Zak.

"Lex, from what you've told me, you never go there like you did before the fire. And I've noticed that you only want to jog with me at a beach or park." His eyes, not shaded by sunglasses, studied her with obvious concern. "Really green parks."

She averted her gaze toward the lake. "I don't go there because it's not like it used to be. Not because the vegetation is gone, but because my parents live there now. Nana and Papa live down the road and they float around like ghosts trying to pick up the pieces from their old life. It's just too sad."

His arm brushed hers and he took her hand.

Add big, strong hands to the list. She said, "I know, I know. Some hot, dry, windy day this place will burn. It's nature's way of cleaning house." She looked at him. "But it's springtime now. We had rain all winter and just last week. Things are blooming. We are sitting next to a lake. You're with me. I am not scared."

"If you were, it'd be understandable."

"Zak!" She whined the syllable into three. "Sorry. Learned that trick from my sister."

"*Bzz!*" He mimicked a game bell. "Subject change not allowed. I'm taking your emotional temperature. Come on, don't groan. I haven't done this for a *long* time."

Maybe because they hadn't seen each other for a *long* time? Not that she was complaining. They were, after all, only friends, thrown together by fate, their shared fifteen minutes of fame used up ages ago.

"Come on yourself," she said. "Give me a break. It's been six months. I'm fine."

"The impact of trauma goes on and on. The other guys and I are still talking to the counselor. He's available to you."

"I know. You told me before. Once or twice."

"Or thrice." He leaned nearer her and pulled off her sunglasses. "And I will tell you again."

"It's different for you. You need to get your head on straight for work. You have to keep going into those situations. You fight fires for a living. I don't."

Humming a sigh, he rested his forehead against hers. "How are the nightmares?"

"Gone."

"*Bzz*. Fibbing not allowed either."

"Well, they are gone. Mostly. Only once in a while, when I'm overtired, and they're not too . . . awful."

"And you're fine with that?"

"Yes!"

"Life is hard enough, Lex. We might as well ease what pain we can."

"I'm fine."

He jerked upright, his eyes wide. "It's here!" He pointed to the mountain across the lake. "That way."

Again Lexi strained to catch the sound. After a moment, it came. A deep rhythmic *whomp, whomp, whomp* grew louder and louder.

Suddenly a helicopter burst into view. Like some prehistoric, monstrous bird it rose straight up from behind the mountain. Clearing the peak, it swooped down and shot directly at them, the roar of its engine deafening.

That was when Lexi knew she wasn't fine. Nope. Nowhere near it.

Terror tasted like bile in Lexi's throat. It smelled like ash. It thundered in her ears.

Still. Two hours after the helicopter had finished its display over the lake.

She and Zak sat on a restaurant's patio. He chattered nonstop about the event, totally unaware of her thoughts because she hadn't shared them.

"Oh, man!" he said for the umpteenth time. "That was so incredibly cool."

She couldn't help but tune him out. Her imagination refused to leave behind the source of her distress: the night of the fire. The night and the morning that followed.

It was the morning, the aftermath, that haunted her even more than the memory of the danger itself. She remembered how she and Zak and the others had walked through what could easily have passed for a war-ravaged land. Instead of bushes and trees there was black and debris. Instead of sunlight there was a sky of pewter. She had trembled uncontrollably, adrenaline drained by then, shock setting in.

A helicopter flew overhead several times, back and forth. It hovered and stirred up ash until they all choked on it. There was no place for it to put down. There would be no help from it. It left, taking with it all hope that the real-time nightmare would ever end.

Now she bit into a french fry, obliterating that other taste. The sun was shining. She was with Zak. There was nothing to be terrified about.

Her reaction had caught her by surprise. Not that it mattered.

She wouldn't be repeating that scenario any time soon. It wasn't like she'd become a groupie and attend SDFD helicopter exercises.

She picked up another fry, part of a late lunch. Or was it early dinner? Her sister Jenna would be appalled. Midafternoon burgers and fries?

Were Lexi and Zak dating or not? According to Jenna's standards, the answer was *not.* There were no regularly scheduled candlelit trysts, not even weekly phone calls. *But,* Lexi thought, *it's no big deal.* So they weren't dating. She and Zak were friends. Who knew? They could be inching their way toward romance and real dates.

"Lex." He grinned and picked up his hamburger. "Tell me, was that the coolest thing you've ever seen or what?"

She swallowed and pasted on a smile. "Sure. Watching a giant hose dangle from a helicopter and suck up lake water and then spray it all over the hillside is my idea of extreme fun. I especially thought it was cool that they could do it at least eighty-nine times without stopping."

"I know!" His eyes did their little-boy number, wide and starry. "It was amazing!"

Clearly she needed to work on her sarcastic tone.

"They're scheduled for a repeat tomorrow. We can go again!"

Whaaa—

Laughter exploded from him. "You should see your face. Gotcha! You thought I believed you!"

"Ha-ha."

"You're a good sport, Short Stuff." His face turned somber. "I know it bothered you. You were kind of clingy out there."

"I'm sorry."

"Don't be sorry. You faced a major fear, and you lived through it. Right?"

"I guess."

He made a show of studying his bicep. "I don't see any bruises—"

"I didn't hold on that tight!"

He smiled, his lower lip curling in its funny way.

She went slushy again. Slowly, like during the fire's aftermath, Zak Emeterio's presence made its impact. The world was not such a scary place after all.

"I bet you're tired of hearing me talk about fire stuff."

She shrugged. "It's your life."

"So how's your life? How was the shopping day with your mom and sister?" He bit into his burger.

"It was a disaster. How could it not be? Mom wants a wedding gown, but surprise! She's already married to my dad, and there's no such thing as a dress for a *re-wedding* ceremony. Jenna insists that as bridesmaids we should dress alike in matching LBDs. Me look like her? Not possible. No way am I going there."

"What's an LBD?"

"Little Black Dress. The kind that makes Jenna look even more perfect than she is. According to her, every woman should have one." Just the thought of trying on dresses with Jenna bugged her like crazy, but Zak's attention drifted.

She said, "It doesn't matter. Anyway, my parents are no longer acquainted with reality. What are we sibs going to do, though, except go along for the ride? I'll have to find a dress."

"I think it's great your parents want to recommit to each other in a formal way. I wish my parents would do something like that."

"Then you want to come with me to the wedding?" *Oh, no.* She didn't say that. She didn't. "I mean, the reception is going to be a huge party. My mom's inviting half the city, probably all the fire stations. You know you're welcome. It's not like you're a stranger. I didn't mean . . ." *Like a date. I didn't mean like a date! I just don't want to go alone.* "I mean it's no big deal if you don't—"

"Lexi." He pulled on his chin and kept his eyes fixed on his plate. "I appreciate the invitation, and I would be happy to come, but— um—there are extenuating circumstances."

She stared at him.

"I've told you about Abbey."

That would be the ex. Really ex, as in out of the picture months before Lexi had met Zak.

At last he looked up and met her eyes. "Things are getting . . . complicated. I may, uh . . ." He cleared his throat. "Be spending time with her. Not that this changes anything between you and me. We'll always be friends. We'll still jog and stuff." He scratched the back of his head. "I just don't know about, you know, a nighttime dress-up thing." His smile slid sideways. "LBDs and all."

"Yeah, sure. I understand." Her own smile attempt didn't even get off the ground. "No big deal. You want those onion rings?"

"Uh-uh." He chuckled and shook his head. "Have at them."

"Thanks." She scooped a handful and transferred them to her plate. The first sweet crunch of crispy breading was like heaven.

No big deal, she thought. Nope, no big deal. As a matter of fact, it was good news. That moony teenager might be put out of her misery once and for all.

Two

"Officer, is there a problem?" The man in the silver convertible flashed a toothy grin and squinted at the policewoman.

Rosa Delgado lowered the flashlight beam from his bloodshot eyes. These guys always asked the dumbest questions. Problem? With red eyes, slurred speech, car weaving like a kite down the road? "Yes, sir, there could be a problem."

"Okay, shoot." His grin stretched to clown proportions.

"Wow! For real? You don't mind?"

The smile went lopsided.

"Aw, shucks, you were kidding," she said. "I don't get many invitations like that to shoot. Hey, this is a great-looking car. But aren't you freezing?"

"Huh?"

"It's thirty-eight degrees, the top's down, and you're in shirt-sleeves."

"Oh. Yeah! I see what you mean. Record-setting polar temps, eh? Who would have thought, in Southern California! Global warming, you know." His left eye closed and stayed that way. "But I'm fine. Just fine. The leather seats are heated." He waggled a hand, dismissing her concern, and then let the hand drop back onto the steering wheel beside the other.

Rosie studied his hands. Though masculine in size, there was a softness to them. The long fingers moved in a graceful manner.

Whether it was his wink gone south or the sight of those hands that for sure never came in contact with dirt, she didn't know, but her hackles rose. Her muscles tensed.

On the other side of the convertible, her partner hummed a distinct "uh-oh" sound. "Delgado." He murmured her name, pushing the last syllable up a notch to convey caution.

Bobby Grey's uncanny ability to read her emotions amazed and annoyed her to no end.

Okay, so she should just request the driver's license and proof of insurance and get things over with. But she wanted to keep playing. Tanked rich guys set her off with their promise of slimy lawyers. She wanted to give this one enough rope to string himself up so tightly that the slimiest of the slime could not untie him and make DUI charges go *poof.*

"Hey." Bobby again, a soft growl.

Still watching the smiley tanked rich guy, she nodded to her partner. *Okay, okay. I'm in control. Just give me half a minute with him.*

In the car, Mr. Slaphappy cleared his throat, an ugly, rumbling noise. His left eye reopened. "So kind of you to inquire after my comfort. Will that be all, Off—" He hiccuped. "—icer?"

"Did you honestly think that was all?"

"Huh?"

Rosie took a deep breath. The scent reached her again. She guessed martini. Made with gin. She willed her expression to stay neutral and her voice to go low. "Sir, you coasted right on past a stop sign."

"Really?" He glanced over his shoulder. "Oh, right. That one." He leaned toward her and whispered, "To tell you the truth, I roll through that one all the time. I live right down the street, and I know from experience there is ab-so-lute-ly no traffic this time of night. I'm usually on my way home from work about now."

"What job keeps you out so late?"

He gave his sluggish wink again. "You don't recognize me?"

"No."

"I'm on television. News anchor. Channel 3. Six and eleven."

"No kidding? That's gotta be an interesting gig. Bet the news gets you down, though, after a while."

"You're telling me."

"You probably like a martini or two after that business."

"It takes the edge off."

"How many did you have tonight?"

Both eyes closed now, and he chuckled. "I don't have to answer that."

Rosie sighed to herself. The fun was over. He'd been here before. "No, sir, you don't have to answer that. But you do have to show me your driver's license and proof of insurance."

"Look, my condo's two blocks away. How about I park right here, walk home, and we'll call it a night? Unless this is a no-parking zone." He peered over the hood at a sign on the sidewalk. "Guess I better move—"

"License. *Now.*"

He tilted sideways and eventually managed to pull a wallet from his hip pocket. With exaggerated movements, he opened it, slipping a hundred dollar bill into plain view.

"I'll pretend I didn't see that."

He handed her his license.

She read it. Erik Beaumont, age thirty, really did live two blocks away, a tiny neighborhood snuggled between downtown and Little Italy and chock-full of San Diego Bay views. "Mr. Beaumont, are you familiar with field sobriety tests?"

"I don't have to answer that."

"Nope, you don't. However, I would like to conduct one."

"I refuse to take one."

"You have that right, too, sir."

He smiled, a flippant "gotcha" expression.

A dangerous stillness settled over Rosie. The guy had crossed the line. She was about to cross one herself. No matter Bobby's warning or the fact that a video camera recorded her every move and word, she could not stop the ensuing, regrettable behavior.

She blamed it on ancestry.

Rosie resembled her father in every which way: Mexican in appearance, chatty as a magpie, a mellow demeanor. At times, though, her mother's Irish temperament erupted, self-control vanished, and words spewed forth like volcanic ash, raining down on anyone within shouting distance.

"You know what I'd like just once?" Her voice jumped to a yell. "I'd like just once for some joker like you to say, 'Yeah! I did it! I admit it. I got drunk as a skunk, and then I got behind the wheel of a car. As a matter of fact, I am still drunk as a skunk. You better lock me up before I hurt somebody!'"

Rosie blew out a loud breath. The verbal explosion ended as quickly as it had come.

Bobby groaned softly in the shadows. "All better?" he murmured.

She ignored her partner and watched the driver's smirk disintegrate.

"Okay." She tuned her voice back down to its usual low pitch. "Where were we? Oh, yeah. Mr. Beaumont, get out of the car."

"I don't have to—"

"Yes, you do have to. You're under arrest."

Rosie, Rosie." Bobby shook his head and *tsk*ed. "You were doing so well. Why did you let him get to you?"

Walking beside her partner through the police station, she shrugged. They were off duty, wearing street clothes, and heading home to sleep away daylight hours.

He touched her arm and pulled her to the side of the noisy room. When Bobby Grey spoke, she listened. Pushing forty, he was the most focused person she'd ever met and the smartest cop. Fifteen years on the force and he was still passionate about being a patrolman. After two years of working with him, she adored him more

than she did that first day when he unabashedly welcomed her, a
scared blustery rookie, as his new partner. He soon became the big
brother she never had.

"You know," he started, his gravelly voice hushed lower than
usual. "You would make some partners nervous."

"I know. I know."

Not much taller than her own five-six and wiry in build, he did
not intimidate through size, but through intense cornflower-blue
eyes that seldom blinked. Though he never lost his cool, there was
always a pulsating undercurrent of physical and mental strength
about him.

"You're profiling, Rosie. It doesn't matter how right you call a situation, if you don't get this under control, you're headed for trouble.
I can't have you shooting some guy's head off just because he's eye
candy, drives a fancy car, and smirks at you."

"I wouldn't—"

"You never, never know for sure. Look, you're a good officer. You
can rise above whatever it is that trips your trigger about this type."

She shrugged again. "My temper only lasts a few seconds."

"Like you couldn't pull your gun and waste him within a few
seconds."

"Bobby, it's not that big a deal. I've told you. I have a bad history
with the Erik Beaumonts of the world, but that doesn't mean I want
to maim and kill them. I just need to spout off now and then."

He glanced over her shoulder. "My wife would have been royally
ticked if you'd hurt this Erik Beaumont."

"What does she have to do with him?"

"She watches him on the news. I think she has a crush on him,
along with half the female population of San Diego."

"I should have shot him."

"You should have shot him." He flashed a grin. "Actually, you've
got another chance. Here he comes now."

She looked over her shoulder. The hot anchorman didn't look so good. Hangover was written all over his puffy face, messy black hair, rumpled clothes. She wondered what his adoring fans would think.

An older man walked beside him, obviously his dad. Though not as tall as the younger Beaumont and fifty-something, his handsome face would turn heads as well.

She should shoot the father, too, for bailing the son out so soon, for not letting him suffer consequences that might remind him not to drink and drive.

As they approached, the scowling duo paid no attention to Rosie and Bobby, but she heard the exchange between them.

"I called Dan," the son hissed. "Not you."

"It's not your brother's job to get you out of jail."

"And since when is it yours?"

"I'm your father."

"Ha! You check out of my life for thirty years and now you're my *father*. That's rich."

They moved out of range, and Rosie caught no more of their argument. Not that she needed to hear more. Her macho police demeanor melted the instant she deciphered the tone of their voices.

"Aw, nuts," she muttered.

Bobby chuckled. "Hit the soft spot, did he?"

"I really hate it when they have *issues*."

"Rosie's Adopt the Hopeless Club, now in session."

"Oh, get lost, Grey." She spun on her heel and walked away, Bobby's laughter echoing in her ears.

Three

Lexi wasn't sure why she agreed to pizza at a restaurant with her siblings. The three of them reminded her of paintbrushes long overdue for a good cleaning: stiff with the old and a few hog-hair bristles shy of being useful for creating anything new.

Jenna was . . . Well, Jenna was Jenna, an unequivocal pain in the neck.

Erik, the oldest of the four of them, was a male version of Jen: gorgeous, talented, bossy.

Only Danny, Lexi's fraternal twin, prevented the evening from dipping into really ugly territory.

"How about we change the subject?" Erik scowled into his goblet. "'Chew on Erik' has become quite boring." He downed half the wine in one gulp.

Jenna had been haranguing him nonstop for twenty minutes. "Maybe being chewed out is exactly what you need! I mean, a DUI? Give me a break! How old are you anyway? You're on television! People look up to you! Danny, tell him how stupid he's behaving."

"Oh, I wouldn't want to be redundant, Jen. How about we move on to the menu? What kind of pizza do you all want?"

"But he hasn't gotten the message! Erik, don't you dare order another glass of wine."

He kept his arm raised and signaled the waiter. "I'm not. I'm ordering a bottle."

"Then I'm leaving. Move." She shoved at Erik, who had her blocked in the booth seat.

He didn't budge. "Nasty habit you have, running away all the time. You haven't left Kevin again, have you?"

"You snot! That was totally uncalled for."

"So is ranting and raving about my habits, nasty as they are. It's not like I get blotto every night and then drive and get caught."

"But you had to do it now? In the middle of Mom and Dad's plans? Their do-over wedding or marriage blessing or whatever it's called. The point is you were so hungover you missed your tux fitting appointment. You can't blow their special time!"

Erik did not reply. Even Jenna closed her mouth.

An eerie hush settled about them. Noise of the bustling pizza joint sank to a background hum. Scurrying waiters slowed to robot pace.

The siblings rarely got together as an isolated foursome. Aside from the special connection between the twins, the four of them were not exactly close friends. They saw each other at family events with brother-in-law Kevin, their parents, and grandparents in tow. There were occasional social doings when their paths crossed with mutual friends. But a dinner like tonight? Not in recent memory. Lexi had no clue why Jenna had insisted on it or why on earth they'd all agreed.

Until now.

The wedding reference brought them all up short. Lexi felt like they'd come upon a neon sign flashing a message: "Now hear this: You are all in the same sinking ship."

Erik sighed in his dramatic way. "Well, gang, I confess. That is precisely why I drank myself into a stupor at this exact point in time. I don't want any part of Mom and Dad's *re-wedding* stuff, and my guess is neither do any of you. Jenna, you've turned into a first-class shrew. Lexi, you're so closed in on yourself, you're going to disappear altogether."

She squirmed. Who wouldn't be tentative with the king and queen of drama? As far back as she could remember those two had always dismissed everything she said with a laugh or some demeaning remark.

Erik continued. "Dan, if you don't have some deep, dark, nasty secret, I'll plead guilty to the DUI charge that the mayor already fixed."

Beside her, Danny piled up sugar packets, his eyes lowered, his lips bunched. People often didn't believe he was Lexi's twin. His brown hair was darker than hers and curly. Unlike her, he had their dad's black-brown eyes. Sometimes, though, people noticed the twin-ness in their ability to read each other.

She knew beyond a shadow of a doubt that he did not have a deep, dark, nasty secret.

Danny folded his hands on the packets and eyed Erik across the table. "I lost a client. My biggest."

An excruciating pain shot through Lexi, as if a rhinoceros had just fallen atop her and crushed every bone and organ in her body.

Danny shrugged. "My fault. I'm surfing instead of working, and the whole time I'm thinking to myself, who gives a rip? Let them design their own stinking software."

Erik guffawed. "You are such a Boy Scout! I was talking booze, sex, drugs."

"Get off your high horse. We're both talking about our living. You'll lose yours if you keep this up."

"No worries. They love me at the station. My fans adore me."

"It'd be Dad's worst nightmare come true, you know, if either of us flopped at our careers."

"Whatever."

Jenna cleared her throat. "Kevin," she whispered. "Kevin's going. Next week. They're shipping out."

They turned as one and stared at her.

She nodded, her face crumpling.

"Next week?" Lexi said.

"No way!" Danny exclaimed. "He's not supposed to go until sometime after the wedding! In June, not March!"

"Stupid, idiotic, incompetent, lousy, rotten marines." Jenna lifted her hands in a helpless gesture.

Erik flung an arm around her shoulders and pulled her close. "Oh, Jen-Jen."

"That's why I'm such a shrew!" she blubbered.

Lexi wanted to slide under the table and slink on out the door. It was all too much. Danny not confiding in her? Erik drinking like a fish? And Kevin? Her brother-in-law? Overseas?

She grabbed a breadstick. Only over her own dead body would she ever agree to get together with her siblings again.

A rhinoceros?" Danny grinned.

Lexi stood beside her twin, studying her unfinished oil painting. No wonder she'd imagined a rhino earlier that evening. She'd been engrossed with the animal, working on its likeness for weeks now.

They were in her apartment, in the spare bedroom she used as a studio. Danny had driven her there after they'd finally eaten dinner—a mushroom-and-pepperoni pizza that still wasn't feeling quite right from the inside. Kevin's news had dominated their conversation. By the time they left the restaurant, Jenna was under control. Erik wasn't, but she and Danny escorted him into his condo and hid his car keys.

"Lex, how on earth do you come up with these subjects to paint?"

"The Wild Animal Park."

"I know that much. But why choose this guy? I mean he is one ugly dude. Horrific. Your work is disturbingly realistic sometimes."

The white African rhino filled much of the sixteen-by-twenty-inch canvas. His head turned slightly, the two horns on his snout were front and center, one menacing eye above them.

Danny stepped nearer the canvas and studied the color photo clipped onto the side of the easel. "Whoa. How close were you to the real guy when you snapped this?"

"A few feet. I took one of those photo caravan tours at the park. He came right up to the truck."

"He's not a true white color, really. Just gray. Is he endangered?"

"Yes." She studied her depiction again.

Except for the shiny dark eye, all the colors in the painting were drab and fading. Light gray armor covered the rhino. There were stark, leafless tree branches behind him, an ashen sky, sunbaked earth beneath him, a few dried-up weeds.

He said, "Everything about this is endangered, isn't it? The ground, the plants. The sunless sky, even. It's like every detail is in the throes of death."

She shut her eyes briefly. Danny always figured them out.

"Lex, I was going to tell you."

She assumed he was referring to his business situation. "You didn't have to. It's okay."

"But it's not okay. I tell you everything."

She shrugged.

"Don't do that. Don't shrug it off. I've been avoiding you, Lexi. You're my other half and I've been avoiding you like the plague. Which makes absolutely no sense at all." Plainly exasperated, he clasped his hands atop his head. "No sense at all except it shows you how tied up in knots I am over this whole mess."

He wasn't talking about the business situation.

Lexi watched him pace the small room in quick, jerky strides. Whenever her twin was wound up like some battery-operated bouncing toy, she waited without comment until the energy drained.

He pressed his fingertips against his temples as he turned again. "Mom and Dad, the perfect couple, churchgoers, outstanding community leaders, high-society members, parents of four fairly normal adult children. Out of the blue, Mom files for divorce. Mom, the one who taught us how much God hates divorce. The one who swore if we followed God's standards, we wouldn't have problems."

Lexi's recollections differed. Their mother's faith had not been so well-defined to her. But then Danny embraced religious things differently than Lexi did.

Danny still paced. "Mom leaves Dad and says the past thirty years have been nowhere near what they were cracked up to be. Okay, so he wasn't around all that much. He provided for us, didn't he? Now he throws his entire life's work away, his passion, and says he should have listened to Mom more? And she says she should have disagreed with him more? What does this say about our childhood?"

Lexi met his glance with an uncertain shake of her head. She didn't know what it said.

"It says it was all a crock. It says if I can't trust my parents, who can I trust?" He blew out a breath and halted in the middle of the room, hands on his hips.

"This is why you're tied up in knots?"

"Yeah."

Lexi let her gaze wander back to the painting. Despite the almost eerie connection she and Danny had on every level, it surprised her whenever he grasped meaning in her work. As a child, she never colored inside the lines. Now, as an adult, she painted her originals in a similar manner. An observer would not mistake the rhino or tree or other things for anything else, but no distinct outlines formed the subjects.

She looked at her brother. "Our parents aren't coloring inside the lines anymore."

He scrunched his lips together.

"According to your standards, they don't look like they're supposed to look."

"So my standards are wrong?"

"I don't know. I only know that you used to have a fit when Mom put gold stars on my coloring-book pages. The ones that had crayon marks all over them. Now when you see her and Max's messy pages, you don't have fits. You just surf and don't work."

He lowered his head. "I've practically been living in the water."

"How bad is the business loss?"

"I can still pay rent and buy food." He toed the carpet for a moment and then looked up. "So, what do we do? Call in sick for the next re-wedding event?"

"Sounds like a plan."

He smiled, his first of the long evening. "But we can't. They're our parents. Guess I'll just surf some more while you keep painting nature on the verge of extinction. We'll get through it. God will get us through it." He turned again to the painting. "It really is very good. Erik says you hold too much inside. Maybe you ought to invite him over to see this."

"Got to catch him sober first."

"Yeah. Okay, I'm out of here, sis."

Within moments of his leaving, Lexi squirted a glob of paint from a tube onto a palette. She pulled out the widest of her brushes. A short time later, the rhino, the tree, the dirt, and the sky were obliterated, disintegrating in a pool of burnt umber.

Four

Rosie sat cross-legged on an ottoman directly in front of the television, elbows propped on knees, chin in hands. A waist-up shot of Channel 3 news anchor Erik Beaumont filled the screen. With an appropriately somber expression on his face, he related a story about a bank robbery.

On the other side of the living room, her dad's recliner creaked. "He is not bad looking."

"For a gringo."

"Rosita, you should not use that word."

She smiled. The gentleness of Esteban Delgado's admonitions tickled her. *"Papi."* The word for "daddy" sounded like "poppy" in English. She'd always called him that. "I'm almost thirty years old. When are you going to give up on me?"

"When you quit talking like a hard-nosed cop. I know what the streets are like. They will ruin you if we don't keep our guard up. I will get to heaven and your *madre* will turn her head in disgust and say she never knew me."

Rosie glanced at him. His facial features reflected his Aztec heritage. His accent spoke of a childhood in Mexico. His ample waist indicated that he overindulged on the yummy dishes served at the restaurant he owned. His mention of her deceased mother meant he was overtired.

"Papi, go to bed. I'll let myself out."

"Take this man here." He pointedly ignored her, nodding toward the television. "Nice and clean looking. Handsome."

Erik Beaumont was all that, dressed in a stylish black suit and royal blue tie. The contrast between his black hair and light eyes produced a startling effect. Like catching a glimpse of sunlight breaking through clouds. She was drawn to study his face. She didn't think the eyes were blue. Greenish, maybe? He was attractive in a cookie-cutter way, nose and mouth and chin perfectly sized and shaped. She remembered handcuffing him. He was tall, over six feet, broad shouldered. Soft hands.

"You'd think," her father continued, "that he was the heart and soul of the United States. Trustworthy. A model citizen. But no. He does not know the meaning of self-discipline. He is a drunk. A bum. *Grosero*. You had to arrest him."

Rosie grimaced. The story had slipped out when she tried to explain why it was she wanted to watch the news all of a sudden. "Forget I said anything, okay? I shouldn't have told you."

"My lips are sealed. But your blessed madre . . ." He shook his head. "*¡Dios mío!* What she will say to me! I never should have allowed you to go to police school."

"Mom would say you should pray for this guy and not worry about me. Right?"

He harrumphed.

Now Beaumont shared the screen with his coanchor, Felicia Matthews. Even at thirty years of age or so, they were material for high school homecoming king and queen in white-bread America. She was cover-girl pretty, blonde, obviously blue-eyed even on the old television. Through the grapevine, Rosie had heard that Beaumont and Matthews were an item offscreen.

Her father lowered the footrest, lumbered out of his chair, and stepped to her side. "You are right." He leaned over and kissed the top of her head. "Lilly would say a prayer for him. I will tomorrow. Good night, Rosita."

"'Night, Papi. Love you."

"I love you too. Be careful going home."

She smiled at his oft-used phrase. She lived in his yard. Typical old San Diego, the modest property included a small cottage tucked behind fruit trees, next to an alley.

For a few more minutes she continued to study Beaumont on the television. Her partner Bobby was right. Much as she disliked what the newsman represented with his slaphappy attitude, he had touched a spot in her heart.

It was the place where God whispered to her to pray for a complete stranger.

It was the place that convinced her she was loonier than half the weirdos she arrested.

"Whatever." Rosie closed her eyes and bowed her head. "Okay, Lord, I'm listening. You want me to pray for this guy, right? Right." For a long moment she sat still, waiting for words. They came. "Swamp Erik Beaumont with Your love. Swamp him until he can no longer stand under the strength of his own power."

Five

"Erik looks well." Claire Beaumont studied her son's image on the small television screen as he announced the late-night news. "His voice is strong."

"Mm-hmm." Seated beside her on the love seat, Max cracked his knuckles, yanking back one finger at a time. After all ten popped, he started the process over yet again. He'd been doing it through the entire program.

She laid a hand on his and stilled the torturous *crick-crack*.

He gave her a tight smile. "Sorry."

"You've been at it for twenty minutes." She winked at him. "Guess I hit my limit."

The knuckle thing was a new habit. Max had picked it up soon after signing the contract that completed the sale of his business. *Interesting,* she thought, *how a piece of paper could end the work of a lifetime and still leave one living and breathing. Or at least gasping for breath.*

Beaumont Staffing, a multimillion-dollar national firm her husband had built from scratch, now belonged to someone else. For over thirty years it had consumed every hour of his day. He said it was like losing an arm. She hardly blamed him for making sure his fingers were still attached.

"Sweetheart," he said, "Erik is not all right."

"But . . ." She pointed to the television.

"He's acting. They pay him to act. Offscreen he's a mess."

25

"You saw him after the DUI and said he wasn't great, but he was okay. He was fine with me on the phone later that day. He and Felicia were going sailing with friends."

"Later that day, long after he missed his appointment for a tux fitting due, no doubt, to a hangover."

"Which reminds me, I've been thinking. Maybe I'm expecting too much from the kids for the wedding-blessing. Erik and Danny don't need to wear tuxedos. Lexi is not crazy about getting a dressy black dress. She doesn't wear dressy black dresses. If she wears a dress at all, it's baggy and bohemian."

"But this is all about what you want, not them. You want fancy and formal. You want a private ceremony in a church with them and my parents and a few friends. Afterwards, you want an all-out bash of a reception, to which you've invited half the city."

"Only a fourth." She smiled. "Yes, I do want that. I really do. It's not so much because we didn't have it the first time. Eloping wasn't all that bad. I mean, we didn't have a clue what we were getting into back then. Now that we've made it, it seems so important to celebrate our marriage, to recognize what we've accomplished. Or better, what God has accomplished in us."

He nodded. "I agree. And I think the tuxes and the black dresses and the whole gang smiling would not be a problem except for one thing."

"What's that?"

"Me."

"Max!"

"If I weren't involved, they'd rally 'round you in a heartbeat."

"That's not true."

"It is." He paused. "I didn't tell you what Erik said to me at the police station." The creases on his forehead deepened. "He said I checked out for thirty years and now I want to be his father. He can't reconcile those two things."

"Oh, hon."

"He's right. We had some good times when he was a little kid, but I've let him down for most of his life. I haven't been there for him. Haven't been there for any of them, not in the deep sense of the term. Danny tries and Jenna comes close, but none of them are exactly embracing the new dad with open arms."

"It'll take time."

"This is called reaping what you've sown."

Claire slid an arm across his chest and leaned against him. "Give it time, Max."

He held her close. "I don't know. I somehow sense that we just don't have the time."

A short while later, after the news program, Claire and Max walked outdoors through the dark cold night. She shivered and pulled a shawl more tightly around herself.

"What did you mean," she said, "that we don't have the time?"

"I don't know if I have words to explain it. It's more of a vague sense. Life feels like it's teetering on the edge of a cliff. It's all going to give way at any moment."

She ignored his gloom and doom and zeroed in on *feels like*. Who would have thought! A few short months ago that phrase did not exist in her husband's lexicon.

Smiling to herself, she gazed up at the sky, packed so densely with stars it looked like the Creator had spilled a giant bag of powdered sugar all over it. *Thank You.*

She slipped her arm through his. "Yes, I agree, life has been teetering. But here we are, starting our new life at the Hacienda Hideaway."

"Yeah. That's the only piece of solid ground I can find. The rest is giving way like a mudslide."

"You're tired, Max. Let's just go to bed."

"No, I want to see Mom and Dad."

Claire didn't argue. She wasn't about to quash the new side of

Max that emoted and actually desired to talk with his parents. Up until last fall he could hardly stand the sight of them, let alone initiate a heartfelt discussion.

They continued their stroll, following the dirt-and-gravel road down to its first bend. Over three hundred acres made up the estate—land purchased by Max's great-grandfather after he discovered gold on it in the 1800s. The original Beaumont built the hacienda that descendents had lived in for more than a century. Max had grown up in the old house. It was Spanish-styled, U-shaped with thick adobe walls and a red-tile roof. In recent years his parents had remodeled it into a retreat center.

Claire knew from her own experience that people came because the place offered a safe harbor from the world. The natural beauty and the comfy rooms provided the ambience, but her in-laws added the essence of safety. Their faith and prayers and loving ways filled every inch with a tangible peace.

In September, not many months ago, a wildfire nearly destroyed everything. Unwilling to start all over again at their age, Ben and Indio Beaumont had planned to sell the hacienda. Max and Claire, desperate to start all over again and to make a safe harbor of their own, decided to leave behind their old life, sell their house, and reopen the Hideaway.

To date, the only completely finished room was the master bedroom suite. It was enough for them. They'd moved in and now worked most days with the construction crew—a high-priced outfit worth every penny because they renovated in record time. Ben and Indio lived in a camper down the road, on the site of their new home.

Life resounded with glorious song.

Except when Max said it teetered on the edge of a cliff.

Son, what do you mean life is teetering on the edge of a cliff?" Ben Beaumont's thick silver eyebrows drew together in a frown.

Max did not reply. Claire noted his tranquil demeanor and mar-
veled at the change. In days gone by, he had been highly expressive,
his gestures nonstop and energetic, his words a rushing stream.
Now, in life's new season, his personality was tempered with calm
moments of reflection.

Max cracked a knuckle.

Except for that.

They were seated on built-in benches around a tiny table in the
RV. Ben and Indio chose to live in these cramped quarters, never
complaining, grateful to be alone again and back on their beloved
land after the fire. Despite delays in the completion of their new
home, they exuded contentment.

Max laid his fists on the table. "Not counting Claire, everything
in my life is a total unknown." He began uncurling one finger at a
time. "One, Danny hasn't asked me a business question in weeks.
Unheard of. Two, Lexi won't make eye contact with me. Who knows
what she's hiding. Three, Erik drinks too much. Four, Jenna is falling
apart. Five, Kevin is going off to war. Six, Phil made two major dumb
moves with the agency." He referred to the new owner of Beaumont
Staffing. "And seven—no offense, Mom and Dad—but you're getting feeble. As you should, since you are closing in on eighty."

Indio bristled, shaking her head and shoulders, pursing her lips.
"I do take offense, Maxwell. Feeble? A little exhausted from time to
time and getting up there in years, yes. But let's not even consider
the word *feeble!* It makes me sound like some witless nincompoop."

Claire couldn't help but laugh at her mother-in-law, a short,
plump woman of Native American descent who wore her salt-and-
pepper hair in a long single braid. "Indio, we all know you are a far
cry from witlessness or nincompoopness."

Ben chortled. "Now that easily applies to me, but not to you, love."

Tall and broad shouldered, he still looked like a strong cowboy to
Claire. She said, "Ben, you don't fit that bill either. I bet you could
rustle a herd of cattle and ride a horse from here all the way to Denver."

He nodded. "Durn right. And eat beans out of a can heated up over an open fire and sleep under the stars." He laughed again.

Claire noticed Max's somber face. "Hon, what are you trying to say?"

"I just don't know what to do with this feeling of helplessness."

She pressed a hand against her lips and squished the grin that kept tugging. *Oh, my.*

"I can't control one infernal thing!" he said.

Ben burst into laughter, a wild, bellowing noise. He slapped the table. Tears rolled down his flushed cheeks.

Indio jabbed him with her elbow a few times, all the while smiling and giggling herself.

Max kneaded his forehead.

Ben cleared his throat. "Son." He chuckled and wiped the corners of his eyes. "You just figured this out?"

"Well, yeah, I guess so."

"Better now than never. To tell you the truth, it took me awhile too. You get used to the fact that you are not in control. It slowly dawns on you that you never were. You just thought you were."

Indio said, "You'll figure out that God is in control. Pretty soon you'll realize He wants only the best for you. He's not trying to make you miserable. That's when the peace comes no matter what things look like."

"I'm sure being miserable is my own fault. It's obvious I'm reaping what I've been sowing. You can't exactly go AWOL on your kids and then expect them to forgive and forget the hurt you inflicted."

Ben and Indio's smiles vanished. They exchanged a look.

Max shut his eyes. "Good grief."

Ben said, "You're a little slow on the uptake, son. I think we've been here before, like when you were growing up and we went AWOL on you."

"Yeah."

"And what did your mother and I do, Max, when we realized we'd unintentionally hurt you for years and years? Unfairly comparing you to your brother, making you think your brother walked on water?"

"You asked me to forgive you." He spoke in a hushed tone. "And I didn't, not right then. Not for a very long time."

"So don't give up hope on your kids."

Indio said, "And remember this: You and Claire have sown good things. My grandchildren have excellent work ethics. They do not take for granted that you provided for all their needs, that you gave them an abundance of opportunities. God's Word was planted in them because you took them to church. They are good-hearted people. Max, you get to reap all that good stuff too."

Ben nodded. "We all sow weeds right along with the flowers. Gather the flowers and give the weeds to God. He does amazing things with our messes."

Max covered his face with his hands.

Claire wrapped her arms around him and held tightly until the shuddering stopped.

Six

Where does this event fall on your fun list?" Danny whispered the question in Lexi's ear.

She glared at her twin, a waste of effort considering he couldn't see it through her sunglasses. "I can't believe you said that."

"Remember how you used to rate everything by the fun list?" he murmured.

"I was a kid."

Pointedly ignoring her, he went on. "Let me guess. If hanging out with Zak Emeterio is at the top of the list—by the way, how is Zak?"

"Go away."

"Moving right along, how about we say Zak is near the top and at the bottom is losing a tube of paint. This would be below the tube of paint loss, right?"

"You're a jerk."

"Just trying to lighten the mood."

She had worse derogatory names for him, but the nauseating ache in her throat choked them off.

The scene before them was from hell. Hundreds of people milled about. They divided themselves into clusters. In the center of each cluster stood one person with a buzzed haircut, dressed in desert fatigues. In the middle of the Beaumont family cluster stood her brother-in-law, Kevin Mason.

Jenna clung to him, grasping his arm with both hands. Her husband had no local family members, but all of his in-laws had come to say good-bye. In a few minutes he would board a bus and be whisked off to an airbase and from there flown overseas so he could live in hell full-time, for at least a year.

Danny leaned again toward Lexi and whispered, "Shall I get my antiwar sign out of the truck? 'Bring 'Em Home Now!' The slogan seems somewhat appropriate under the circumstances, don't you think? I mean, everyone here wants these people to come home ASAP. And they haven't even left Pendleton yet."

Lexi ignored him. She wanted to be sick. She wanted to curl up on the concrete and sleep until this nightmare was all over. She wanted her brother-in-law Kevin to change his mind. The marines did not need him. The war would go on just fine without him. What difference could one really nice guy make?

She turned to Danny. As was their habit since they were little kids, they stood apart from the family, carrying on their own private conversation. It was time to end this one.

She said, "Stop clowning around. This is killing Jen."

"It's killing a lot more people than Jen. Do you know how many thousands we've lost to date?"

"I don't want to know!"

"You have a crush on him."

"So what?" Her feelings toward Kevin were obvious. Besides being a hunk, he was down-to-earth, friendly, and thoughtful. He never teased her like her brothers did. Lexi had no idea how snotty Jenna had snagged him, other than the fact that she was gorgeous.

"Yeah," Danny said, "you're right. So what if you have a crush on him? We all do. We all think the world of him."

He went still.

Her twin rarely went still. If he wasn't jabbering, he was moving some body part. He'd sway, bounce, stretch, do the moonwalk, always in motion.

She looked at his profile. His jaw muscles tensed. She could see through the side of his sunglasses. His eyes were narrow slits.

"Danny, don't be mad at Kevin. It's not his fault."

"He enlisted. He *re-enlisted.* That's his fault. That's totally his fault."

"The war is not his fault."

"Yeah, well, call me a wuss. I can't seem to get into assassinating the president or blowing up Congress, so I gotta take it out on old Kev."

Lexi noticed Kevin gazing over heads at her, trying to get her attention.

It was her turn.

Slowly she made her way between her mom and grandmother, dreading the moment. It would be an awkward, one-armed hug. Jenna wouldn't let go, and she would hear whatever Kevin said to Lexi and vice versa.

Not that Jenna could be blamed for clinging to her husband. She hadn't married into the military. She had married a marine who was no longer in the service. But as the war intensified and Kevin watched the boys he coached in football graduate from high school and enlist, he could no longer sit on the sidelines. He signed back up.

Lexi reached him. He pulled her to himself with one arm, and she sank against him, her face buried in his chest, her arms around him. His chin rested atop her head.

"Lex, you're the best little sister I could ever ask for. You'll write, won't you?"

She nodded. There was so much to say, but the words wouldn't come.

"Shh," he said. "It's okay. I love you too."

His other arm came around her and he hugged very, very tightly.

Kevin was gone.

Jenna sobbed in their mother's arms.

Nana, their grandma, rubbed Jenna's back and talked in a soothing tone. Their grandpa rubbed Nana's back, his lips moving silently. Lexi knew both her grandparents were praying.

She could not comprehend what they felt. Over thirty years ago they'd sent their son, her Uncle BJ, off to Vietnam. He never came home. Not even his remains came home. He was still officially listed as MIA.

Fate added a stupid twist. Just days ago they'd passed the thirty-fifth anniversary of his disappearance. As usual, Nana and Papa spent the day alone, in mourning. Now they had to send off a grandson-in-law, maybe to the same fate. Or an unequivocal death. She didn't know which would be worse.

Erik scurried off without a backward glance. Danny moved away, throwing a quick "'Bye" over his shoulder. Lexi followed in his footsteps.

Until her dad called out, "Lexi, can we talk a minute?"

She stopped cold in her tracks. "O-okay."

He stood before her and removed his sunglasses.

Eye contact with Max Beaumont was not a common thing. He seldom stood still long enough for it to happen. When he did slow down, his eyes quickly glazed over, evidence of a disengaged mind. It was like making eye contact with a brick wall.

At least that was his demeanor until all the re-wedding business started. Now he was in her or some other family member's face all the time. She preferred the brick wall to a stranger overly eager to be her best buddy.

He said, "Where are you headed now?"

"To work."

"It's Saturday."

Like he hadn't worked on Saturdays for the twenty-six years she'd known him? She glanced in the direction Danny had taken. He was long gone. No help there. She sure didn't want to hang out with Jenna.

"Are you going to the office?" he asked.

"No." She looked at the January sun and estimated a few daylight hours remained. It should be enough. It was the best way she could think of to pass the awful time following Kevin's departure. "There's a site in Oceanside I need to check on."

"Mind if I tag along?"

What was it about him that produced discomfort in her? He wasn't tall like Erik or Kevin. He was Danny's size, but broader, more solid somehow. His eyes were a deep brown-black like her grandma's. But Nana's were velvet; his were obsidian. Rock hard.

He blinked. "I have my own car here. I'll just come for a few minutes. I need to tell you something."

She lowered her head and dug in the pocket of her baggy pants for keys. She wanted to grieve over Kevin in private. She wanted to work in private. She did not want to hear about anything to do with her parents or her lack of interest in wearing a little black dress to the wedding.

"Please?" he said.

Please?

That was a first.

She gave him directions to her work site.

It happened five minutes down the freeway. She couldn't wait any longer.

Gunning her small SUV, she flicked on the turn signal and glanced over her shoulder. She yanked on the steering wheel, careened across three lanes of heavy traffic, and braked on the shoulder. In quick succession she shoved the half-empty cookie bag off her lap, burst out the door, and dashed around the car. Leaning against its fender, head bent forward, she was sick.

Then, after a bit, she was okay. She could put aside Kevin's departure, Danny's lousy attitude, and drama queen Jenna's behavior. Now if only her dad lost the directions to her work site, she'd be totally, absolutely fine.

No such luck. Her dad found her.

"I've been here before." Max approached her from the parking lot.

Kneeling on a mound of cedar bark chips, Lexi glanced at him and then continued pushing aside the mulch with her glove-covered hands. Of course he'd been there before. Max Beaumont knew everyone and every place of business in San Diego County.

He stopped near her. "After all those years of placing temporary workers, I suppose I've called on a large percentage of local companies."

"Probably."

He gestured toward the nearby building. "This brokerage firm is still a client. They hire through us now and then."

"Nice." She picked up her trowel and began digging a hole.

He cracked a knuckle, an annoying habit he'd started in recent months. "So," he said. "What are you doing for them?"

Duh. She worked for Pierce Gardens, a small landscape architect firm. Owners of commercial buildings like this one hired them to design their grounds. Obviously what she was doing was landscaping.

"I mean," he said as if reading her mind, "I thought you created landscapes on paper. I didn't know you still planted the flowers."

"Our crew finished up here yesterday. I didn't have time to check on their work."

"You're digging."

How observant of him. She crawled a few feet and slipped the trowel under a clump of fragrant sweet alyssum. "Transplanting the *Lobularia maritima*. It's in the wrong place."

"You remind me of myself."

Oh, I hope not.

"I'm always looking over shoulders, making sure all the i's are dotted, the t's crossed."

She gently lowered the white flowers into their new home.

Max plopped down on the ground, the flowers between them. "Alexis, please look at me."

Reluctantly she sat back on her haunches. "You'll get your good pants dirty."

"It doesn't matter." Again he removed his sunglasses.

She felt safer with hers on, as if the slice of tinted plastic warded off unwanted attention from a man she did not know.

"Honey, I don't know where to begin. I don't know how to say it—well, I guess I should just say it." He paused, took a breath, and exhaled. "I love you. I'm sorry for hurting you, for not being the dad you needed me to be. I'm sorry for always looking over those employees' shoulders because all the time I spent doing that was time I stole from you. I'm sorry, and I hope you'll forgive me."

Oh boy. The campaign to get her to jump onto her parents' bandwagon continued. "Um."

"You don't have to say anything." He smiled. "It was what I needed to say—"

"You paid for everything I needed." She shrugged. "Mom tried not to spoil us, I know, but she gave me every crayon and paintbrush I ever wanted. I was the first on the block to have an easel. You did your best."

"I didn't do my best, hon. I did my best with Beaumont Staffing, not with my family. I hope you can forgive me, more for your own sake than for mine."

Breaking their quasi-eye contact, she trailed the small trowel through the mulch, making zigzag patterns.

"I want to make it up to you, Lex. I want to be a part of your life."

She stabbed the trowel into the ground. "I'm not a kid anymore."

"No, you're not. I'm not saying I'll drive you to music lessons."

"I never took music. I took—"

"You know what I mean."

Gymnastics, she finished her sentence silently, yanked the trowel out and thrust it in again. *I took gymnastics.*

"Maybe I could, like, um, I could help you transplant this stuff right now?"

"I really don't need any help—"

"That's not the point."

"I don't need any help." Lexi rubbed her hands down her thighs, streaking the pants with soil from the garden gloves. "Thanks anyway."

"Okay. The thing is I just needed to tell you all that. I need to tell you that you are a beautiful young woman and you matter to me. This might not make sense right now, but maybe . . . maybe someday it will." He stood.

She looked up at him. "You did your best."

"Yeah. All right. I better go." He put on his sunglasses. "We'll see you later."

"Mm-hmm. 'Bye."

"'Bye." He walked away through the grassy area and onto the parking lot.

Lexi turned back to the plot, a showy area that softened the effect of the glass and brick building behind it. The azaleas weren't quite right. Given the overall picture of the new landscape, the azaleas were a minor detail. But such details could make or break the entire effect.

The scene before her turned fish tank-y. She wiped a gloved hand across her cheek and felt the dirt dissolve, probably into a muddy streak down her face. Her dad was a jerk. Always had been. Always would be.

After making sure Max's car was gone, she went to her own and pulled a bag of cheesy puffs from the trunk. Munching, she returned to the flower bed, sat down, and imagined what flowers belonged where.

Seven

The glitter in Max's eyes shone all the way across the dimly lit kitchen.

Claire set the tea tray back down on the island countertop and gazed at him as he walked toward her from the doorway. An unfamiliar expression smoothed his face, erasing even the crinkles of his fifty-five-year accumulation of California sun.

He gave a thumbs-up sign and the tiniest, briefest of smiles.

She melted into his embrace, into him.

Throughout a day of emotional upheaval that had begun with their son-in-law's departure, she had been harassed by a distinct sense of unease. Now, in the blink of an eye, it vanished, a drop of water exposed to a blast of desert heat.

She peered up at him. "Something's different about you."

He nodded as if in agreement and then shook his head.

"Yes, no? What?"

His chest heaved with a deep sigh. "It's like a two-ton weight rolled off my back. But . . ." His voice caught. He whispered, "But getting rid of it nearly killed me."

Wordlessly, she leaned into him again.

They held each other for a very long time.

Max, it's near midnight. Save your stories for tomorrow." Claire handed him a mug of hot tea.

"No, I want to tell you now."

Tucking her legs beneath herself, she sat down beside him on the love seat and glanced around the master suite. Logs burned in the fireplace, keeping the January chill at bay and cozying the room. "I like this room a lot."

"Yeah, it's great. But I did notice you were in the kitchen when I got home."

She smiled. "And not in here behind bolted doors?"

"Does that mean you did okay being all alone at night?"

"I did fine." She smiled. "Just me, the howling coyotes and mountain lions, and my violin. I played up a storm."

"I knew you could do it."

Max wasn't gone much anymore. Business travel seldom occurred. His parents were only a holler away down the road. Still, though, her first few times alone at night in the sprawling hacienda set in the middle of hundreds of acres had unnerved her. It wasn't so much that she was by herself or that Max was out of cellular phone reach. What sent chills down her spine were haunting memories of a night spent there narrowly escaping a wildfire.

She winked. "Well, this place is, after all, a safe harbor. Especially when I'm on my knees."

He grinned. "Prayer makes a difference."

"Listen to us. It's still hard to imagine, isn't it? We pray about everything." She exchanged a look of wonder with him.

"And go to church without thinking about how to network with business contacts."

"And trust that God is right here with us."

"And confess to my kids what an idiot I've been for most of their lives. Or, as Erik would phrase it, a putz."

"I am so proud of you. Today you went to each one of them and asked for forgiveness."

"Well, it's not like I had a choice. Once God gets hold of you and you realize how dead you were before, you don't want to go back to being dead. Forward is the only direction." He set the mug on an end table. "Forward meant clearing the air with them."

"And now you're two tons lighter."

"Yes." He rested his elbows atop his knees. "While I was driving to meet Lexi, I thought about the pastor's sermon last week. Remember he talked about how we need to examine our beliefs?"

"Vaguely."

"He said what we believe about ourselves—whether it's true or false, conscious or not—determines our emotions and our behavior."

"Mm-hmm."

"I realized my actions toward the kids shaped their beliefs about themselves. My absence must have communicated that they weren't important, that they didn't count as people. Isn't that awful? I mean . . ." He rubbed his forehead. "That is so despicable. What right did I have to . . ." A choking sound overtook his voice.

"Oh, hon. We all make mistakes."

"Claire, don't let me off the hook. Lexi, Danny, and Jenna all tried to let me off, saying I did my best. Granted, I'm not totally responsible, but my impact on them was huge. I'm their dad, for crying out loud."

She reached over and touched his damp cheek. "Their loving dad who asked for forgiveness."

"Yeah. It didn't seem to be a big deal to any of them, though."

"It was, Max. Trust me. It had to be." She moved into his arms, her head on his chest, and let him cry.

His stories could wait.

Max again insisted he did not want the stories to wait.

Claire made more tea and settled back onto the couch with a mug and a box of tissues. "Okay. You saw Lexi first?"

"Mm-hmm. I did my thing. Told her I was an idiot. I got no response. She just kept on digging in the dirt."

"Digging?"

"I met her at one of her work sites. She was transplanting flowers."

"That's Lexi. Always planting or painting. It's how she copes."

"What do you mean, copes?"

"I suspect she's more lonely than she lets on."

"Lonely? She has friends. And I thought she was dating that guy Zak."

A painful realization dawned on Claire. Max had missed out on years with Lexi. While he connected with Danny via business interests, their youngest daughter remained outside his purview. But surely her personality had registered with him.

Claire said, "You know how withdrawn and quiet she is."

"Uh." His face contorted, as if he searched his memory for snapshots of Lexi.

"She's never really had friends, Max. She did poorly in school because of her dyslexia. Except for Danny, her closest relationship is with Vivian, her boss, who's my age. And Zak?" She shrugged. "I'm not sure. He's a fireman and works odd hours and lives in North County. As far as I can tell, they get together only occasionally."

"I should know this stuff."

"You will. It's a new day for you."

He pressed his lips together, unconvinced.

"How'd things go with Danny?"

"The same, but different. I met him at Kono's, at that coffee cart on the boardwalk. Then we walked out on the pier."

Claire blinked consciously, in slow motion, and reminded herself God's ways were not hers. Neither were Max's. Why he would carry on such a deeply personal dialogue on a busy pier rather than in Danny's apartment two blocks away was far beyond her comprehension. But that was okay.

She blinked again and waited.

"Dan heard me out. Told me I did my best. That he appreciated all the opportunities I provided, all the business insights I give him.

I insisted I had let him down by being an absent dad. He hugged me and said don't worry about it."

She smiled. "And that's Danny."

"Yeah. He's like me in many ways when it comes to business, but thank God he's got your soft side."

"He's been ahead of both of us in the faith department for years."

"He's always been open about his Christianity, but the thing is . . ." He paused. "We know how he is, so black-and-white, so into following the rules. If he thinks he's supposed to forgive me, he will say the right words. I don't know if they're registering in his heart, though. I guess this is where God does His thing?"

"Yes. We sure can't do it."

"No." He shook his head. "Okay. Dan had someplace to go; he left. I stood there until after the sun went down."

"And then you went to Erik's?"

"We met at a coffee shop in Little Italy."

Again with the public confession.

"We sat outside. Didn't bother getting coffee. Like always, he was in an obvious hurry to be elsewhere. So I gave him the short version of my spiel. 'I'm sorry. I hope for your sake you can forgive me.' He called me a putz and walked off. I don't know how long I sat there."

They exchanged a despondent gaze. Erik's reaction was no surprise either.

"And Jenna?" Claire said. She had spent the day with their daughter, leaving her a short while before Max's expected arrival. Jenna appreciated their visits, but she couldn't be talked into coming to the hacienda. She insisted she had to get used to Kevin's absence starting immediately, his first night away.

"I picked up Chinese and went to her house. Made her eat a little something. She's so sad about Kevin, isn't she?"

Claire nodded.

"I almost didn't get into it with her, but then I figured maybe it'd give her something else to think about."

"You two have always had an open relationship."

"I think we've been straight with each other. Anyway, she wanted to let me off the hook too. She said there wasn't anything to forgive. I said someday she'd understand that there are things."

"You did good, Dad." She leaned over and squeezed his hand. "And you're two tons lighter."

"I feel better, but . . ." He shook his head. "Maybe it was all a ridiculous effort. I doubt it'll make an impact on any of them."

"Max, you did what you had to do. You made confession to them. Now it's their choice whether or not they'll forgive you. Remember your own reactions to your parents?"

He frowned. "It's obvious where Erik got his 'who cares' attitude."

She smiled softly. "And remember you and I discussed how the kids might react. We were not surprised. We imagined in one way or another everything you described."

"But—" His voice thickened. "If I could just erase those old tapes in their heads, then they could stop believing the lie that their dad ignored them because they're worthless, unimportant people."

Through a shimmer she saw tears spill from his eyes.

He rubbed the heels of his hands roughly across his face. "They should believe healthy things about themselves."

"Hon, you started erasing the old tapes today."

"I don't know—"

"Yes. You most definitely did. With your apologizing, you loved on them. You loved on them like crazy. That in itself records new over the old."

He frowned, clearly not buying her interpretation.

"Max!" Hearing her frustrated tone, she stopped talking. What was his problem? *Lord, can I have some insight here?*

"It's too little, too late," he said.

"Oh, hush up." She scooted closer, rising on her knees until she was almost nose to nose with him, and wrapped her arms around his neck. "You sound just like them. God is your Father, Max. He's trying to love on you like crazy and you won't let Him. He's trying to record in your heart that you matter. That He is wild about you even if you are imperfect. That He totally forgives you for being an absent dad."

Max tilted his head back, as if to focus better on her face.

"You know this, hon. Jesus took care of it all on the cross. Right? Maybe, though—" She tapped his chest. "Maybe you don't *know* it know it."

His frown eased into a wary expression. "What do you mean?"

"You're having trouble receiving love."

"Like the kids are?"

"Ach!" She screamed in jest. "Let's stop talking about the kids!" She drew his face closer to hers and kissed his cheek. In a husky voice, she whispered, "Let's talk about us."

"Huh?"

"I might be able to help you practice receiving love." She kissed the corner of his smile.

He chuckled. "Are you saying what I think you're saying?"

"That my husband turns me on because he's so incredibly honest and vulnerable?"

Max burst into laughter. "Well that wasn't exactly what I was thinking. But . . . ." He kissed her in a slow, leisurely way. "I think we can go with that."

Eight

"This is a familiar address," Rosie said.

Bobby pounded on the front door of the home again. "I don't remember ever being in this building. Police!" He raised his voice. "Open up!"

They were on the third floor of a condominium complex. Someone from the second floor had called in, complaining about loud voices and crashes above them. At the moment no sound came from the other side of the door. Still she tensed. Domestic disturbances were the worst. More than once a berserk couple had turned from beating on each other to physically attacking her or Bobby.

She said, "No, I don't think we've been here before. The street and number seem familiar is all."

Her partner thumped the door again.

"Coming!" a female voice called out.

A long moment passed before the door finally opened. A smiling woman greeted them. "Hi!"

Thirtyish. Blonde. Blue-eyed. Homecoming queen material. Black cocktail dress, above the knee, plunging neckline. Local television news personality. Felicia Matthews, in the flesh. Plenty of flesh.

Aw, nuts. Matthews plus the familiar address equaled Erik Beaumont's place. Not that Rosie had memorized his address from his driver's license. She just remembered numbers.

"You're the police?" Matthews cocked her head.

Maybe the question was rhetorical. Rosie thought of how she and

Bobby looked like twins dressed in their uniforms, short cold-weather jackets with telltale insignia, and ten pounds of equipment hanging at their waists making their hips look wide as a squad car.

Rosie hoped to spit that they were the police.

Bobby said, "There was a complaint about loud noise coming from your condominium."

"Oh, the condo is not mine. It belongs to my boyfriend."

"May we come in?"

"But we're fine, Officer. He was fussing maybe a bit too loudly, but he's settled down now."

"Ma'am, we really need to check things out if you don't mind." He smiled his real smile, not the cop one.

To keep from laughing, Rosie pressed her tongue against her cheek. Obviously he recognized the woman too. He had told Rosie that, like her, he'd watched the Beaumont-Matthews TV news show after they'd arrested the guy. Bobby asked his wife if she would tape the news when he was at work; he didn't want to miss a chance to ogle Felicia. His wife didn't think he was funny.

"Certainly." Matthews backed out of their way. "Please come on in. Erik! We have company, dear!" She shut the door behind them.

Although lamps were dim and gas flames danced in a fireplace, Rosie felt an instant coldness, a harshness about the place. The tiled foyer opened into a combination area of kitchen, dining, and living rooms. Uncovered floor-to-ceiling windows dominated one wall, black except for distant city lights. Daylight hours would provide a spectacular, big-bucks view.

A spiral staircase led to a small landing with one door, presumably a bedroom. Furnishings were ultramodern, all gleaming stainless steel and glass and sharp edges. Upholstery was black. The place was a mess with newspapers, clothes, and whatnot scattered everywhere.

"By the way," the woman said, "I'm Felicia Matthews." She said the name in an offhand way, making it obvious that she knew they knew her identity.

Bobby shook her hand. "Nice to meet you in person. I've seen you on the news. I'm Officer Bobby Grey. This is Officer Delgado."

Rosie nodded to her, not reaching for her hand since it was still clasped with Bobby's.

Erik Beaumont appeared, emerging from a hallway at the back.

Felicia said, "This is Erik Beaumont."

Although he seemed alert and his white shirt was tucked neatly into his jeans, he did not look well. He'd probably been drinking at some point that night. He stopped a few feet from them, making no effort to engage in conversation, his arms crossed.

Felicia went on, "So, as you can see, everything is fine and dandy. No disturbance going on here. What else can we do for you?"

Rosie said, "Mr. Beaumont, there's blood on your shirt. Are you all right?"

"Hm?" He looked down at his white shirt. "Oh, that." He held up a hand, a large bandage across its palm. "Just a little accident. We dropped some plates on the hearth and I was picking up shards of glass. Cut myself."

"'Dropped' plates on the hearth?" Rosie asked.

"Actually, they may have been thrown."

Felicia made a huffing noise.

He looked at her. "What?"

"Isn't this humiliating enough, having the police come to your door? Why would you say anything about plates being thrown?"

"Because you pitched them at my head, Felicia."

"Only after you shouted at me, Erik."

Obviously the argument wasn't finished.

"Officer Grey." Felicia twirled on her heel. "I don't want to talk to him anymore. I'd like to go home now. Can I do that?"

"That sounds like a good idea. Unless either of you want to file charges?"

"File charges?" She laughed, a tinkly sound. "Of course not! We just had a minor spat. We'll make up tomorrow."

"Mr. Beaumont?"

"Yeah. Ditto."

"Ma'am, do you have a car?"

"Yes." She waltzed to a coatrack and lifted a white furry thing from it.

"Officer Delgado will escort you to it."

"That would be sweet, but . . ." She batted her eyelashes.

Rosie batted her own, not quite believing what she was seeing.

Matthews said, "To tell you the truth, Officer Grey, I'd feel safer with a man. I'm parked way down the block and it is the middle of the night."

"That's fine. I'll be happy to walk with you."

Rosie cleared her throat. Bobby hustling off with a woman was never part of their game plan if they could help it. It provided too much opportunity for the appearance of impropriety.

He mouthed, "It's okay."

She made her eyes go wide. He raised his brows in reply, telling her not to worry. She imagined he couldn't wait to brag to his wife.

Men!

Speaking of men in that exasperated tone . . .

There was Erik Beaumont, shuffling off toward the kitchen. He was barefoot.

A confused mishmash of emotions hit Rosie. In another day, she could have fallen for a guy like Beaumont. Correction: She *had* fallen for a guy like him. Scratch that noise. Never again. He was a waste of oxygen.

But she understood enough about human nature to catch on that Beaumont was one hurting puppy. That led to compassion. And that unlocked the door to her Adopt the Hopeless Club, prompting her to pray silly things like, "Swamp him with Your love."

Bobby's voice echoed in her mind. *"Balance, Rosie. Find the balance. Don't give up on him, but don't lose your mind over him either."*

Rosie sighed to herself and headed to the kitchen.

Erik was pulling a brandy snifter from a cupboard, his back to her.

"Mr. Beaumont."

He turned. "Thought you left."

"No. I need to make sure you're all right." She walked over to him. "Can't go off and then have you bleed to death. Bad publicity for the department, you know. By the way, you are still bleeding, sir."

He held his bandaged hand up again. Blood had soaked through the wrap. "It's nothing."

"Let me see it. Why don't you sit down?" She pulled latex gloves from her back pocket and put them on.

He sat at a nearby glass-and-chrome table.

Kneeling in front of him, she took his hand and began to lift the wide bandage.

He said, "You seem vaguely familiar."

"You don't recognize me?" She smiled to herself, remembering that was the question he asked her.

"Should I?"

"DUI. About ten days ago."

"Eww. That was an ugly night. Sorry. I wouldn't recognize my own mother if she'd been the one arresting me."

"I think you need stitches." The half-inch gash was deep and crossed the fleshy part of his right palm. "We can transport you to the ER. You could take a cab home."

"No. It's fine."

"Well, let me wrap it better than this."

"Then will you leave?"

"Promise. Where—"

"Top cupboard, left of the sink."

She found a first-aid kit and carried it to the table.

"You creak and clink when you walk."

"Yeah." She knelt before him again. "I don't see any broken plates on the hearth."

"One good thing about Felicia is she cleans up her messes. Guess I should have let her do it by herself."

Rosie found everything she needed in the kit and went to work on his hand. "So I was wondering, Mr. Beaumont, why is it we meet twice within two weeks? Your neighborhood is part of a large area I patrol, but I've been at it for over a year and have never seen you before."

"I guess up until now I've been a very good boy."

"Or you just haven't gotten caught."

"Did you always want to be a cop?"

"Nice change of subject." She smiled. "No, I did not always want to be a cop."

"What changed your mind?"

"Bad guys like you. Drove me round-the-bend bonkers what they got away with. I quit law school. Figured making arrests would be a lot more fun than practicing corporate law." She paused. "Making a charge stick can be a challenge though."

"The mayor is a friend of my dad's. That's how I got out of the DUI."

"I heard."

"Bet that drove you round-the-bend bonkers."

"Soon as I finish bandaging your hand, I'm going to shoot you in the leg."

He laughed.

She looked up at him. His eyes were greenish, his teeth white and the kind of even that came only from orthodontic work. His black hair was just long enough to be mussy. She glimpsed the little boy he must have been.

Nuts. She really didn't care to see him in that light.

When he stopped laughing, she said, "Did you always want to be a bad guy?"

"Every good boy wants to be a bad guy. You should know that, Officer."

"But what makes them want to? I can never understand that part."

He didn't reply.

She placed another butterfly tape across his cut. "If these don't hold, you better see a doctor in the morning. A couple stitches might be necessary."

"My dad is a putz. Felicia's cheating on me. NBC hired someone else."

She unwrapped a large bandage. "So what you're saying is other people's behavior makes you want to be a bad guy?"

"I'm not blaming them. That stuff simply proves good guys don't win. Why should I bother?"

"Because the world needs more good guys, especially ones in the public arena." She pressed the bandage into place. "There. You really should let the air get to it tomorrow, but keep it covered for now. My EMT skills are not the greatest. It'll probably all fall apart and gangrene will set in."

He chuckled. "Thanks anyway."

"Sure." She gathered the wrappings, closed up the first-aid kit, and peeled off her gloves. "Trash can?"

"Under the sink."

She deposited the trash and returned the kit to its proper place. "Okay, as promised, I will leave now."

He followed her to the door. "What's your name again?"

"Delgado."

"You're Latino."

He didn't need a name to go with her appearance to figure that one out.

A lifetime of hearing racial references had tuned Rosie's ear to nuance. She discerned tones. Erik Beaumont's carried a hint of surprise, as if her heritage precluded her role as a cop.

No problem.

No problem if she gave herself to the count of five.

She started counting.

It stung. It always did. But she recalled her parents' admonition,

drilled into her psyche from an early age. She didn't have to let someone else's prejudice define her.

Five.

"Latin*a*." Rosie winked. "Got my green card and everything. See
you."

He held up his injured hand and smiled. "DUI and medical
attention. Let's hope you don't see me again."

"Amen to that." She opened the door. "Good night."

"Good night."

He shut the door behind her.

A few yards down the hall, she halted and turned to gaze at his
door. Several deep breaths later, the stomp dance going on in her chest
finally slowed.

"Lord," she spoke aloud, "he's a prig. A first-class prig. You're going
to have to get somebody else."

Nine

Lexi lifted her brush from the canvas and stepped back several paces to study the painting. Full orchestral music rebounded off the walls, some high-velocity piece with the words "fire" and "dance" in its title.

The recomposed rhinoceros was thinner than the first one. Emaciated even, with countable ribs. Nothing at all like the real animal in the photo she'd snapped.

She didn't often stray quite so far from the photos. It forced her to create out of thin air and taxed her limited abilities. She lost balance in the process. Cohesiveness.

Blame Kevin.

Blame Danny.

Blame Max.

Blame Zak.

Mostly blame Zak.

In the week and a half since Kevin shipped out, she had come to terms with her brother-in-law's exit. The wedge Danny had driven between himself and her would go the way of a lifetime of spats, its intensity fading. She doubted that Max's uncharacteristic display of *fatherly concern* would be repeated.

Life went on. Grateful for a break from family, she buried herself in landscape work by day, painting by night, and wishing Zak would call.

He had, that morning. Sort of. He texted a message to her cell phone. "Dinner, our beach, six p.m.?" Her workday pretty much ended at that point. She left the office early, changed into sweats, and jogged off the tension.

"Their" beach was a stretch in Solana, the midway point on the freeway between their homes. Dinner would be at a casual hamburger place. Nothing all that special. Nothing worthy of "date" status.

Still, Zak had contacted her. He wanted to see her.

Dinner never happened. He greeted Lexi in an exasperated tone, something along the lines of, "You're going to jog yourself to death, and, oh, by the way, Abbey the ex doesn't want me to see you. She knows you saved my life. She's just a little insecure."

It was all civil, all shrugs and yeah, sure, she understood. No problemo.

In the hours since then she had consumed enough carrots to feed an army of rabbits for a week and lost herself in reconstructing the rhinoceros.

Now she dabbed her brush on the palette, into a glob of charcoal-gray paint, and wondered how many ribs a rhino had.

Through the pounding music, she became aware of a tiny voice. She cocked her head, listening.

"Pick up the phone!" Danny. His muted shout came from the answering machine in the other room. The phone ringer was turned off, explaining why she hadn't heard it.

She set down the brush and hurried from the studio, twisting the volume knob to low as she passed the CD player.

"Lexi!"

"Okay, okay, I'm coming." In the living room, she picked up the cordless phone. "What?"

"Turn on the news!"

Erik. Her stomach twisted into a knot. "What's wrong?" She lunged for the remote next to the television and turned it on.

"He's going to flip out this time. Is he still on the air? I'm getting in my car."

"Just a sec. It's coming on. What's wrong?"

"Just listen. I'm heading to the studio."

The familiar image of Erik and Felicia filled the screen. "He looks okay."

"Listen to his voice."

"Felicia's talking."

"They should keep her talking and get him off."

"Shh."

The "Darling Duo of Newscasts"—as they'd been dubbed in a local magazine article—was engaged in casual banter, segueing from one report to another.

"Well, Felicia," Erik was saying, "as you know . . ."

Lexi said, "He just called her 'Flee-*sha*.' His smile is goofy. Now he's got his elbow on the desk. He's about buried his chin in his bandaged hand, like if he doesn't hold up his head, it'll fall off."

Danny groaned. "They're not cutting to a commercial, are they? They are going to let him make a complete fool of himself."

"Great for the ratings."

Danny swore under his breath.

Her twin never swore.

"Lex, meet me at the studio as soon as you can. We gotta get him out of there."

"Okay."

Danny broke the connection.

Mesmerized, Lexi remained in front of the television. It was obvious that Erik was feeling no pain. But as usual, he projected the charm that was second nature to him. Maybe the general public would not notice.

Felicia noticed, though. Her complexion flushed. She interrupted Erik again and again. She stuttered.

"Erik!" she said at last in a loud, strident voice. "It's time for a commercial break!"

"Right you are, Flee-*sha*. Stay tuned, folks." The camera picked up a full-face shot of him, his eyes all but closed, his mouth a grim line. "Next segment, we'll learn exactly how long Ms. Matthews has been two-timing me."

At last, a commercial replaced the newsroom.

The entire thing took less than three minutes.

Wow. One could commit professional suicide in the blink of an eye.

Ten

"Ouch." Rosie cringed at the television.

From his recliner, her father grunted. "I think my hearing is going bad."

"No, it's not, Papi." She muted the volume. "Erik Beaumont really did say what you heard."

"That his girlfriend is two-timing him? That is not a nice thing to say in front of the whole world." Esteban rose from his chair. "He is not a nice man. Look at his hand, all bandaged up. How did that happen?"

She wasn't about to answer. The less he heard about her work, the better.

He plopped down on the ottoman next to her. "You think he was digging in his garden?" He snorted a noise of disbelief. "He does not have the look of a man who digs dirt or scrubs his kitchen sink or cooks his own food. No, he injured his hand while up to no good."

Rosie knew her dad was a smart cookie, but sometimes she was truly surprised at his ability to read people.

"Rosita." He leaned forward until his forehead nearly touched hers, locking eyes with her. "Why do you come on your nights off and watch him on my television?"

Several replies sprang to mind. In the first place, to be with her father, of course. She spent much of her time off with him. She helped out at his restaurant, waiting tables or prepping food. She made sure he got home at a decent hour for a sixty-five year old. His capable manager did not need Esteban hovering until closing time.

And then there was the fact that she didn't own a television.

But something told her he would dismiss those . . . excuses.

She cleared her throat. "I'm praying for him."

Esteban sat up straight. "Ah!" he said in disgust.

"God told me to."

"You are crazy."

She grinned, waiting for what always followed.

"Just like your madre. Ah!"

"Thanks."

He shook his head. "Why don't you find a nice boyfriend and go out more?"

"I go out plenty."

"With police people."

"So? They're my friends, and they're nice."

"The ones you mention are all married."

"Their spouses are my friends too."

"You are lonely."

"Papi! I am not. Stop worrying."

"This Erik Beaumont reminds me of"—if thunder had a physical expression, it would look like what came over her dad's face—"Ryan Taylor."

"Nah. No way. Taylor had blue eyes."

"Do not make jokes about this. Ryan Taylor was evil. So is Erik Beaumont."

"Papi, yes, Taylor was evil. I fell for his blue eyes and his lies, and I never prayed for his soul. Beaumont is a stranger toward whom I am not in the least bit attracted. It's only when the news comes on that I'm reminded of him." *And when I take domestic disturbance calls to his condo.* But that wasn't the point.

"This is true?" he asked.

"It is true."

He kissed her forehead. "My heart is heavy. You need a good man."

"I have you."

He chuckled. *"Te amo, mija."*

His term of endearment always warmed her. *"Te amo, Papi."*

"Good night. Be careful going home." He left the room.

Rosie stared at the muted television. The weatherman and sports-caster now sat in the chairs usually occupied by Beaumont and Matthews. They appeared harried and uncertain.

She wondered why Beaumont had been left on air so long. It was obvious from the start of the program that he was not quite sober. He must have the entire staff wrapped around his little finger, else how in the world did he get on the set in the first place?

Unless the powers that be wanted him there because they needed a reason to fire him.

Oh, well! It wasn't her problem. He wasn't her problem. If he got fired, then she wouldn't have to watch him anymore. She wouldn't have to think about praying for him.

Except when she couldn't get him out of her mind.

Like now, when he wasn't on the screen in front of her.

"Aw, nuts, Lord. Please take care of him. Let him be fired or not. Whatever. Whatever will open his heart to Your divine love and mercy. Amen."

Eleven

"Mom!" Jenna's voice pierced through the phone line.

"Hi." Claire clicked off the television and wrapped an afghan more tightly about herself.

"Did you see him?" her daughter cried.

"Yes, I—"

"Erik's life is ruined! What are we going to do?"

"Oh, honey."

"It is!"

On any normal day Jenna's emotional outbursts were over the top. It was her personality. Since Kevin's departure, though, she'd been hitting the stratosphere on a regular basis.

"Now listen to me, Jenna. First off, we're going to pray."

"You sound more like Nana every day!" Jenna's words were not a compliment.

"Well, what can I say? Prayer works. The fact that your father and I are not divorced is proof that God exists and He wants the best for us."

"Erik doesn't believe that."

"It doesn't matter. Do you know how long your Nana and Papa prayed for us before we really believed that? A long time. So first off, prayer. Second—" An image of Erik came to mind, of his pathetic effort on television to function normally. Claire's throat constricted.

Her eldest was plunging headfirst down a slippery slide. Most likely he had already hit the low levels of alcoholism and job loss. What was next? Jail? Homelessness? The gutter?

"Mom!"

"Hm?" The word was more a cry of despair than a question.

"You said 'second.'"

She took a quick breath. "Right. Second. Second, we cry."

"Oh, Mom!"

Claire grabbed a tissue from a nearby box and pressed it to her face. She and Jenna did not speak for several moments.

"Mom, where's Dad?"

She blew her nose. "Outside, walking off . . . whatever."

"He talked to Erik, right?"

"Tonight?"

"No, I mean the day Kevin left, Dad came over and apologized for . . . for stuff. I figured he met with Erik too."

"Yes, he talked with all of you. Why?"

"It did a number on me, Mom. I mean, it was, like, *whammo!* All of a sudden Dad's nearly in tears, apologizing for missing my piano recitals three lifetimes ago. I told him he was crazy and who needed to talk about that? Then he made me realize he was serious, and he really needed me to listen. I reminded him that he always apologized when he didn't show up for something or was late, like to my wedding rehearsal. My reaction was always to tell him where to get off. Then he'd threaten to wash my mouth out with soap. In the end, we'd make up."

Claire couldn't help but smile. Dramatic and mouthy traits served Jenna well when it came to her relationship with Max. She usually didn't bury her anger or her hurts.

Jenna went on. "Dad said he just wanted to clear the air once and for all. So I said there was nothing to forgive, and asked him when he'd joined AA. He kind of laughed and said the steps were good even if alcohol wasn't involved. We talked about him starting his own group: Absentees Anonymous."

Claire blew her nose. Hearing Jenna's version of their conversation tore off a corner of the scab again. Would the wound ever completely heal? When the kids were little, she had made excuses for their dad's absence, for his seeming lack of interest in their lives. She should have confronted him and let the chips fall. By not being real herself, she had handicapped her babies.

"Mom, you asked me for forgiveness, too, last fall. I didn't get it then. I still don't. But I guess you both need to hear it, so okay: I forgive you and I forgive Dad for not being perfect. All right?"

Claire nodded, as if Jenna could see her. "All right."

"And I take full responsibility for my actions from here on out. I won't blame either one of you if I'm unhappy or do something majorly stupid."

"Honey, that's a mature attitude."

"I just don't want to sound like my students. All day long they gripe about whose fault it is they didn't do their homework. Anyway, the reason I asked about Erik is I'm wondering: how did he respond to Dad?"

"I'd rather you talked to your dad than hear my secondhand rendition."

"The thing is, was he upset? I mean, I was upset. It's just so emotional, you know? Erik doesn't do emotion. Lexi doesn't do emotion. Danny expresses it and probably handled Dad's whammo better than I did."

Claire nodded again. Jenna's opinion of her siblings mirrored Max's report. Lexi and Erik had blown him off. Danny emoted, quickly offering forgiveness to the dad he'd nearly idolized since childhood.

Jenna said, "My guess is Erik is upset and that's why he did this tonight. He's working it out. And if what he said about Felicia is true, there's a double whammo."

"Do you think she would?"

"Cheat on him? In a heartbeat. She's a— Well, never mind. So what are we going to do, Mom? Besides pray and cry?"

"Love on him."

"How do we do that?"

Claire looked around the room. The kitchen was large. She sat on a couch at one end of it, near a fireplace, dining table, and television. One wall was part of the original chapel in the more than one-hundred-year-old adobe building. It still displayed her mother-in-law's collection of crosses, a constant reminder of God's faithfulness.

She thought of the hacienda, of how it had suffused her with warmth and hope the first time Max took her there to meet his parents. She didn't have words for it until many years later. The place had been her safe harbor. People who came for retreats found it so. In recent weeks she could see how, at last, it was becoming the same for Max. It had been for her children as well, especially when they were little. Could it offer safety to them now?

"Jen, one of the guest rooms is almost finished. In another week or so, a second one should be done. Maybe . . ." *Oh Lord, please?* "Maybe it's time for a family retreat here. A weekend thing. Everyone would have a place to sleep. What do you think?"

"I think I'd be the only one who'd come."

Claire grabbed another tissue. What happened to the good old days when they all pretended life was just fine?

Twelve

Lexi entered the television studio not long after Danny. Via cell phone, he directed her to the producer's office and told her to ignore the closed door.

Still, she knocked.

None of the voices she overheard called out, "Come in."

She hesitated. What was she doing there? She would do anything for Danny, which was why she'd said yes to him without question and raced downtown. It didn't matter that it was after eleven p.m. or that she had to quit painting, her most important activity relegated to precious few hours a week, a thing she would not interrupt for anyone else.

But this was really all about Erik. Why would she stay for him?

Because he was her brother.

She figured the sibling thing was innate, reinforced by Nana's stories. According to her grandmother, Max and his brother BJ were always at odds unless somebody threatened the other one. Even in Lexi's lifetime her dad had gone to Washington to urge congressmen to insist Vietnam hand over MIA information.

Funny. He'd missed her eighteenth birthday because he was in D.C. defending, in a sense, his brother, most likely long dead.

Lexi shook her head and opened the producer's door. Danny's loud voice covered the noise of her shutting it behind her.

He stood in front of a desk, red faced and hands on hips. "You can't do this!"

Beside him, Erik sprawled in a chair, arm over its back, his legs

66

crossed. His smirk was typical *laissez-faire*, as if the whole scene bored him.

Lexi assumed the man behind the desk was the producer. He shrugged and said, "Yes, we can do this. I defer to our legal counsel. Jackie?"

A woman seated next to him flipped through a stack of papers. She wore blue jeans, a sweatshirt, her brown hair in a ponytail, and sleep folds still puffed at her eyes. "Uh . . . yes. Mr. Beaumont." She glanced up at Erik. "Your contract becomes null and void if you, uh, if you did what they say you did tonight."

He flashed his charming smile. "You missed it?"

"Sorry." She flushed. "I mean . . ." She cleared her throat. "My husband just returned from a two-week overseas business trip and we—uh, I don't always catch the late news."

"Jackie," Erik purred. "My own family and friends don't always catch the late news."

Danny leaned across the desk toward the producer. "Kipler, you can't get away with firing him. What you did was let him go on air when you shouldn't have, and then you kept him there. That makes it your responsibility."

"How were we to predict his idiotic behavior?"

"Because he was drunk!"

Erik lifted an arm and shook his finger. "I beg to differ. I only had a few."

They ignored him.

The producer said, "He didn't act drunk when I saw him. It wasn't obvious he was out of control until he accused Felicia of—that was when we cut him off."

"You're a liar!"

"I think this meeting is over!"

"You let the cameras roll long after the usual time for the commercial break. You trapped him on purpose. You've been after him for months!"

"Prove it."

"We will, you—"

"Dan." Erik laid a hand on Danny's arm and sprang to his feet. "Let's go. Jackie." He thrust his other hand toward her. "It's been a pleasure, my dear."

Shaking his hand, she smiled and blushed.

"Kipler." Erik shook his hand next. "It's been . . . well, whatever. Say good-bye, Dan." He turned. "Ah, Lexi! Everyone, this is my little sister, Alexis."

She ignored their stares, stepped to Danny, and grabbed the back of his jacket. "Come on."

While Danny fussed and muttered, Erik somehow got the three of them ushered out the door and down the hall.

"Wasn't that fun?" Walking between them, he swung one arm over Lexi's shoulders, the other over Danny's. "My heroes. Thanks for coming, guys."

"Erik, can't you be serious for one minute? They're railroading you. You've got to fight this."

"Let the lawyers unravel it. The night is young, and we have miles to go before we sleep."

Lexi slid an arm across his back. "You're our brother, Erik. We love you. Please stop hurting yourself. Please don't go out drinking tonight."

"Drinking?" He chortled. "Wouldn't dream of it. I have other plans. I'm going to kill my best friend."

"Brett?"

"Yep. Gotta stay sober for something like that, don't you think?"

Danny said, "Brett? What are you talking about?"

"Dan, Dan. My Boy Scout. What do you think I'm talking about?"

Lexi felt a sudden loss of energy. She knew what he was talking about. "Not Brett."

"Oh yes, Brett. Of all the males in San Diego panting after her, you'd think Felicia could have found somebody else."

It was going to be a long night.

They escorted Erik outdoors to the sidewalk for some fresh air. Lexi believed he was fairly sober. He'd been more hurt and angry than blitzed during the news.

"Brett Abbott?" Danny's shoulders sagged. He looked like a deflated balloon.

Erik said, "Having a hard time assimilating that, aren't you? Took me awhile."

"I always liked Felicia. Brett too."

"Tell me about it." He chuckled.

Lexi said, "Okay, guys, what's next? Food?"

They both frowned at her.

Erik said, "French fries instead of vodka?"

Danny turned to him. "You're not serious about Brett? I mean, you wouldn't really attack him."

"We had enough fistfights growing up, I'd know how to do it. If he were standing right here, I'd punch his lights out." Erik's voice went deeper than normal and he spat an expletive. All facade of cool, calm, and collected vanished. "I still can't believe it. We played base-ball together!"

Watching Erik fall apart while he was sober hurt worse than the other way. Lexi gazed down the sidewalk. They should probably just take him home and hide his keys again.

From a few yards away, a woman moved toward them. She was bundled up against the cold night and wore, like other street people, a stocking cap and long coat. She carried a gym bag.

"Excuse me," she called out.

Erik and Danny stopped talking.

She reached them. "Excuse me." Her soft voice carried a slight accent.

If not for the presence of her brothers, Lexi would have tensed. Even in the daytime the homeless frightened her. She never knew what they wanted from her. This woman was taller than Lexi.

Something about her seemed Asian. The shape of her eyes? The ends of her black hair stuck out beneath the cap, short and straight.

"You are Mr. Beaumont?"

"No." Obviously Erik was in no mood to sign autographs. "I've been told I look like him."

"But this is television place." She pointed to the tall building. "You are wearing same tie you wore on news tonight."

"Sorry."

"I believe you are Erik Beaumont. My name . . ." She paused and straightened her shoulders. "My name is Tuyen Beaumont. Your uncle was pilot in Vietnam. He shot down in 1973. He was . . . my father."

Thirteen

In her wildest dreams, Rosie never could have imagined she'd be standing outside Erik Beaumont's door again, and certainly not at seven a.m. wearing blue jeans and a hooded sweatshirt.

The door opened. He wore black sweats and a stone-cold sober expression of sheer confusion. "Hey."

"Hey."

Stepping outside into the hallway, he pulled the door shut behind himself.

She frowned. "On the phone you promised me coffee."

"Yeah." He finger-combed his hair, more a helpless gesture than an attempt to detangle and smooth the black mop. "In a minute, okay?"

In a minute. All right, she could give him a minute. *Then I'm out of here. Are You listening, Lord?*

He had phoned the police station in desperate need—according to Sgt. Susie Hall—to speak with Officer Delgado. Fans of the heartthrob-slash-newsman had been coming out of the walls since his DUI, Susie foremost among them. Once she'd deciphered that no crime or medical emergency was involved with Erik's phone call, she told him she could pass his phone number along to Delgado.

Half asleep, half in tune with the previous night's concern that haunted her dreams, Rosie had called him.

She rubbed sleep from her eyes now. "No more bandage on the hand."

He turned it palm side up. The cut was still evident. "Won't need to cover it today. No chance of it bleeding all over the news desk since I won't be sitting at the news desk." His chuckle sounded bitter. "Anyway, thanks for coming."

"Sure. Why don't you tell me what's going on?"

"I don't know where to begin."

"Cut to the chase, Beaumont. Did you do it or not?"

"Do what?"

"Murder Ms. Matthews and/or the person with whom she's two-timing you."

He barked a noise of disbelief. "Yeah, right! If only it were that simple."

"And I was going to apologize for being flippant. I'm sorry. Did they fire you?"

"Yes. No. Who knows? The suits have to sort it out."

"So the job and the girlfriend aren't the issue right now?"

"There's a woman inside." Speaking seemed difficult for him. He kept pausing, as if not sure what words to use.

Suddenly Rosie wished she had her gun. She knew better than to leave home without it. People were just plain weird, most especially the spoiled rich and famous. Why had this man called her? Why had she come?

Because she prayed for him and he asked for help.

Her dad warned that she let her faith cancel out her common sense. Someday, he feared, she would regret it.

Beaumont said, "We didn't know who else to call."

"We?"

"My brother and sister are here too. 911 didn't quite fit. I told them I had met this helpful cop. I thought you'd be in uniform." He wiggled a finger at the back of his neck. "And the bun."

She glared at him. "Last night was my night off. I should be sleeping right now so I can work tonight. Go call someone on duty if you want official."

"Sorry."

She made a show of glancing at her watch. "You're thirty seconds over time."

"Okay, okay. This woman says she's my cousin. That my uncle was her father. Benjamin Charles Beaumont Jr. He's MIA. Vietnam. Over thirty years ago."

Rosie blinked, taking in the enormity of what he had said. "Wow. Just out of the blue?"

"Yeah. Last night, when we were leaving the studio, she approached us. I guess I was the easy one to find."

"Well, it seems like good news. In a way. At least it makes your uncle no longer MIA. You'll find out what happened to him now."

"She's got papers, but how do we know she's telling the truth?"

"You need to call Immigration or the Department of Defense. Start with one of them. They're in the phone book."

"This is going to be a major blow to our grandparents."

"That would be your uncle's parents?"

"And our dad's."

"It's closure, Erik. Closure is always part of healing, distressful as it can be." *Nuts.* Had she really just called him by his first name?

"I suppose." He gave her a small smile, borderline authentic. "See how helpful you are? We've been basket cases all night. You show up and within two minutes you've calmly put everything into perspective."

"That's a cop's job."

"Officer Delgado, will you come inside and calm my brother and sister and this strange person who says she's our cousin?"

Rosie crossed her arms and looked at the floor. Meeting the family of a DUI dodger was not part of a cop's job. Her dad would say this was when her common sense should kick in. Her partner would say the neon welcome sign for her Adopt the Hopeless Club flashed big-time. He would say it was overdue to burn out.

What did they know?

She looked up at him. "Is coffee involved?"

He grinned and opened the door for her.

Beaumont's living room area still had the look of a hurricane's aftermath. The kitchen fared better. Rosie noticed a young guy at the sink, up to his elbows in sudsy water, and figured he was the reason for a semblance of order.

The scent of coffee beckoned, and she followed Erik toward it.

"This is my brother, Danny," Erik said.

He turned with a polite smile and wiped his hands on a towel.

"Dan, this is Officer Delgado." He looked at her. "I don't know your first name."

Danny shook her hand, grinning. "You're not supposed to, dork. Nice to meet you, Officer. Can I get you some coffee?"

"Yes, please. Black."

Erik said, "How come I'm not supposed to?"

She shrugged at him.

Ignoring his brother, Dan poured coffee into a mug. "Thanks for coming."

"Sure."

Her immediate impression of Dan was that he didn't resemble his brother in the least. He was shorter and friendly without the phony charm. His shaggy hair was brown, his eyes dark.

He handed her the cup. "It's been a long night. Did he tell you?"

"Yes. I don't know what I can do to help, except suggest which agencies to call."

"That'd be great."

He filled two more mugs and gave one to Erik.

"Um," she said, "you guys could have figured that out for yourselves. Why call me?"

Dan looked at Erik. "You didn't tell her."

"I was getting to it."

Dan said to her, "Plain and simple. This woman, this Tuyen, is scared to death. She wants a police escort to meet her grandparents."

"Why?"

"We haven't figured that one out yet. All she says is 'police, please.'"

A police escort? To meet family?

Rosie went to the table and sat, hoping the caffeine would deliver a heavy dose of common sense.

Fourteen

The stranger was creeping out Lexi.

There were many reasons she produced the heebie-jeebies, not the least of which were her eyes. Desert-sky blue. The exact shade as Lexi's grandfather's. Right there, smack-dab in the middle of decidedly Asian features.

With a shake of her head, she shut the door to Erik's bedroom and started down the spiral staircase, hoping against hope one of her brothers had made a breakfast run. The Pit, aka Erik's condo, had stuff crammed everywhere except in the cupboards and fridge. They were bare as Mother Hubbard's.

Crossing the living room, she spotted a woman seated at the kitchen table with Erik and Danny.

"Lexi," Danny said as she approached. "This is Officer Delgado, the policewoman Erik told us about. This is our sister Lexi."

Officer Delgado smiled and shook her hand. "Hi."

"Hi. Guys, is there any food yet?"

Blank stares met her question.

"Guess not."

"Help yourself to coffee," Erik said. "Where is she?"

"In the shower." She poured coffee. They all seemed to have difficulty saying her name. *Tuyen.* It didn't easily roll off the tongue.

"Well." Officer Delgado cleared her throat. "This so-called cousin wants a police escort, but none of you know why?"

"Nope." Lexi sat at the table.

Wearing blue jeans and a navy-blue sweatshirt, the woman did not look like a cop. Her hair was dark brown with reddish highlights and pulled back in a bouncy ponytail. Although she was obviously Hispanic, her speech pattern was not that of a recent immigrant. She spoke with authority, too, in a no-nonsense tone. A wrinkled sheet of paper and a pen lay before her. Not exactly professional tools of the trade.

Delgado eyed each of them in turn. "Do you mind telling me the story from the beginning?"

Danny described their meeting outside the studio the previous night.

"And why were you all three there together?"

"Uh, well—"

"She saw it," Erik said, referencing his TV performance. "It's a sibling thing, Officer. Dan's been watching my backside since I was in fifth grade. A baseball coach yelled at me. My pip-squeak of a brother told him where to stick it. Lexi stood right behind him, frowning with her hands on her hips." He smiled at the memory. "They're twins; they travel as a twosome."

"So, Dan and Lexi, you went to the studio to . . . ?"

"Chew out the powers that be." Danny shrugged. "Don't know if it helped any."

"Okay. Then you all went outside and this woman approached you?"

"Yes. She blew us over with her announcement. Man, we had no idea what to do. But we sure didn't want to wake Nana and Papa up in the middle of the night with that bit of information."

"Nana and Papa?"

"Our grandparents. Ben and Indio Beaumont. They live outside of Santa Reina."

"Where the fire was last fall?"

"Yeah. The Rolando Bluff Fire almost destroyed their estate. Our parents live there now too. It's called the Hacienda Hideaway. They're reopening it soon, a retreat center."

Delgado took notes as he spoke.

Lexi said, "Not that she wanted to go there. That was why she found Erik first. She said it would be rude to show up at her grandparents' unannounced. They would feel like they'd been pounced on by a tiger. Or something to that effect."

"Her English is good?"

"Pretty good. You have to listen closely. She said she's been in San Francisco for a couple years."

"Doing what?"

"She didn't say."

"So she made it clear she didn't want to go to the grandparents yet, and you brought her here."

Erik said, "She didn't want to go to a hotel. She seemed frightened about losing us. My place was the closest."

"What'd you guys do all night?"

Lexi exchanged glances with her brothers. It had been an incredibly, indescribably long night. Danny had suggested she call Zak. Maybe a fireman's uniform would fill the woman's odd request for a police escort. Lexi hadn't told Danny about her split-up with Zak. There were no words to explain how they could split up when they'd never been together. She told him Zak was out of town.

Now she said to the policewoman, "We got a pizza. Mostly we talked. She insisted she wanted the police to go with us today. Finally Erik promised to call you. I convinced her to use the bedroom upstairs. We sort of crashed in the living room. It was just totally weird."

Erik said, "She had papers. She knew all the right stuff. The year Uncle BJ disappeared in Vietnam, that he was a pilot. Our dad's name. Nana and Papa's names. She said she was born in 1980, which means . . ." He paused.

They'd all agreed, it was the worst point of her story.

"Which means," Erik continued, "that he would have been there for a long time."

"And where is he now? And her mother?"

"They're dead." He shrugged. "No clue when that happened."

"Didn't the U.S. pull out of 'Nam in seventy-three or so?"

"Yeah. BJ was shot down in January, days before the signing of the Paris Peace Accords. Of course things didn't end overnight, but still, the timing stinks."

Delgado winced. "I'm sorry."

No one said anything. Lexi was used to such silences. They occurred whenever a conversation went to Uncle BJ, even with total strangers.

"Yet," Erik said, "we don't know whether we can trust her or not. We decided to call in the pros. What do you think?"

"A crime hasn't been committed."

"But do we trust her?"

"Play it out. Take her to your grandparents. She must have talked to officials who helped her find you. Get in touch with people who know about this sort of thing."

"Will you come with us?" Erik asked.

"It's not exactly what I do. If she wants some sort of official protection, you could hire a private security person."

"We would pay you."

"That's not the point."

"Then what is the point? You're a police officer and this wacko wants help from a police officer! Aren't you into building community relations?"

The exchange between Erik and the cop grew curious. Lexi sat back in her chair to watch. Some undercurrent flowed, some undefined tension.

Normally by now, Erik would have switched on his charm to full blast. By now, the recipient would have been kissing his feet. But none of that was happening.

Officer Delgado was not his type. His girlfriends had always been Felicia clones: blonde, blue-eyed, attractive in spandex, feet kissers.

The policewoman was plain looking. Her shape, though hidden in the sweatshirt, appeared more solid than curvy. She was a Latina, a culture that usually brought out Erik's snooty side. Lexi never could understand why he acted prejudiced at times, like he forgot Native American blood ran in his own veins.

To top it off, something in this woman's attitude said she'd never so much as touch his little toe, let alone kiss it. Maybe she hated newsmen. Maybe she had her own issues.

No wonder there was an undercurrent.

"The point is," Delgado said, "no crime has been committed."

"You already made that observation."

Danny whistled softly. "Wow."

Lexi followed his gaze and looked over her shoulder. Wow was right.

"Hm," Erik murmured.

The stranger, their so-called cousin, glided down the staircase, a vision of Asian elegance.

She wore what Lexi thought must be a traditional outfit, a long tunic with side slits and a standup collar. It fell over pants of the same color, a sunburst yellow gold. Down one side of the tunic, from top to bottom, flowed an intricately embroidered floral design, white petals and spring-green leaves and stems. Her black hair was smooth, freshly shampooed, falling just so in a blunt cut.

Lexi noted the one off-key note. Despite the dress, the young woman did not resemble a typical Southeast Asian. The shape of her eyes and face hinted at it, but she was too tall and large-boned. It was obvious one of her parents could have been American. And then there was the blue. They said Uncle BJ's eyes were that color, like Papa's.

For the first time since their bizarre meeting, Lexi admitted that Tuyen could very well be her cousin, a person whose existence had never even been imagined by any of her family.

"Okay." The quiet word came from the policewoman. "I'll go with you."

Fifteen

Rosie, Rosie." Bobby set down his hammer and wiped sweat from his brow with his T-shirt sleeve. "Didn't I tell you to close up shop? This Adopt the Hopeless junk leads nowhere."

Ignoring her partner's disapproval, Rosie sat beside him on the wooden step. "It's looking really great." She referenced the deck he was in the process of building behind his house.

"Thanks, but let's not change the subject."

"I didn't stop by to ask your permission. I just wanted to let you know why I was taking the day off."

"Because it makes so much sense. You're using up your personal time to impress a loser."

"Rephrase: to develop community relations."

"With a family up in the hills? In case you haven't noticed, that is not your community."

"Think big picture, Bobby. I was all set to say no, and then this young Asian woman walks into the room and I realize, hey! We're talking about a real human being who wants me to help her unite with grandparents she's never met. You would have said yes too."

"Did you tell your dad?"

She gazed at the sky and shook her head in disbelief. "He asked if I'd told you."

"Your two guardians. We drive you round-the-bend bonkers, don't we?"

She punched his arm. "The thing is she made me think of my

81

own family. I remembered when my two cousins came up from Mexico, ages ago. We'd never met them before, and they were so terrified, so desperate for a new start in the States. They lived with us for a while and Papi gave them work."

"You're talking about your cousins at the restaurant? Ramón and Raúl, the chefs?"

"Yes."

"I thought they were born in California, like you."

"They weren't." She felt the hackles. "And they're legal."

"I wasn't implying—"

"Sorry." She took a deep breath and blew it out. "I know you weren't. For a second, you sounded like that prig Beaumont."

"I take it, then, you're not getting involved with this situation because you've got a thing for him?"

She glared at him. "Yeah, right. I have the hots for a spoiled-brat borderline racist who went on air drunk, shredded his girlfriend's reputation to pieces, and knowingly threw away his life's work."

"Just making sure." Bobby smiled. "Did she say why she wants the police escort?"

"She didn't directly answer the question, but I know why. It was the terrified look in her eyes. It was the same one my cousins had. They'd witnessed death and destruction in the homeland. There was nothing for them to return to. Their only hope lay in our hands."

"You're not this woman's family, though."

"No. But I think Tuyen Beaumont, for some reason, can't trust her American family like my cousins could trust my dad. Maybe she heard bad stuff about them. Maybe, for some reason, a uniform symbolizes safety." Rosie glanced at her dark-blue slacks and long-sleeved shirt with its patch and her badge pinned on the front.

"A uniform, like her GI father," he offered.

"Maybe."

Maybe. She sighed to herself. *Lord, why is it I sense it's more like You're sending me?*

The answer came clearly, as it sometimes did. It was the same as turning a page in a book and reading the last half of a sentence.

"Bobby, I just know that she's at the end of her rope and I'm in a position to help keep her from letting go."

They met in a parking lot a couple blocks from Erik Beaumont's condominium. Rosie got out of her SUV and walked over to them.

She smiled at Tuyen and received a shy one in return. The young woman still wore the beautiful *ao dai*, probably because the occasion was extraordinarily special. She would want to make the best impression on her father's parents.

"Are you ready?"

Tuyen nodded.

The Beaumonts stood in a semicircle near Erik's car, its rooftop up. The twins were nothing like their brother. By comparison, they seemed fairly normal, not uppity or obnoxious. Dan was seldom still, Lexi seldom moved much at all.

Dan said, "Thanks for the uniform."

"Sure. Sorry I couldn't use a squad car."

"No problem. Tuyen prefers to ride with you."

The woman nodded again.

Rosie said, "That's fine. Does the family know you're coming?"

"Yes. I talked to Mom. They'll all be there. They probably think it's about Erik's fiasco last night."

Erik chuckled. "Won't they be disappointed. They've probably been checking out rehab centers and putting my name on waiting lists."

Lexi ignored him. "And I called our sister, Jenna. She's getting off work early so she can come. Her husband's overseas. She's so miserable, she didn't even ask why."

"Anyone else included?" Rosie asked.

"No."

She studied their faces. "You three look like you're ready to keel over."

The frown lines deepened.

"Okay, listen. You didn't sleep well last night, if at all. You probably haven't eaten right today. This news is too much to take in.
You're fearing for your parents and grandparents because they will be
as upset as you are, probably more so. Why don't you all give it a rest
and ride with me?"

They exchanged glances and half nods.

Dan said, "We can hitch a ride back with Jen."

"Okay then. Let's go." Rosie caught the tone of her own voice. She
might as well have said, "Chop, chop! Get a move on so we can get
this over with." That was Bobby's influence, always telling her to stay
on task. By which he meant it was time to disengage her feelings.

Which made sense, to a certain degree. Getting personally involved
blurred the lines between her job as a professional and her life as
a woman with hang-ups and opinions. The potential for disaster
loomed in such situations.

But . . . there were these hurting people in front of her without
an obvious bad guy to arrest.

When in doubt . . . *Lord, I'm listening. You know the pain they're
in. Why can't I be a help to them?* Shouldn't *I be a help to them?*

They climbed into her car, Erik up front with her, the other three
in the backseat. As she slid the key into the ignition, he leaned
toward her.

"Thank you, Officer."

Her hand stilled. The sincere voice and somber expression held
her attention. Perhaps the man was not beyond hope.

To heck with Bobby's advice.

"Call me Rosie," she said.

The corners of his mouth lifted slightly.

Sixteen

Her mind in overdrive, Claire surveyed the large room. Within moments her family would be gathered in it. And she would tell Erik, her firstborn, that she was sorry. So very, very sorry for failing him.

Max draped an arm across her shoulders. "Sweetheart, his wrong choices are not entirely our fault."

In spite of his sensitivity to her unspoken fears, she could not melt into the comfort he offered.

"Claire," Indio said, "you've got to let the guilt go."

Let it go? But she hadn't even admitted it yet, not to Erik, not to the one who needed to hear it.

She ignored their words and eye contact. "Do you all think this room is the best place for . . . for . . . ?"

Indio chuckled. "For a powwow? Yes."

They still called the room by its old Spanish name, *sala*. It was a combination of sitting and dining rooms. Evidence of the fire that had scorched it was gone. Newly paneled walls and new terra-cotta tiles on the floor freshened its appearance. The ceiling was a clean white between the oak beams. Even the stonework around the enormous fireplace had been scrubbed clean of black streaks.

The room lacked a finished ambience. There was a barrenness to it, probably because no rugs or window coverings or artwork had been added yet. Nor was there enough furniture to accommodate future guests. The Spanish décor was haphazard, caught in the leather couch and wrought-iron chandelier, but not in the brass lamps.

"Mom." Jenna sat between Indio and Ben on the couch. "We all have a place to sit. What else do we need?"

"I don't know exactly. Something's missing. What's an intervention supposed to look like?"

"Claire." Max hugged her close to his side. "I know we sent the construction workers home early so we'd have complete privacy. But this is more of a powwow than a formal intervention. We're not prepared for that. We would need a counselor to help, a plan of action—"

"But, Dad," Jenna protested. "We do plan to confront Erik, right? Tell him we love him and that we refuse to let him drink himself to death?"

Ben said, "It's what he needs to hear."

Max said, "How do we back up what we say? How do we not let him drink himself to death? It's not like we live together. I don't pay his bills, so it's not like I can cut him off."

Claire rubbed her forehead, weary of the questions that had no answers. Erik was bent on self-destruction. He was probably an alcoholic. She did not know how to fix him. Thirty years of mistake-riddled mothering stabbed at her soul. Life seeped out through pinprick punctures.

"Claire's right," Indio said. "Something is missing and it's not curtains. We haven't invited the Lord to join us." She closed her eyes. "Holy God, I invoke Your presence right now. Dwell in our midst, direct our conversation . . ."

Claire gazed at her mother-in-law, wishing she could absorb Indio's faith just by watching it in action. Why couldn't she turn her thoughts like that, quick as a wink, to God and expect Him to answer?

"Amen," Indio said with a smile directed at Claire. "Dear, I just remembered something. When Ben and I came to the realization that we had hurt our sons, we were sitting in this room. Since then, I've thought it a perfect place for mending hearts. I believe it will work just fine."

Claire nodded in agreement. Riding the coattails of Indio's wisdom sounded better than curling up in a fetal position.

E rik, Lexi, and Danny appeared without warning at the wide doorway of the sala. Its door had been left open to the courtyard, as it often was on sunny winter afternoons.

Claire took a step toward them, eager to hug Erik and to confess her mistakes and to get past the initial pain and pour unconditional love onto him—

Others came into sight. Two strangers. Two women.

Claire halted, her mouth half-open, her leg muscles tensed.

A policewoman.

And a tall woman of obvious Asian descent, wearing a formal dress of the Far East. Of . . . of *Vietnam*.

In that split moment, at some unconscious level, Claire knew what was going on. Her mind could not quite grasp it, though. Words failed to take shape to explain what "it" was.

She felt herself go very still. She sensed Max beside her go very still. She sensed Indio and Ben behind her go very still.

None of them had been watching at the windows. They had not seen or heard the group approach. That wasn't unusual. There was no front door or doorbell. Given the U-shaped layout of the place, it was easy for people to roam in and about the hacienda unnoticed.

Claire imagined Erik and the others walking along the exterior entryway, a narrow hall that cut through the U between the parking lot and courtyard. The flagstones would have muffled their footfalls, the thick adobe walls their voices.

Indio spoke first. "Erik?" Her voice was more of an exhaled puff.

Erik's smile kept slipping out of place. "Uh, we have some, uh, surprising news. Nana, you might want to sit back down."

Claire made eye contact with him. Sorrow flowed through her, a steady stream of regrets mixed with words meant to heal. But she understood that they would not be spoken today. The meeting was not about him or her.

The stream pooled in a corner of her heart. She closed it in, shut it off, and hoped the dam would hold.

Seventeen

Chasing after suspects would have been easier. In the dark through city streets, on foot, blindfolded. Having a tooth pulled without benefit of a numbing agent would have been a treat by comparison.

Rosie sighed to herself. She didn't have a choice. She was stuck witnessing a pain she could not begin to fathom rip its way through a family.

She watched the woman who stood nearest the door they had entered. On the ride up into the hills, Rosie had asked Erik for names, and so she figured this was the mother, Claire.

She wore stylish glasses, comfortable-looking khakis, and a long-sleeved T-shirt, no makeup. Her hair was chin length, brown going gray. She was of average height and weight, in her low fifties, attractive in an understated way that money made possible.

Her face spoke volumes. In light of Erik's performance the previous night, Rosie imagined Claire's forehead creases and sad mouth expressed a mother's pain at her son's humiliation. As the woman's gaze passed over Rosie and landed on Tuyen in her oh-so-obvious Vietnamese dress, something shifted. A light went on.

According to Erik, Claire had never met BJ, the missing guy. But his mother had the appearance of an intelligent woman. She was probably bright enough to put two and two together. She would have heard the crazy stories about MIAs being spotted alive, and she would have wondered now and then about BJ's fate.

Claire turned and touched Max's arm as she walked past him. The grandparents, Ben and Indio, and the other sister sat down on the couch. Lowering herself to the floor, Claire sat at Indio's feet and placed a protective hand on the older woman's knee.

Like she knew.

Tuyen held a large, padded envelope. Erik took hold of her elbow and drew her gently a few more steps into the room. They both looked over their shoulders at Rosie and the twins. Glances were exchanged, half nods given. They had all agreed Erik should be the spokesman. It was time now.

"Uh, everyone. Dad, Nana, Papa, Mom, Jen. This is Tuyen." He paused. "Tuyen Beaumont."

Dead silence. And then a whimper from Indio.

Rosie shut her eyes momentarily. The unspeakable agony of not knowing for thirty-five years what had happened to her son was wrapped up in the older woman's soft cry.

"Uncle BJ was her father." Erik added the unnecessary explanation.

"Was?" Ben croaked out the word.

Tuyen moved a step away from Erik and bowed slightly toward the others. "I am pleased to meet my grandparents and my uncle."

Rosie's heart thumped in triple time. She ached for the foreigner as she spoke in her thickly accented, gentle voice the words she must have rehearsed for years.

"My father killed when I am child. I very sorry for your loss."

Ben moaned a long, low cry.

Indio wailed, a soul-shattering sound. Before it ended, before she could take another breath, she was rushing across the room and scooping Tuyen into her arms.

Wordlessly, the short, round woman of obvious Native American descent and the tall Amerasian in her beautiful traditional dress held on to each other, tears flowing unabashedly from both.

Rosie sank onto a chair near the door, suddenly overcome with gratitude that she was there to see such an incredible sight.

Danny tapped her arm and held out a box of tissues. She helped herself to a handful.

Several moments of quiet sniffles passed. After a bit Indio introduced the others to Tuyen, filling in their relational names for her. Papa Ben, Uncle Max, Cousin Jenna, Aunt Claire. Although everyone's cheeks were damp, only Claire clasped her in a big hug as Indio had.

Max suggested they all sit back down. Indio ushered the girl to the couch. Claire offered to make tea.

Across the room, Tuyen caught Rosie's eye. "This is my friend."

Rosie met their puzzled looks with a little wave. She really needed to get out of there. "I'll help with the tea."

Claire gave her a slight nod and they walked together through the door.

The woman turned to her. "I'm Claire Beaumont."

"Nice to meet you. I'm Rosie Delgado."

"How do you know"—she hesitated, no doubt getting used to not only the newcomer's name, but her existence as well—"Tuyen?"

"Erik, Danny, and Lexi introduced us."

"What?" She stopped in her tracks. "How did they . . ."

"Mrs. Beaumont, why don't you sit down for a moment?" Rosie spotted a bench and led her to it.

She took the opportunity to glance around the place. It was a lovely old hacienda with white stucco walls and a red-tile roof. From the living room they had stepped directly outdoors onto a covered verandah. It surrounded a courtyard on three sides.

They now sat facing it. Dried-up flower beds and a broken fountain filled the space. She remembered the Rolando Bluff Fire of the previous fall. On the ride up the long driveway, she had noticed evidence of it having swept through the Beaumont grounds. It must have hit even inside this courtyard.

"Mrs. Beaumont—"

"Please, call me Claire."

"All right. Claire. I'm here because Tuyen asked for a police escort." She shrugged. "At this point I don't know why."

"But how did my children . . ." Again, her voice trailed off. The woman seemed to be in a daze. No wonder, given the circumstances.

"Tuyen tracked down Erik at the television studio last night. She made her police request, and he called the station and asked for me because, um . . ." Did the mother know about the DUI? Or the domestic disturbance call? If not, Rosie sure didn't want to be the one to unload those surprises on the poor woman at that moment.

She continued. "Because we had met on a previous occasion. I patrol his neighborhood."

Claire raised a palm. "Enough said." She sighed. "I always wondered if BJ had survived, and if so, for how long. The details were sketchy about him being shot down. Then there were all those reports of MIAs being spotted." Another sigh. "Well, the etiquette books never covered this one, did they?"

Rosie smiled. "Tea is a good idea."

"I'm not sure, but my mother-in-law always makes tea. In the middle of the big fire here, she was making tea." She placed a hand over her mouth, holding back a cry. "Dear Ben and Indio," she whispered. "I feel so bad for them. They've been through too much, and now this."

Rosie blinked back her own tears. *Dear Lord. Help us.* "Claire, the best thing you can do for them right now is hold yourself together. We'll make the tea, and you will all get through this day. Everything will be okay."

Claire removed her glasses and pressed a sleeve to her eyes. After a moment she nodded. "Thank you."

"No problem. It's just part of my job." She grinned. "Boiling water is what I do best."

Eighteen

Lexi couldn't even lose herself in the fantasy of how to capture the moment on canvas. The whole scene was just too bizarre to compare to any known occurrence in her life. It was worse than anything. It was more devastating than the wildfire. Uglier than her parents' breakup. More confusing than their reconciliation. In a different solar system from trying on little black dresses.

Knees pulled to her chest, she sat on the rug, leaning against the big stone hearth, a pillow cushioning her back. She fought down nausea one minute and tears the next. She imagined telling Zak about it, and then remembered he wasn't her friend anymore.

By the time her mother and the policewoman served tea, it all seemed so ridiculous she wanted to laugh out loud hysterically to drown the noise in her head.

"Tuyen." Her dad leaned forward in his chair, speaking in a gentle voice. "Will you tell us about your life?"

Typical Max; he had taken charge. Not that anyone else seemed capable at the moment.

The ripple effect went round and round the room. Nana whispered her favorite phrase, "God is good," about five hundred times. She and Tuyen held each other's hands until their knuckles were white. Papa blew out one breath after another until Lexi asked him if he was all right. She got a fierce scowl in reply. Erik and Danny had gone totally quiet, rearranged chairs, and twiddled their thumbs. Jenna kept shaking her head as if to knock something loose in it.

"Tuyen?" Max prompted again.

She lifted her gaze from the padded envelope on her lap and looked at him.

"Maybe you could start with your birth. When were you born?"

Lexi held her breath and traded panicked looks with Danny. Here it came, the worst part. She wanted to press her hands over Nana's ears and make loud noises.

Tuyen said, "I was born in 1980."

It took less than a split second for them all to do the arithmetic. Lexi knew they were finished when Nana gasped, Papa put his forehead in his hands, and her parents went bug-eyed and slack-jawed.

"Seven years?" Nana cried.

Max held up a hand. "When . . ." His voice was hoarse and it faltered. "When was your father killed?"

"Nineteen eighty-two."

Lexi lowered her face to her knees, unable to watch the fresh wave of anguish roll through her family. She slipped her fingers into her ears, but that scarcely muffled the laments.

At least the worst was over. Now they knew everything. Uncle BJ disappeared, but he hadn't died. No, he had lived for nine more years. *Nine.* And none of them were aware of it! He obviously was involved with a woman. He became a father. And then he died.

Yes, the worst was over. That was the final blow.

As far as Lexi knew, anyway.

What about your mother, Tuyen?" Max asked after things had quieted again.

Lexi lifted her head. From the expressions on their faces, her family appeared in a suspended state of shock. At least the tears had slowed or stopped altogether.

"My mother die with my father."

Nana touched Tuyen's cheek. "Oh, my. I am so sorry. You poor,

poor child. You must have been only two years old. Who raised you?"

"My grandparents. My mother's parents." She leaned into Nana's hand and closed her eyes for a long moment.

Lexi noticed the large, unopened envelope still lay on her lap. She kept a protective hand over it as she had in the car on the ride to the house, but she was definitely more at ease than she'd been. Strange to think that they'd met less than twenty-four hours before.

Nana said, "Did they tell you about your parents?"

Tuyen nodded. "My father come from the sky. My mother see parachute, and she find him. He is hurt. Very hurt. Burned." She traced a finger down her left arm, across her chest, over the left side of her face. "His leg wrong." She reached down and made a twisting motion at her shin. "My mother take good care of him. She hide him from Communists. He get well. My grandparents don't like, but she love him."

A silent minute passed as that news sank in.

Max said, "Why didn't they leave? Why didn't he bring you to see us?"

"My village too far away. Far, far. Up in mountains. Enemy all around. Someone betray them. They kill them. My grandmother hide me."

"In 1982?"

"Yes, 1982."

"Do you remember your mother and father?"

Tuyen shook her head, but her face softened. "She was beautiful. He was tall. I have blue eyes like him." She pointed to her eyes. "You want see photo?"

"You have a photo?" Max nearly shouted in surprise.

She nodded eagerly and reached inside the envelope. "My grandmother say more Americans in village before I am born. They have camera."

"What happened to those other Americans?"

She shrugged. "Some go to Cambodia, not come back. Some die

with my father." She pulled things from the envelope. "See? Benjamin Charles Beaumont Junior and Niang Tam."

As one, Lexi and her family swooped to the couch and surrounded it. Tuyen held the picture gently between her fingers and smiled.

The color photo was bent and cracked, the finish grainy. Lexi guessed it had been taken with an old Polaroid Land camera. Two people stood in it, a jungle scene as backdrop.

Uncle BJ almost did not resemble the pictures Lexi had seen of him. He was tall, like Papa, but he sort of tilted, as if one leg was shorter than the other. He was no longer handsome. Dark slacks and a baggy short-sleeved white shirt hung from him like rags on a broomstick. And he was burned, scars obvious on his arm and one side of his face.

Nana began to weep again, very softly. She whispered, "My son."

Lexi wished she could run away and hide for a very long time.

Tuyen must have sensed they needed awhile to absorb each new thing she revealed. Whatever else she had pulled from the envelope, she kept hidden from their sight.

They all lingered in silence for a time, each dealing in their own way. Lexi noticed how close her parents sat together on the love seat, their hands entwined. Jenna had squeezed onto the end next to their mother. Danny and Erik alternately sat on the hearth and paced.

"Excuse me." The policewoman spoke.

Lexi had forgotten she was even in the room.

Officer Delgado sat in an armchair near the door, apart from the semicircle of seats around the couch. She looked at Max. "Do you mind if I interrupt?"

He shook his head, still with a dazed expression.

"Tuyen," Delgado said, "I am curious. Why did you want the police to come here with you today?"

"Because I am afraid. My grandparents always hate Americans.

They say Beaumont family will hate me. They say Beaumont family will hurt me. Grandparents die, I come to San Francisco. Police protect me in San Francisco. Help me find my father's family."

"I understand." Officer Delgado spread her hands. "Well, I think the Beaumonts are kind people. They will not hurt you."

Tuyen grinned. Her face lit up. "No. They not hurt me." She reached under the envelope. "I have necklace."

Nana stared at the silver chain with its clinking little rectangles. Dog tags. Tuyen handed them to her.

Lexi crossed her arms, hugging herself tightly. Nana kissed the dog tags, unable to read them without her glasses. Danny went behind the couch and peered over her shoulder.

"Oh, man." He whistled softly. "There it is."

No one else moved. Another long, quiet moment passed.

Then Papa stood abruptly and glowered at Officer Delgado. "Blast it all!" he barked. "How do we know she's telling the truth?"

Lexi flinched, but the policewoman didn't bat an eyelash.

Nana spoke up quickly. "Ben." The tone wasn't her gentle one.

"Indio, I've got to get this off my chest. We cannot just swallow this nonsense whole."

Delgado said, "Well, sir, you are right. We can't verify the details at this point. But there are agencies to help. I was told she has papers, probably from Immigration."

"A paper isn't going to tell me one dang thing! Anybody in Vietnam could have picked up his dog tags. Photographs get doctored all the time. Anybody with half a brain could have gotten this information about BJ and found us."

"Yes, but the question is what does Tuyen hope to gain by coming here?"

Nana put an arm around Tuyen, who cowered against her. "She doesn't have a family. She wants a family."

"And what if she's not a Beaumont?" Papa shouted. "What do I owe her then? What if—"

"Sir." Officer Delgado leaned forward in her chair. "It would be best for everyone if we all remained calm."

"And who are you to tell me what to do in my home? Why are you here anyway?"

"I was invited by your grandchildren. Now I realize blue eyes are a dime a dozen, but Tuyen does have the same blue as you do. There's a possibility of DNA testing, comparing yours and hers—"

"Officer." Papa growled now. "There's only one thing that does not add up and it will never add up. My son would have come home, or he would have died trying, long before 1982 rolled around!"

He stomped across the room and through the door.

No one said a word. Maybe they were all as stunned as Lexi. Maybe they were all thinking what she was: *Yeah, Papa had a point there.*

Nineteen

I need a drink."

Erik muttered the remark more to himself than to Rosie. But she heard it and it rankled. The guy had so much going for himself, not the least of which was a caring family. Why did he insist on throwing it all away?

They walked through the cold dark toward her car. A row of solar lights softly lit the flagstone path across the front yard. Stars shone, the sky dense with them. Thick quiet enveloped the place like a silky blanket.

Rosie could not reconcile the peace with Erik's crummy preoccupation with himself. "Beaumont, give me a break. You've got so much to be grateful for. Granted, I have not walked in your moccasins. And it's true, looks and money don't equal fulfillment. But you have a family who dropped everything they were doing because you needed help. Your brother and sister last night. The others today probably thought you were coming up to be with them for your own sake. Now they embrace this hapless stranger."

"Not totally. My grandfather will never do so. Lexi and I have doubts. Dad's uncharacteristically quiet. He's not sold, I can tell."

"I'm talking generalities. You're all at least willing to give her the time of day and her story a chance. Except maybe your grandfather." The old man never had reappeared.

She and Erik went down the few railroad-tie steps to the parking area and walked across the gravel. She could almost feel Mr. Cool, Calm, and Collected bristle beside her.

Oh, well. That was his problem. It was time for her to exit the scene.

She'd declined Claire's kind invitation to stay for dinner. Tuyen was in good hands. Indio and Claire just assumed the stranger would stay with them. Rosie saw the beautiful guest room where she would live for the time being. Danny had already carried Tuyen's lone gym bag into it.

Rosie stopped near her SUV and turned to Erik. "The point is they are rallying around you and now around Tuyen."

"Officer, who asked you?"

The guy was such a loser. "You invited me, remember? My opinion comes with the territory."

"You don't know diddly-squat about my family or about my life."

"I know they care, and I know that the perfect family does not exist. We all have to deal with whatever hand we're dealt."

He jingled a set of keys before her. "I am dealing with it." He spun on his heel and strode toward one of the other cars in the lot.

Visions flashed through Rosie's mind. She could see him sitting on a barstool in nearby Santa Reina and then swerving along the narrow two-lane back to the hacienda.

"Erik!" She snapped his name.

He paused, his hand on the open car door, and looked back at her.

"Promise me something." *Aw, nuts.* Was she really saying this? Was she really swinging open the door to her Adopt the Hopeless Club? How grossly unprofessional! She was an idiot.

But she couldn't help it.

She said, "Promise me you will buy your alcohol in town and bring it back here to drink."

Without a word, he got into the car, started it, and peeled out of the lot, gravel spewing from the tires.

Dear Lord, please keep him safe!

Lost in thought, Rosie drove more cautiously than Erik had. The long road down to the highway was dirt and gravel. It wound through the dark hills, lit only by stars and her headlights.

At a bend in the road she saw a figure standing near a turnoff and assumed it was Ben Beaumont. She remembered Erik pointing out the spot on their way up. His grandparents lived in an RV on the site, next to their future home.

Lowering her window, Rosie drew up alongside the tall elderly man and braked. "Mr. Beaumont."

"Officer." He wore a heavy jacket. His hands were stuffed into its pockets. Shadows played across his face.

"Are you going to be all right, sir?"

"Depends what you mean by all right."

"'All right' as in you're not going to do something you'll regret? Something that will require the sheriff to pay a visit here?"

"No."

"Glad to hear that. Sir, I really am sorry for the loss of your son. I cannot imagine the hell you've lived through all these years or the shock that just hit you today."

He mumbled something indecipherable.

"Anyway, I hope things turn out for you all."

"I wish the kids hadn't brought her here."

"They had little choice."

"It's a cock-and-bull story. I can't believe they fell for it. 'Course, they never knew BJ. He was long gone before they were even born." He shook his head. "I tell you, BJ would have gotten out of there if he had to crawl on his belly the whole entire way."

Rosie had no words to empathize with the depth of his pain.

"He was nothing like Erik. That kid is a basket case. BJ was the star student, star athlete, star navy pilot. He had character, you know? Integrity. They just don't make 'em like that anymore."

"I'm sorry." She paused. "What will you do about Tuyen?"

"Stay out of her way. Max and Claire can track down her information if they want. Indio can fawn all over her however much she wants. But nothing's going to change my mind."

"Not even the facts?"

"There's only one fact that matters, and her name is Beth Russell. BJ's fiancée. He never would have done this to her. Never. Not in a million years."

Rosie watched the old man shuffle away, his shoulders hunched. Her heart ached for him and for all the Beaumonts and for Tuyen and now for someone named Beth Russell.

"Lord, don't You think this prayer list is getting a little long?"

Twenty

"And then there's Beth Russell," Max said. "How do we deal with her?"

"Who's Beth Russell?" The question exploded from Danny, Jenna, Erik, and Lexi all at once.

Claire looked over at Max. He looked back at her, his fork midair, his eyebrows halfway up his forehead.

Approximately four hours earlier, Tuyen Beaumont had entered their lives. The situation still felt a bit awkward. A stranger was in their midst. BJ's fate had finally been revealed. Was it a time to cry or celebrate?

Life went on. They got hungry and tired. With her daughters' help, Claire prepared a light supper. Indio cloistered herself and Tuyen in the lone refurbished guest room to eat by themselves. Ben never returned to the house.

Claire and Max ate dinner with the kids in the kitchen. They sat at a long table in a corner near the fireplace. Against the walls were built-in benches, down one side of the table and one end, making it a snug family spot. The fire crackled and popped.

Max said, "Sweetheart, you know the story. Why don't you tell it?"

"You're the one who brought it up."

"Technically, Mom did." Earlier, out of everyone's earshot, Indio had told Max they would think about Beth tomorrow. "I'm only repeating what she said because I think the kids should know what's going on."

"I never even met BJ. He'd been missing for ten months when I met you."

"Please?"

She traced her fork around the half-eaten omelet on her plate. Since Tuyen's arrival, Max had withdrawn more and more into himself. Although they hadn't yet had a chance to talk alone, she understood that the news about BJ pained him and his parents beyond measure. They flailed about, searching for ways to cope. Max became uncharacteristically silent while his parents hid away.

Claire suspected that once they got used to the fact of BJ's death, they might find a joy in the existence of his daughter.

Seeing Max's tired demeanor, Claire felt a sense of being set apart. A realization swept through her: The mantle had been passed, the mantle of being matriarch. Its heavy weight and its suddenness caught her by surprise. Shouldn't such a thing be passed on gradually? The closest thing she had to a wise response was to make tea.

Beyond Max's shoulder, Indio's wall of crosses came into focus. There were about sixty of them, in every style, size, material, and color imaginable. Framed sketches of Jesus also filled the space, from floor to ceiling. When the fire had torn through the house, it didn't touch one cross or one picture.

Claire had told her mother-in-law to take her things into her new home, but Indio insisted they belonged in the hacienda itself, on the wall that had once been part of the early Beaumonts' chapel.

Now Claire caught a glimpse of the power they represented, the one that Indio always called upon.

Claire smiled to herself.

Dear Father, Indio would say that You are here and that You are good and that You love us and want the best for us. All right. I say that too. And I ask that You help us. Thank You.

Erik cleared his throat loudly. "Will somebody clue us in sometime tonight?"

Claire looked up and became aware of tears seeping from her eyes. She wiped them away with her napkin, nodding at Max. He mouthed a thank-you.

She gazed at her children, one at a time. Her vision seemed different somehow. She wasn't afraid to see what was there.

Erik's pupils were too large, too glassy. Although he was not overtly drunk, yes, he had been drinking. And yes, that often was the case.

Jenna appeared much older with new crow's feet and a worry crease between her brows. The wear and tear of Kevin's absence was taking its toll. The fears for him at war chewed away at her self-sufficiency.

Danny's eyes darted too much. He was hiding something from his dad, something he might acknowledge to Claire if she pressed the issue.

Lexi pretended to eat. An unopened half-gallon carton of mocha fudge ice cream was missing from the freezer. It wasn't the first time two such circumstances collided.

Claire turned to her husband. "Max, fill in the blanks, okay?"

"Sure."

She took a deep breath. "Beth Russell was engaged to Uncle BJ."

"Oh, man," Danny said.

Claire went on. "I met her a few times. She used to come and sit with us at that memorial Nana and Papa made for him, when we'd remember his birthday. The last time she came, you two, Erik and Jenna, were very small. Beth eventually got married and moved to the Northwest. Seattle, I believe. Anyway, she and Uncle BJ had been inseparable since they were five years old. He proposed the day after they graduated high school. From what I've heard, she was the female version of him: beautiful, popular, homecoming queen, valedictorian."

Erik scoffed. "Engaged? How big a deal is that?"

Max said, "For them it was huge. They were seriously committed to God."

"Yes." Claire agreed. "Their faith was important to both of them."

"That's putting it mildly," he said.

She smiled. "They were over-the-top committed, right?"

"Borderline perfect. For real." Max rolled his eyes. "Jesus in blue jeans."

"They held Bible studies right here in this kitchen, all through high school and college. They planned to be missionaries in Latin America. They both got degrees in Spanish and Portuguese."

Jenna blurted, "Then why did he join the navy?"

Claire hesitated and turned to Max.

His face went hard. "The war news did him in. He couldn't reconcile his life with the suffering. Being a missionary in the jungles of Latin America didn't seem sacrificial enough. Even marrying Beth was out of the question until he settled the issue. He chose the war. He thought he could put an end to it, all by himself."

Danny huffed a noise of disbelief. "That makes perfect sense. Go bomb North Vietnam and win souls for Jesus?"

Claire said, "It was more complicated than that. He had his pilot's license by the time he was sixteen. Part of his missionary dream was to be a bush pilot. He was always fascinated with jets and the navy. Two of his best friends joined the navy right after high school. He met others in college who had already fought in the war. He felt he should serve his country before getting on with the rest of his life."

Jenna leaned across the table, her features scrunched in earnest. "Did he tell Beth he was going?"

"Oh, honey." Claire grasped her hand. Jenna was talking more about her own husband. Last year, Kevin had rejoined the military without telling Jenna until after the fact. "Kevin apologized for not telling you."

"That doesn't exactly help at the moment while he's over there getting shot at!"

"I know." She squeezed her hand and let go. "According to Nana, BJ and Beth made the decision together."

Max said, "He promised her he would come home." His voice cracked. His dark eyes shone. "That's what she told me. He was such a purest, I know he never broke a promise in his life."

Claire watched him blink back tears. "And that's why Papa can't accept Tuyen's story. Uncle BJ always kept his word. Even if he couldn't make it home, he wouldn't have cheated on Beth. Their commitment was old-fashioned, like in ancient days when people were betrothed. It meant the same as being married."

Danny fidgeted in his seat. "It doesn't take a rocket scientist to know war does strange things to a man's mind. Would he have wanted her to see him burned and maimed? Would he have wanted to dump that horror on her? Saddled her with that kind of future?"

Claire stared at him.

Danny kept talking. "Not to mention the psychological scars. I mean, he flew Phantoms, right? It's no secret he bombed and killed people. Add to that getting shot down and not being rescued by your own country. Imagine the number that would play on your psyche. Who knows what was going on in the poor guy's head?"

No one said a word.

Danny shrugged. "I vote for Tuyen. It doesn't subtract anything from Uncle BJ's reputation. Not for me anyway."

Of course Danny had heard the same stories Claire had. BJ attacked life with a zealousness that both charmed and annoyed others. If he got into trouble, it was only because of his great big heart.

Odd. She'd never noticed before how that description sounded an awful lot like his nephew Danny.

Danny's summary ended the conversation about Uncle BJ and Tuyen and Beth Russell. There seemed to be nothing to add.

Abruptly, Erik stood. "Well, I vote for going home. Jen? You're the one with the car."

"We should help Mom clean up first."

Wordlessly Erik began to collect plates. The other three followed suit. Carrying things to the counter, they all appeared to be in a hurry. Claire didn't blame them for wanting to get away from the difficult talk as soon as possible.

The thought crossed her mind to tell them they needn't bother with the dishes, but then she saw Max massaging his fingertips against his forehead. Was he getting a migraine? He hadn't had one in several months. She felt a twinge of panic. Had they even unpacked his medication since moving to the hacienda? Where would it be?

The panic tied itself into an anxious knot in her stomach.

And what of the kids? They needed her. She should stay with them, help in the kitchen that was still unfamiliar to them. She should comfort and hug them, walk them outside to the car.

She should check on Indio and Tuyen. And Ben! She should call. Had he made supper for himself? The dog and the cat usually hung out with him. Surely he'd fed them?

Max rose slowly to his feet and moved across the room toward the door.

The matriarchal weight pressed in upon her again.

"God is good." She echoed her mother-in-law's old phrase. The words slipped out with no conscious thought.

Scattered about the kitchen, her family turned as one and looked at her.

The heaviness lifted. The knot untwisted.

She shrugged. "Well, He is good. What else can I say? We will get through this."

Swiftly, she went to her children and, in turn, planted a kiss on four cheeks and said four times, "Love you. Thanks for cleaning up. Good night."

Then she went to Max by the door, kissed him, and whispered, "Let's go tuck you into bed, honey."

His eyes mere slits, he said hoarsely, "You just quoted my mom."

"You have a problem with that?"

"If you start dressing like her, we will have a huge problem."

She laughed.

Twenty-One

The morning after delivering the bombshell to the hacienda, Lexi, Danny, Erik, and Jenna met at a restaurant for breakfast. The previous day still hovered over them like a dark cloud.

"Hey." Danny whispered in Lexi's ear.

She ignored him. Like that would stop him from speaking.

"I thought you swore to never, ever, *ever* meet with all your siblings at the same time again?"

She wrinkled her nose and took another bite of waffle.

"Does this mean sib socializing has been promoted? Oh wow. No way! Is it true?"

Danny could recite Hamlet's soliloquy in a hoarse whisper and not miss one dramatic nuance.

He continued at her ear. "Sakes alive! It might be true! Sib socializing is now officially"—he inhaled sharply—"an acceptable activity?"

"Danny!" The exasperated complaint burst from Jenna.

Erik said, "Dan, can you pay attention and not mouth off for just two minutes? Huh?"

"Sure." He leaned back against the booth, one arm stretched behind Lexi. "I didn't think I was interrupting. I mean, we've rehashed this scenario for the past forty-five minutes. Do any of you have anything new to add to the conversation?"

Glares went round the table.

Lexi noticed a busboy hovering nearby and wondered if he wanted to clear their table. "Jen." She lifted her fork. "You want that pancake?"

"How can you eat at a time like this?"

Erik set down his water glass. "Give us a break, Jen, and drop the huff. We're all getting through this in our own way. I drink, Lexi eats, you turn shrew, Danny does an incredible imitation of two magpies yapping at once."

Danny said, "I'm praying too."

"Uh-oh. Now he's going into his Nana routine."

"Make fun all you want, Erik. But God knows what's what. He works something good out of even the messes we make, if we let Him."

"Aye, there's the rub."

"What have you got to lose except your false sense of being cool?"

"Whatever." Erik seldom rose to the bait when Danny challenged him on faith. "So what do you and God propose we do with this new cousin of ours? Besides drink, eat, yap, and be shrewish?"

Lexi swallowed a bite of pancake and resisted an urge to scoop bacon from her twin's plate. When had Erik noticed her eating habits?

Danny said, "I think—"

"God and I aren't on speaking terms." Jenna interrupted. "Kevin is running around in a blazing-hot foreign desert wearing a flak jacket and a helmet and carrying a loaded rifle, all of which will do so much good if a bomb blows his truck to kingdom come."

As usual, Jenna positioned herself as the center of attention. Lexi snagged bacon from Danny's plate—he'd never minded sharing with her—and popped it into her mouth. She could always skip lunch.

Danny said, "Jenna, joining up was Kevin's choice. God didn't make him go."

"He could have stopped him."

"He doesn't make us do or not do anything. We get to choose. Kevin did what he thought he was supposed to do. Just like Uncle BJ did."

"Don't you dare compare him to Uncle BJ!" Jenna wailed. "Uncle BJ got shot down! And now, come to find out, he wasn't all that missing, was he? And we're stuck with some stranger invading our family! And of all times! With Mom and Dad's life in an upheaval. Selling their house. Selling the business. Moving up to the hacienda, of all places. Getting remarried. What a royal mess!"

"Hold on, Jen," Danny said. "It's not exactly a mess, royal or otherwise. We have to admit, Mom and Dad are doing better than ever. Why not let them do their thing? Whining about a re-wedding isn't going to help. And what is Tuyen to us? We may never know her full story or even if half of it's true. Maybe she'll show up for Christmas dinner. I vote we all just calm down and give the poor girl a chance. At least welcome her to America."

Erik laid money on the table and slid from the booth. "I vote for getting on with my life. I think I need a job."

Jenna said, "I vote for moping and grading papers."

Lexi set down her fork. "You okay?" She made eye contact and felt a brief connection with her sister.

"Moping alone does wonders for shrews." She twisted her mouth into a crooked smile. "What's your vote?"

"Um, to paint, I guess. It's Saturday. It's raining."

Danny said, "I'm going up to the house, see how everyone's doing. You want to come, Lex?"

Suddenly she'd had enough of Danny's opinions. Maybe it was lack of sleep. Maybe it was a stranger from Vietnam. Whatever.

"No, I don't want to go," she said.

"Papa could probably use your company," Danny urged. "The gardens always need attention these days."

"Danny, I don't want to go. I don't think I ever want to go there again."

He stared at her.

Erik let out a low whistle. "She speaks."

And she continued to speak. "Papa's a grown man, and it's too rainy to work outdoors. Tuyen may be a long-lost cousin, but I don't care to see her today or tomorrow. I'll think about Christmas. Excuse me." She pushed at Danny's arm until he moved off the bench seat.

With her heart in her throat as well as breakfast, Lexi hurried from the restaurant.

That was definitely the last sib socializing with any of them, together or separate, forever.

Wiping her paint-covered hands on a towel, Lexi looked through her apartment door's peephole and saw Erik, hand poised to knock again. Or rather pound. With her music blasting at eardrum shattering levels, she wouldn't have heard him otherwise.

She opened the door, motioning him inside.

He mouthed an exaggerated hello. His dark hair glistened with the rain.

She went to the CD player and lowered the volume.

"No need for that, Lex. We could just read lips." He grinned. "Don't your neighbors complain?"

"No. The nearest one is an old woman who's half deaf. How did you get inside the building?"

"Someone was leaving. So much for security, huh?"

"I guess."

"You've got a dazed look on your face. Either I'm interrupting your work or you can't believe I'm here."

"Um."

"Alexis." An odd tone in his voice set her name apart, as if it were spoken by a stranger.

She stared at him. Erik was four years older. His life never really intersected with hers beyond family gatherings. She couldn't remember ever being alone with him in the same room. In her imagination, she pictured him as existing on some far edge of her world, all but out of her peripheral vision.

He'd been the smart, popular athlete. Now he was the charming handsome guy on television. There was no reason for him to pay attention to his mousey little sister who'd barely graduated from high school, dug holes for a living, and painted strange images in her spare time.

But he always spoke her name with the familiarity of a brother. No big deal. Until now.

"Alexis," he said again.

"What?"

"Let's sit." He sat in the overstuffed chair.

She sat on the couch and twisted the hand towel.

"I don't bite," he said.

"I know that."

"Seriously, I don't."

"Okay."

"Okay. Now, will you try to be straight with me for once? Either I'm interrupting your painting or you're flabbergasted that I'm here. Which is it?"

"Both."

He smiled. "Thank you for speaking your mind. Again. You got a good start at the restaurant."

She shifted, folding one leg underneath herself. "You've never stopped by before."

"I was in the neighborhood."

Of course he was in the neighborhood. Her apartment was most centrally located. The four of them had met at a restaurant near her place.

He winked. "Besides that, I've never been fired before. Nor have I ever been cheated on by my girlfriend. I never knew I had a cousin from Vietnam. And I never realized before how much you and I are alike."

How weird.

"You just got a funny look on your face, Lex. What are you thinking?"

She shrugged.

"Come on. Stay with me here. Stay open. What are you thinking?"

"That it's so weird you'd say that. Max said the same thing."

"You still don't call him Dad." He held up a hand. "Totally under-standable. So what did he say?"

"That he and I are alike."

"I presume you got the 'woe is me, forgive me' speech too?"

She nodded. "He was talking about work ethics."

"Oh, that." He waved a hand in dismissal. "It's a curse we siblings share. Everyone of us works our tails off. It's how we win his affec-tion, you know, because that's what's important to him."

"I hadn't thought of it that way."

"Kind of a nasty way to think of it, isn't it?"

"Well . . . It's not exactly warm and fuzzy."

"Nope." He leaned forward, his elbows on his knees, his hazel eyes intense. "Unfortunately, what you and I have in common isn't warm and fuzzy either."

She glanced around the small living room. "We have the same last name that belongs to a wacko family." Her stomach knotted.

"Lexi." Again he pulled her back.

She looked at him.

"I drink too much. You eat too much and you don't gain an ounce."

She shrugged a shoulder and twisted the towel, unable to turn from his gaze.

"An eating disorder?"

She tilted her head, a half acknowledgment.

"Can I help?"

She shook her head.

"How long?"

How long . . . She didn't want to add up the time.

"Years?"

She nodded.

"Danny doesn't know, does he?"

Her eyes stung.

"Your twin should know. You two are closer than two pods in a pea."

At the old family joke, Lexi's breath caught. If she didn't exhale, the sobs that felt like bricks in her chest would dissipate. They needed air to survive.

Erik moved from his chair and knelt on the floor before her. "I still remember the first time you said that. 'Two pods in a pea.'" He untwisted the towel from her fingers and laid it on the floor. "I think you were three years old. It was so funny. You were the cutest thing I'd ever seen."

Her tears spilled over. "Don't tell him."

"But everyone knows about me. It's so freeing not to have to pretend."

She was shaking now. Her teeth chattered. "Don't tell him!"

"All right. But that leaves only me to help. Which isn't saying a whole lot."

"Can I help you?"

"Oh, Lexi." Erik smiled gently and traced a thumb across her cheek. "There isn't anything anybody can do. Except maybe cry with me?"

Air hit her lungs then and gave life to the sobs.

Her brother—the one who had nothing in common with her but a last name—pulled her into his arms.

Twenty-Two

"Mm." Bobby Grey closed his eyes and chewed, lost in a state of pure bliss. "Mm."

Across the table from him, Rosie nodded vigorously. "Mm." She swallowed a tasty bite of an enchilada. "Papi, this is the best ever. You've got to put it on the menu."

Her father's grin stretched until his cheeks nearly enfolded his eyes. He leaned back in his chair, fingers laced together atop his ample midsection.

"Mm," she murmured again. "Exquisite. Featherlight tortilla. Luscious, creamy white sauce. A hint of garlic. Tasty baby shrimp. Scrumptious buttery scallops that melt in your mouth."

Bobby wiped a napkin across his face. "Esteban, my man, thank you. Is this one of your own creations?"

"No." His grin remained fixed.

Rosie chuckled. "Tell him whose it is."

He held his sides and laughed loudly.

They sat at his restaurant in Old Town, a tourist hot spot. Mexico resonated everywhere in red-tile roofs, museums, menus, and shop wares. Bougainvillea, lush colorful flowers, and wide-leafed subtropical plants grew high and low wherever the eye could see.

Esteban had been a successful proprietor for years. His Casa del Gusto encompassed half a block. It had several dining rooms, two patios, a festive ambience, and a reputation for great food.

Rosie smiled at him. They were on the back patio, and the early evening sun peeked out from behind rain clouds. It lit his face, making him appear years younger. "Well, Papi?"

"Okay, okay." He nodded. "Bobby, I have a new cook."

Rosie hooted. "Esteban Delgado, stop acting like a coward!"

"Rosita, please. This is a sacred moment." He patted his chest. "Yes, it is true, Bobby. I have a new cook. Her name is Helen, and she created this magnificent dish."

Rosie leaned across the table. "And she's his sweetheart."

Bobby smiled.

"Rosita!"

"Well, if you're not going to say it, I will."

"I will say it."

"When? Next year?"

Bobby said, "Does she know it?"

"Now that's a good question."

Esteban frowned. "You two are not funny. Of course she knows it. We do not have to broadcast our business. We are not like your TV news friend."

"He is not my friend."

Bobby said, "Kind of quick with the denial there. The guilty ones always do that."

A mean retort nearly jumped off her tongue. She clamped her mouth shut.

"You were going to say something?" He grinned.

"He is not a friend. How many times do I have to say it?"

"Until you convince yourself, I guess."

She kept her face passive, but inside the anger simmered. It wasn't Bobby's fault that he hit too close to the truth. The fact that Erik Beaumont had sidled up alongside her heart was her own fault.

Good grief, the guy wasn't even likable.

Bobby said, "You know, Rosie, what you did yesterday could be considered 'friend' activity."

"Or just friendly. As in kind. As in community angel."

"So what happened up there at the Hacienda Hideaway yesterday?"

She'd put off the question from him and her dad for the past hour. The cop in her had not been able to disentangle her emotions from the visit. Not a good situation.

"Rosita?" Esteban leaned across the table, no trace of a grin on his face.

"I guess I'm not sure what happened." That about summed things up. "It was . . . It was a heart-wrenching event, especially for the grandparents. Such a high and such a low. They gained a grand-daughter, but lost a son all over again." She gave them an overview of what happened.

"Whew." Bobby let out a low whistle. "Imagine learning you have a relative via someone you figured was long dead."

Her father said, "You are a good girl. I am proud you helped this family."

"Thanks, Papi. I'd like to be a fly on the wall so I could watch how things play out." She bit her tongue. She shouldn't have said that.

"Why not call them?" Bobby asked. "I think you've earned the right to do that much."

"No!" Esteban shook his head vigorously. "No. You are not to get any more involved with this Beaumont family. You did your duty. You played angel. You are done with them."

Bobby slipped a hand in front of his mouth, not fast enough to hide a grin. He always cracked up when Esteban pronounced rules for his adult daughter.

But Rosie wasn't laughing. Her father had been the one to pick up the pieces just a few short years ago. "Papi, it's not like that."

"He is another Ryan Taylor."

"Not exactly."

Bobby raised a hand. "Excuse me. Either of you care to clue me in on what you're talking about?"

Rosie frowned at her dad.

He opened his mouth to speak, closed it, and then he started again. "It is Rosie's story to tell. An old boyfriend. Rich and hand-some. A no-good. He hurt my Rosita."

Bobby looked at her. "That's your bad history with guys like Erik Beaumont."

"Yeah." Sort of. Details aside.

She caught the look on her dad's face and knew he would not shut up until he'd told Bobby everything. She'd rather do it her own way.

"We were in law school together. He was total WASP, through and through. Never in a million years would he ask me out. I'm sure he did it just to horrify his parents. Or win a bet with his friends. I mean, me. An unattractive, Catholic Latina. Was I an idiot, or what? Anyway, things got ugly. Real ugly. I dropped out of school. Ryan was a . . . a mean person."

"Evil," her dad corrected.

"Probably. Beaumont is an okay guy, not mean or evil. He's just in a bad way."

Bobby said, "So you open your Adopt the Hopeless Club to him."

"Yeah. Entirely different thing than falling for him."

The men exchanged a look and then they gazed at her. They weren't buying into her conclusion.

"It is!"

"Explain, Rosa." Esteban tapped a finger on the tabletop. "Your heart is your heart. You care about this TV man."

"As a human being!" She shoved back her chair and stood. "Good grief. It's time to go to work." She walked around the table and kissed her father's cheek. "Good-bye, Papi. Thank you for the great meal. Tell Helen thank you."

Without a backward glance, she walked across the patio and down the steps to the parking lot.

Bobby caught up with her. "Delgado, you're not unattractive."

"Give me a break. I look like my dad. Well, not the belly, but the too-wide nose and thick coarse hair and solid build—"

"Rosie." He grasped her elbow, halted their walk, and turned her toward him. "You are a beautiful woman. Your heart's made of gold and you've got this thing going with God that permeates the air with—I don't know how else to put it but, well, with holiness."

The intensity of those cornflower-blue eyes held her attention, as did his words. Bobby didn't talk that way. He wouldn't say such a thing unless he meant it.

She smiled, warmed by his care. The ugliness that took hold whenever the subject of Ryan Taylor came up melted like butter in the sunshine.

"Ohhh!" She drew out the word in a singsong tone. "You're talking about *inside* beautiful. Shucks, I knew that."

"You're really annoying too."

"I try."

Twenty-Three

That's enough for one day." Lexi rubbed her hands against her pants and surveyed the dusty, cluttered room.

Rain pattered against the unadorned window, its panes black with evening.

Erik walked past and ruffled the top of her hair. "We might as well finish it, Lex, as long as we're here."

They were at the house. The House, capital letters. The place she'd called home for all but a few years of her life. The place her parents had sold to strangers at the drop of a hat.

The room was her studio. Or rather, it had been her studio. Located off one side of the garage, the room was a small workshop that held no interest for their dad. When she and Danny were youngsters, they claimed it for their own toy room. Eventually art supplies replaced Barbie and GI Joe.

Furnishings were sparse: one stool, tall wooden workbenches, shelves, a dorm-room-sized fridge, a piece of indoor-outdoor carpet an ugly shade of taupe. A portable heater hummed, warding off the dank night air.

Erik pulled a canvas from a group of eight-by-tens shelved upright like library books and inspected the painting on it. "Hey, it's the Crystal Pier."

"Mm-hmm. My pier phase."

"It's great. Can I buy it?"

She raised her brows.

"I'm serious."

She never knew with him. "It's not any good."

"But I like it. Isn't that one way to interpret art? If it speaks to me, there must be some merit to it."

"The tones are all wrong, and the—"

"It's where I first kissed what's-her-name."

"Felicia?"

"No. This was back in high school. She was blonde and older. Actually it was the only time I kissed her." He sighed in his dramatic fashion. "Anyway, what do you think is a fair price? Three, four hundred?"

"Erik, it's been sitting in here since I was nineteen. You can have it."

He began flipping through the paintings. "Maybe there's another happy memory tucked away. I could fill my walls. The few paintings I have are nouveau crap."

"I've noticed."

He grinned over his shoulder at her. "I bet you have."

She turned from him and gazed around the room again. Like Erik, she hunted for a happy memory.

Out of the entire house, including its big yard, pool, abundant gardens, and canyon backdrop, she adored this spot the most. It had been her hiding place. In it she felt safe from the world's terrors, most especially teachers, homework, failure. She would get lost in her art, paint to her heart's content, and store food and munch whenever she wanted.

The new owners would soon take possession, but Lexi had avoided going through her things. It was only at Erik's insistence that they'd come. He figured it would be a constructive way to deal with their demented coping mechanisms. After all, he had nothing scheduled for the evening except to beat up his best friend.

They had already filled several trash bags with garbage and loaded a filing cabinet and an easel into her SUV. Although more things remained, she was finished. Saying good-bye was just too hard.

Her stomach rumbled.

"Wow, Lex. Did that come from you?"

"I'm okay."

"Well, that's debatable. Neither one of us is okay."

"Do you have to keep saying that?"

"Admitting we have a problem is the first step—"

"I don't have your problem."

"Aha! The little girl votes for denial."

She stuck out her tongue.

He smiled. "Denial can be a nice break from bawling."

"Don't you ever shut up?"

He laughed long and hard. "Now I know why you've been so quiet your whole life. Between me, Dan, and Jen, you never had a chance to get a word in edgewise, did you?"

"No, I didn't." A smile tugged at her lips.

"It's good to hear from you. Finally."

"Thanks." Her tongue had loosened considerably during the hours spent with him. Not only did he not bite, he didn't judge. But she was done. "Can we go now?"

"Let's at least pack up the paintings. You can't pitch these."

"I have nowhere to put them. Let the new owners do whatever they want."

"With your work? I don't think so."

"It doesn't matter."

"It should. Listen, I really want to hang some on my walls. Meanwhile, we can put them in the storage space in my building. So here." He handed her a stack of canvases and pointed at a box. "I promise, we'll eat soon. And drink."

For a moment they stared at each other.

He made his lopsided self-deprecating grin. "Hey, let's look on the bright side. We made it through the afternoon, right? A leopard can't change its spots overnight. Come to think of it, it probably can't at all. Anyway . . ."

He turned again to the shelf of paintings. She began to pack some in the box.

No, a leopard could not change its spots at all, but why would it need to? Camouflage worked so well. Just blend into the surroundings and keep attention off of yourself. That kept life bearable.

At the sound of the automatic garage door rattling up, Lexi and Erik paused in their work. Lexi peered through the workshop's open door and saw their mom's car enter. A moment later, the big door went back down and Claire emerged, looking like a teenager in blue jeans, faded green barn coat, and suede boots.

Catching sight of Lexi, she smiled. "Hi, Lexi! I didn't expect to see you here."

"Mom."

Claire entered the room and gave her a hug. "And Erik!" She hugged him. "Hey, you two. I called both of you today and left messages."

Lexi exchanged a glance with Erik. They'd turned off their cell phones hours ago.

"The truth is," Erik said, "neither one of us felt like talking to anyone, so we shut off our phones. I haven't even checked for messages. Have you, Lex?"

She cringed. How could he just come right out and say something like that to their mom? It'd hurt her feelings. "Uh—"

"I don't blame you," Claire said.

Huh?

She went on. "I mean, yesterday was pretty draining, wasn't it? And things started even earlier for you two, considering you met Tuyen the night before." She gazed around the room. "Looks like you're all packed."

"Mostly."

"This is great, hon. Don't worry about the stuff you don't want to keep. We'll have a cleaning crew come in to finish up. I don't think I can work in this house anymore."

Erik eyed Lexi, as if he expected her to say something.

She couldn't imagine what.

He gave his head a slight shake. "Lex says being here is an emotional nightmare."

She glared at him, but he wasn't paying attention.

Claire sat on the old stool and propped her feet on a rung. "I'm not talking about the emotional impact. It's a physical thing. I'm just plain pooped out." She smiled. "Taking care of the hacienda is more major than I imagined it would be. And most of the rooms aren't even refurbished yet."

Lexi toed the scruffy rug. *Emotional nightmare* floated like an invisible mobile strung from the ceiling. Maybe she didn't want to be Erik's friend. He said too much. He revealed things that were best left tucked out of sight.

Erik said, "What brings you down here?"

"Scrabble. Danny thought Tuyen would enjoy playing it tonight. Then we discovered there are no board games at the hacienda. So I offered to run down to the house. I wanted to pick up a few other things anyway. When I left, Nana was teaching Tuyen how to make spaghetti." Claire crossed her arms, holding shut the jacket. "Speaking of emotional nightmares, your grandpa didn't show himself all day."

The heater hummed noisily.

Their mom sighed. "Can we talk, kiddos?"

Lexi scrunched down on the floor.

Erik hoisted himself up onto the workbench. "Shoot."

"Your dad looked over Tuyen's papers today and called some agencies. As far as he can tell, her story is probably legitimate."

"Hm," Lexi murmured.

Erik cleared his throat.

Claire said, "It seems you have a new cousin."

"Hm," Lexi said again.

Erik didn't bother to make any response.

"But that's not what I want to talk about. There's more going on here. I know about the emotional nightmare, Lexi. And I know about yours, Erik. I know addictions are rooted in deep hurts. Dad already gave you the speech, but I'll add my two cents." She wiped a sleeve at her eye.

"Mom," Erik said. "You don't—"

"Let me finish. I admit, I didn't come close to being a perfect mother. I'm sorry. We wounded you, most recently by almost divorcing. And now, by selling your childhood home. Even if that is just a normal part of life, it still hurts a place in your heart."

Lexi hugged her knees to her chest.

Claire said, "But we can't fix the damage. Only God can. I hope you'll forgive me." She took a breath and released it. "Okay, that being said . . . Erik, did you get fired?"

"Uh, yeah. Unless my attorney can wangle some loophole out of the contract."

"I'm sorry. And is it true about Felicia and Brett?"

"I'm fairly certain she admitted it on the phone last night." He had told Lexi about calling his girlfriend while not quite sober. "Or was it this morning?"

"I'm sorry," Claire said.

"Mom, it's not your fault."

"No, it's not." Her voice caught. She whispered, "How much do you drink?"

He gazed back at her for a long moment, clearly measuring his response. "On a somewhat regular, frequent basis. There are times I can't have just one drink. I've been known to black out on occasion."

Claire's lips almost disappeared. The flesh around them went white.

"Mom, it's my life."

She gave a slight nod and turned to Lexi. "Honey, I think you're struggling with an eating disorder."

Lexi shrugged and propped her chin on her knees.

Claire slid off the stool and sank onto the floor next to her. Wordlessly, she wrapped her arms around Lexi.

She would not cry. She would not cry. She would not. She would not.

Her mom kissed her temple, laid her damp cheek against Lexi's, and rocked her like a baby.

Twenty-Four

January rain pelted against the stained-glass windows. Claire could think of nothing else—other than the much-needed, thorough soaking rain—for which to give thanks that Sunday morning.

She glanced down the pew to her left. Somehow she had ended up on the aisle with Tuyen next to her. On the other side of the young woman sat Indio, then Danny, Max, and Ben. It was an odd seating order, the result of Ben rudely barging his way first into the row, Max on his heels trying to calm him.

Claire's attempts to focus on the service fell flat. Snippets of conversations intruded on her thoughts. They were like annoying ditties from commercials. The more she struggled against them, the more insistently they replayed in her mind. Again and again and again.

There was one from the previous evening. *Erik, how much do you drink? Lexi, I think you're struggling with an eating disorder.* Their faces etched with pain, wordlessly expressing a hopelessness. Later, Erik's reply, speaking for both of them: *No. No counseling. Not interested.*

There was Danny's voice. He was the only one to come up to the hacienda. He had made excuses for the others. "Lex really wanted to paint. Jen had papers to grade. Erik needed to talk to his lawyer." Ever the champion of the underdog, he hovered over Tuyen, teaching her about the hacienda. He even spent the night on a couch so he could be available for whatever they needed.

A short phone chat with Jenna. "Mommy, it hurts so bad. I miss Kevin so much . . ."

And dear Max. The only words she could remember him saying were, "The dots connect." He spoke them in disbelief, a confused expression on his face. Technically, Tuyen's story might be factual, but it was not settled in his heart as truth.

Claire closed her eyes. *Why now, Lord? He was just getting acquainted with his heart. He was just beginning to open up.*

Then there was the new voice. Tuyen's halting speech grew familiar, its cadence finding a rhythm in Claire's ear.

The girl had very few clothes in her bag, and so Claire shared some with her. When Tuyen undressed to try on a sweater, Claire noticed yellow-green bruises on her ribs.

"Tuyen?"

"It not hurt now. My friend say it 'come with territory.'"

"Friend? Territory?"

She nodded. "Some men bad. They not like how we do things."

"Do things?"

"Serve them."

Claire realized she wasn't talking about being a salesclerk or a waitress. BJ's daughter worked as a prostitute.

Getting her mind wrapped around that revelation took some moments.

Tuyen touched her own cheek. "Sometimes they hate my face. Vietnamese and American. So ugly . . ."

Late last night, Indio spoke privately with Claire, her eyes wide with concern. "She's never heard of Jesus! Buddha yes, but not Jesus. Imagine! BJ's child not knowing . . ."

Then there was that morning in the kitchen. Ben finally showed up, in need of coffee. The face-off between him and Indio unnerved Claire. Her in-laws had been the only safe harbor she'd known.

Indio said, "Benjamin Beaumont, it does not matter one whit who her parents were! She is a guest in our home. You will be civil. You will come to church with us."

Claire opened her eyes. What was she supposed to do with all of it?

The mantle of matriarch weighed heavy again on her shoulders. Her neck ached. She stretched it, tilting her head this way and that.

A light caught her attention. Although rain still thumped against the windows, a stained-glass pane—a spot on Mary's shawl—brightened from pewter to sapphire. Sunlight must have created the effect.

Sunlight while rain poured?

Sunlight plus rain equaled a rainbow. Somewhere outside. And what did a rainbow mean but hope?

The mantle moved, as if cosmic hands fluffed it, releasing its burdensome weight, repositioning it until it settled about her shoulders, featherlight.

Claire smiled to herself. *Thank You.*

Twenty-Five

"Come on, Lex." Danny stood on the other side of her desk, hands on his hips. "You can take a short lunch break."

With him and Max? She didn't think so. "I told you, I have too much work to do."

"We'll eat across the street, at that Thai place. You can just pop in, pop out. Half an hour, tops. You have to eat something."

All of a sudden everyone was mentioning food to her. Danny's invitation to a meal was her fourth to turn down in two days. She'd said no to Nana twice and Jenna once. Had her mother blabbed to them all that maybe she had some sort of food issue?

She said, "No, I don't have to eat some—"

"I wonder if Tuyen likes Thai." His mouth yapping nonstop, he sat in the only extra chair in her small office, crossing his legs, ankle to knee, in one unbroken motion. "I invited her to lunch, too, but she and Mom were going shopping. Mom said that would be complicated enough in itself. She didn't want to factor in a lunch date."

"Shopping for what?"

"Clothes. I guess she doesn't have many. She wore one of Mom's dresses to church and looked a little schoolmarmish. But wow, Lex, you should have seen her face. All bug-eyed, like a kid in a candy store. The service was totally foreign to her, but I think she sensed something that's going to taste sweet once she gets hold of it." He chuckled. "Maybe the smell of incense hit her like chocolate does us at See's."

Lexi rolled a pencil between her fingers. She didn't want to talk about Tuyen. "Why aren't you working?"

"I am. That's why I'm having lunch with Dad. He's got some ideas for me."

"So you told him?"

"About the losses?" His foot bopped in time to her music, a primitive African piece, lots of drums. "Yeah. He's totally cool with it."

She didn't want to talk about Max either. "I have to finish this." She looked down at the sketch, a landscape idea her boss hoped to show a potential client.

"What's it for?" He leaned across the desk until his head blocked her line of vision.

"A new housing development in Escondido."

"A new housing development. Lex, this is big stuff, isn't it?"

She laid a hand on his head and pushed him back. "You're in the way."

He looked at her, his nose centimeters from hers. "It's big stuff."

"It pays the bills."

"It's big stuff." Light from the window reflected in his unwavering, dark brown eyes. He was paying attention. Too much.

"Danny, what do you want?"

"I want to know what you're so mad about."

"I'm not mad."

"You didn't come up to the hacienda last weekend or all week."

"So?"

"So, you practically lived there before."

"Before the fire."

"Before Mom and Dad moved there, you mean."

"Things are different."

"How?"

"They're just different. Everywhere. Every which way."

"What do you mean?"

She glanced beyond his shoulder, but was drawn immediately

back to the eyes she'd stared into for as long as she could remember and probably even before then. In their mother's womb. In the playpen. They'd always centered her, always made her feel safe.

Like hanging out with Nana and Papa at the hacienda did. Before.

But then things changed. Danny didn't tell her about losing clients. Nana found a new granddaughter from Vietnam. Her dad acted crazier than weird. Her parents sold The House. Her mom finally saw her as she really was: a real loser who couldn't even manage to eat correctly.

Danny should know all that. If he didn't, it wasn't her job to tell him.

She shrugged. "I don't know what I mean." She lowered her gaze to the sketch. "I really have to get this done."

"It's all good, you know. Everything has changed, yes, but it is good." Danny stood. "You're sure about lunch? We could bring you something— "

"No!" She looked up at him.

"If you want to come up tonight, Nana and I are teaching Tuyen how to make meatloaf."

Wasn't that sweet? "I'm busy."

For a fraction of a second his eyes scrunched. "Lex, why are you so angry? You almost got killed last fall, but you didn't. You're alive. You have this great job. You paint amazing things. You have a boyfriend. Mom and Dad are together. We have a new cousin. Life is good. Embrace it."

In a flash, the anger she could not admit mushroomed into a fury. "Get over yourself, Mr. Know-It-All!" The words hissed from her like air escaping from a punctured balloon. "Maybe your life is good. You get to be pals with Max and Nana and that so-called cousin. You get to tell Mom the re-wedding baloney is wonderful. You get to ignore Papa and me and Jenna and Erik."

"I'm not ignor—"

"Yes, you are!"

"I am not. You're the ones who chose not to show up and get to know Tuyen better. I'm just recognizing the part of the glass that's full. Which you could do, too, if you ever got that chip off your shoulder. We're witnessing miracles right and left. I mean, Dad selling the business and asking for forgiveness from his kids? Mom, happy as a bride with him? Uncle BJ living on in his daughter? You don't see them because all you can think about is how you have to share your grandparents and your private space at the hacienda."

"I don't want to talk to you!" She cupped her hands over her ears. "Get out of here!"

"Fine! I don't really want to talk to you either." He strode from her office and shut the door with a loud thud.

He was so wrong. So totally wrong. Those weren't the things she thought about at all. What she thought about was Zak dumping her and about what food she would binge on next and about where she could purge it and about the nightmares full of smoke and fire.

The shaking slowed and she opened a desk drawer, bottom left. The cracker stash. A whole-wheat brand. At least it had some food value.

She tore apart the cellophane and started eating.

Twenty-Six

"Give me a break, Delgado." Bobby drove their squad car into a 7-Eleven parking lot and braked outside the entrance. "Get the frappucino here. They got those bottles in the case."

"Nah." Rosie shook her head. "It's not the same. Come on. Two more blocks to Starbucks."

"You're a coffee snob."

"So?"

"So I have a wife and three kids, one in braces. I can't afford to be a coffee snob. I like this manager's free drinks."

"My treat."

Bobby gave her a sidelong glance.

"Pretend I'm a guy, Officer Macho."

"Ha-ha."

Her cell phone rang. "It's Susie." She referred to a sergeant at the station and answered. "Hey."

"Hey, Rosie. I've got another Beaumont insisting on talking to you. Lexi. Same family as the Hot One?"

"Yep."

"Maybe you ought to give these people your number? Anyway, she sounded distraught, but refused to talk to me. Said it's personal. She's on her cell."

As Susie rattled off the number, Rosie memorized it. "Thanks."

"What's up?" Bobby asked.

"Lexi. Erik's youngest sister." She punched in the number. "Distraught. Probably something to do with the other night."

"You might as well give all of them your number."

"Tuyen has it. I figured she'd be the one who might need—Lexi? Rosie Delgado—"

"He's going to kill him!" The words burst out between screeches and gulping sobs.

"Calm down, Lexi. I can't understand you." She shrugged at Bobby and turned on the speakerphone so he could listen in. "Who's going to kill whom?"

"Erik! He's going to kill Brett! He's going after him! He is so out of control. You've got to stop him!"

"Who's Brett?"

"His friend. The one Felicia's—Oh! Please go get him! He ran out before I could do anything."

"Where is he going?"

"Her house!"

"Felicia Matthews?"

"Yes. He thinks Brett's there with her. He is so drunk. He might have a gun. He said something about getting a gun."

"What's the address?"

"I don't know! Somewhere up the hill from Erik's."

Rosie turned off the speaker as Bobby radioed the dispatcher for an address for Matthews, Beaumont's coanchor and ex-girlfriend. She overheard him say "armed" and "need backup."

Nuts. Beaumont wouldn't really. Would he? The morning she went to his condo all tired and cranky, she hassled him, asking if he'd murdered anyone. He sloughed off the idea.

But he was sober then and more important things were going on, like the arrival of an unknown cousin from Vietnam.

But now?

Nah. No way. He wouldn't have a gun. He was not the violent type.

Of course she'd thought the same about Ryan Taylor.

Rosie slammed a mental door on the pointless speculations. "Lexi, where are you?"

"In my car." She sobbed. "Downtown. By a stoplight. I couldn't catch him! I tried. Some guy kept harassing him about Felicia and he went berserk. They both ran out of the bar. Oh, please help! I don't know how to get there!"

"It's okay. It's okay. Take a breath. Thatta girl."

Bobby nodded to her now, and they peeled out of the parking lot.

"Lexi," she said into the phone, "we've got the address. We're on our way. You go home and wait there."

She sobbed, undeniably hysterical now.

"On second thought, don't move. I'm sending someone to help you get home. Where exactly are you?"

"I don't know! The Gaslamp District?"

While the midnight streets blurred past her and the siren wailed, she managed to pinpoint Lexi's whereabouts, get another patrol dispatched to her, and berate herself for not going through channels. The phone call should have been recorded. It wasn't personal business as she'd thought.

What was wrong with her? She heard the name Beaumont and instantly slid over into private life mode. The family did not belong there. Most especially Erik Beaumont did not belong there, no matter how often he'd come to mind in the past seven days.

Bobby hit the brakes.

Rosie was halfway out her door, the siren winding down, still ringing in her ears. Yet she heard the screams. A woman's. Bone-chilling sounds of sheer terror pierced the night.

According to Lexi, the guy was armed and dangerous and threatening to kill.

Rosie drew her gun from its holster, unlatched the safety, and ignored Bobby's shouts to put on her vest.

Felicia Matthews lived in a single, one-story dwelling on a street lined with similar gingerbread houses complete with white picket fences. Probably built in the 1920s and refurbished in recent years, they made for a cute neighborhood.

Windows on both sides of Matthews' place lit up. Residents would be accustomed to the whine of jets on way down to Lindbergh Field, but not to bloodcurdling shrieks and police sirens on their doorstep.

The observations more or less registered themselves as Rosie flew along the short sidewalk and up onto the small, old-fashioned porch. Bobby was breathing at her neck when she turned the front doorknob.

It wasn't locked.

"Beaumont!" she yelled as they crossed the threshold. "Police! It's Delgado!"

Another shriek replied, a woman's. A male voice ranted and raved, the words indecipherable, the tone of one totally checked out of reality.

They stepped into a dimly lit living room. Hardwood floors, scatter rugs, floral upholstery, soft classical music, potpourri scent. Dining area at one end, lace tablecloth. Soft light through the kitchen doorway.

Comfy. Homey.

Except for the fact none of it was in order. Lamps lay on the floor, shades askew. Chairs were overturned, rugs balled up, lace cloth bunched at one end of the table.

"Police!" Bobby shouted as they moved in the direction of the cries, into a shadowy hallway. "Beaumont, show yourself! Now!"

The radio crackled at Rosie's shoulder. A backup team was on the street. She heard the sirens.

Three doors rimmed the hall. Two on the left, one open, revealing a bathroom, the other shut. The third one, shut as well, on the right, far end.

Determining which room the screams emanated from was easy. They came from the door on the right, the one with the body lying near it.

Rosie and Bobby moved in tandem, attempting to bring order to chaos, the whole time creating more with their own shouts and squawking radios and thudding booted feet and bulky uniformed selves crowded into a tiny hallway in a house built in the 1920s for a family of three. At the most.

Everything happened at once, at lightning speed.

Bobby knelt at the man's body.

More shouts and foot stomps resounded as the backup team entered the front room behind them.

Rosie stepped over the body. "Beaumont!" She kicked open the door, arms extended, gun pointing, knees bending into a crouch.

Somewhere between the sight of Felicia huddled on the bed and Erik yelling incoherently at her, his arm swinging up toward the helpless woman, Rosie lost it. Her emotions broke loose. Like wild horses, they stampeded through her. They crushed everything in their path, every safety protocol and well-rehearsed response so carefully hardwired into her second nature.

And then she pulled the trigger.

Twenty-Seven

Through the interior windows of the hospital waiting room, Claire saw the surgeon walking toward them. He wore blue-green scrubs and a smile.

She appreciated the smile. They already knew Erik was going to be all right. The ER doctor had told them when they first arrived that things looked good for him. But she appreciated the smile. It was like dotting an *i* and crossing a *t*.

Beside her on the waiting-room couch, Max squeezed her hand and stood. She wanted to stand. Her legs refused to cooperate, though. Even seated, she felt them tremble and wobble, as sturdy as gelatin.

"He's going to be just fine."

A sigh went around the room. They were all there: Ben, Danny, Jenna, Tuyen, Indio. Lexi hunched against her grandmother, half asleep with the sedative the ER guy had given her.

"Thank you, Doctor," Max said. "Thank God. Can we see him?"

"Not just yet. He'll be in recovery for a while."

Claire said, "When can he go home?"

"My guesstimate is within a week. He has two broken ribs and contusions about his face. But the bullet . . ." He raised his right arm straight out and pointed with his left hand at the shoulder. "It went in here, just in front of the armpit, and lodged itself in muscle. We extracted it. There's some tissue and muscle damage, of course. Actually quite a bit, but nothing that won't heal. It missed the lung."

Indio said, "God is good. Hallelujah."

Claire whispered, "Amen."

Jenna harrumphed loudly. "I still can't believe that woman shot him!"

"Jen," Lexi mumbled. "You're an idiot. He was full-on wasted."

"Then he should have been full-on mellow. He's never mean when he drinks. He's never mean, period. As a matter of fact, I've seen him—"

"He beat up Brett!"

"Who beat him up!"

Max said, "Jen and Lex, please."

The doctor cleared his throat. "At any rate, a few centimeters to his left"—now he touched his chest—"and it would not have been good."

Claire winced.

"Aunt Claire." Tuyen smiled shyly at her. "That not happen."

Her words parted the dark clouds. It wasn't the first time that had happened in the past week. With a quiet dignity, Tuyen often spoke light into a conversation.

Claire rose and, her arms wide, stepped over to the young woman. "Oh, Tuyen." Chuckling, she pulled her close. "Thank you. You are absolutely right. That not happen. That not happen indeed."

Only a night-light above Brett Abbott's bed lit the hospital room. Claire sat beside her friend Tandy, the injured man's mother. Their hands were clasped together on the arms of the chairs between them.

"We've been here before, Claire." Tandy spoke in soft tones. "Well not quite, but almost. I guess it's only been to ERs, huh? Not an overnight hospital stay."

"They never managed a concussion before. Erik did break Brett's nose one other time though."

"And Brett cracked Erik's ribs at least twice. Not to mention all the bruises they gave each other through the years."

"And our silly arguments over them." Claire gave her a sad smile.

Tandy returned it. "I'm not mad at you this time."

"I'm not mad at you."

They sat in silence, still clutching each other's hands. Brett was going to be all right. His ribs and nose were taped. The concussion was mild. He had spoken with Tandy earlier.

Claire said, "Did the doctor talk about baseball?" Brett played professionally for the Padres.

"He said he's in excellent shape. He'll heal quickly." Tandy squeezed her hand. "It's February. There's *plenty* of season left." She winked.

Another long silence passed.

Tandy said, "Did they ever fight over a girl before?"

"Not that I recall."

"They're thirty years old, Claire. They should be grown up by now!"

"Max thinks we're in a reaping season, that he's reaping what he sowed by being an absent dad."

"Well, I'd be the first in line to blame Brett's dad and, just for good measure, I'd even throw in Big-Hair Bimbo from Bishop as partly responsible." She referred to her ex-husband and his second wife.

"Your sarcastic tone has lost its sharp edges."

"Old age. Seriously, I've done my own share of sowing seed that wasn't exactly the best for my kids."

"Me too. But you know, at some point they need to take responsibility for their own choices. Good, not so good, incredibly stupid like this one."

"Figuring out how to let them go is like dancing to music I can't hear. The radio signal is blocked or something."

The bedcovers rustled as Brett stirred.

Tandy said, "Is he humming?"

Brett chuckled. "The Byrds."

They hurried to his side. Claire's stomach ached at the sight of his eyes swollen shut and the bright white bandage across his nose.

He murmured, "'Turn! Turn! Turn!' 1965."

Tandy touched his shoulder. "'To Everything There Is a Season.' Pete Seeger, 1962, before the Byrds. And before that it was in Ecclesiastes, you knucklehead."

A corner of his mouth went up and down. "Tell Erik I'm sorry."

"Tell him yourself tomorrow. He's just down the hall."

"Mm-hmm." He quickly dozed off again.

"Claire." A tear trickled down Tandy's cheek. "How do we let them reap their own stuff when they look like this?"

Claire put an arm around Tandy's shoulders. "By spending a whole lot of time on our knees."

"You sound more like Indio every day."

"Yeah. I figure it's about time I grew up too." She wrapped her other arm around Tandy and, on impulse, began to pray aloud, a thing she had never done before with her friend.

A new peace filled her. A new certainty took up residence in her heart: God was with them in all their sowing and reaping. Yes, they had to gather weeds with the flowers. As her father-in-law said, though, God could do amazing things with weeds.

And, as her mother-in-law said, God was good.

Hallelujah.

Twenty-Eight

Rosie sat with Bobby in the lieutenant's office.

Behind his desk, their boss hung up the phone and grinned. Davis was a fit-and-trim, no-nonsense guy with a full head of black hair turning to silver. At the moment, he let his grandfatherly demeanor come out to play. "Okay, now it's official: Beaumont's fine. Cheer up, Rosie. There's nothing to worry about."

"I shot him."

"The Padres are going to thank you for saving their first baseman from further injury."

"I should have—"

"Put a lid on it. The guy had a gun."

"A toy gun!"

He glared. "Beaumont pointed a gun at you. You told him to drop it. He didn't. And there's more." He paused, his glare softened. "I just found out his blood alcohol content was high, but not by much. Here's the thing though: they found PCP in his system. He had no idea what he was doing, not a clue. The lab guy is surprised one bullet stopped him."

Bobby whistled. "Me too."

Erik Beaumont on drugs? She found no space to file that information in her mind. It would explain his violence that didn't make sense either.

"So," Davis said, "take some time and get over it. I want you back on the street ASAP. Your mandatory suspension won't last long. As

144

far as I'm concerned, the investigation is over." He pushed back his chair and walked around the desk. "I'm going home. It's Saturday. That means pancakes with my wife followed by the grandkids' soccer games."

Bobby stood and shook his hand. "Thanks, Lou."

"Sure." He patted Rosie's shoulder on his way out the door. "See you."

She had no response but to continue biting her lip.

As Davis left the office, Bobby leaned back against the desk and looked at her. "They oughta outlaw that toy he used. It's too realistic. Anybody who knows guns could mistake it for a Glock at first glance."

"Don't go there. Just don't go there." She leaned forward, squishing her palms against her eyes.

Bobby sighed. "Do you want company or do you want to be alone?"

"Yes."

"Okay."

"It wasn't my temper." She looked at him.

"Rosie." He crossed his arms. "We just talked through this at least sixteen times with something like sixteen different people."

"Not all of it." She hesitated.

"What do you mean, not all of it?"

"I mean . . ." She bit her lip again. With those other people he mentioned—all of them related to law enforcement, most of them men—she had held back.

Bobby sighed again, more a sound of settling in for the duration rather than impatience. "I was there with you, remember? What'd I miss?"

"The lapses." She sat up, holding a shrug and her breath. "I don't remember yelling 'Drop it.' I don't remember seeing a gun." There. She'd said it. She let her shoulders relax.

"It'll come back to you." He slid up onto the corner of the desk. "This is your first shooting. In spite of the training, you can't get around the fact that it's traumatic. It all happened in a split second.

But I was there too. I distinctly saw the gun coming our way and heard you yell. The other guys coming in heard you. And I distinctly remember kneeling behind you thinking, if she doesn't take this guy out, I'm in deep yogurt and so is Brett Abbott because Beaumont's shot will most likely miss you and hit us."

She shook her head. "I still can't believe you recognized a baseball player in the middle of all that."

"That was the easy part. The tough part was deciding whether or not I should throw myself in front of him and take a bullet for the Pads." He smiled. "He had a decent season last year."

"It's not funny."

He stopped smiling. "No, it's not. It's how I deal with it. You know this incident has a fairly happy ending only because you're a crack shot. Nine out of ten couldn't have hit him like you did. He would have been in the morgue."

"I made tea with his mother!"

"Huh?"

"I know him! I know his family!"

"Come on, Rosie, don't go irrational on me."

"I already did! That's what I'm saying. It was a totally irrational thing."

"It feels like that now, but give it time—"

"Bobby, listen. Something happened to me in there. When I saw him. When I saw Beaumont with his arm raised, I felt."

"Felt what?"

"I *felt*. Cops don't feel."

"Well—"

"We don't. But I did." She rubbed her hands together, trying to knead away the tingle left in them since the gun had gone off hours and hours ago. "Remember we talked about Ryan Taylor?"

"The old boyfriend, the one your dad calls evil."

"Yeah. It all came back to me, the ugly thing I didn't want to tell you about before. Seeing Beaumont." She shut her eyes. "Wham. All of a sudden he was Taylor and I was the one on the bed screaming."

There was only the sound of her ragged breathing, the ticking of a wall clock.

Bobby said, "Did he . . . did he hurt you?"

"He beat me and he raped me." She opened her eyes and watched the emotions play across a face trained to not reveal them. Compassion. Anger. Back to compassion. On to the inveterate neutral. Disgust never showed up.

"How old were you?"

"Twenty-two."

"Is he behind bars?"

"No. Not one day."

"Oh, Rosie."

She gave him half a nod. "I swore I would not let that happen to another woman if I could stop it. For a long time, whenever I practiced at the shooting range, I aimed at Taylor's face."

"Probably why you're so good at it."

"But it wasn't right. I finally got around to asking God to help me forgive him. Good-looking rich white guys still tick me off, so there's a grudge lingering somewhere inside of me. I thought it was all taken care of."

"It's not a grudge. It's your halo slipping while you give a quick nod to your human side. It never lasts long."

"Tonight scared me, Bobby. They should never give me back my gun. I should quit. I'm not cut out for this."

"Hey." He slid off the desk and sat in the chair beside her, leaning close to her, his eyes intent on hers. "You did not lose control. You did everything you were supposed to, by the book. It was automatic. You even aimed well, impossibly well under the circumstances. You could not have done anything better. You got that?"

"No."

"Well, you better get it because I need my best partner working with me."

She tried to smile.

"You want to come over for breakfast? Elise's waffles."

"There's one other thing."

He groaned and hung his head.

"In the ambulance." She had ridden with the unconscious Erik to the hospital. "I prayed for him."

Bobby peered at her from the corner of his eye. "Out loud?"

"Yeah."

"Medic hear you?"

She nodded.

"There goes your reputation." He grinned and sat up. "But I still want you riding with me as soon as possible."

For a long moment she studied his intense cornflower-blue eyes gazing back at her. He meant it. He really meant it.

She whispered, "Thank you."

Twenty-Nine

Lexi gingerly pushed open the door to Erik's hospital room. While she slept away most of the day in her apartment, her family had kept watch over him. They were gone for the time being.

Evening had fallen, and the illumination inside the room was dim. Lights flickered from the muted television mounted on the wall.

"Hi, Lexi."

Lexi hadn't noticed the woman seated in a chair on the other side of the bed. "Hi. Officer Delgado?"

She stood. "Please, call me Rosie."

Lexi pushed the door shut and went to Erik's bedside. Her mother had warned her, but the sight of him made her cringe. He was white as the sheets and almost hidden between all the tubes and monitors and wires and IV bags. Even if he were awake, she wondered if he'd be able to open his eyes in such a swollen face.

She touched his leg. "Oh, Erik."

"Of course," the policewoman mumbled, "you might have some other names you'd prefer to call me."

Lexi glanced over at her. "Why?"

"Um, I should go." She moved around to the foot of the bed. In blue jeans and a sweater, her wavy hair loose to her shoulders, she looked like any regular person.

"Thank you for helping me last night."

"I don't know how much I helped." She tilted her head toward Erik.

"Erik freaked out. You got to him before things got worse, and you took care of me. The guys you sent parked my car and drove me here to the hospital."

"Lexi, why did you call and ask for me? Why not just call 911? The dispatcher could have done the same."

She shrugged. "I freaked out too. It wasn't exactly an emergency. I mean, it wasn't like an accident happening right in front of me or a fire. He really hadn't done anything wrong. Yet. And you know him personally. It was easier to explain it to you. I'm sorry."

"No, don't be sorry. It's . . . it's okay. You're right. It would have taken longer for you to explain it all to someone else. Then they probably would have gotten there after he—I'm sorry. I'm not sup-posed to talk about it. Forget I said that. Forget I said anything. Nuts. Forget I was here."

"Why aren't you supposed to talk about it?"

"Cockeyed rigamarole." Rosie placed fingertips at her mouth. "I can't even tell your family how sorry I am." Her voice cracked.

"Why not? We know you are. Well, except maybe Jenna, but Miss Drama Queen doesn't count."

Rosie just stood there blinking rapidly, pressing her hand against her mouth, as if she was trying to get herself under control.

Suddenly Lexi did not want her to leave. Like the day she'd shown up at Erik's place, she brought an air of order to the chaos. Order and something else. Kindness? Understanding? Acceptance? She was so easy to talk to.

"Lexi." Rosie lowered her hand. "When an officer shoots some-one, there's an investigation. I'm suspended until it's decided whether or not what I did was acceptable under the circumstances. Someone will ask you questions about what happened. If I talk to you or Erik and say something like I should have seen it was a toy gun in his hand and not shot him, and then you all sue me and the police depart-ment, and you say that I said . . ." She sighed. "It just gets real com-plicated. It's best we don't talk yet."

"We wouldn't sue you."

"Sometimes it's not your choice. Insurance companies have different ideas. The media will influence things. They're going to have a heyday with this. They already are. Five o'clock lead." She pointed her thumb at the television.

"But we know you wouldn't have done it if you didn't have to. For crying out loud, you know him. And Jenna did have one valid point: you made tea with our mom."

Rosie smiled. "Yes, I did." She paused, frowned, and then spoke again. "How is everyone?"

"Fine. Well, I mean they're upset, naturally. But Erik's okay. Brett's okay. Felicia's okay. "

"Will you tell them I'm sorry, please? So very sorry that it happened."

"Yes." She glanced at her brother. The walls with their sick odors closed in on her. "Could we . . . could we go have coffee or something?"

"I—" Rosie clamped her jaws together. Her forehead wrinkled again. Her wide mouth turned in an upside-down *U*.

"I promise not to tell anyone," Lexi said.

Slowly, Rosie smiled. "Do you know what perjury is?"

"It won't come to that. I need—uh . . ." *Need?*

The word sounded foreign in Lexi's ear. She never said *need* out loud. Probably because the only thing she ever thought about needing was food. But now, with Erik totally out of commission, Zak out of the picture, and Danny and Nana off the deep end ad nauseam over Tuyen, maybe she needed to not be alone.

She took a deep breath. "I need to hang out with somebody who understands last night."

Rosie studied her for a moment. "Yeah, I do too."

They sat in a booth tucked away in a corner of the busy hospital cafeteria. Rosie drank coffee. Lexi succumbed to the gnaw in her stomach and filled her tray with a selection from every food group offered.

"Lexi, do you know how he got to Felicia's? His car wasn't found in the vicinity."

"No. He and this other guy ran out the door. Maybe he drove him?"

Rosie shrugged.

"How long will you be suspended?"

"I don't know. Maybe a week. I'll still work, but behind a desk."

"I'm sorry."

"It's not all that bad of an idea. I can't exactly think straight after this. Forget I said that. Anyway, my dad owns a restaurant in Old Town."

"Really? Which one?"

"Casa del Gusto."

"I love it."

"I do too. I like to cook and wait tables. And I like to keep an eye on my dad. He's got a great manager and staff, but Papi refuses to give up control and he wears himself out doing things other people could do. Now he's got a crush on a new employee, so he's spending even more time there. It's really kind of cute. This woman is almost his age and adores him."

"Your mom's not around?"

Rosie shook her head. "I was nineteen when she passed."

"I'm sorry."

"Thank you." Rosie leaned forward. "Lexi, you don't have to feel obligated to apologize for everything."

"Sorry." She rolled her eyes. "Danny tells me it's a bad habit. You said 'passed.' I've only heard my grandmother use the word that way."

"It totally fits my mom. She was so in love with Jesus. After her second time going through chemo and then getting sick again, all she could talk about was going Home. Capital *H*. It was like she just went through the veil, passed from this world on to the other one."

Rosie sat back again and sipped her coffee. "In the kitchen at the hacienda I saw your grandmother's wall of crosses. That's an incredible collection."

"Did Mom tell you about them, how they didn't burn during the Rolando Bluff Fire?"

"She did. She also told me about how you saved the family and those firefighters."

Lexi felt the flush creep up her neck. It hadn't been that big of a deal.

"Then I remembered the story. I read about you and your family miraculously making it through that night. You were a heroine."

Lexi shrugged a shoulder and pushed aside the thought of Zak. He'd never, ever be absent from the memory of the fire. "It wasn't that big a deal."

"Of course it was. Actually I was nearby, working traffic control when Santa Reina was being evacuated. I got far enough up the hill to see the flames. Of course the smoke was everywhere. The wind was horrendous. I can't imagine how awful that must have been for you being right in the middle of it all. Do you have nightmares?"

The question startled Lexi. How did Rosie know? "Sometimes."

"Understandable." Rosie spun the coffee cup around in a nervous gesture. "I'll probably be having some of my own after this." She tapped her temple. "I can't stop seeing your brother with his arm thrust out. Things happened so quickly, it's a blur. My partner saw the gun, heard me say 'Drop it,' saw Erik swing it toward us." She shook her head. "If only I'd looked at it more closely."

"But if it had been a real one . . ."

"Yeah." She shut her eyes briefly. "I am so grateful I did not kill him."

"The doctor said if he had to get shot, that was the best way for it to happen."

"It could ruin his tennis game forever."

"He doesn't play tennis."

"Another blessing."

"Our dad plays. That's why Erik doesn't. The thing I don't get is why Erik was so crazy. I haven't been around him a whole lot while he's drinking. Jenna says he always gets more mellow. This wasn't mellow."

"No, it wasn't. Fist-fighting with his friend and threatening others with a toy gun is not mellow. I did see him wasted once—"

"Really?"

"Arrested him for a DUI. That's how we met the first time, not that he remembered." She shook her head. "Gracious and charming and witty. I'm not saying that in an admiring way. It was my impression that's his personality no matter what."

"It is."

"Does he ever use drugs?"

"Drugs? I don't think so. But then, would I know? We're not all that close."

"But you were out with him last night, in a bar downtown?"

"I don't usually do that. I've never done it with him. I don't even drink. But . . ." But Danny had been such a snot. "But . . ." How to explain that one to a stranger?

"That's okay. We're not supposed to be talking." Rosie smiled and her dark eyes twinkled.

Lexi couldn't help but smile back. It felt so good to talk about things. "But to tell you the truth, Tuyen has disrupted everything. And we were already upset about other stuff. Now Papa's always scarce. Danny's on my case about this and that. Erik lost his job— Why did you ask about drugs?"

"Oh, you know, that would explain his bizarre behavior."

Lexi felt her eyes widen. "It would."

"On the phone you said some guy was hassling Erik about Felicia?"

"Mm-hmm."

"Did he know him?"

"It's hard to tell with Erik. Everybody knows him, and he's one of those people who never meets a stranger."

"What did this guy say?"

"He called Erik a moron and bought him a drink. People act plain weird in bars. Why they even talked to each other, I have no clue. The guy said everybody knew Felicia Matthews and Brett Abbott were together, had been for ages. They argued. Erik got louder and louder, more and more out of control."

"Would you recognize this man if you saw him again?"

"Maybe."

"Where do you think Erik got the gun? Not that it matters, considering it was a stupid toy—"

"That guy gave it to him."

Rosie stared at her.

"I think he did, anyway. I didn't hear the whole thing. Something about he could get Erik a gun. They left, I couldn't keep up with them. I went to get my car." She blew out a breath. "It was so awful."

"Lexi, you might have to go through all this again. If Matthews or Abbott file charges, a defense attorney will need to know everything. Writing it down is a good idea while it's fresh in your mind."

"All right. They probably won't send you to question me?"

Rosie smiled. "Probably not."

"It's easy talking to you."

"But we didn't talk."

"Oh, yeah. Um, in case I don't want to talk to you again, can I have your number? Though it's probably stored in my cell now."

"I'll give you all my numbers." Rosie unsnapped her purse and rummaged in it, noticing the message light on her cell. "Oops. Missed a text." She handed Lexi a business card while reading her phone display. "It's from my dad. 'Where are you?'" Laughing, she stood. "He gave me a curfew and I'm late."

Lexi shook her hand. "What time is curfew?"

"Six thirty! If I don't shoot anyone this week, he says he'll change it to eight o'clock. 'Bye, Lexi. Thanks for the chat we didn't have. I needed it."

"Me too. 'Bye."

"Tell them I'm sorry."

Lexi nodded and watched her walk away.

She wished she had a dad who gave her a six thirty curfew and sent text messages and made her laugh.

Thirty

Claire watched the policewoman make her way between the vacant patio tables at the Casa del Gusto. Rosie Delgado did not resemble the same woman who had come in her uniform to the hacienda with Tuyen. Nor did she fit what the newspaper described: a record-setting, in-your-face sharpshooter. She wore a flouncy embroidered top and knee-length black skirt, looking like other waitresses in the restaurant.

Like them, except for the distinct expression of sorrow creasing her face.

Lexi, seated beside Claire, pushed back her chair. "Rosie."

"Hi." Rosie greeted Lexi with a hug and then turned to Claire. "Mrs. Beaumont."

"I'm Claire, remember?" She stood on legs still shaky days after the shooting and stepped around the table.

Rosie pressed her lips together.

"Oh, honey." Claire hugged the young woman. "It's all right."

"I am so, so sorry."

"I forgive you. We all forgive you." She squeezed Rosie and, over her shoulder, returned Lexi's smile.

"Thank you."

Claire stepped back. "Can you talk a few minutes?"

Rosie smiled at Lexi. "Yes and no. Please, let's sit." As they all settled in around the table, she said, "How is he?"

"Great," Lexi replied. "He's going home Thursday."

"And his friend?"

"Brett got out Saturday, but he's been to see Erik every day since then. I guess they're working through things."

"He must be filing charges."

Lexi shrugged. "Not that we know of. They go way back, best friends through thick and thin since they were about ten."

"How about Felicia?"

"We heard she's out of town. She got a temporary restraining order against Erik, but she didn't file charges either. Don't ask me why. I never took her as the forgiving type."

"Happens all the time." Rosie's eyes closed briefly, as if she was weary.

Claire said, "How are you?"

"I'm . . ." She blew out a breath. "I'm okay. They've got me seeing a counselor, and I've talked with my priest. And the department's attorney. I'm on desk duty until next week. The investigation cleared me. Which means what I did was acceptable." Her face scrunched up again. "Which I cannot fathom."

Lexi said, "So they'll let you go back to your old job?"

"The counselor says I have to fathom it first. I mean, this is part of a cop's life. This happens. If I can't live with that—Is Erik really all right?"

Compassion for this hurting woman filled Claire. She and Max figured Rosie would have a rough go of it. When Lexi told Claire about the restaurant where she worked sometimes with her father, they thought it might be the place to unofficially contact her.

"Rosie, why don't you come and see for yourself how he's doing? I twisted his arm until he agreed to spend at least his first few days out of the hospital at the hacienda. Will you join us for dinner Thursday?"

"Uh, well, I want to apologize to him and everyone, but . . . Dinner? I don't know if that's appropriate."

"Max and I see things differently. We believe Erik put himself into that situation, you were just doing your job. Rosie, the point is we want to show some token of our appreciation. You took care of our kids Friday night."

"I shot your son."

Claire saw the pain in the sparkly eyes. "You facilitated a desperately needed wake-up call."

Rosie blinked. "That's creative. You want to talk to my lawyer? Maybe he could use it as defense strategy."

"Do you need one?"

"So far, technically, no."

Claire smiled. "Please come."

"What does Erik think about it all?"

She felt her smile fade. "He doesn't remember anything."

Rosie nodded as if she knew.

Claire figured she probably did know but hastened to explain. "They say there were hallucinogenic drugs in his system. Erik swears he doesn't do drugs. Well, not counting alcohol. He also says he doesn't own a gun, toy or otherwise. I know he hardly ever played with them when he was a child. The police are trying to find that guy Lexi said was in the bar with them."

Lexi said, "Erik is horrified at what he did. For the record, he's joined our club." She paused, her lips dancing in a little smile.

"And which club is that?" Rosie asked.

"The 'I Can't Believe She Shot Him!' club."

Rosie groaned and put a hand to her forehead.

Claire exchanged another smile with her daughter. A familiar verse from the book of Romans sprang to mind, the one about loving God and then being able to see good come from even the most awful situations. Positives had already emerged from Erik's fiasco. He couldn't drink while he was in the hospital, and Lexi, too distraught to work, wanted to spend time with Claire.

"Seriously, Rosie," Claire said, "the Beaumonts owe you. Tuyen is eager to see you as well. How about Thursday?"

She lowered her hand. "Okay. Okay. I really want to say I'm sorry in person. Thank you for the invitation."

"You'll come then?"

"Yes." She smiled brightly now. "Speaking of meals, you haven't had lunch yet, have you? I want my dad to meet you, and he will insist on feeding you."

Lexi said, "I'm ready for lunch. Mom?"

"Are you sure?"

"Mom." Her tone added, *Give me a break.*

Claire raised her brows, hesitant.

Lexi nodded vigorously.

"All right." Claire looked at Rosie. "Yes. Thank you."

While the young women discussed the menu, she gazed around the patio. It was a pleasant place, full of plants and flowers and brightly colored tableware and umbrellas. Tables were filling up with a noonday crowd.

Despite her effort to avoid the anxiety, it plowed its way through to her conscious mind, obliterating the Romans verse and the sweet anticipation of the whole family getting together later in the week.

Lexi ate mountains of food. She refused to talk about it or to seek help.

A silent wail filled Claire.

Thirty-One

Thursday evening, Rosie drove into the wide graveled area at the Hacienda Hideaway and turned off the engine. By the light of one pole lamp, she saw five other parked vehicles. Erik's fancy convertible was not among them.

Maybe he had not come.

Of course, he shouldn't be driving yet.

Given his arrogance, though, she would not be surprised at how many doctors' orders he had already disobeyed.

Rosie felt the death grip she had on the steering wheel. "Let go." She lifted her hands, holding them up midair. "And let *it* go, whatever 'it' is. Lord? Could we have a little help here?"

With fingers extended, she gingerly rested her palms back on the wheel and breathed deeply.

She was fine. Or she would be fine once she made it through the next few steps. She reminded herself about her personal "backup team": Papi, Bobby, and her priest. They'd sent her to the dinner with their blessings.

When Claire and Lexi came to the restaurant, Papi had met them. His initial standoffishness almost embarrassed Rosie, but Claire won him over. Elegance, poise, and a reference to God's faithful hand keeping them all safe did it.

Rosie's priest was an old confidant, wise and wizened Father John. He told her what she already knew—that confession to the ones she hurt was in order. It just always helped to hear his affirmations. Or maybe it was to see his gentle smile and the love shining in his eyes. He'd been there for her when her mother was ill, when she told Jesus He could take a hike. And he'd been there years later, pointing her to the counselors who lived out in the desert—the ones who'd carried her along the path back to Jesus.

Bobby had been more difficult to sway. He kept throwing legal ramifications at her until she agreed it made no sense. Finally she exclaimed, "Bobby! I answer to a higher authority. If I don't take care of this, you can forget about me ever getting back out on the street."

"You are certifiable, Delgado, you know that?" he had said. "Certifiable. All right, go. Just tell him you're sorry he got hurt and then get out of there. Other than that, keep your mouth shut."

"Okay."

Now, in the car, she murmured to herself, "Okay. I can do this. I have to do this."

She glanced around the darkened grounds. Solar lamps lit a pathway up a few railroad-tie steps from the parking area, then along a walk to the front opening of the old house. Lights shone through the large kitchen and living room windows.

A new sign had been erected since the previous week. Low to the ground, next to the stairs, it proclaimed simply in rounded letters: *Hacienda Hideaway ~ A Place of Retreat.*

She understood it was not yet reopened to the public. Construction work remained unfinished. Considering recent developments, she imagined family work remained unfinished as well.

But she remembered the indelible peace imprinted on Indio's face even as she heard the worst possible news about her son. And in the midst of it, she'd enfolded Tuyen into the family with grace to spare. Rosie thought, too, of Claire's sincere demeanor, Dan's friendliness, Lexi's guarded openness.

Maybe it already existed, this *Place of Retreat.* If anybody needed one that evening, it was Rosie.

S o." Rosie leaned forward, the better to hold eye contact with Erik. "I am sorry you got hurt." The sound of Bobby's exact words tripping off her tongue almost made her gag. "Nuts. Scratch that."

Seated in a recliner, its footrest up, Erik propped an elbow and cupped his chin in his hand. "You're not sorry?"

"Of course I'm sorry you got hurt, but you got hurt because I shot you. Therefore, what I'm really sorry about is that I shot you."

"What's the difference?"

"The difference is if I say I'm sorry I shot you, that begs the question: did I have to? And that opens a whole Pandora's box of lawsuit-type propositions."

"You're overreacting."

"Hazards of the trade. These things happen."

"But you've been cleared."

"Technically, but—never mind."

"Nope." He wagged a finger at her. "'Never mind' is not allowed. You nearly killed me. You owe me at least a teensy glimpse into your anguished soul."

She sat back. "I do not."

"Then it is anguished?"

"Anybody's would be."

"Even a cop's?"

"We're human."

"Hey!" He grinned. "I've got a brilliant idea. I could do a documentary, an in-depth study into the psyche of a policewoman. What makes her tick? More important, what makes her pull the trigger?"

Rosie stood. "I have to go."

"You just got here. My mother will be so hurt if you leave. And my grandmother. And Lexi. And Tuyen. The poor girl was ecstatic about you coming."

"My partner said I had to leave after apologizing." She thrust out

her hand to shake his, and then, flustered, pulled it back. He couldn't
stretch out his right hand. His right arm was in a sling.

"Uh, good-bye," she said and turned.

He grasped her arm with his left hand. "Rosie, please."

She looked at him and noticed everything she had tried to ignore.
His handsome face a deathly pale, his hazel eyes rimmed in dark cir-
cles, his long body spilling over the recliner as if poured there,
devoid of all strength.

He smiled. "I promise to put my insolent self to rest for the remain-
der of the evening."

"You have another self available?"

"On rare occasions. Are you sure you don't want to do that doc
with me? You really would be an intriguing subject."

"Yeah, right. Seriously, I have to—"

"Seriously, my family would be immeasurably disappointed if
you left. And I was so hoping to give them the night off from dis-
appointment."

She sighed. "We can't talk about what happened."

He let go of her arm and fell back against the chair as if exhausted
by the movement. "What happened when?"

She smiled and told herself it wasn't guilt over his condition that
persuaded her to stay for dinner. Nor was it his disgustingly charming persona focused on her.

No. It all boiled down to that sign out front: *Hacienda Hideaway -
A Place of Retreat.* What else could one ask for? Especially a cop on
suspension who could not fathom the desire to ever pick up a gun
again.

Thirty-Two

Lexi had always viewed Beaumont family dinner conversations like Amtrak trains gone amok: hurtling along one moment at breakneck speed, derailing the next with discordant crunching noises.

As if that weren't unsettling enough, there was the added pressure of luscious food prepared by the world's best cooks—her mom and grandmother. To eat or not to eat? How much? How little? How to rearrange things on the plate to give the correct impression?

Lexi had hoped that Rosie Delgado's presence at the table might change the dynamics, but no such luck. The policewoman fit right in, going at Erik like an express train making up for lost time.

Rosie was holding up a hand, her fingers spread apart. "Five miles, Beaumont." She kept calling Erik by his last name.

"No way." He grinned. "It's in feet or yards or meters. Five meters?"

"This is nothing to laugh about! You better think of it as five miles. If Felicia Matthews can see you, if she can even vaguely make out your likeness in the distance, you are in violation of the restraining order. Got that?"

They all sat at one end of the sala, around the new dining table. It was huge, rectangular and rustic, made of rough hewn pine with eighteen chairs—enough to accommodate future guests when the Hideaway reopened.

The ten Beaumonts sat, spread apart along the table, Max and Ben at the far ends. There was too much space, but the kitchen table was small and her mother insisted they all sit together.

One big happy family.

Ben scowled. "Erik, don't you dare go near Felicia. You've filled your quota for stupid actions this year."

Jenna touched their grandfather's arm. "Papa, this one wasn't entirely his fault. Somebody did this to him. Rosie, do you think the police will ever find that guy?"

Beside Lexi, the policewoman stared bug-eyed across the table at Jenna as if she'd lost her mind.

Erik burst out laughing. "Our resident cop cannot believe you actually said that. Jen, I was hammered and a raving lunatic. I don't remember a thing. I don't remember what he looked like. You can't lay this off on some sap who gets his kicks from taking advantage of willing dupes."

Ben said, "Eh, there is hope yet for the eldest."

Danny chimed in. "Erik, this went a few steps beyond getting kicks. He intentionally harmed you and it could have been a lot worse."

"It wasn't intentional. Guys like that don't think of consequences. Shoot, guys like me don't think of consequences."

Danny ignored him. "Right, Rosie? It could have been worse."

Rosie pressed a finger against her lips and shook her head.

Erik said, "She's not talking."

Next to him, Tuyen said, "Why not talking, Miss Rosie?"

Lexi *tsk*ed in disgust. She was so tired of the so-called cousin, of everyone kowtowing and explaining things umpteen times in umpteen different ways. Well, everyone except their grandpa. He showed up for some dinners, but he still ignored the woman.

As Rosie leaned forward and attempted to clue in Tuyen on the intricacies of the law, Danny shot Lexi a glance that said he heard the *tsk* and disapproved.

Yeah, well, so did she. In reply, she narrowed her eyes at him. Since their argument in her office last Friday morning, they hadn't talked. That night in the hospital, while they all waited through

Erik's surgery, Danny had hugged her, but there had been no verbal connection between them, no glide back into that easy twin rapport.

One big happy family.

Ben said, "Jenna, did you hear from Kevin this week?"

Lexi's stomach did a double backflip. She reached for the serving spoon in the large casserole dish in front of her.

"Yes," Jenna said. "He e-mailed last night."

E-mailed. A bitter tone underscored the word.

Lexi scooped cheesy potatoes onto her plate. They were Nana's specialty. One of her specialties. She was a great cook.

"You know." Ben went on in that voice he'd been using since the Vietnamese woman's arrival. It was so not his own. "We used to wait weeks to get a letter from BJ. No such thing as e-mail back then. Talk about gut-wrenching."

Jenna shook her head. "I'm not sure how helpful it is to read that he's so exhausted he can hardly stand up. Or that he's going to a place he can't name and can't e-mail from. Or that it's something like two hundred degrees. Or that he saw more starving children today he wasn't allowed to feed. Or that—"

Erik swung his good arm around her and pressed her face against his shoulder.

From the other end of the table, Indio glowered at Ben.

One big happy family.

While her grandparents exchanged frowns, Erik's sweatshirt soaked up Jenna's tears, Rosie and Tuyen continued their talk, and Max asked Danny something about a work project. Lexi savored a bite of potatoes, creamy in a delectable blend of cheddar cheese and sour cream. She figured she could jog them off later, take the starlit road down to her grandparents' place and back up before driving home.

"Well!" Claire smiled, a bright headlamp on yet another speeding train. "Only three weeks until the wedding!"

Lexi wondered what her mom's point was and stabbed a fork into a slice of ham on the nearby platter. Not that she cared what her point was, but evidently Claire thought somebody did because she kept talking.

"Yesterday, Tuyen and I found a beautiful black dress for her to wear to it."

Danny stopped midsentence. "Excuse me, Dad." He turned to their mom. "But we ordered that black dress online, the traditional one. What's it called again?"

Max filled in the blank. *"Ao dai."*

Her father did not remember that Lexi took gymnastics and art lessons, but he remembered obscure phrases in Spanish and Vietnamese and whatnot languages because he'd spent his life with non-English speaking people who needed jobs.

Claire said, "Yes, we ordered that and she can use it for other occasions. But for our reception, she decided she doesn't want to stand out so much. She wants to wear something similar to Jenna and Lexi. I think it's a great idea. It'll help her blend in more with the family."

The meat on Lexi's tongue dried up into stringy, tasteless threads.

"Lex." Her mom leaned around Danny to face her. "Nordstrom got in some new dresses. Lots of different styles. You might find one you like now. Tuyen's is simple and really pretty, not slinky. Maybe you can shop this weekend."

Tuyen swiveled to Claire and smiled. "I not look like prostitute."

"No you don't, hon."

Huh?

Jenna said, "Huh?"

Something indecipherable rumbled in Ben's throat.

Nana grasped Tuyen's hand on the table.

Max tilted his head, his mouth half-open. He knew. He was just searching for the right words.

Danny rescued him. "She used to. She had to. It makes horrible sense. I mean, people in her country despise her mixed race. Even her own grandparents shunned her." He raised a shoulder. "She had no other way to support herself."

It was the derailing moment. Whistles shrilled and metal screeched against metal. Lexi flinched.

Her mom talked about dresses and shopping while her grandparents argued, while her relationship with Danny disintegrated, while Erik recovered from almost being killed, while Kevin was probably getting himself killed or worse.

While a prostitute was welcomed into the family.

Lexi pushed her chair from the table and bolted across the room and out the door.

Racing madly from the site of the family train wreck, Lexi tore around the outside of the house and down the front sidewalk. Cold night air slammed into her lungs. Darkness enveloped her.

"Lexi!" Her dad yelled her name.

She ignored him. Her feet scarcely touched the railroad-tie steps. She dashed across the gravel parking area to her car and grabbed the door handle.

"Wait!" Max's hand slammed against the car door.

She let go and turned, her chest heaving.

"What is going on with you?" He wasn't the least bit out of breath. That was because he played tennis. Through it all, he played tennis. Through Erik's baseball and Jenna's recitals and Lexi's once-in-a-lifetime art show senior year and the near-divorce and the fire and—

"Lexi! Talk to me! For once, just talk to me!" His face inches from hers, he nearly shouted.

Cool, calm, collected, always-in-control Max Beaumont never raised his voice.

Lexi stepped back against the car and crossed her arms.

"Please," he said in a lower voice. "I want to know what's going on with you."

They faced each other in the shadows. Except for the string of ground solar lamps, the only light came through windows in the distance.

There, in the cold and dark, it struck Lexi: she'd stopped coming to the Hacienda Hideaway because it was gone. It no longer existed. It wasn't that the spotlights on the parking lot were not yet replaced. Nor was it the lack of bushes and flowers and trees. Nor the unfinished guest rooms that meant there was no space for her to sleep.

No, it was not a physical thing. Her parents and the stranger from Vietnam had invaded the home and annihilated its very essence. The peace and safety she'd always known with her Nana and Papa were gone. That was what she meant when she told Danny that everything had changed.

"Lexi, what's wrong? Why are you leaving in the middle of dinner?"

"I can't stay!" She huffed out the words, her breath shallow from running, from trying not to be sick, from fleeing a rage that tore through her.

"But why?"

"Nothing's the same!" Things went dreamlike. As if she were another person, she watched herself lean against the car and blurt things she did not recognize as coming from her own mind. "I don't belong! I don't fit in. Not that I ever did. She's a prostitute?"

"Was. What do you mean you don't fit in?"

"For one thing, I'm not a hooker."

"Is this about Tuyen?"

"No!"

"About all the attention she's getting? If it helps any, it's hard on all of us. To think that BJ survived all those years—of course you fit in."

"Yeah, right. It doesn't look or feel that way, okay? It just doesn't. It never has. And I'm sick of pretending. You and Mom can have your fancy wedding with your long-lost niece. Danny can go soak his head. And everybody else—oh forget it! It doesn't matter."

Her dad wrapped his arms around her. He wasn't a tall or big man, but he engulfed her.

Cool, calm, collected, always-in-control Max Beaumont did not bear hug.

An image of a smoky morning came to mind. Okay. Not counting that time she survived a wildfire, Max Beaumont did not bear hug.

Lexi felt soft cashmere against her cheek. She inhaled a faint scent of Polo. His chin grazed the top of her head.

"Lexi, it does matter. What can I do to fix it?"

The world tilted. Like a washing machine changing cycles, her insides jerked into a spin. She pushed herself away from him.

"Honey—"

"I—" She gagged and bent over, missing his sweater and his slacks, but not the tips of his shoes. As she slid to her knees, he knelt beside her and rubbed her back.

"Lexi, you're not well."

She shook her head and coughed. "Happens all the time."

"Come inside."

She wiped her mouth with the back of her hand and stood. "I have to go. I'm fine."

"Come in—"

"I'm fine! Just let me go. I'm fine." She yanked open the car door and climbed inside.

"I know all about it, Lex. Your mom told me."

"Whoop-de-do." She picked up the keys where she'd left them on the console. Her jacket and bag lay on the passenger seat. No reason to lock up in the middle of three hundred uninhabited acres.

"We'll get help."

"Nope. Not interested." She started the engine, shifted into reverse, and pulled on the door.

He held it fast. "Lexi."

She looked at him.

He gazed back for a long moment. "Are you okay to drive?"

"Yeah."

"You're sure?"

"Yes!"

"Please call when you get home."

"I'm almost twenty-seven!"

"Call." He shut the door on her protest and stepped away.

She drove off, trying not to think about the shimmer in those brown-black eyes that, for as far back as she could remember, had been rock hard.

Thirty-Three

T uyen, do you understand?"

Tuyen studied the woman she called "Nana." Of all the Beaumonts, Indio made her feel the most comfortable. She was as short as Tuyen's other grandmother, but the resemblance ended there. Her mother's mother had been scrawny with beady eyes and a thin, down-turned mouth, and a hand quick to slap.

"I understand, Nana." She heard her own speech, halting, dropping hard consonants, skipping entire words. But that would not stop her from shaping her mouth around the sounds that felt so strange. She had to practice. She had to be accepted into her father's family.

She simply *had* to because there was absolutely nowhere else on the face of the earth for her to go.

Smiling at Indio seated beside her on the couch, eager to please, she said, "Word 'prostitute' upset Lexi because is against law. Police arrest. But police help me in San Francisco. They keep me safe from bad men."

"Yes. They didn't see you take money from the men."

"No." Of course she'd known the police would arrest her if they caught her soliciting. She and the others weren't fools. They knew they had to keep their work secret. It was only that one time when the beating was severe that the police came. Neighbors called them and they protected them.

After that, one of the officers took a personal interest in her story because his father, too, had fought in Vietnam. Officer Jay put her in a shelter, found the Beaumonts, gave her money to travel to San Diego. He probably would still be her friend if not for his jealous wife.

Yes, Tuyen understood the law. It wasn't exactly the point, but she reassured her grandmother. "I keep law now. Miss Rosie not arrest me."

"Right. It's also against God's law, dear."

Indio spoke often of God and how good He was. Tuyen learned that this God was bigger than the Buddha worshipped by her other grandparents. According to Indio, when God lived on earth, His name was Jesus. He was killed but then He came alive again. He taught that God loved everyone and forgave everything that was wrong in the world. People could accept His love and forgiveness if they chose to, and then He would work in their lives for good things.

That was the mysterious part. God caring about her, Tuyen Beaumont? She liked the mystery of it.

"How prostitute against God's law?" she asked.

Indio continued, like always, in her patient tone. She never hesitated in trying to explain things to her. "He gave us this beautiful gift of physical intimacy. But He meant it as an expression of love between a husband and a wife. It makes two people one. It unites souls."

"Souls?"

Indio touched her chest. "Essence. Core of our being."

"I look in dictionary."

Indio laughed. "Yes."

Tuyen had a dictionary. She had many books and clothes and her own large room and as much food as she needed. She had friendship with Indio and Claire and Danny. They taught her about the Hacienda Hideaway and gave her work to do preparing rooms for guests in the coming months.

But a despair clung to her, leechlike, sucking away what little hope still managed to pump through her veins.

Claire and Danny had their own lives to live apart from her.

Uncle Max, her father's brother, kept his distance, as did Jenna and Erik and Lexi. They were polite to a point.

Ben, her father's father, the one called "Papa," completely and unabashedly ignored her. She understood that she created a rift between him and Indio. Sometimes he ate with them in the big house, most often not. Sometimes Indio went home with him down the road for the night, sometimes she did not. Sometimes Indio cried inconsolably over the photograph of her son BJ.

Yes, hope that things would work out with the Beaumonts steadily drained from her, day by day.

"Tuyen?"

She blinked and focused again on her grandmother's face.

"I love you, dear."

The words had never before touched Tuyen's ears, not in English, not in any language.

"Do you understand?"

Tears welled. She felt an odd sensation, as if a deer leapt within her chest. Was that her soul moving?

Indio smiled and nodded. "I love you very much."

Tuyen leaned into the woman's embrace. The deer jumped again and again until she could hardly breathe.

Sadness and despair would engulf her again, but for now she rested, awash in the mystery of love.

Thirty-Four

Morning." Max handed Claire a mug of coffee.

"Thanks." Wrapped in an afghan, her legs curled beneath her, she closed the Bible she'd been reading and watched Max sit at the other end of the love seat.

As usual, he'd risen before her, made the coffee, and joined her in their master suite. After a lifetime of hitting the floor running their separate ways, the glide into a daily habit of conversing with each other first thing had been surprisingly easy.

But something was off.

"Hmm," she said. "I was kind of getting used to the 'good morning, sweetheart' with a little lip action."

He smiled briefly, leaned over, and planted a solid kiss on her mouth. "Good morning, sweetheart."

"Ahh. Much better. Okay, what's up with you?"

He sat back, his eyes nearly creased shut. "How do you do that?"

"Do what?"

"Know things. You didn't used to read me like this."

"I did. I just never felt safe enough to tell you."

He sighed.

"So what's up, hon?"

"I'm going to the office."

She stiffened.

He drank from his mug and avoided eye contact.

176

With a deep breath and a long, loud puff to exhale, she let the tension go. "I don't think so."

"What?"

She smiled. "I said I don't think so. It's a new phrase Tandy suggested. I still haven't got the attitude down, though. Let me try again." She cocked her head and made her voice gruff. "I don't *think* so!"

He squinted as if totally baffled.

"It's to remind myself not to react in old ways. Like just now, when you said you're going to the office, I instantly got all uptight because you used to say that on evenings and weekends and holidays. It meant you're choosing work over family. It meant I had to carry on without you. It meant I played second fiddle."

"Yeah, well." He rubbed his forehead. "It might mean that today."

"I don't think so!"

"No, it's true. I admit it."

"It might be true, but I'm still talking to myself here. Give me a second." She half teased, half stalled, not wanting to hear his plans. "Okay. Not only am I not going to get a stomachache over this, I am going to tell you exactly what I think and how I feel."

"That's good. Keep our communication lines open." He quoted the counselor who had talked and prayed with them through some rough spots after their decision not to divorce.

Claire nodded and offered another quote. "And reassure each other that we're on emotionally safe ground."

"Right." He gave her a small smile. "This is the hard part, huh?"

"Mm-hmm."

"I promise to listen. I promise to value your feelings and opinions and not attack you for having them. Okay?"

"Okay." She rested back against the cushions, her fingers entwined around the mug on her lap. "After the fire, I couldn't handle being a violinist with the symphony. Emotional trauma and all that. I had to step down. Since more or less recovering, I've been able to go back as a sub, now and then. For fun I play once a month with Tandy and the others. I adore playing. But my priority is creating our new life together. It's a joy to work alongside you to get the hacienda in shape. And guess what? The symphony and my little group get along just fine without me and my violin."

"Duly noted. Where's this going?"

Tell him, Claire. Tell him. Nobody else will. "You've caught that germ again."

"Huh?"

"The micromanaging germ."

"That's ridiculous. I've—"

"Max, what else can you call it? You've been to the office three times this week. Three. Full. Days. What happened to the agreement with Phil? You work as a consultant, meaning you go in now and then. He bought the company. Good grief! Let him have it. Let him deal with it."

"The thing is . . ." He closed his eyes and pinched the bridge of his nose. "The thing is I can't deal with life here. The emotional chaos is beyond me."

As if a fist slammed into her stomach, it clenched.

No way! I don't think so! Lord, we are not *going* backwards.

Max looked at her. "I mean, I apologize to my kids and then two of them stop talking to me altogether. My brother's illegitimate daughter shows up out of nowhere. This whole house reconstruction thing is one big never-ending headache. And the final kicker: I hold Lexi and she gets sick." He shook his head. "It's total chaos."

"Hey, welcome to the real world."

"Give me a few hundred people who need jobs."

"Nameless, faceless people."

"At least I know how to help them." He pressed back his forefinger. The knuckle popped.

"Max, your presence in itself helps us. You don't have to say or do a thing. We just want you up close and personal. It makes all the difference in the world."

"I need a break, Claire. I'm sorry." He cracked another knuckle. "I just need a break."

"Your mom is calling Beth Russell today. She needs us for emotional support."

"If she can wait until later, I'll be home by three."

"Famous last words." Tiny hot bursts prickled every inch of her skin. Evidently hot flashes were not a thing of the past. She untangled herself from the afghan. "You wimp."

"I'm sorry."

"I know you are. But I am so disappointed. No, let me rephrase that. I am so really ticked off."

He glowered at her, the apology gone from his eyes, his mouth a compressed line. "So am I, Claire. Royally. All I'm asking for is a time-out and you go berserk. A little understanding might be helpful. I'm doing the best I can here!"

"I don't think so! And that is not me talking to myself."

"Thanks for the vote of confidence."

"You're welcome."

They fell silent. The exchange replayed in her mind. She heard Max's promise not to attack. She heard him accuse her of going berserk.

His shoulders heaved. "Truce?"

Shaking her head, she stood. "Nope. Just a time-out. You're not playing fair, Max. I did not go berserk."

She left the room and headed to the kitchen. Tears burned. Coffee gurgled in her stomach.

"I don't think so."

Her fingers twitched around the mug still in her hand.

Hmm . . .

She strode across the kitchen, through the mudroom. Flipping the light switch, she exited the back door. Spotlights pierced the predawn gray and illuminated the cobblestones. A few feet down the path she stopped, dumped coffee from the cup, and drew back her arm. Taking aim at a boulder the size of a Volkswagen Beetle, she hurled the mug with all her might.

It hit with a satisfying crash. Ceramic chunks splintered.

Claire smiled and brushed her hands. "Well. That sure beats having knots in the stomach and bawling my eyes out."

So he's not coming?" Ben asked.

Claire kept her expression as neutral as her tone had been in relaying Max's schedule. She shook her head and slid onto the couch next to Indio in their small RV.

Her father-in-law harrumphed. "Men!" He nearly spat the word. "Lord, help us. We're like hound dogs on the scent of a coon, except we skedaddle the opposite direction. First whiff of something we can't fix or control, we're history."

Indio exchanged a surprised look with Claire.

"Yeah, yeah," he said and paced the room in two strides. "I'm talking about myself."

Indio said, "So you'll stay while I call Beth? Maybe talk to her too?"

"I always loved Beth."

"You always loved BJ. His daughter is right up the road, wanting to get to know her grandpa."

"Don't press it, Indio."

"Just getting in my licks while I've got your attention."

They frowned at each other.

But Claire saw the give and take in their scowls. Deep, abiding love was not lost in their disagreement on how to treat Tuyen.

She felt another hot stab of anger. Would she and Max ever find that balance? Right now, as far as she was concerned, if Max chose to live at the office, her response would be "good riddance." She'd already started a mental list of who to call to cancel the wedding blessing ceremony.

"Blast it, woman!" Ben muttered.

"So." Unruffled, Indio turned to Claire. "How is Erik today?"

"Still pretty spaced out on pain medication. He and Tuyen are having an English lesson. They're watching *The Sound of Music.*"

"That must be her fifth time through that movie." Indio smiled and brought her hands together in a soft clap. "Well, enough chitchat. I'm all prayed up. I trust angels are surrounding Beth Russell, ready to comfort her. You two pray while I talk, okay?"

Claire nodded in unison with Ben.

As Indio picked up the telephone, Claire propped her elbow on the back of the couch and cupped her cheek, watching her mother-in-law. The woman's shoes were too big. Claire felt silly at the thought she was meant to fill them, to be the Beaumont matriarch.

"Hello, Beth. It's Indio." She smiled, her eyes focused elsewhere. "It's good to hear your voice too . . . Yes, we're well. And you? . . . Your husband? . . . And how about the children?"

Indio continued the chitchat, as she called it, mentioning Beth's family members by name. The two of them had kept in touch through the years, via Christmas cards and infrequent phone calls.

Indio's eyes began to shine. She reached out for Ben.

He took her hand and sat on the arm of the sofa beside her, his face unreadable.

"Beth, dear, we have some difficult news."

The story unfolded again, tripping lightly from Indio's lips with grace, achingly beautiful and bittersweet.

Unable to absorb any more, Claire shut her eyes and begged God to carry them all through it.

Thirty-Five

Rosie grabbed the receiver of the wall phone. Some-one was waiting for her on the other end of the line, but she hesitated answering.

Across the noisy, bustling Casa del Gusto kitchen she spotted her cousin at the stove in his white chef's jacket and hat. "Ramón! If this is a reporter, you're in trouble!"

He grinned, threw a handful of herbs into a stockpot and stirred.

"I mean it!"

"Do I look like your secretary?"

Laughter rippled through the kitchen.

She shook her head and put the phone to her ear. It was Friday noon, every table filled with people wanting tacos yesterday, and the staff cracked jokes.

"Hello."

"I hope you don't hurt Ramón. I am a reporter, but that's not why I'm calling."

She'd recognize those dulcet tones anywhere. "Beaumont."

"Yes. The one you shot."

"You don't have to remind me—"

"I just didn't want you to think it was my brother or my dad or my grandfather. All of whom found you, as I did, a delightful addition to our family gathering last night."

"You are so full of baloney."

"I am." Erik chuckled. "Seriously, I don't know what they thought, but I am indebted to you for hanging out. I'm watching *The Sound of Music* with Tuyen. It's our English lesson for the day. Anyway, I find the parallels amazing. Here we have Mary Poppins coming in—"

"Mary Poppins?"

"No, that's not right. Tuyen? Excuse me, Officer. Tuyen, what is her name?"

Rosie heard a muffled reply.

"Right," Erik said. "Maria. So here we have this odd little nunlike woman coming into—nay, *bursting* into—the lives of the von Trapp family, waving her magic guitar like a wand and before you know it, everyone is happy. Don't the parallels just jump out and grab you?"

"You're calling me an odd little nunlike woman."

He roared so loudly, she had to hold the phone away from her ear for several seconds.

"Erik, are you still on medication?"

"Oh, yes! Sweet, sweet oxy!"

His reference to painkillers sold illegally on the street sent a chill through her.

"Delgado." He chuckled. "I have a prescription."

"I really need to get back to work."

"Wait, please. I'm sorry. There really is a point to this phone call." She sighed to herself. "But can you remember it?"

"Yeah." His voice turned somber. "I can remember it. It's the reporters. I know why they do it. I mean I've done it myself, but man, enough's enough. The station keeps calling, like I owe them. In their dreams. This morning, some newspaper guy showed up here. My grandfather cut him off at the pass. Luckily Papa didn't have his shotgun in hand."

"It might have been my *LA Times* guy. He tried to eat dinner here last night. My dad overheard him questioning a waitress and tossed him out on his ear, refused to let him take his half-eaten burrito with him. Face it, Beaumont, we're big news. Somebody else will take our place tomorrow."

"We could join forces and make a ton of money. We'll do a book and then the documentary. Or a movie. Yeah, a movie would rake in the most dough."

"No comment, and now I'm going to hang up. I really have to—"

"She's filing something."

"What?"

"Felicia. Some reporter just called and asked me what I think about her lawsuit. I don't have the foggiest notion what he's referring to."

"Did you call your lawyer?"

"Not yet."

"Maybe it's not true."

"I'm sure it is. That's why we need to do the book and the movie. Felicia adores money. She'll want us to buy her off with the big bucks."

"We? Us?"

"She's suing the police department too. Evidently my blood on her carpet is their fault. They gave you a gun and let you out with it. *Bang, bang.*"

"She can't—oh!" Her voice hit soprano. A few select Spanish phrases embellished her rant. "She can't do that! That conniving, ungrateful, despicable—oh! She won't get away with this. She will not. I will not lose my job over some moronic, bottle-blonde parasite who thinks she can flounce her skinny—oh!"

The kitchen went dead silent.

Rosie glanced around. Everyone stood perfectly still, watching her, concern evident on each face.

"My, my," Erik said. "You have a temper, Maria."

She closed her eyes. *Maria.* The guy was nuts.

"I'm sorry," he said. "I just wanted to give you a heads-up. And to thank you, from the bottom of my black heart, for last night."

"Beaumont, just call your lawyer and don't go near her." She slapped the phone against its base. The third time it stayed put. She spun toward the waiting crowd. "What?"

Her cousin glanced at one of his cooks, pointed to the long-handled spoon in the pot, and let go of it. He walked over to Rosie and wrapped his arms around her.

It was Friday noon, every table filled with people wanting tacos yesterday, and the staff dropped everything to comfort her.

She buried her face in Ramón's shoulder.

Every odd little nunlike woman should have such a family.

You really think we'll see him?" Lexi twiddled the straw in her glass. Ice cubes whirred, soda foamed. Her eyes, the same brown-speckled green as her brother Erik's, darted continually, scanning the noisy, crowded bar.

Across the tall pub table, Rosie wondered again if her plan was half-baked. Who did she think she was trying to nab the alleged guy who allegedly harmed Erik? While on suspension? With the help of an apoplectic private citizen?

Lexi puffed a breath. "What if he recognizes me?"

Forcing a calm she didn't feel into her voice, Rosie said, "Relax. I observe people all the time. Generally speaking, they are so into themselves, they really don't notice others, especially not those quiet blenders around them."

"Quiet blender. Like me."

"It's not a bad thing."

Lexi shrugged a shoulder.

"You said the guy didn't look directly at you, that he was totally zeroed in on Erik, who was ignoring you by then, not giving any indication he was with you. Trust me. This stranger won't recognize you tonight, a week later."

"Why would he come back here?"

"He had a hand in creating big news. He'll need to gloat. My guess is Friday is the busy night here with regulars winding up their work week."

"But nobody knows this person exists."

The investigation remained under wraps. The fact about drugs in Erik's system at the time of the attack had not been reported. Thanks to his airing of dirty laundry on television, the public assumed they knew his motive. Of course he went after his cheating girlfriend. What self-respecting notable figure wouldn't? Although a pesky reporter had traced his steps back to the bar, no one had relayed the conversation Lexi overheard.

That thought always brought Rosie up short. Was Lexi telling the truth? Could Erik even remember what happened? Who knew about either of them? Lexi would go to the mat for her brother. He was a hotshot, a type that might pop pills and threaten his girlfriend and beat up an old pal.

She said, "It doesn't matter that no one knows what this guy did. People are talking. He'll want to hear it. He'll want to talk. Maybe he'll even confess. That'd be a gift. Aw, nuts."

"What?" Lexi looked over her shoulder, following Rosie's gaze.

Which focused on Bobby doing a good impersonation of a Jet Ski slicing through the ocean.

"Nuts!" she muttered again.

"Who's that?"

"You don't want to know."

On his way past a nearby table, he grabbed a stool in one hand. Reaching their table, he plunked it down backward and straddled it. He dangled his hands over the high ladder back, clasping them. The knuckles whitened. His face was tight, closed up—like when he cuffed the slimiest-of-the-slime pimps and pushers.

Rosie swallowed.

"Delgado, tell me I'm hallucinating."

She grimaced.

"What in the—" He clamped his lips together and gave a slow blink. "What are you doing here?"

The scene grew vivid. Music, heavy on the bass, rumbled, an

undercurrent to the cacophony of a hundred voices. It all ricocheted off brick walls, black chrome décor, and a two-story-high ceiling. Sweet mixtures of designer perfumes chased on the heels of sour mash.

At last her throat opened. "I'm having a drink."

His eyes skimmed her coffee mug and settled back on her face. The cornflower blue all but disappeared.

"With a friend," she added.

He looked at Lexi.

Rosie said, "This is my partner, Bobby Grey."

Under his glare, Lexi seemed to shrink. "H-hi."

He ignored the greeting and turned his gaze back on Rosie.

"Bobby, you look like a yuppie." She touched the sleeve of his tweedy sports coat. He never dressed like that. He was undercover. "Nice. You fit right in with this crowd."

"You shouldn't be here. We have things under control. Go home."

"It's my job that's on the line."

"It's my job to save your job. For crying out loud, Rosie, the whole department is behind you. This outrage is a reflection on all of us. Now go home and let us work."

At the word "outrage" she flinched, awash in guilt.

She assumed others were there, in search of the mystery man, the missing link who could explain away Erik's bizarre behavior and maybe help place Rosie's actions in a more favorable light.

She wanted to tell Bobby her idea to identify the guy, but she hesitated. Lexi was her ace in the hole. He'd blow a gasket if he knew who she was. Rosie was suspended and had no business getting involved with the Beaumonts.

A voice hallooed. Rosie looked toward the sound.

And then she slid halfway off the stool, wishing to disappear underneath the table.

Resplendent in a V-neck dress of jaguar print spandex, blonde hair cascading from a jeweled clip on top of her head, Felicia Matthews strode toward them, arms spread wide. "Lexi Beaumont!"

The world moved at warp speed, everything happening at once.

Bobby hissed in her ear. "*Lexi Beaumont?* As in Erik Beaumont's sister? Are you crazy?"

A camera flashed.

Felicia embraced Lexi. "Oh! Please tell me he's fine?"

Rosie's leg bumped against Bobby's as they both twisted off their stools and hit the floor running. They were quickly brought up short. People had closed in and blocked their escape. She resisted the urge to lift her elbows and charge through them.

"Officer Grey!" Felicia's voice rose again. "Is that you?"

Bobby swiveled back around.

He never should have done that.

Rosie kept going, pushing her way through a wall of bodies.

"Ohmygosh!" Felicia squealed. "Get out of town! It is you! I can't believe this! Brett!"

Brett? Rosie stopped and turned, peering between shoulders.

Yep. There he stood, the Padres first baseman, one eye still bruised, white tape across his nose.

A camera clicked.

"Brett! This is him!" Felicia's voice carried easily above the noise. "He's the one who saved us."

Rosie cringed at Bobby's mottled face as he shook hands.

A week ago, medics had loaded an unconscious Brett into one ambulance and Erik into another. Rosie rode with the gunshot victim to the hospital. Bobby stayed with other officers at Felicia's house, attending to details at the crime scene.

It was how they worked. They made a good team. With little discussion they looked out for each other.

Until now.

Rosie didn't have a clue how to cover his back in the present situation. The situation she had created.

More cameras flashed.

Rosie turned away. Head down, she hurried to the exit.

Thirty-Six

Lexi finally disengaged herself from Felicia's syrupy piffle and left the bar.

Honestly! The woman had cheated on Erik—with Brett!—and then was concerned about his welfare? Yeah, right. The cameras were rolling, or at least clicking. It was all about Felicia. Gauging from the crowd's smiles and applause, two-timing enhanced the woman's public image. Go figure.

And what was with Brett? Was this a publicity ploy for him as well? He'd only briefly greeted her, the mousey little sister Erik's friends had always easily ignored.

Biting a thumbnail, Lexi scanned the busy downtown sidewalks, looking for Rosie. They had ridden together in Rosie's car. If she left her stranded, how would she get home?

She spotted her then, with her partner, across the street and half a block down. They stood in shadows, away from restaurants and storefronts.

Lexi sighed in relief and hurried toward them, glad to see Rosie hadn't abandoned her. She didn't seem the type. She was so friendly, so confident, so in control.

So in tears?

Lexi paused, one foot on the curb, one in the gutter.

Rosie motioned to her to come closer, but she spoke to Bobby. "I'm sorry."

He slapped his hand on the wall and moved his head back and forth, a mock banging of it against the bricks. "Numbskull. Numbskull."

"I'm sorry."

He faced her. "Stop apologizing and agree with me. I knew better than to come. I wasn't here officially."

"But I created the whole entire situation. You wouldn't be here otherwise." She swiped the back of her hand over the tear streams on her cheeks. "It's all my fault."

"Tonight is not your fault."

"If you weren't here, she wouldn't have seen you and recognized—"

"It is not your fault that she recognized me." He barked some indecipherable word and slid his hand over his almost-bald scalp. "It is not your fault that I made sure she would recognize me. Don't you get it? I flirted with her."

"Bobby—"

"I did! Twice. After the shooting and—"

"Typical hero-damsel-in-distress syndrome."

"Just let me say this. I went above and beyond the call of duty dispensing comfort that night. Okay? No other officer was going to help my damsel in distress. And don't forget the time we got called to Beaumont's place and I walked her to her car." He placed his hands on his hips. "There. I said it. Thanks to my idiotic response, she would have known me tonight even if I hadn't been sitting at the same table with Beaumont's sister."

"Bobby, you do not flirt. I've seen you in all sorts of spots with women way more attractive than her, falling all over you, giving you every opportunity. You're Mr. Professional Stoic. What did you do? Make eye contact with her? Smile?"

"This was different. I felt something. A connection. A spark. I don't know."

Lexi had to interrupt. She stepped closer. "That's just Felicia vibes. She does it to all men. My brother—not Erik, the other one—

thinks she's a horse's hind end, but he's affected the same way. If she interviewed Danny, he swears he'd spill out everything he's ever said and done and embellish it all."

Bobby stared at her for a long moment. "You're kidding."

"It's true. She's bad news. No pun intended."

"Thanks. I'll tell my wife." He threw a glance at Rosie. "So. You're Lexi Beaumont."

She nodded.

"I take it you're here to ID the guy."

"I want to help."

"Yeah, well, unfortunately, he probably ID'd you tonight."

"What do you mean?"

"If he's in there, he couldn't have missed the Felicia-Brett show. He might not have known you before, but she practically told everybody who you are. Including the *Snapshot USA* reporter and photographer."

Lexi stared at him. *Snapshot USA* was a weekly magazine available at every checkout stand in the nation.

Rosie sniffed. "Yeah, for real. They're here, along with *San Diego in Motion.* Another officer just told Bobby. I'm so sorry, Lexi. I never should have asked you to do this."

Bobby said, "She's right. We've got a sketch based on information you gave to our artist. We'll bring in anyone matching the description and you can find him in a lineup, behind a two-way mirror." He emphasized the last words.

"But he doesn't know I was here last week with Erik."

Bobby and Rosie exchanged a look. He said, "Unless he saw you last week."

"I-I don't think he did."

"Depends on how calculating he was. If it helps any, I think he's just a mean prankster, jealous of the famous folk, not a full-on psycho. He found an opportunity to stick it to your brother."

"Still," Rosie said, "he might have noticed you last week."

Bobby nodded. "And witnessed tonight. Heard I'm a cop, thanks to Felicia."

Rosie said, "And then figured we're on to him. He'll not want to be noticed."

"Bottom line, we don't think he'll bother you, Lexi."

They did their look-exchange thing again.

Lexi pulled her sweater more tightly about herself and crossed her arms. A vague unease twisted into a physical sensation. Fetal curl on the sidewalk seemed imminent. "You 'don't think.' That's not exactly a guarantee."

Rosie held up her arms and let them drop at her sides. "No. No, it's not a guarantee. Could you go to your parents' house?"

Lexi cringed.

"Or," Rosie hastened to say, probably because she had witnessed Lexi's abrupt exit from the dinner table the previous night, "you're welcome to come home with me. Spend the night. I live in my dad's backyard, in a small guesthouse, with an alarm system and dead bolt locks. It's yours for as long as you need it. I'll sleep in my old bedroom inside my dad's."

Lexi felt the earth move beneath her, a quake's ripple. Her legs trembled. The whole world was disintegrating before her very eyes, from the wildfire destruction of her grandparents' safe harbor to her parents' weirdness to Danny's aloofness. Not to mention the Zak debacle. Now she couldn't go home to her own apartment?

There were nightmares there, yes, but also her only bits of solace: painting and food, the latter exactly what she wanted, available exactly when she wanted it. She couldn't go to Danny's. Nor Jenna's, nor Erik's. She couldn't go to the hacienda. She thought of her boss, a couple of friends. It wouldn't work with any of them. She had to go to a stranger's place?

"I'm sorry, Lexi. It's only temporary. The undercover guys are good. Bobby and I aren't—"

"Rosie, why wouldn't this guy recognize you and find me through you? Your picture has been all over the newspapers."

She smiled. "Do I look like that picture?"

Even in the shadows, Lexi could tell that she did not. The photo was an official police department shot. In contrast, Rosie now wore her hair loose, full and wavy, down to her shoulders. A hint of makeup softened her eyes. Her lips were fuller, with a touch of cerise-red gloss, and they curled upward frequently. The fuzzy turtleneck removed the last traces of her cop-like persona.

"No, you don't."

"Besides that, some people think we Latinas all look alike." She winked. "What do you say? I don't want to frighten you, but in all honesty, I'd feel better."

"Ditto," Bobby said.

Lexi squeezed her arms more tightly over her stomach and nodded. She would go home with Rosie.

Thirty-Seven

M r. Erik." Tuyen felt sorry for her incapacitated cousin, but he was making a mess out of the lettuce. "Not do that way."

His right arm still in the blue sling, Erik awkwardly wielded a large knife with his left hand, chopping away at a pile of leaves on the island countertop. He grinned. "Not say 'Mr. Erik.'"

As usual, she giggled at his gentle banter. "Nana say tear lettuces gently. We not want kill vitamins and minerals. Like this." She picked up a leaf and demonstrated.

"But whacking is so much more fun." He laid down the knife, tried it her way, and blew out a frustrated sigh. "Especially when you don't have two good hands. If I'm making the salad, we'll just have to skip on the vitamins and minerals tonight." He reached for the knife.

"Ah!" She pulled the cutting board away from him. "I make salad. You set table."

"Deal. And who, may I ask, has decided to deign us with their presence tonight?"

His words flittered through her mind, searching for a recognizable comparison. Unlike the other family members, Erik never labored over his speech or increased his volume for her. He assumed her hearing was intact and expected she would catch up to his meaning sooner or later.

"Take your time, Tutu." His eyes sparkled.

She nodded.

This man was a surprise to her. He pretended not to care about anything that happened to himself or to anyone else. He was disrespectful to his elders. He argued with his brother and sisters. But . . . for her he had a nickname. For her he was patient and calm. For her he sat fairly still and watched movies to help her learn English.

Perhaps the pain medication aided his careless behavior. Still, he'd become the single thread to which she could cling, her only source of hope.

Danny meant well, yet he hovered, wanting to make things just so, wanting her to understand right now, wanting her to agree with everything he said. He always had a better idea.

Nana poured her love into Tuyen's dry heart. And yet there was that haunted expression about her eyes, the one Tuyen caused by just being there.

Aunt Claire was sweet when she was not too busy with her own life. She and Uncle Max seemed very much in love. Her aunt was not helping with dinner because the moment he'd come home from his office just now, they'd embraced for a very long time. After that, Aunt Claire asked her to prepare what she could for the meal, and then she disappeared behind closed doors with him.

Papa, Jenna, and Lexi all but spat at Tuyen.

And Uncle Max . . . aloof and distant did not begin to describe him.

Tuyen thought it was probably wrong, but she was grateful for Erik's accident.

She smiled at him. "'Deal' mean I do your job, you do mine."

"Bravo."

"Other words mean who coming tonight."

He clapped and whistled. "Woo-hoo!"

"Thank you. All right. This is dinner lineup."

He smiled at the word he'd taught her.

"Papa not come. Mr. Danny not come. Miss Jenna and Miss Lexi, no. Uncle Max, yes."

"Got it. Small and intimate." He went to the cabinet where the plates were stored.

"Oh. And Beth Russell not come."

Erik turned to her. "Nana told you about her?"

"Yes."

"You know who Beth Russell is?"

"My father's fiancée before he meet my mother."

"Right. Maybe she'll come another time. She lives far away, in Seattle. She has a husband and kids. A busy life."

Tuyen nodded. The woman was just another person close to her father who did not want to know Tuyen existed.

"I never met her." He pulled plates from the shelf. "I hear she and BJ were the best of friends, from the time they were very young." He smiled. "She'll want to meet his daughter."

Lowering her eyes, she concentrated on tearing the lettuce leaves into symmetrical, bite-size pieces full of vitamins and minerals.

"For real, Tuyen. Well, for sure she'll want to meet me anyway. I'm Mr. Hotshot Famous Newscaster."

She giggled. He often referred to himself in that disparaging tone with silly phrases. "*Ex*-Mr. Hotshot Famous Newscaster."

He laughed. "Good one."

"You say it one time."

"And you remembered. You are an excellent student."

She beamed.

"And you have a beautiful smile."

Shaking her head, she covered her mouth.

"You do. Don't hide it."

"Amerasian ugly."

"You have got to stop saying that! Promise me you will not say it again. Never ever, from this point on."

"But it is true."

"It is not true! Now promise me. Or else I won't take you driving."

"Driving?"

"You want to drive?"

"Me?" She stared at him and gestured as if steering a car. "Drive?"

"Yeah. One-armed as I am and drugged half out of my gourd, insane with boredom out of the other half, I need a driver. I need to go to Santa Reina. Just a quick errand. One stop. We'll be back before the chicken goes into the oven. What do you say?"

"Oh, yes! I dream of driving! I dream I drive truck."

"Truck? You like Papa's big honkin' mean machine?"

She nodded. "We come in it to see you at hospital. Max and Claire take own car." Despite their fearful destination, the ride had been cozy. The cab smelled of her grandfather's pipe, a sweet scent like oranges. He helped her climb up into it and back down again. For a short while, she felt a member of the Beaumont family.

"Um, we better start with something a bit smaller. We'll take my mom's car. Okay?"

"Okay. I put food away. Nana not want it left out." She gathered the salad ingredients and quickly put them in the refrigerator. "Bacteria grow. Mr. Erik?"

He frowned and shook a finger.

"Erik."

"Yes?"

"I not know what I do without you." She blinked so the stinging tears would not fall.

His smile disappeared and he studied her face for a long moment. "I did not hang the moon, Tutu."

"What mean 'hang the moon'?"

"It means you give me too much credit. I'm an unemployed drunk. As soon as I can live through half a day without a pill and a nap, it's so long, farewell, *auf wiedersehen, adieu.* To you and you and everybody."

"Where you go?"

"To my condominium."

Her chest felt like the time Ben galloped by on his horse, so fast and hard and oblivious to her. "What you do?"

"Think about a job." Erik shrugged. "Or not."

"You come back." Her anxious voice rose. "You come back, visit! You come back for blessing on wedding! Aunt Claire want you here."

"Sh. Sh." He stepped around the island and placed his free hand on her shoulder, lowering his face toward her. "Yes, I will come for blessing on wedding. It'll be all right, Tutu. I promise to say good-bye to you before I leave. You know I don't normally live here."

Her heart boomed more loudly, pounding against her chest and echoing in her head. "You not go tonight?"

"No, not tonight. Tonight you drive, I buy self-medication treats, and then we have a cozy family dinner. Okay? Take a deep breath now."

She tried to do what he said, tried to keep at bay the old terror of abandonment. "You good friend. You bring me to my grandmother."

"Hey, what's a cousin for if not to facilitate homecomings?" He smiled and straightened. "Just remember, though, I did not hang the moon. I am not God."

She followed him into the mudroom located off the kitchen, where coats and boots and keys were kept. Erik thought too little of himself. If he had a fault, that was it.

Tuyen slipped her jacket from a hook. "I beg to differ."

He laughed at the phrase he'd taught her that afternoon. "What do you beg to differ about?"

"Nana say God strong and kind and He love me very much. He take good care of me. He watch over me all the time. He make me feel safe. You much like God."

He paused, his hand on the doorknob, and stared down at her. It was a rare moment when his features relaxed and his eyes lost their guarded expression. "Well, I can declare without hesitation that I have never, ever been accused of that before."

"It good thing."

His burst of laughter warmed Tuyen. Fears retreated into the shadows of her mind, thwarted if only for a while.

Thirty-Eight

"What, no flowers?" Claire's sarcastic tone grated, painful to her own ears as fingernails scraping across a chalkboard. "No jewelry?"

From his own corner of the love seat, a pokerfaced Max cracked his knuckles. "Thought I'd try something different."

"By hiding away at the office all day?"

"By not using gifts to earn your forgiveness. That never really worked, did it?"

Struck with the enormity of what he was saying, she swallowed a sarcastic retort. Max's behavior was a direct answer to prayers: she'd asked for a transformed husband, one who understood that all the diamonds and roses in the world did not make up for the pain his absence caused.

His brows rose slightly. "If the counselor were here, she'd suggest we try that exercise. Remember how—Sweetheart, you're doing the Jenna eye-roll thing."

She squeezed her eyes shut. "Okay, okay. I remember how."

"I just think we should slow down here and have a productive dialogue."

"I don't want to." She looked at him. "I want my pound of flesh."

He smiled. "All right, let me have it. You be the extractor of flesh and I'll be the listener."

"A heart-to-heart instead of flowers?"

"Yep."

"My mind has nowhere to place that scenario. This is the first time you blatantly let me down since . . . since . . ." She waved a hand, not knowing what to call that time during which she'd left him, moved out, looked for comfort from another man, filed for—

"Since our mending."

The tension fizzled. Her muscles relaxed. "We've come a long way."

"An incredibly long way."

She sighed. A short while before, when Max walked in the door after being gone all day, she'd received his bear hug. She'd felt great comfort in his return, but it also reignited anger.

So they withdrew to the master suite for privacy. Three hundred acres and it was the only place available to them on a cold winter's night. Claire knew she had to get used to that idea. The presence of Erik, Tuyen, and her in-laws was nothing compared to a dozen guests inhabiting the place. Maybe it was all a pipe dream, thinking she could grow into the role of matriarch and keeper of the safe harbor.

"Claire, what is it?"

"I wonder if I've bitten off too much. I know God is my safe harbor, but most of the time I still can't grasp that as a reality. How can I run a retreat center? I'm at my wit's end with the four people who are here right now, and they're family!"

"What I heard you say was . . ." He smiled crookedly as he echoed the prescribed phrase that was supposed to help them communicate better. "I heard you say you're scared. I heard you say we are a team and I let you down today. Did I get that right?"

Claire replayed his words. They wove themselves in and around her agitated emotions. Like gold embroidery floss they stitched and designed. Finally a pattern emerged. He understood.

She nodded.

"I am so sorry," he said.

Again she nodded.

"Can I talk now?"

"Sure."

"I had an awful day. Nothing went right. I wasn't a help to anybody. I just got in their way, but I kept at it, not wanting to admit what a gutless wonder I was to leave here this morning."

"Hm. Hm. This is when I have to keep my opinion to myself, right?"

"Yes, for now. For this exercise. I suspect you see things the same way."

She smiled, but kept herself from bouncing up and down in ecstatic agreement that yes, indeed, he had behaved in a cowardly fashion. "Okay. What I heard you say was that you're scared too."

"How's that?"

"You're afraid to live in this emotional space where you can't fix a thing. Where your dad is falling apart, your niece is crying for help, your son is a wreck, and house reconstruction moves at a snail's pace."

"I guess so, considering the mere mention of all that makes me shudder."

"So, we're both afraid. Fear is sin. It means we're not trusting God. We should both confess it and move on."

"Move on together."

"Yes."

He scooted across the love seat and took her hand. "You're okay with a gutless wonder on your team?"

"Oh, Max. It beats a fool all puffed up with machismo."

He tilted his head and peered at her through squinched eyes. "Are you saying what I think you're saying?"

She laughed until tears ran down her face. "Yes, Max. I love you just the way you are."

Thirty-Nine

The Saturday afternoon following the incident at the bar, Lexi grasped the fence-like guardrail that encased the back end of a pickup truck. With about a dozen other people she bounced along as the vehicle rumbled across rough terrain on its way toward a herd of giraffes at the Wild Animal Park.

Eyes shut, she leaned out from under the canopy, catching the warm winter sunshine full on her face, glad to have gotten a spot due to a last-minute cancellation.

Funny, she thought. Zak had never gone on the Photo Caravan Tour with her. It was her most favorite thing to do, but he always declined. Why was that? She would watch a stupid helicopter circle around a lake with him, yet he would not visit a zoo or an art gallery with her.

It had been Rosie's idea that she lose herself in some fun pastime. The overnight in the little guesthouse had not been all that restful. Comfortable as the tidy home was, and secure as Lexi felt with an alarm system and a cop not twenty yards away, she wrestled with thoughts of that ugly man chasing her.

He wasn't ugly, not literally. The guy she had seen talking with Erik reminded her of her brother: Armani suit model material. Erik had him beat, though. Dumbo ears disrupted a perfect flow of tall, dark, and handsome in the man.

She now recalled Erik's phone call a short while before. He'd reached her as she drove into the park's lot.

"Are you home?" she asked in surprise. Cellular signals weren't available at the hacienda.

"No." His breathing was labored. "Just hiked up the north hill a ways until my phone worked."

"You're feeling stronger then."

"Well, yes and no. It's the best place to stash my stash, if you get my drift."

"Erik."

"Don't feel bad, Lex. I've been dry for one entire week. A record. I foresaw an emergency last evening and offered to give Tuyen a driving lesson. We ran up to Santa Reina. She's not bad behind the wheel."

Pursuing the topic of alcohol abstinence would be like suggesting she fast for a month. No reason to go there. "What was the emergency?"

"Dinner with Max. Now, moving right along. Nana talked with Beth Russell, the fiancée. She took the news rather well, but didn't commit to coming down from Seattle to meet the young 'un. I can't imagine why she'd want to."

Beth Russell and Uncle BJ and Tuyen were the furthest thing from Lexi's mind. "I had an emergency of my own."

She filled him in on the previous evening at the bar with Rosie and her partner. He didn't comment and remained quiet for so long, she figured the signal was lost.

"Erik?"

"Brett came up here yesterday. He told me he and Felicia are in love. Deeply, truly, madly. Isn't that a laugh? She hates baseball. He never wanted to hang around if she was anywhere in the vicinity." He sighed. "Who knows? Maybe it's true. In some bizarre way it stands to reason. I mean they're both my best friends. *Were.* Oh, I don't even care anymore. They deserve each other."

"I'm sorry."

"Yeah, I know you are, Lex. And I'm sorry you're in the middle of this. My opinion is that Rosie's job is to be overly cautious. She had to warn you. End of story. There's no reason why that imbecile would cause more trouble. He got his jollies by making a fool out of me. I don't think that's against the law. They couldn't charge him with anything."

"But to expose him would validate you."

"You're sounding like Jenna."

"That's not nice."

He chuckled. "I'm not a nice person. There is no validation for me. Back to you. Are you scared?"

"N-no."

"Alexis."

She wrinkled her nose. "A little, maybe."

"Come up here."

"You're joking."

"I'm not. Nana and Papa move into their new house today. As of tonight, they won't need the RV. You could sleep in it."

"Still too close. How long are you staying?"

"Until that worried look on Mom's face goes away or I get plastered enough not to be able to see it. I could leave today and you could stay with me."

"I . . ." She hesitated. The time she'd spent with Rosie stood out in such a sharp contrast to her other relationships. There were no words to describe it, only a sense that she felt different with Rosie. She behaved differently with Rosie.

"Talk to me." His voice went soft.

"I-I don't think we're good for each other."

"Youch!" He shouted, flippant tone back in full force. "That hurt!"

She bit her lip.

Erik laughed. "And bravo for saying it. You are absolutely right. Besides keeping each other company in our addictive behaviors, you'd trash my condo with your slew of paints and canvases."

"Like it's possible to trash your place?"

"Pot calling the kettle black." He blew out a noisy breath. "Seriously, Lexi, that guy is long gone. Your family is toxic to you. We love you, but you don't have to take care of us. Get on with your life. You're cute and intelligent and incredibly talented. I'm here if you need me. All right?"

Now, as the breeze blew her hair from her face, she felt another rush of hope. It was okay that she and Erik shouldn't spend much time together. The thing was he believed in her. It canceled Danny's exit from the scene. It canceled Zak's about-face.

And, to top it off, she was on a photo shoot at her favorite place in the world.

Maybe instead of endangered rhinos, she'd snap photos of giraffes. Maybe she'd even capture one in that precarious, most awesome of awesome milieus: a perfect balance of light and shadow, the condition that gave shape and tone to her paintings.

Maybe, just maybe, the world wasn't such a bad place after all.

Wow!" Rosie gazed over Lexi's shoulder at a photo on her laptop computer. "I didn't know giraffes were so gorgeous. This one has got to be female. Check out those eyelashes."

"Pretty cool, huh?" Lexi smiled. "I think I'll name her Gigi."

"You can actually paint her?"

"Well, a version. It won't look like a photograph." Lexi eyed the policewoman. "I'll start as soon as it's safe for me to go home."

Rosie leaned back in her chair at the table. Her typically assured demeanor kept slipping from her like a shawl that wouldn't stay put. She'd come over to the guesthouse with a bowl of homemade salsa, a bag of tortilla chips, and vibes way beyond tense.

"Sorry, Lexi, nothing to report on that front. I vote we just give it a few days. Are you comfortable enough here?"

"Sure." The small one-bedroom with its bright hues met her craving for physical safety. "I don't want to put you out, though."

"No worries. I'm fine next door. I'm making points with my dad too. He thinks I've finally taken his advice and made friends with a regular person, somebody who isn't a cop or related to one." She grimaced. "I pointed out to him that with a friend like me, you don't need an enemy. Be that as it may, do you want go to a movie or something? Unless you have a date?"

Date. Right. In her dreams. "I don't have a date. You don't either?"

Rosie shook her head. "I usually work on Saturday nights. Besides that, all my guy cop friends are either married or otherwise engaged. Anyway, if I don't get my mind off things, I'll go crazy."

"Things like last night at the bar?"

"That and the fact that Bobby dragged me off to the shooting range today and the fact that it took me a good ten minutes to even pick up my gun." She exhaled a loud breath. "They want me back on the street tomorrow night. My captain says time's up. Or not-so-nice words to that effect."

Lexi didn't know how a female only a few years older than herself could do what Rosie did day in and day out as a police officer. Such courage and decisiveness were qualities Lexi had tasted of only once, the consequence of making it through the wildfire the previous fall. Rosie's personality brought back the memory of what it had been like to live in that rare atmosphere of confidence. It whet her appetite to experience it again.

Maybe hanging out with Rosie could pave the way.

"Sorry, Lexi. I'm dumping on you."

"Hey, what are friends for?" She smiled. "A movie sounds fun."

Forty

By the time Rosie lost herself in an offbeat movie, consumed a large buttered popcorn and jumbo soda, and polished off half a Chicago-style deep-dish pizza with extra cheese, normalcy returned. The only downside to the process was the number of fat calories involved.

"Really?" she said to Lexi across from her in the booth. They were discussing the film. "Your dad was like the one in the movie?"

"Unavailable? Yes. Sometimes I think Erik got the worst of it. I mean, Max was there for him when he was little and then, *poof*, he wasn't. For me, he just always wasn't, at least not by the time I was old enough to notice. I never knew the difference."

"I'm sorry. I don't know where I'd be without my dad being who he is."

"But you lost your mom, you said."

"That's a different story." She smiled. "Nobody has the perfect parental situation, huh? We all get thrown for a loop by one thing or another. I guess that's what life is all about—finding our way through the loops, hopefully coming out better for the zigzaggy trip."

"You obviously did."

"You think?" Rosie's smile fizzled. "My mom first got sick when I was sixteen. I was an okay kid up until then. *Hellion* best describes what came next. She died three years later. Somehow all that anger got me through college and into law school, until everything went south."

"What happened?"

"I fell in love, which sounds on the surface like a good thing. But it was an unhealthy relationship and I knew it. I just couldn't stop it. There was an ugly date rape. I was hospitalized. Then it was his word against mine and since his family was rich and powerful and white, his word counted. I believed I deserved my mother's death and this guy's treatment. I deserved to die." She paused. "I wanted to kill myself."

Lexi paled. "How did you get from there to here?"

"God. My dad. Father John, a wise old priest. Counselors. They never stopped loving me, never stopped praying. Eventually God helped me forgive the guy and my mom."

"Your mom?"

"It sounds goofy, I know. It wasn't her fault she died, but the end result was a major wound inside of me, something to let God heal."

"How does that happen?"

"Slowly. By His power. Through prayer. I had to let it all go, over and over again."

"My dad asked us to forgive him."

Rosie felt her eyes bug out. "You're kidding!"

"I don't know why he did. There isn't anything to forgive. I mean, he was just being a dad, working, supporting all of us. He didn't abuse us. He just wasn't around much. Big deal."

"Lexi, don't let him off the hook. His actions, whatever their cause, hurt you. They made you believe he rejected you, and nobody can feel good about themselves if Dad rejects them." She shrugged. "Sorry. I'm preaching. Bad habit."

"That's okay. My mom and grandma do it all the time." The seam between her brows said it wasn't really okay.

Rosie bit the inside of her lip to stop the didactic stream of verbiage. But it was all so obvious! Erik and Lexi were bent on self-annihilation. Lexi's chosen method might be more subtle than Erik's, but it was not lost on Rosie. She easily recognized the signs of an eating disorder.

Adopt the Hopeless Club, now in session.

Not true, Bobby! There is hope. There is always hope. And there is help.
Not if they don't ask for it.
I'm just being a friend here.

"It's not like he didn't try." Lexi toyed with a fork.

"Hm?"

"Max. I remember he came to my gymnastics meet when I was nine. It's memorable because I broke my leg. I saw him walk in when I was on the balance beam." She shrugged. "Wham. On the floor. Is that my phone?" As she pulled her cell from an oversized leather bag, a jazzy beat intensified. "It's Erik." She glanced at Rosie and answered. "Hi."

Rosie watched emotions play across Lexi's usually stoic face. Impatience and anger creased her forehead and tightened her mouth.

"Erik, what is wrong with you? You couldn't stay dry for one night?" She flipped her straight hair over a shoulder. "Call a cab . . . I know it would cost a fortune! Then call Danny. I can't handle— What? No . . . Yes . . ." Her voice faltered. "No . . . I'm with Rosie. I don't have my car. Okay." She smacked her phone shut.

"What's up?"

"He was drinking at the house. Max kicked him out. Mom cried, but it seems she sided with Dad."

"Where is he?"

"At a bar just outside Santa Reina. He hiked down to the highway and thumbed a ride."

"That's quite a distance, isn't it?"

"Yes. He's going to end up back in the hospital. I have to go get him. Take him home. Danny and Jenna already told him no."

"Don't do it."

"He's my brother!" Her voice rose. "I can't leave him there, wasted, his arm in a sling."

"He's got to hit bottom, Lexi. As long as we keep picking him up and dusting him off, he won't get the help he needs. In the meantime, look what this does to you."

With a shaky hand, Lexi wiped at tears. "I have to help him. I have to keep him safe. No one else will."

"I will." Rosie met her friend's gaze and tuned out Bobby's nagging voice. "But he has to do it my way."

"All we have to do is get him home."

"No. He hits bottom tonight and in the morning he checks himself into a treatment center."

"What do you mean, hits bottom?"

"Crash-lands. Whatever. The place where he admits he needs help."

"Like he could pass out on the road and freeze to death?"

People at a nearby table turned at her screechy voice.

Lexi kept going. "Or pick a fight and get beat up or—"

"Exactly. You get the picture."

"He could die!"

"I'll go up to Santa Reina and play guardian angel, watch over things." *Call an ambulance when he gets hurt.* "I'll take you back to my place first."

"I'm coming with."

"No." Rosie felt her eyes constrict, heard her voice go soft. "You're not."

Lexi recoiled as if she'd been slapped.

It stunned Rosie how easily she could slide into cop mode with someone she considered a friend.

Maybe she was ready to return to work after all.

An hour later, Rosie drove behind a sheriff's car, following it into the bar's parking lot just outside the little town of Santa Reina.

The show had already begun?

Rosie breathed deeply and reminded herself that she'd promised her dad not to act in a hasty manner. Chasing down the deputy and asking what Erik Beaumont had done would be breaking that promise. After all, maybe the guy wasn't there for Erik Beaumont.

Sure. And maybe polka-dotted heffalumps really did exist.

She got out of the car, glad that Lexi had agreed to stay behind with Papi. He was in the kitchen, experimenting with new recipes, and—at first sight of Lexi's red eyes—insisted she help him figure out what was wrong with the *mole*. Not enough chocolate? A missing spice?

Rosie smiled. He'd even cut short his lecture about her idiotic plan to play guardian angel.

In the dim light of a few pole lamps, the deputy strode toward the low cinder-block building. Neon beer signs brightened its small windows. Situated in the middle of nowhere on the edge of the highway, it appeared to be a hopping place. Several pickups and cars sat in the gravel lot. As the officer entered, a country-western beat fluttered through the air until the door swished shut. Thick, nighttime quiet returned.

Vulnerability swamped over her. It was total idiocy, stupidity, lunacy. Who did she think she was? No uniform, no weapon, no backup, no undercover agenda. No official capacity whatsoever.

Just a desire to help a hurting family, in particular the eldest son who—when sober—made her laugh and made her heart skip a few beats. Who made her forget his rich white boy persona. Who called her Maria after a nun who saved a family.

Nuts.

Rosie shook her head and marched toward the door.

"Not even a nightstick, Lord." She patted her shoulder. "What do You think about a set of wings?"

Forty-One

Claire laid the phone in its cradle on the kitchen counter and sighed loudly.

The other side of the island, seated on a stool, Max crick-cracked his knuckles. "What did Lexi say?"

She gathered her thoughts. Lexi had phoned and said so much more in what she didn't say than in what she did. First off was the fact she called. It spoke volumes of her desire to stay connected with her mom. Second, she sounded calm in the middle of another Erik trauma, which meant she'd found help, probably in Rosie's friendship. Third, that nice man Esteban Delgado spoke in the background, asking her to stir the sauce. Lexi was in good hands for the night.

"She said Erik called her from that bar up the highway, near town."

"The Lonestar?"

"Yes. He wanted her to take him home. She was with Rosie, who talked her out of racing to his rescue. Both Jenna and Danny told him no too." Claire touched her stomach. The ache had lessened with her daughter's call. It remained, though, as did the scene of Erik ambling down the darkened driveway, huddled in a too-short ski jacket.

"So he made it to Santa Reina," Max said. "Or almost. And everyone refuses to give him a ride?"

"It must be contagious, this decision to say no to him."

"I hope so." He reached over and touched her cheek. "We have to stop enabling him."

Easy words. What if he had gotten lost and hurt? What if he had died in the wilderness?

"Sweetheart?" He lowered his hand. "What else from Lexi?"

"Rosie's on her way to him."

Max's jaw went rigid.

"Not to rescue, but to watch over, like a guardian angel. So he . . ." She waited for the lump in her throat to dissipate. "So he doesn't get . . . hurt or-or worse. Rosie said she wouldn't even let him know she was there unless . . ." Another lump.

"She's not going to shoot him again?"

"Max."

"I wasn't trying to be a smart aleck. Actually, I thought another bullet might do some good. It seemed like God had his attention there, you know, for a short while, anyway. Oh, Claire. I'm sorry."

She sniffed.

He walked around the counter and pulled her to himself. "Not funny, huh?" He held her close, his chin brushing the top of her head as he spoke. "Rosie is an intelligent, caring young woman. She'll do what's best for him."

"Watching him suffer consequences is so hard."

"It's a time of reaping weeds, planted back when I didn't know the difference between them and flowers."

"You're not taking full responsibility for his choices, are you? You tell me not to."

"No, I'm not." He kissed her forehead. "I am so grateful we're going through this together, you and me and God and now an angelic policewoman. Remind me to write her into the will."

As he grew quiet, Claire listened to his heartbeat. He was a good man, his heart a garden of exotic flowers. She hadn't seen them in full bloom, though, not until he'd uprooted the choking weeds, those steadfast refusals to extend and receive forgiveness.

Surely it would be the same with their son.

Lord, give Erik his time to gather flowers.

Forty-Two

Evidently a smoking ban had not reached the outskirts of Santa Reina. Or else nobody bothered to enforce it. Rosie watched Erik and the deputy sheriff through a smoky haze, Toby Keith's gusty twang reverberating in her head.

She wove through the crowd to get closer, wondering if the conversation was as friendly as it appeared. The burly officer nodded, his mouth nearly hidden in a full reddish-brown beard. Erik grinned in a lopsided, one-too-many way. Mellow. Nothing at all like the night she confronted him.

A small group surrounded them, consisting mostly of females. There were giggles and polite boos and lots of spandex.

Staying out of earshot, Rosie sidled up to a young woman. "What's going on?"

She turned, full, glossy lips stretching to reveal teeth smudged in red. "Do you know who that is?" Not waiting for a reply, she leaned toward Rosie, excited to share gossip. "Erik Beaumont. The TV news guy? Called his girlfriend." Her dark eyebrows rose and she shook her head, long raven hair swishing. "That's a no-no."

Rosie played ignorant. "A no-no?"

"She's got a restraining order against him. Now the sheriff is here. Says he's gotta haul his cute you-know-what off to jail."

Rosie gritted her teeth. How could Erik be such a dork? Undone by a stupid phone call. "Brainless nitwit twerp."

214

"Yeah." The woman snorted. "If that guy was calling me, no way I wouldn't invite him over. Come on down, Mr. Beaumont! Yow!"

Rosie didn't bother to explain she wasn't talking about Felicia.

Two minutes later, she sat in her car again. Assuming the officer had things under control, she waited nonetheless to make sure Erik's cute whatever was thrown into the back of the sheriff's SUV.

She should call Lexi, put her mind at rest.

She would do that.

As soon as the sensation of fire burning in her lungs stopped.

What was she so angry about anyway? Erik had shelter for the night. So what if it was provided courtesy of Felicia Matthews?

So what if he went after that woman again, the one who'd broken his heart?

So what if Felicia Matthews still held sway over him?

Why did Rosie even care?

"Balance, Rosie. Find the balance. Don't give up on him, but don't lose your mind over him either." Bobby's voice again.

Bingo.

"The thing is, Bobby, it's not my mind that concerns me."

Rosie gave up trying to find balance. She just shut down.

"You will not regret it, Delgado." Sitting in her car across the street from the Santa Reina substation, she calmly lectured herself. "Trust me on this. Distance is the key. This guy is starting to resemble old Ryan."

Beaumont was inside. Five more minutes and she would assume he was staying put for the night. She waited, not wanting to call Lexi too soon.

"Admit it. Okay, okay. I don't want to talk to Lexi until my voice stops warbling like a canary on antidepressants."

The cell phone rang.

It was probably Lexi.

Rosie hummed a long, low "hmm," smoothing out the telltale huffy tone before answering.

It rang two more times.

She flicked it open. "Hello."

"Hey! Maria!"

No way.

"Wassup?"

Absolutely no way.

"Maria, you there?"

"What do you want?"

"Mm. Bad news. I mean, I don't want bad news. I have bad news."

"You are bad news, Beaumont."

"Yes, I am." He sighed dramatically.

Rosie shook her head. *Do not help him. I repeat, do not help him in any way, shape, or form.*

"I messed up. I messed up big time. Did you realize that order thing meant not to even call her? Not even to say 'hi, how ya doin'?'"

"You didn't call her."

"Yeah, I did. On a dare. This lovely group in the bar thought I'd blown it with her so I—"

"Give me a break. You're still blaming others for your actions?"

"Mmm, lemme think. No. I was showing off. I admit it. So then dear Felicia called the police, and here I am, stuck in Santa Reina's holding tank for the night without any pain meds for this aching shoulder."

"You deserve it."

"I do. I admit that too. Being shot and being arrested and living with excruciating pain."

"Why on earth are you calling—how did you get this number?"

"Tuyen had it. I, in an astoundingly clearheaded moment, committed it to memory. Just in case. You know."

"I don't. Just in case what?"

"Just in case I needed you."

"You need a lawyer. Is this your one phone call?"

"You got it. But I don't need a lawyer, Maria. I need you."

"How many sheets to the wind are you?"

"Not all that many." His voice lost its mocking cadence. He sounded stone-cold sober. "You're the only one who can help me."

Heat seared her lungs again. In a flash, it spread through every nerve in her body. She gripped the steering wheel and fought back images of marching inside and smacking him.

"Rosie, help me. Please?"

Help him? As in bail him out? Tell the court he didn't mean to harass Felicia? That he was under duress because he'd been shot? By one of their finest?

"I'll help you, Beaumont. I won't stand in your way. You can rot in jail first and then you can rot in hell."

She slapped her phone shut, tossed it on the passenger seat, and started the engine.

Forty-Three

Sunday afternoon Lexi zipped shut her gym bag on the floor and straightened. One sweeping glance covered the living area of the tiny guesthouse. Through the bedroom's open door she noted the stripped bed.

"Rosie," she said to her friend seated at the table, "I'll wait until the sheets are dry and make up the bed."

"Don't worry about it. Papi will probably find them in the dryer while I'm at work tonight and take care of it. He still spoils me like that."

Lexi smiled. "Can I adopt him?"

"He said the same about you. We're glad to have you stay longer."

"Thanks." She sat at the table. "But I'm kind of a homebody. Two nights away . . ." Her voice trailed off. Two nights away. She'd survived two nights away . . . from everything, all the comforts of home.

Rosie said, "I probably overreacted Friday night. I really don't think there'll be a problem. Nothing has been in the newspapers about the incident with you and Felicia. The mystery guy will most likely remain a mystery. In the big picture, nobody cares if drugs were slipped to Erik. It doesn't change the outcome."

"I suppose not. What about the lawsuit?"

"Against the department?" She shrugged. "A flash in the pan the suits will settle out of court. It was news for a day."

Lexi nodded. "Rosie, I don't know how to thank you."

"Good grief, giving you a place to stay after what I put you through was the least I could do."

"It was more than that. Your friendship, sharing your papi." She paused. "It just all meant a lot. Your talk, about what happened to you and about me not letting my dad off the hook . . . It-it helped. I know I have some issues to work through."

"Anytime you want to kick it around, call."

Lexi didn't shy away from the steady eye contact. She imagined not much was missed by those dark pools staring back at her. Most likely Rosie even perceived Lexi's biggest issue, the food thing. Yet she treated her with respect.

"Thanks, Rosie."

"You're welcome. At the risk of sounding like your mom and your grandma, God adores you and He's listening all the time."

Adored her?

"End of sermon. Hey, thanks for being my regular-person friend." She laughed.

It had been a long, long time since she laughed. Maybe life would be different, as in okay for a change.

Danny's phone call earlier had helped. Although the conversation was brief and to the point, it was significant because it broke their week-long silence. He told her he'd talked with Erik, now at home after paying a cab driver a mint. He'd been jailed overnight for disorderly conduct; he expected to be fined for breaking the restraining order. Lexi agreed with her twin that telling Erik no went against natural tendencies, but it was the right thing to do for his sake.

And, she knew, it was right for her own sake. Erik stressed her out too much. Stepping away from him as well as Danny and every other family member—including Nana and Papa who hadn't acted like themselves in months—felt like a major move toward something positive. Something like emotional health maybe?

She didn't even want to stop to buy ice cream or cheese curls. She just wanted to get home and paint that gorgeous giraffe in the full glory of nonendangered life.

Hi, Lex."

Cordless phone in one hand, paintbrush in the other, Lexi froze in the center of the room. A few feet in front of her, the canvas blurred from view. *Zak?*

She was painting in absolute quiet, windows shut, stereo off. It was an experiment. The idea sprouted from hanging out with Rosie's dad. Esteban Delgado's philosophy of life and of cooking revolved around upsetting what he called the "applecart of routine." He was the most gracious, contented man she had ever met.

Due to the lack of music blasting through her apartment, she heard the phone ring. She picked it up because, well, because it just seemed like the thing to do. Not waiting for the machine to pick up was another experiment in dumping that applecart.

"It's me," he said. "Zak."

"Hi." Neutral. Cautious. Their last conversation replaying in her mind loud and clear, complete with references to his ex-slash-no-longer-ex *girl*friend.

"How are you?"

"Okay."

"Good. Um, listen. I'm at work, so I only have a minute. Some reporter came by. He's working on a follow-up story to the Rolando Fire. A human interest piece, sort of where are they now, several months later. He interviewed me and Chad and Eddie."

"Shadrach, Meshach, and Abednego."

He chuckled. "Yeah, I told him about that. I'll never forget your grandmother's nicknames. How is she?"

"Fine."

"Good. Anyway, this guy's focus seemed to be on heroes, so I told him who the real hero was that night."

She bit her lip.

"Heroine, I should say. I didn't want to give him your unlisted number, so I told him I'd call and give you his number."

"Why?"

"So he can interview you."

"I'm sure he only wants to hear stories from firefighters."

"Lexi, you're doing it." Exasperation filled his voice. "Preempting what could possibly be a good thing. You were interviewed right after it happened by everybody. Why not give it a shot? People like reading about heroines. It gives them hope that something's right with the world."

"I wasn't a—"

"Yes, you were a heroine. You saved our lives. Here's his number. Just write it down. Do you have a pen?"

She looked at the paintbrush.

"It's seven—"

"Wait." She stepped to a tall bench that held her art supplies. The palette lay there, a large sheet of paper with dabs of oil paint arrayed in rows, a spectrum of hues, dark to light.

As she dipped the brush into her creation of a henna tint that just might work in the giraffe's coat, she was struck with a sense of beauty. It was as if the colors swirled, a sudden, vivid burst of magnificence showering about her like fireworks.

She inhaled sharply.

"Lexi, are you there?"

Yes, she was there. She *was there*. She existed. God adored her. She had been—for one night—a heroine. And Zak was for that past moment, not this present one.

"Yeah," she breathed. "What's the number?"

Y ou must be Lexi Beaumont." The man set his grande-sized coffee on the table, slid the leather backpack from his shoulder, and offered his hand. "Nathan Warner."

"Hi." Returning his smile, she shook his hand.

"Zak Emeterio said to look for the cute one with long hair."

She stopped smiling, released his hand, and let the *Nice to meet you* die on her lips. Why did they always have to go for a line?

"Zak really did say that and it would have been enough to recognize you." His eyes crinkled. "So it's not total bull, which I gather from the expression on your face is what you're probably thinking. May I?" He nodded toward the empty chair.

"I don't know yet."

He flashed a grin. "Okay, God's honest truth: I did my homework. I saw your photo in an old newspaper, from right after the fire." He bunched up his shoulders and kept them there like a question mark.

Lexi tilted her head, as if weighing his words. God's honest truth? She savored the moment.

Her experiment with upsetting the routine applecart that had started the previous night continued. It spilled over into Monday work habits and, to her surprise, she designed an awesome landscape. Her boss and the client couldn't praise it enough.

Interesting how everyday life had lost its threat. She felt downright feisty and flirty. With a start, she realized she didn't have to talk to this guy.

Likewise, she could. Her choice.

"Have a seat, Nathan."

"Thanks." He hooked his knapsack on the chair back and sat.

She guessed him to be not much older than herself, maybe thirty-ish. He had that kid-next-door flavor going with rumpled jeans, oversized white button down, and chubby cheeks. His coppery hair was moussed messy, but not in a deliberately stylish way.

"Uh-oh." He tapped the side of her clear plastic cup. "Strike two. I'm supposed to buy your coffee. Or whatever that concoction is."

"You're making fun of my venti iced caramel macchiato, extra shot, extra whipped cream? Strike three."

"At least I'm on time."

"You are. Which I guess might cancel strike two. I came early and didn't wait for you to buy my venti iced caramel macchiato, extra shot, extra whipped cream."

"Hot dog! That leaves one strike to go. There's still hope for an interview then?"

She smiled. "Sure. Who do you write for?"

His eyes, a curious tawny color, twinkled. He took a business card from his shirt pocket and handed it to her. "I freelance. Newspapers, periodicals. I'm trying to get a column syndicated. My specialty is human interest. I've been doing a lot on disasters. They intrigue me—not the event itself, but its impact on people months and years after the fact."

"The Rolando Bluff Fire last September."

"Exactly. Anything else?"

She shook her head.

"Cool." He pulled a notepad from his bag. "I should warn you that I've been accused of sounding like an interrogator when I talk to people about tragedy. So please tell me if you don't want to discuss something or if you get uncomfortable at all. Okay?"

Din from jazz music, a dozen conversations, blenders, and coffee grinders meshed into white noise. Lexi sensed vibes roll from Nathan Warner. They touched her in the same way that sliding her feet into a favorite old pair of comfy Birkis did.

She leaned back in the chair. "Okay."

Lexi described the night of the fire. Although she relayed vivid details, the event had taken on surreal qualities over the past months.

"Sometimes I wonder if it really happened to me. It could have been a dream or a story I read."

"Can you compare the Lexi Beaumont before the fire and the Lexi Beaumont after she led her mother, grandparents, and three firefighters to safety, thereby saving their lives?"

"Don't forget the cat and dog."

"Willow and Samson." His smile was soft. "It's a tough question."

"I don't feel like a hero."

"What does a hero feel like?"

"I don't know."

"Me neither. Try to think about how you view life since that night."

"After that night, I was flying high. It was like I couldn't even come down. I didn't want to sleep because I didn't want to miss one minute of life. The world was a totally new place." She stopped. She didn't know what else to say.

"Past tense?"

She glanced away. "It . . . it faded, I guess."

"Common occurrence. After a while, our lungs notice the air is too thin on the mountaintop. We can't survive up there."

She thought she had changed in such a huge way, life would never ease back into the old ways.

"Is that your phone?"

She heard it then and started digging through her purse, a bag the size of a small suitcase. "Excuse me. Normally I wouldn't bother." She shoved aside everything but the kitchen sink, vowing once again to get a smaller bag with compartments, and at last her fingers touched it. "But we're in the middle of issues. Family junk." She glanced at the caller ID and groaned. Erik. "I have to take—Hi."

"I think." Erik's voice was faint. "I think I need help."

"I can hardly hear you. What's wrong?"

"There's blood. I'm bleeding."

"Where are you?"

"Home. I don't know what hap—It's my shoulder."

"A lot?"

"Sort of. I wonder if I bumped it?" His voice sounded odd, neither loaded nor sober.

"I'll call an ambulance."

"No, it's not that bad—It's just—Oh, nooooooo."

"Erik!"

The phone went dead.

She was on her feet, frantically digging for keys, quivering from head to toe, stumbling toward the door.

"Lexi, can I do something?"

"Huh?" The keys were in her hand. She noticed then the journalist at her elbow. "Uh, no. I have to go. It's an emergency."

"I'll walk you to your car." Nathan Warner stayed beside her through the winter dark. He helped her find her car in the lot and get inside it. "Want me to drive you?"

She shook her head. Should she call an ambulance? Erik's place was less than ten minutes away. If he had just bumped the wound, maybe stitches came loose. No big deal. The sight of blood had always made him woozy.

"Hey, Miss Heroine." Nathan squeezed her shoulder. "Call me, okay? I'll buy the next venti iced caramel macchiato, extra shot, extra whipped cream."

That "ah" sensation oozed through her again, tingles of hope prickling from head to toe. Grateful, she smiled at the source.

He shut her door, stepped back, and waved, his feet in plain view: thick white socks and Birkenstock sandals.

Lexi knew then that she could handle whatever was going on with Erik.

Forty-Four

Erik Beaumont was not going to bleed to death on her watch.

Rosie bounded up the steps two at a time, two flights covered, one to go. She huffed and vowed to never ever again skip gym time.

Minutes before—several, thanks to Bobby's mulishness—Lexi had phoned her, saying she was on her way to Erik's. Considering what she reported about him, she had sounded surprisingly calm.

Rosie, however, lost it. She let Lexi disconnect. In hysterical tones she relayed the situation to Bobby beside her in the squad car. He made matters worse by serenely suggesting they send another unit.

Rosie screeched at that. "We patrol his neighborhood! At this moment we are on duty!" Like her partner didn't know such things.

He dawdled further until she got herself under control and was able to radio dispatch. He dawdled until she informed them in a professional manner where they were going and to please put an ambulance on standby. He dawdled while she phoned Lexi. When she didn't answer, he made a U-turn and flipped on the lights.

They had rushed into Erik's building. While Bobby waited for the elevator, Rosie found the stairwell.

Now she bolted across the third-floor landing.

Erik Beaumont was not going to bleed to death on her watch.

As the elevator dinged behind her, Rosie reached Erik's front door, which was ajar. She pushed it open and went inside.

On her two previous visits, she'd described Erik's condo as "untidy." The adjective no longer applied.

The combination living area and kitchen was basically trashed, everything from dirty dishes on countertops to an overturned lamp. It smelled of garbage and dirty clothes and stale booze.

A windstorm? Party out of control? Thieves? Or a blitzed tenant at the end of his rope?

"Lexi!"

"Up here!" Lexi's voice came from above.

"Do we need an ambulance?"

"No." Lexi poked her head through the single doorway located at the top of the open spiral staircase. "But we need you." She ducked back inside.

More steps to climb.

Rosie stared at them . . . at the trail of red-black spots marring the thick ecru carpet.

She followed them up, gingerly planting her feet around the blobs.

"No ambulance?" Bobby's voice came from below.

"Nope."

"Yell if you need me."

Rosie went inside the bedroom. Fresh sea air greeted her, a welcome whiff through the open balcony doors. Like the downstairs, the room was chaotic.

Erik lay on a king-size bed, clothed in black sweat pants, atop the covers. His eyes were shut.

Lexi sat beside him, pressing a towel against his wounded shoulder. She looked up. "He always barfed whenever somebody on his ball team got hurt. He'd faint at the sight of blood."

"Has he fainted?"

Erik cleared his throat, but didn't open his eyes. "No. Just feel . . ." He raised his left hand and waggled it. "A little off."

Every nerve in Rosie's body crimped up as if she'd stuck her finger in an electrical socket. "Beaumont, you pathetic waste of oxygen!

You snooker your sister into racing over here because you feel a little *off*? Because of you she calls me because you feel a little *off*? People are out there getting robbed and beaten and worse while I'm here because you feel a little *off*? Give me a break!"

Lexi burst into tears. "He didn't snooker me! Rosie, he needs help."

"That's the understatement of the year. But the truth is, Lexi, he is never going to get help because he will not come straight out and ask for it!" Who in the world did not know that basic psychological fact? Everybody knew it! What was wrong with this family?

Lexi rushed past Rosie to the door. "Why don't you just shoot him again?"

"I just might do that!" she yelled at her retreating back. "Put him out of his misery."

Bobby appeared at the top of the stairs and pressed himself against the wall to allow Lexi by. He looked at Rosie. "That was professional."

Words of retort caught in her throat. Bobby's tone did not banter nor condemn. He did not lift his chin in the way that communicated he was Mr. Patience. He could wait for her to get over the huff and puff before offering a soft reprimand.

Nope. None of that. She had crossed a line, one big giant step from where she belonged as a cop right on over into the ethereal never-never land of personal involvement.

Rosie gulped. "I need more time off," she whispered.

He gazed at her, his face unreadable.

"One day. Starting now. I'll call in."

"Don't bother." He shoved himself away from the wall. "Just get yourself straightened out, Delgado. You've got twenty-four hours."

She watched him pound down the stairs.

How had she gotten into such a tangle? She had only meant to pray for a needy person who crossed her path, a rich, good-looking guy with issues for whose sake she had now probably lost her job and her friendship with Bobby Grey.

None of it made sense, but she knew her choices had narrowed themselves down to one.

"Lord, have mercy," she muttered and turned back into the bedroom to take care of Erik Beaumont, that man she referred to as a pathetic waste of oxygen.

Forty-Five

"Y ou okay in there?"

At the sound of Officer Grey's voice from the other side of the bathroom door, Lexi lowered the towel from her face. According to her reflection in the mirror, she was anything but okay. Her straight hair had gone stringy, her hazel eyes colorless orbs rimmed in puffy reds.

"I'm fine," she lied.

"Can you come out, please?"

The sight of Erik's filthy bathroom made her want to be sick again. She opened the door and followed him into the living room. He was not a big man, but in the blue-black uniform, arms akimbo and jaw set, he appeared larger than life.

He said, "What happened here tonight?"

"I-I don't know." Lexi squirmed under his gaze. "When I got here, he was sitting on the floor upstairs, bleeding from his shoulder wound. Not much, but enough to make me think he should go to the ER."

"There's a stool overturned in the kitchen."

She nodded. "I think he fell off of it. He's not really coherent, but he said something about standing on it, searching those high cupboards for boo—for whatever. He's such a mess. He needs help."

"Did he say anything about another person being here with him?"

"No."

"All right. We can assume he was alone, inebriated, had an accident." He exhaled heavily. "Delgado is going to stay with him. We should leave."

"But he needs—"

"Rosie will take care of him."

"How? What will she do?"

"I don't know exactly, but we can trust that she has the situation under control."

"She said she might shoot him."

He started to say something but clamped his mouth shut. His face glowed red.

Lexi bit her thumbnail. Tears burned her eyes. "She didn't mean it."

"No, she didn't. Is there anything I can do for you? Give you a lift?"

"I should stay and help her."

"She's a one-woman show. You can help him and yourself best by leaving." The creases in his forehead smoothed out and his voice hushed to a gentle tone. "Lexi, sometimes we're just too close to a situation. We need to step back and let others take over for a while. Nonfamily others."

"I should clean up this place."

"No, you should go home. Why don't you go to your parents? They must be as concerned as you are about him. He's taken you all through a rough time of it. I imagine you're feeling pretty alone right now, maybe afraid too. You may not know this, Miss Beaumont, but misery and anxiety love company." One corner of his mouth lifted.

"But my parents . . ." The protest fizzled. Her parents what? Made her crazy? No longer fueled her soul with warm fuzzies? Not that her dad ever had, but her mom and grandparents knew how to care for her.

Knew. Past tense.

"Lexi, a crisis makes for a good catalyst. It pressures people to look at life differently, to make changes."

Resistance drained from her. She felt a twinge of gratitude that she and Erik had not been close in earlier years. He exhausted her. She felt like a lone warrior carrying him for weeks now, ever since they'd acknowledged mutual self-destructive habits.

Where was everyone else? Of all weeks Danny could camp, he went this one. The rest of her family—

Well, who knew? She was the one angry with them.

Maybe it was time to go home.

Lexi drove slowly up the road from the highway through Hacienda Hideaway grounds. The evening was pitch-black. Distanced from city lights, stars shone brilliantly. As she rounded a bend, house lights came into view. They emanated from the new bungalow where her grandparents now lived.

How odd that they'd moved in before she'd even seen the finished product. She, the grandchild who spent more time in their home than any other family member.

Before the fire.

"Can you compare the Lexi Beaumont before the fire and the Lexi Beaumont after . . ." The reporter's question came to mind.

Before the fire she came and went as she pleased, to and from the estate at least two or three times a week. She worked on the landscape. She helped Papa with the horses. She played canasta with him. She rested in Nana's serenity. She learned the old ways from her, how the Kumeyaay lived off of the desert. She heard about Jesus' unconditional love and she received it from the old couple.

She seldom ate herself into oblivion at the hacienda. She seldom made herself sick.

Then came the fire. It diminished Nana and Papa, somehow made them smaller. And that development—even more so than her parents' stupid re-wedding rigamarole—was what had wrung the life out of Lexi's world.

Not exactly a lucid answer for Nathan Warner and his article.

She stepped on the gas pedal. Dirt swirled behind her, and the new home faded from view.

It was time to find her own new home. Not the house she'd grown up in—that had been sold. Not the hacienda her grandparents used to live in—that had burned and been refurbished.

No, it wasn't a physical thing. It was her parents and her grandparents, waiting now for her up at the big house, longing to hear news about Erik.

She hoped they longed as well to welcome her home.

Forty-Six

Claire held Lexi tightly. Her youngest was shorter by a few inches, small boned, petite.

When Claire was pregnant with her and Danny, the doctor did not suspect twins. Always it was one heartbeat, one large baby doing gymnastics in the womb. He waited full-term to arrive. Some minutes later, Lexi surprised them all, slipping quietly into the world as if she were her brother's shadow. Too tiny to go home with him, she remained at the hospital for a few weeks.

"Oh, Mom!" Lexi choked.

"Honey, what's wrong?" Claire took half a step back, hands on Lexi's shoulders, and looked at her.

They stood alone outdoors, near a kitchen window, on the verandah. Patio lights strung along the overhang cast a warm glow in the evening.

"He is such a mess!" Lexi cried.

"You said Rosie was with him. That's all I need to know for now about Erik. I asked how *you* are, Lex. Tell me, please? Last week you left here so upset. Then you didn't return my calls. I miss you."

Lexi's breath caught. Her eyes widened. "I miss you! I miss Nana and Papa. I miss Danny something awful." The words tumbled from her. "I just miss the way life used to be. Oh! I sound like such an idiot!"

"No you don't. Emotional, maybe, but not an idiot. What did you mean 'used to be'?"

Lexi blinked. "Before the fire."

Before the fire. But so much good had come after the fire! Eventually, at any rate. Lexi, obviously still stuck in the losses, did not have the eyes to see those things. It was an old tune with her: change meant trauma.

Claire chose her words carefully. "It's true the fire precipitated a lot of changes."

"A lot? Absolutely nothing is the same anymore. Nobody is the same anymore."

She nodded. Lexi had always struggled with change, no matter how insignificant. Everything from a new classroom to a new tooth- brush disturbed her in equal proportions. Thank goodness she'd hooked up with Vivian, her boss, in a business she adored, at the age of sixteen. She hadn't needed to change jobs. Moving her from home to her own apartment hadn't happened until just a couple years before and had been nothing short of amazing.

Recent developments would be wreaking havoc in her.

"Lexi, there have been huge adjustments to make. I know how hard it is on you. Your childhood home is gone. Nana and Papa have aged considerably. Their place, your home away from home, can't possibly feel the same to you."

Lexi hung her head, and Claire knew she'd hit the soft spot.

She knew because it was her own. "Honey, Nana once told me that you came to the hacienda for the same reason I did."

Lexi raised questioning eyes that brimmed with tears.

"It was a safe place for us. Hm?"

Lexi nodded.

Claire drew her close. "Well, I think it's supposed to be one again. For you and me and the others. Even for strangers who visit. It's a tall order and not one I can fill. But I'm learning that God is a God of tall orders."

"You're sounding more and more like Nana."

"Thank you."

Lexi backed out of her embrace, wiping at her eyes, a tiny smile on her lips. "You're welcome."

Claire returned the smile. Her baby was home, at least for now, vulnerable enough to express her heartache, open enough to receive her mother's hug.

Had God begun to fulfill that tall order?

The proof lay in Lexi's reception of Max.

Dinner had been put on hold for over an hour after Lexi phoned. Now Claire put the finishing touches on it, praying that her daughter would sense a safe harbor with the dad she really didn't know well at all.

Tuyen sat in the corner at the table, not entering in on the welcoming of Lexi. She remained visibly upset about Erik. Jumpy, she asked question after question about him. Her Vietnamese accent thickened by the hour until she was almost unintelligible.

Indio comforted her new grandchild as best she could, but she appeared tired and unable to put her whole heart into it.

Ben had deigned to join them, making one of his rare visits to the family dinner table since Tuyen's arrival. His behavior toward the girl still bordered on rude. No wonder Indio was worn out.

Claire pulled baked potatoes from the oven, piled them into a bowl, and murmured softly to herself, "Not my job. Not my job."

What a perfect phrase! The pastor had used it the day before in his sermon, and she'd already repeated it umpteen times, whenever an old thought pattern attacked and suggested she was responsible for Max and Ben, Erik and Lexi, Jenna and Danny and now Tuyen. The old Claire—the one before the fire—majored on trying to fix things so that family and friends would not know one minute of unhappiness.

Of course that was an impossibility and—to top it off—it was never intended to be her job!

At the stove now, she lifted the lid from a pot, forked the broccoli in the steamer, and saw Lexi greet Indio and Ben.

Big hugs were passed all around. Perhaps almost as big and warm as in the old days, the days before the fire had changed everything? Lexi asked if Danny was coming; her face fell at Indio's negative answer.

At last Max approached her from behind, touched her arm, turned her away from her grandparents.

"Hey." He spread his arms apart. "Welcome."

Claire paused in her work, spatula midair above the baked chicken pieces, and held her breath.

She held it for a long, long moment.

Then Lexi shifted her weight onto the other foot, and the narrow space between her and Max was filled.

She sort of disappeared inside Max's arms. His width enveloped her small frame.

A blink of an eye later, the hug ended.

But, Claire thought, it was a hug, given and received.

Yes, God seemed to be filling that tall order.

Claire prayed for further proof. Lexi's sense of a safe harbor would lay in her consumption of food.

They sat at the cozy kitchen table, Claire, Max, Ben, Indio, and the young women. Tuyen resembled a spooked deer, Lexi a sated kitty.

"Okay," Lexi said, "first I have to tell you about Friday night. But Mom, you've got to promise you will not freak out."

"Why?" Claire set down her fork. "Why would I do that?"

"Lexi, don't worry." Max's voice was tender. "You're here with us, safe and sound. No one is going to freak out over something that might have happened to you three nights ago. Okay?"

Her brows went up as if in surprise at his words. She gave a half nod. "Okay. So, Rosie had this brilliant idea to identify that guy who gave Erik the drugs." She described the implementation of that brilliant idea, which concluded with Lexi's need of a safe house.

Brilliant? Claire could think of more appropriate adjectives, but swallowed them along with the mental tone now rising to freak-out levels.

Max sat back in his chair, a calm expression on his face. "Rosie and her partner really thought you might be harassed by this guy?"

"They see such crazy things." She popped a bite of broccoli into her mouth and shrugged.

Indio said, "Lord, protect Lexi from demented people."

"Amen," Claire said. "So that explains why you were with Esteban Delgado last night when you called?"

"Right. Nana, you've got to meet this guy. You would love to cook with him. I have a new recipe for *chimichangas*. Anyway, back to Erik." Her voice faltered when she said his name, but she pressed on. "I was at a coffee shop downtown with this journalist, Nathan Warner." She went on to explain the reason for the interview, speaking in between bites.

Bites from normal portions. Not her usual huge ones.

Max smiled and held up his water glass. "The legend lives on! A toast to our resident heroine!"

Lexi grinned.

Indio said, "Is this Nathan good-looking?"

"Nana!"

"How about Esteban?"

"Indio," Ben growled.

"He's okay." Lexi winked at her grandmother.

"Which one?"

Lexi laughed. "So in the middle of the conversation with Nathan, Erik called." She described what happened after that, which concluded with her leaving him bleeding and more or less passed out.

Max said, "What was Rosie going to do?"

Lexi shook her head. "She didn't say. Her partner said we can trust her, though."

"Yeah. I believe that. And she'll call when it's time."

Silence filled the table.

Lexi pushed her plate away.

No second or third helpings.

"I'm stuffed and I don't want dessert. Papa, how about a game of canasta?"

Ben gave her a thumbs-up.

Claire breathed a prayer of thanks. Lexi felt safe. God was indeed filling that tall order.

Forty-Seven

Tuyen watched the Beaumonts smile and laugh, and she once again sensed a curtain draw shut between her and others.

She was not a Beaumont. She never would be a Beaumont. Her father's name was not hers.

The fear that had pursued her for as long as she could remember smothered her now. With increasing clarity she understood she was destined to live on the opposite side of that curtain. It was how she had always lived. In her homeland she existed separate from her mother's parents, separate from everyone in the village, separate from Vietnamese nationals. In San Francisco she existed separate from Americans.

A despicable castoff.

And now her final vestige of hope died, killed by one blow after another at the hands of the Beaumonts. It felt as if she were being entombed.

Lexi, the cousin she hoped would one day befriend her, had not even greeted her directly tonight.

Max and Papa Ben, the ones who never made eye contact with her, turned compassionate faces toward Lexi. Papa Ben put an arm around her shoulder and they left the kitchen to play a game.

Claire tried to show concern for Tuyen, but it fell short. Always her own children were first in her conversation, in her choices.

Nana's warmth had cooled since her phone call to Beth Russell. There was, too, her question. Were Tuyen's mother and father married? Her confusion grew more pronounced at the negative answer.

Danny, who at first visited every day, had not come to the hacienda in many, many days. His presence at the family dinner last week was not personal to her.

With Jenna there had never been even a slit in the curtain between them.

The fatal blow, however, hit Saturday night. Erik left. He left sooner than he said he would. He did not say good-bye as he promised. He had not called her as he promised. Not one word from him to her, in spite of the camaraderie they'd shared.

A despicable castoff.

It was time for Tuyen to leave, once and for all, the world that was not her home.

Forty-Eight

Lexi peered over the cards in her hand at her grandpa. They sat in the sala at the huge dining table, the replacement for a smattering of small tables. Before The Fire, she and Papa had played their perpetual game of canasta at a small table, Samson curled at his feet, Willow on her lap. Now the furniture felt all wrong. Not even the dog and cat had shown up.

"I miss the small tables in here."

Papa snorted. "I miss a heapful more than a lousy table. And it ain't necessarily made up of things, if you get my drift."

She got his drift, all right. That was exactly what she'd been telling her mom. "I know. Life before The Fire was good."

Papa laid his cards down, spread his hands against the table, and leaned toward her. His expression was the one used for warnings about snakes and mountain lions. "Alexis Beaumont, that was not my drift."

Only once in her post-toddler life had Lexi crossed him. It happened at the time of The Fire, when he'd behaved as if struck with a sudden case of dementia, making him totally irrational.

Obviously that was not the case at the moment. She kept her mouth shut.

"Life before The Fire was like always," he growled. "It just was. Good and bad, easy and hard. God blesses us with it all mixed together. The good stuff makes us feel happy for a while, but it's the crap that shows us what kind of people we really are. Exposes those black spots on our hearts, the ones He's in the business of healing." Papa's jaw went rigid.

"Th-then what did you mean? What do you miss from before?"

242

He blinked, loudly sucked air in through his mouth and held it as if trying to keep control. "I miss not knowing my eldest son went back on his word. Turned into a man I would not recognize." He blew out the breath.

"But, Papa—"

"God could have let me die without that information."

"But the circumstances—"

"Circumstances! Hogwash. That's situational ethics. No such animal." He pushed back his chair. "I'm going to bed."

"Do you see a black spot? On your heart?"

The glare in his eyes dimmed. His jaw went slack. "Don't know. Don't much care at this point. I'm just a tired old man. My Maker can clue me in when I see Him. Finish the job then."

Lexi watched his retreating back as he left the room. His formerly broad shoulders were rounded under the plaid flannel shirt that appeared a size too large.

She sank back in her chair, feeling like a tired old person herself. The day had held too much. Too much good and bad, easy and hard. Dawn's first rays had fallen on her giraffe painting, a promise of good things to come. And come they had—first at work, then with Nathan Warner. Both invigorated. The difficult stuff—Erik, Rosie, choosing to go to the hacienda—served her well. They somehow created hope.

Until reality sank in.

Being with Max wore on her. Responding to the dad who hadn't paid her attention in twenty-some years frazzled her. Her mother listened to her, but still she seemed distant, entwined in her new life as hacienda hostess, occupied with the care of Max, Papa, Nana, and now Tuyen.

Nana wasn't her old self yet. Papa had been—for about twenty minutes.

If Papa was right, it was all designed to reveal some black spot on her heart. But she already knew what that was: like Erik, Lexi was such a mess.

Forty-Nine

In the parking lot near the hospital's ER entrance, Rosie sat on squishy, pearl-gray leather behind the wheel of the silver convertible. Top up. It was a late-model Mustang, one powerful piece of equipment. If given the opportunity, she would consider paying a large sum of money in order to drive it, open it up out on a desert highway. Top down.

She traced her finger around the steering wheel and spoke to the man sprawled in the passenger seat. "I'm sorry I called you a waste of oxygen."

"I think that was 'pathetic waste of oxygen.'"

"Yeah. Whatever. I apologize."

Silence filled the car again. The clock read ten fifteen. They'd spent hours inside the ER getting Erik repatched up. He was good to go. The question remained as to where.

He shifted, reached over, and turned the key in the ignition. "It's freezing."

"You could have asked me to do that."

He flipped on the heater. "Rosie, I did ask for help."

She rubbed her forehead. He wasn't referring to the heater.

"I got arrested in Santa Reina on purpose. I needed an excuse to call you. I told you I didn't need a lawyer. I said I needed Maria. I said, 'You're the only one who can help me.'"

So upset about his arrest, Rosie hadn't heard his thinly veiled cry for help.

*Upset about his arrest? Get over yourself, Delgado. You were upset
because he called Felicia. That's not even upset. That's jealousy.*

"Tonight," he said, his voice low and quiet, "I asked Lexi for help.
I shouldn't have done that. She's not well herself."

"Beaumont, just come out and say it. I'm listening now."

For a moment he didn't respond. "I need help. I don't know who
else to ask. You're the only one who talks to me straight and at the
same time seems to give a hoot."

Rosie shut her eyes.

"I'm . . . scared. I'm in serious self-destruct mode. The last thing I
remember was tearing my place apart trying to find another bottle.
Have no clue how I hurt myself. Have no clue what day it was. Or
is. The blackouts have gotten worse."

She looked at his profile. He stared straight ahead, his shoulders
hunched, as if talking to some unseen confessor.

"I had such good intentions. Forget you along with my family—
I can do this by myself. That lasted all of thirty minutes. I came
home to my agent's message that all the feelers he put out for jobs
got the same reply—something along the lines of 'in your dreams'—
and then he more or less fired me as a client. Okay, I can take a hint.
Nobody in news broadcasting is going to hire me."

He paused. "Things got fuzzy real quick after that. I ran out of
booze at some point. I left to buy more and tripped over a copy of
that ridiculous rag *Snapshot USA* tucked under the welcome mat.
Guess what page was earmarked?" He turned toward her.

Her throat constricted. She shook her head.

"You got it. My two former best friends, full color, arms locked,
grinning like they won the biggest lottery in history. 'San Diego's
Hottest Couple Sizzle.' Tiny insert photos, one of yours truly and
one of an ambulance. They didn't really get a shot of my ambulance,
did they?"

She shrugged.

"You're mentioned, too, by the way, but not by name. Fortunately they totally missed the part about you and Lexi and your partner being at the bar with the sizzling couple." He pinched the bridge of his nose.

"Thank God." She swallowed and coughed, trying to relax her throat muscles.

"You are such a Maria, and I mean that respectfully." He gazed toward the windshield again. "So, I give. What's next?"

"You tell me."

"I-I . . ." His eyes closed. Tears glistened on his lashes. "Do they teach you how to torture at the academy or do you just come by this naturally?"

"Tell me what you want, Erik."

A long moment passed. "I want to check myself in. Somewhere."

"Okay. Somewhere. I assume money is no problem. Which means you could go anywhere. Maybe you want to dry out up in Malibu. You know, at one of those really nice, posh places where all the big names go."

"That's me: big name, posh to the nth degree. Wouldn't consider anything less than first-class all the way."

"It's hard work, no matter where—"

"Revolving-door rehab is the only way to go." Sarcasm overtook his earlier defeated tone. "I'll join the parade of people who get fixed, suffer relapse, and repeat the whole cycle again. Why, the headline guarantee alone is priceless. And it sort of maps out my future, don't you think? I'll know where I'll be six months from now. Well, not specifically. I'll either be on the mend or relapsing." At last his voice ran out of steam.

"I just wanted to make sure you were aware of all the options."

"You think I haven't thought about this?"

Rosie inhaled deeply. "I have another option in mind, one you might not know about. It's very small, very private. Its only guarantee is that the experience will be the most painful you've ever had. It's two hours from here, in the desert. I can take you right now. If you're ready."

He covered his face with his hands and nodded. At the first sound of a sob, Rosie shifted the car into gear.

Erik unbuckled his seatbelt. "From the looks of this place and considering how fast you drive, I'd say we've landed on the other side of the moon."

Smiling to herself, Rosie turned off the engine.

The nighttime desert did not resemble the busy community they'd left behind. It wasn't only the bleak landscape that separated the two, however. Inside the lone ranch-style stucco house before them lived a couple who danced to a tune not many people could hear.

"Talk about desolate," he said. "What am I getting myself into?"

"The rest of your life, Erik." She met his gaze.

They hadn't talked much during the two-hour drive. He'd recovered his composure and remained silent, dozing off and on. She focused on driving and praying. To talk about his decision to seek help could have led him into talking himself out of it.

She sensed they still tiptoed around that possibility. "Trust me, it's a good thing. Let's get out. I have to stretch."

They climbed from the car and walked around its front. The night was gorgeous: cold, clear air, the sky a sequined canopy.

"Where are we besides the middle of nowhere?"

The house was the only place in sight. Lamplight shone through the windows. An exterior light over the front door bathed a small stoop in a soft yellow glow.

"Welcome to Greg and Jillie Hennison's home," she said.

"This is somebody's *home*?"

"You turned down posh."

"Yes, but—"

"Don't worry. It's rehab with a cozy twist. Do you know who St. Francis of Assisi was?"

He thought a moment. "Was he the wild guy who renounced family and money and ran off naked into the woods?"

She smiled at him.

He stared back at her. Even in the shadows he looked a wreck. His eyes were slits in puffballs, his hair matted, his jeans and long-sleeved henley shirt something beyond the slept-in phase.

A smile tugged at his mouth. "Got the family and money renunciation down pat. Do I get to do the naked part too?"

She grinned. "Actually, I packed some clothes for you. Grabbed a few things at your place while you were out of it."

"You never cease to amaze me, Maria."

"It was an act of faith, expecting you would need them." She went back around the car and retrieved a grocery bag from the backseat. Unlike the rest of his condo, his closet and drawers were organized to the point of fastidiousness. Gathering a few basics had been easy. The guy was into personal appearance. No surprise, she imagined, considering his public role.

She handed him the paper sack.

"This is it?"

"Trust me, there are no adoring fans out here. Besides that, Jillie does laundry and Greg is about your size."

"I'm going to miss your smart mouth."

"And I yours. Ready?"

"Shouldn't I know more about these people?"

"Nope."

"A quick synopsis."

"They're different."

He chuckled. "Come on. I promise I won't wrestle you for the keys and hightail it out of here."

"The Hennisons are deeply spiritual. Common vernacular: they're Jesus freaks."

He waited a beat, as if letting that information sink in. "What do they know about drunks?"

"Alcohol abuse is their specialty."

"How do you know them?"

"We met through a hospice group. They lost an adult child when I lost my mom. A few years back, they helped me through a difficult situation. Okay?"

He tilted his head, clearly second-guessing his decision.

"Erik, you've come this far. Go inside and meet them. They're expecting you. I called from the ER."

"You pack for me and make reservations. Why are you doing this, Rosie?"

She sighed. "I don't know. God told me to."

"You're crazy."

"Certifiable, according to my partner. Can I put the top down?"

"You're taking my car?"

"I need wheels to get home."

"What if I want to leave?"

"You won't." She smiled. "You're not a prisoner, Erik. They'll give you a ride. Most likely, though, I'll come pick you up when it's time."

"Like in twenty-eight days?"

"It varies. I'll tell your parents not to worry. Now go."

"You're not coming in?"

"You're a big boy, Beaumont." She walked to the driver's side, got in, and shut the door on any more questions.

Slowly Erik made his way along the stone walkway, through the wide dirt-and-rock yard, toward the light. As he approached the front door, it opened.

The Hennisons did not disappoint Rosie's expectations. Greg enveloped Erik in a bear hug. Jillie reached up and laid a hand on his back.

Rosie drove away, wiping at her eyes.

Fifty

Lexi, you're welcome to spend the night." Claire kept her voice light, not wanting to pressure her daughter out of the comfort zone she seemed to have entered that evening at the hacienda.

"I know, thanks." Lexi rose from the couch and stretched. "But by the time we make up the bed in the RV, I can be home, in my own pj's, and much nearer the office. I'd rather drive home now than early tomorrow morning."

"You've always been a night owl. Still, we need to designate a guest room as yours, as soon as one is finished. Like you had before the fire."

"'Before The Fire.' I am so sick of that phrase. Everything keeps coming down to this was"—she sliced the air with a karate motion—"*Before The Fire.*" Another slice. "And this is *After.*"

Claire caught the undertone in Lexi's voice, the complaining note of a victim. In her past life, *Before The Fire,* Claire would have apologized for the situation. She would have taken responsibility for the construction workers not completing another guest room in time for Lexi's use that particular night when she just happened to show up and stay late—a first since Claire and Max had moved into the house.

But now it was *After The Fire* and impatient retorts like "deal with it" sometimes sprouted on the tip of Claire's tongue. She scrambled for a gentler version.

"Well, Lexi, like we said earlier, the fire brought change, no doubt. But . . ." She raised her shoulders in an exaggerated shrug. "What can we do about it? *C'est la vie.*"

250

Lexi rolled her eyes.

Claire accepted it as a hint of progress.

One of the large oak doors opened and Indio appeared. "Is Tuyen in here?" Out of breath and red-faced, she scanned the room. "Have you seen her? Oh, dear Lord. She's not here! Oh Lord!"

"What's wrong?" Claire strode toward her.

"I went to her room, to tell her good night. And found this." A piece of notebook paper fluttered in her hand.

Claire took it and read the childish block letters. "'To Beaumont family. I leave now. No hurt you more. No hurt me more.'" She watched Indio's eyes widen and her mouth tremble.

Nothing scared her mother-in-law.

Nothing whatsoever under the sun.

Not even *during* the fire. Good grief, the woman served tea during the fire.

"Indio, Tuyen would not leave by herself," Claire argued, as if denial would wipe the fear from Indio's face. "Where would she go? We're the only people she knows. The only family she has."

Lexi touched Claire's shoulder. "Mom." She looked at the paper, her face contorted in pain. "It's a suicide note."

Indio moaned. "No!"

Horror gushed through Claire. Its force nearly buckled her knees.

Lexi nodded. "You said it. Where would she go?"

"But I meant . . ." She pressed a fist against the sudden pain in her stomach.

"She's going to a place where she thinks she won't hurt anymore."

Claire shut her eyes for a moment and let the obvious truth of Lexi's words sink in. "That poor child. She found us at the end of her road, that awful, awful road she's had to follow her whole life. We were supposed to be her safe harbor. But we let her down, just like everyone else did. We have to find her!"

No one stated the obvious, but Claire saw it in the hopeless expressions that mirrored her own. Outside the door lay over three hundred acres of Beaumont property alone. Bordering that were countless more uninhabited acres of wild land and neighboring ranches. Where did one begin to search for a lost soul?

Indio sank onto a chair. "Lord, have mercy." Her lips continued to move, forming silent pleas.

Claire said, "She can't have gone far. We just saw her—when? An hour ago?"

"More like two," Lexi said. "I'll see if there's a car missing. Erik took her driving once."

"Driving! He took her driving?"

Not bothering to answer, Lexi hurried out the door.

Driving?

Those countless acres just got infinitely multiplied.

"Yes, Lord, have mercy."

Claire scurried out behind Lexi and yelled at the top of her lungs into the night air, "Max!"

A short while later, their voices raspy from shouting Tuyen's name, Claire, Max, and Lexi rejoined Indio in the sala. She still sat hunched in the same chair.

Claire flinched at the sight of Indio's face. It was almost unrecognizable, not so much because of the presence of agony, but because of the absence of peace.

Lord, please don't do this to Indio, please. Tuyen is her only link to BJ. A flesh-and-blood touchstone. Please!

"Mom." Max knelt before Indio, his voice softly urgent. "You've spent the most time with her. Where would she go?"

She did not respond.

Claire sat with Lexi on the love seat.

No vehicles were missing. They'd searched a wide area around the hacienda and horse barn. Lexi had left a message on Ben's answering machine, but he hadn't appeared. Hopefully he was awake and had heard it. Hopefully he now scoured the area down the road, near his and Indio's new house.

"Mom, think." Max took hold of her hands. "She probably wouldn't go far. Was there anything special about the property to her? Some place that made an impact on her?"

Claire crossed her arms and held them together tightly, pressing against the ache in her stomach that stabbed relentlessly. Beside her, Lexi breathed heavily.

Father, what is going on? This whole thing is supposed to be about emotional safety, right? Max and I move here to build a haven. We want people to come and experience what it is to dwell in a safe place, where they don't have to be afraid to reveal their true selves, warts and all.

She sighed to herself.

We thought the dream was from You. It's looking like it wasn't. Everybody keeps running the opposite direction. Ben is a wreck. Erik could only handle two days here. Lexi had one good evening. A few hours. And now Tuyen wants to . . .

She squeezed shut her eyes.

Lord, if my family can't feel safe here, I want no part of a retreat center for strangers! This must, first and foremost, work for us. It has to!

A muted wail came from Indio.

Claire skipped the "Amen" and looked across the room.

Indio whispered, "BJ's place."

Max said, "The memorial? You took her there?"

She nodded.

Technically BJ remained MIA. He was missing. His body was missing. His remains were never buried, his life never memorialized at an official service because his parents never knew when to say good-bye.

But they'd needed something. Over time they created a space on the property devoted to him. It consisted of rock and dirt and whatever native vegetation grew in a given year. There were huge boulders piled high. On one that had a flat side facing the rising sun, Ben had carved a cross. Later they had a professional add "Benjamin Charles

Beaumont Jr." and his birth date. Every September ninth, Ben, Indio, Claire, and Max gathered at the spot and fought to keep the memories from fading.

In daylight it was a fifteen-minute hike through rough terrain.

Max hurried to the door, calling over his shoulder, "I'll get the lanterns."

Claire rushed to take his place at Indio's feet. "Indio, you know what to say."

"I can't." She shook her head vehemently. "I can't."

"Then I will say it for you. God is good. God is *good.* And He—" Her breath caught and her voice failed. An inexpressible sense of otherness overwhelmed her.

Indio leaned toward her and blinked, as if to focus at last on the scene before her instead of the ugly one in her imagination. "He what?"

Tears stung. She couldn't speak.

"It's the Holy Spirit, Claire. He's giving you words. Let them come."

A sense of peace washed over her. For a split second it shoved aside the pumping adrenaline. It consumed her litany of complaints and demands. It replaced anxiety with irrational hope.

Trust Me.

She said, "I think . . ." Did she dare believe that still small voice? Why not? Wasn't it something Jesus would say if He were standing there in the flesh before them? "He says to trust Him."

Indio blinked again, twice, slowly. Then she gave a half nod. "I'll call the ambulance."

Lexi was halfway out the door, Claire on her heels.

Fifty-One

Disconnected thoughts pelted Lexi with every step on the rock-hard path.

She knew the mental activity was a coping mechanism. It kept debilitating terror at arm's length. She knew because the same thing had happened the night of the fire as she trudged through the darkness, lantern in hand like now.

Again with the talk of fire. Before. After.

And now—*during*?

Prayers formed again, too, darts flung skyward.

God, keep us safe.

God, keep Tuyen safe.

I really don't like Tuyen. I wish she hadn't come.

But Nana . . .

God, keep rattlesnakes away. Mountain lions . . .

Lexi wondered if Nathan Warner would contact her. Should she call him? He was nice. Easy to talk to. Easier than Zak. Zak the fireman was all about that night, that night of The Fire. Zak was *during*.

They had tramped a different direction that night, to the east, a much farther distance from the house. There'd been no semblance of a path. No stars shone because of the smoke.

"Tuyen!" Max shouted for the umpteenth time.

Like someone in the middle of killing herself would yell back, "I'm over here! South of the big oak."

She wondered what method Tuyen had chosen. Lexi always figured the easiest would be to drive off the highway, at the last S-curve on the way up into the hills to the hacienda. It would be the fastest at least. The easiest was probably food. Binge and purge. Binge and purge. Year after year after year.

"Tuyen!" Max was relentless.

Her dad had not been there that night. Max was not *during*. Nor was he *before*. Why was it he thought he could be *after*?

For a fleeting while just after, it seemed the entire family slipped into a Norman Rockwell series of illustrations. "The Beaumonts— A Real American Family." Scene One: Max embraces a soot-covered Lexi as if she was the most important person in the world to him. Scene Two: Joined by grandparents and brother-in-law Kevin, the siblings camp out at their childhood home. Scene Three: Mother bakes chocolate-chip cookies.

By Scene Four, old dad was checking out again. Lexi could imagine his dress-slacks-covered backside in the picture. It would be a shadowy detail poised exiting the kitchen door.

Four scenes. A meager series.

Lexi scrambled now to keep up with her parents. They neared Uncle BJ's memorial site. She recognized the bend in the path, the point where Papa had neatly laid rocks along both sides. There was the huge oak, damaged but not condemned to death by the fire. And then the outcropping of boulders.

"Tuyen!" Her mother screamed the name.

Even through the bobbing shadows Lexi could make out the letters chiseled out of the boulder's face many years ago: Benjamin Charles Beaumont Jr.

A dark stain cut through the "Beaumont."

Moments stretched into eternal expanses.

Tuyen lay on the ground, a motionless heap at the base of the boulder. Max and Claire knelt beside her. Lexi held two lanterns aloft. Blood was everywhere.

Sirens wailed in the distance.

Her mother cradled Tuyen's head in her lap.

Her father yanked the laces from his shoes.

Unintelligible speech came from both, Claire's in a begging tone, Max's in sharp commands. Prayers and pleas, denials and urgings all mixed together.

Please God. Please God. Please God.

Max made quick work of tying tourniquets on Tuyen's arms, and then he scooped her up. "Lexi, go in front of me. Quickly now."

The scene embedded itself into Lexi's mind with the permanence of a branding iron.

They reached the barn behind the house at the same time the medics did, stretcher and equipment in hand. Spotlights blazed, illuminating the area.

Illuminating the deep reds that smudged her father's cheek, her mother's gray sweatshirt.

Lexi leaned against the corral fence. Claire and Max stood nearby, her mother in the shelter of her dad's broad shoulders.

The two young men worked over Tuyen, their movements smooth, coordinated, confident, quick as lightning. They talked to each other and to her as if she were not unconscious.

Lexi spotted Nana in the distance, standing at the edge of the courtyard, but could not summon the strength to go to her.

"Okay." One guy stood. "Great job on the tourniquets. Did you do it?" He looked at Max.

"Yeah."

"You probably saved her life."

"She's going to make it?"

"Good chance of it. Want to follow us to the hospital?"

"Can I ride with?"

"Are you her dad?"

"Uncle. Sort of a stepdad. Her dad's . . . dead."

"Let's go."

As Lexi watched them leave—covers tucked neatly around Tuyen on the stretcher, Max beside her, Claire moving toward Nana—a memory presented itself.

She remembered being carried on a stretcher and transported to a hospital. If she allowed herself, she could recall details. But why?

With a shake of her head, she pushed herself away from the fence.

And then she felt something shut down, an essential something deep inside of her being.

It was almost as if she'd slit her own wrists and caused life to drain away until not one drop remained to keep her heart beating.

Fifty-Two

Rosie flew west along the freeway, heading back to the city. Erik's vehicle was one incredibly cool ride.

The top was down, windows up, the heater on full blast, her hair loose and whipping wildly in the wind. The stereo volume was cranked to its limit, heavy on bass, the Gipsy Kings' Latin beat rip-roaring across the desert. Stars were so dense the sky resembled a crocheted silvery afghan thrown across a black velvet canopy.

She smiled, still surprised that she'd found one of her favorite CDs in his collection under the seat along with the likes of Bob Marley, Motown, Alicia Keys, and Enya. Was Erik a closet nonracist and nonsexist?

Rosie suspected that he deliberately projected those false images of himself. He enjoyed goading others. It was part of his self-destructive mechanism. If he pricked others enough, they'd not get close enough to hurt him.

"Lord, You're laughing, aren't You? You just had to break my own prejudices by hooking me up with a rich white guy. That's funny."

The 805 exit signs appeared. It was probably time to reenter the real world. She turned down the music and flipped open her cell phone. Two voice mails awaited.

As hoped, she heard Bobby's voice first. "Just checking in." Short and totally neutral in tone—a positive step up from his earlier growl that she get herself straightened out.

Lexi came next, her voice low and hesitant. "Sorry to bother you. It's not about Erik. We guess since you haven't called, he's okay." A long pause. "Mom wanted me to call. Tuyen." A noisy breath. "She tried to kill herself. They think she's going to be all right. Since, you know, you're sort of involved with her, Mom thought you might care." She left Claire's number and the name of the hospital.

Rosie glanced at the dashboard clock. Lexi's call had been recorded around midnight. It was now after two a.m. Knowing the Beaumonts, somebody would still be at the hospital, waiting through the night as a stranger clung precariously to life.

She flicked the turn signal and headed for an exit.

Rosie spotted Claire in a corner of the waiting room, a good sign that Tuyen was alive.

Erik's mother wore her glasses and appeared to be reading a Bible. Her hair was disheveled, her light-gray sweatshirt inside out over a white turtleneck.

A few people occupied some of the scattered chairs and couches. Some of them dozed. Lights were too bright for the middle of the night. At least no television blared.

She walked over to her. "Claire."

"Rosie!" The older woman stood and grabbed her in a quick hug. "Oh! It is so good to see you. So good."

"Crummy circumstances."

They exchanged sad smiles and sat in two corner chairs, a table between them.

Rosie said, "Is she okay?"

"Yes. Is Erik okay?"

"Yes. He got stitched back up no problem, and then he checked into rehab."

"Oh!" Claire's hand flew to her mouth. "Thank you, Jesus."

"Amen. I can give you the number of the place. It's best he doesn't communicate just yet, but the couple who run things there will be glad to answer questions."

Claire nodded, blinking rapidly.

Rosie gave her a moment to collect her emotions.

"Thank you," Claire whispered. "When Lexi told me about tonight, about the condition he was in, I wanted to crawl in a hole. But she said you were with him and then I knew things would be okay."

"God was in it. I was simply there at the right time when Erik asked for help. Is Lexi here?"

Claire shook her head. "She said between Erik and Tuyen she'd seen enough blood for one night."

Erik and Tuyen. Was there a connection? On Friday, just a few days ago, the two of them watched a movie together. He said it was Tuyen's English lesson. The next day, Erik left the hacienda. Rosie tucked the thought away for later.

She said, "Tell me what happened tonight."

"You sound like you look, on duty."

"Occupational hazard. Sorry."

"No, don't be. It's not so much police duty I see as it is holy duty. I sensed it when you served us tacos and when you ate dinner in our home. You have a compassionate concern for others. It emanates from you like audible sound waves. That's why I totally relaxed about Erik's situation. Max feels the same."

Rosie went speechless. The woman must be punchy from lack of sleep and the night's trauma. Did she forget what Rosie had done to her son?

"And," Claire went on, "you brought Tuyen to us and have taken Lexi under your wing. We're awfully glad God brought you to us."

"But I—"

"I know." She reached over and squeezed her arm. "You shot him. Now get over it."

Rosie laughed. "Okay. So what happened?"

Claire sighed. "It was awful. A nightmare. But I think angels intervened." The story poured from her: Tuyen's note, how they found her, what Max did, the ambulance, the timing of it all.

Claire said, "I convinced Indio to stay at home. She was looking every bit of her seventy-five years. Ben slept through the whole ordeal." She sighed again. "Max is in with Tuyen. She's still unconscious, but she's all right. Physically anyway. I've been asking God how we can help with whatever it is that drove her to this."

"Any answers?"

"I'm getting glimpses of an abandoned, fatherless child."

Rosie nodded. "And then Erik left her."

"Erik? What do you mean?"

"Uh." She shrugged. "I'm just thinking out loud. Bad habit."

She noticed Claire gazing at her with an open, almost childlike expression. It was obvious from her words and the Bible on the table next to her that she had a working relationship with the Lord. She was listening and seeking. Rosie figured she could muse all she wanted with Erik's mother. They were almost, if not exactly, on the same page.

Claire smiled. "I just made a fresh pot of coffee over there. Can I get you some?"

Yup. The same page.

Rosie sipped from a Styrofoam cup. "What did you do, bring your own freshly ground beans and bottled water? This is the best coffee I've ever had in a hospital. Or outside of one for that matter."

"Thanks." Claire sat again. She had carried the carafe and cups around the room, serving a few other sleepy folks. "It's Indio's secret concoction. Works even with well water."

"Please don't give any more away. I will want another cup."

She smiled. "You were saying, about Erik?"

Erik. Where to begin? He was the type of guy she avoided. How on earth had he gotten under her skin?

That wasn't exactly the place to start.

"Well, I'm wondering about the timing of events. He called me on Friday. He was watching *The Sound of Music* with Tuyen. I imagine a bonding time occurred between them. He was the one Tuyen sought out in the first place. Because of his help, she made it to the hacienda and met the family."

"That's true. He and Tuyen were enjoying each other's company. I haven't heard Erik laugh like that in a long time. He reminded me of when he and the others were little. He absolutely basked in his role as big brother. He was like that with Tuyen, carefree and funny. He taught her English phrases the rest of us wouldn't touch. She taught him about cooking. I just learned he even gave her a driving lesson Friday night."

"And then the next day he leaves. Abruptly?"

Claire nodded. "Tuyen didn't know he was gone until I told her."

"Has Ben come around yet? Does he accept her?"

"No, not really. He's civil, but standoffish."

"How about Max?"

Understanding crept into Claire's expression. "The same." She set her cup on the table. "In the father-figure slash male department, I'd say Tuyen has had a bad time of it. The worst. Her dad. Two grandpas. One uncle. A cousin who took her under his wing. Or make that two cousins. Danny's just busy with work, but to her it could appear he's backed away as well. Throw in the men she encountered in her line of work and no wonder."

"No wonder." Rosie eyed the collar of Claire's sweatshirt. Even with it turned inside out, a dark stain was visible. "Speaking of which, you and Max probably weren't wearing gloves?"

She shook her head. "The doctor said he would test her."

Another matter for prayer. *Lord, in Your mercy, hear our prayer . . .*

Claire went on. "They said Max saved her life. Watching him with her now, so tender and concerned, vowing to take care of her, I'm wondering if she saved his life too. BJ was his rival but also his idol. He hasn't wanted to believe Tuyen's story about him. It gives BJ feet of clay. I think he might be ready to forgive his brother for being human. He might be ready to fill in for him with Tuyen."

"Amen."

"Amen."

Definitely the same page.

Fifty-Three

Lexi recognized his little red truck as it tore into the far end of the parking lot, dirt swirling all around it.

Normally Danny didn't drive with an attitude. She braced herself for more bad news.

And wondered how much more she could take after last night.

In spite of only a couple fitful hours of sleep, she'd gone to work. Determined to keep her mind far from family matters, she'd turned off her cell phone, driven the company pickup to a distant whole-sale nursery, and spent the morning lost in the world of plants.

Danny's truck kicked up gravel and skidded to a halt. He jumped out and stomped toward her.

"You could have called me!" He stopped before her, hands on hips. "Tuyen almost died? Erik's in rehab? And you were there? And why aren't you answering your phone? The office couldn't even reach you."

She tossed her handbag through the cab's window.

And then she knew how much more she could take.

Not much.

She turned to him. "Stop yelling at me."

"Lexi!" His voice screeched, his dark eyes nearly scrunched shut. "You could have clued me in at some point!"

"Stop yelling at me."

His jaw jutted out.

"I was a little *upset!*"

"I would have come."

"Yeah, right. You said we shouldn't help Erik. But I had to. He told me he was bleeding. By the time I took care of him, it was over and Rosie's partner was walking me to my car. I didn't know she took him to rehab until Mom told me this morning. I didn't know Tuyen was going to slice her wrists until I saw her note, which was about ten minutes before we found her, which was just in time."

"Mom said twenty."

"Stop being so literal, Danny! Everything has to be black and white with you! The point is there was no time to clue you in!" She burst into tears.

"Oh, Lexi." He wrapped his arms around her. "I was talking about after the fact. Why didn't you call me after? I would have been there for you. What a horrible night! And why on earth are you working today? You should be at home, recovering. Did you even sleep? Erik's right. You bottle too much inside."

He went on and on, Danny style, rocking her gently. She rested her forehead against his chest, trying to collect tears in her hands instead of his shirt.

She had never been a crybaby. On rare occasion, when other kids' teasing got too hurtful or her hormones too crazy, she'd experience meltdown. Danny was usually there . . . jabbering too much, but there, sometimes with a hug.

"Hey," he said now. "Watch the snot."

Her giggle instantly gave way to a sob. He'd always said that. It was exactly what she was thinking. It was why she kept her hands over her face.

"See, Lex? This is what I meant. You should have done this hours ago. I should have been there. I yelled because I'm upset I wasn't there to tell you it was all right to let it go. That it was all right to spend the day at home getting over last night's scares."

"I need a tissue." She stepped to the pickup, up onto the running board, and reached through the window for her bag.

"Lex, I miss my twin."

Another sob threatened. She dug through her bag and pulled out a wad of tissues.

"What's happened between us? In the old days you would have managed to call me, even as you raced off to Erik's, no matter what I said about helping or not. You certainly would have phoned when you left the hospital in the middle of the night."

Blowing her nose, she glanced around. There were no people in sight, only a handful of other vehicles in the lot. Rocky hills ringed the area. The noontime sun shone in a clear sky. It was a perfect February hiking day. If she kept driving east into the desert—

"All right," he said, "I apologize. I'm sorry you've felt left out since Tuyen came. I'm sorry you feel estranged from Dad. I'm sorry you're uncomfortable about wearing a black dress in the wedding. I'm sorry Kevin got sent overseas." He lowered his face until they were almost nose to nose.

She rolled her eyes. "Okay, okay. I get it. None of those things are your fault."

"Exactly. But you're taking them out on me."

She looked at the ground, remembering their argument in her office over the same stuff. That was ten days ago. Not that she was counting.

"Lex, what's really wrong? Is it all the change? I know how you hate change. And I know way too much has changed too quickly for you since the fire. You need time to adjust. But why beat me up over it? Am I letting you down somehow? What do you expect from me?"

She peered up at him. "Maybe one question at a time."

He spread his arms in an "I give" gesture. "Pick one."

"Listen to yourself, Danny. You don't even take a breath between questions. You're always badgering. You always know what's best for everybody. You may be right ninety-nine percent of the time but so what?" The words spurted from her, soda fizzing from a shaken can. "I will never measure up to your standards. You're perfect and I am such a loser. I don't confide in you because if I did, then you'd know what a loser I am and I'd disappoint you more than I already do."

His brows rose. "I am not perfect."

"Yes, you are. You've got that black-and-white thing going. You figure out what's right, what's wrong, what's healthy, what's not. Then you choose correctly and come out on top."

"Not always."

"Close enough."

"You don't disappoint me."

"You know what's best for me. Same difference."

"I would never think of you as a loser."

"Zak dumped me. Not that there was really anything to dump. It wasn't like we had a relationship." She bit her lip.

He frowned. "That makes him a loser and a jerk."

"No, it means I'm not good enough."

Danny stepped close and pulled her into another hug.

A silent hug.

Lexi listened to his quiet breathing, waiting for a retort, a question, a comment.

A long moment passed. And he didn't speak.

Another long moment. Still he didn't speak.

Tension seeped from her. As nerves untwisted and muscles slackened, exhaustion set in. She recognized the enormity of what she'd experienced. Trying to ignore it, she'd eaten her way through the hours, busied herself with work.

The thought of Erik hidden off somewhere in the desert with strangers disturbed her. She couldn't imagine him in such a setting. What was he doing? Was he changing his leopard spots? He'd said they couldn't be changed overnight, probably not even at all. How long would he be gone? And why had he finally asked for help?

At any rate, the awful days ahead of him must offer him hope to get out of the hole.

Did she want to get out of her own? Not that it was as bad as his . . .

Telling Danny, though, might bring a sense of relief. To not have to pretend with him. She'd gotten a start, telling him about Zak and her loser status. She wouldn't have to give him details, just clue him in to the fact that sometimes she ate too much and made herself sick.

He'd say she didn't have to lose weight. She'd say it had nothing to do with weight. He'd say then just say no. She'd say—

"Hey." Danny straightened, his hands on her shoulders, eyes intensely searching hers. "Listen to me. You are not a loser. It's a common malady to think of ourselves that way. Remember when I didn't want to tell Dad about losing clients? How upset I was over that? And over him and Mom and all the upheaval they've been through?"

"Mm-hmm."

"Major loser here. It all came down to not forgiving Dad. At first I didn't see anything to forgive, but he asked for it. He said he didn't prioritize us above business. Consciously I saw no problem. Unconsciously, though, if it was true, then something inside of me was hurt as a result of his actions." Danny smiled. "So I have forgiven him and it's made all the difference."

"There isn't anything to forgive him—"

"I'm not explaining it very well. You want to come with me to church? I told you about the new pastor, how fresh he is. He's teaching a series on forgiveness that is totally awesome. It helped me understand things better. Lex, I don't mean to preach at you, but your issue with Dad needs to be addressed."

"You're doing it again." She smashed the tissues against her face, shrugging his hands from her shoulders.

"What? Badgering? I'm not—I don't mean to—aw, Lex."

She wiped at a new batch of tears, overcome by a great wave of sadness. Danny would never quit on her, which meant he would never let her be herself.

"Lex, I'm only trying to help."

"I know. You're just being you. The Danny you've always been. It's okay."

"You are not a loser. Stop thinking that way."

"It's okay," she said more forcefully, telling him in essence to stuff it.

She knew neither one of them believed it was okay, but pretending it was put them back on speaking terms. Why mess that up again by trying to be real with him?

Fifty-Four

Tuyen awoke.

She *awoke.*

Not to nirvana nor to a rebirth, that land of her ancestors according to her Vietnamese grandmother. Not to the heaven with Jesus' welcoming arms, that land of her other ancestors according to her American grandmother. Not, obviously, to the state of total unawareness, the land she longed for.

No, she awoke to the world she had always known, that harsh, cruel, violent place that offered no respite.

She had not escaped it. What went wrong?

She felt as if she wore a dress, an *ao dai* with long sleeves and trousers, made of clay so thick and wet it weighted her down, tied her to the earth. She couldn't move a muscle. Her throat felt scorched, as if she'd swallowed fire.

The sound of hushed voices reached her, growing more distinct although she could see no one. Twilight and fog filled her vision.

"I don't know why I didn't realize it before." It was her uncle Max. "It all became clear riding in the ambulance."

They transported her in an ambulance? Uncle Max rode in it?

"When you thought we might lose her." It was her American grandmother. Indio. *Nana.* "Epiphanies sometimes require extraordinary circumstances in order to happen."

"A simple two-by-four alongside the head would have done the trick. You or Dad could have swung it."

271

"It's not a mother's place. And your father, well . . ." She sighed. "His moral compass got wound so tight, he couldn't find his way out of the barn. He's lost his true north, where God dispenses so much grace into our hearts it just has to overflow to others."

"Mom, why is he having such a hard time accepting Tuyen?"

"He thinks this child would mean admitting that BJ made wrong choices, that he intentionally hurt us and Beth by not coming home."

"That's ridiculous. We've got no idea what BJ was up against. How can Dad judge wrong choices—for crying out loud, he doesn't still believe BJ was perfect, does he?"

"I think his struggle lies in realizing that is exactly what he still believes and knows is wrong. He just hasn't gotten down on his knees to confess it."

"I did a lot of confessing in the ambulance. I've been so angry at the whole situation. Things like that asinine war. Things like all the lives wasted, all the families torn apart. All those years of not know-ing what happened to my brother, of imagining him being tortured. The government doing squat to find him and the two thousand-plus other MIAs. All the homeless vets."

They both fell silent. Tuyen thought she heard the rustle of tissues.

"Anyway." Uncle Max spoke, his voice lower. "Since Tuyen arrived, it all came to the forefront again. I've been living out of that angry center, but pretending like I wasn't. It kept me from getting close to her."

Silence again.

"You want to know what the kicker was, Mom? I saw myself in the same old rut. Like Dad is, I guess. He asked me to forgive him for placing BJ on a pedestal, but he's still got him there. I ask my kids to forgive me for being an absent dad, but my idiotic behavior continues. I'd rather work than step up to the plate with Tuyen."

"What do you mean by that?"

"I need to spell it out?"

Indio laughed softly. "Yes, Max."

"It's just too painful. Tending to heart connections is more diffi-cult than negotiating with some giant corporation about hiring a hundred temporary employees nationwide to count inventory. Mix pain avoidance with anger and you get one ugly guy who won't be there for his brother's daughter. Who contributed to this tragic event."

"And who confessed in an ambulance to God the Father, the Almighty One."

Max exhaled loudly.

"Son, you know what comes next, after confession."

"Yeah, yeah. The ugly guy is history. A new guy with a clean slate gets to try again."

The voices grew muffled, as if cotton balls were wedged into Tuyen's ears.

She did not comprehend all their words, but her heart grasped the intent behind them. She heard regret. Anguish. Hope. And . . . what was it? Something not so much heard as unheard.

The fog thickened, the twilight darkened. She began to drift away—

Condemnation! Yes, that was it! *Condemnation was not heard.*

A golden glow splintered the fog. Unseen hands gently lifted from her the heavy dress made of clay. Tuyen felt clothed in warm sunlight, weightless as a feather.

She slept.

Tuyen, are you awake?"

At the sound of Uncle Max's voice—so near, so tender—Tuyen peered through her eyelashes. She tried to speak, but only a faint scratching noise came.

"Are you thirsty? Here."

She felt the tip of a straw at her lips and drank water. It tasted sweet and it soothed her parched throat like a balm.

"Better?"

"Mmm." She forced a hoarse whisper. "Thank you."

The bed shifted as he sat on its edge. Jostled, she became aware of her body. It ached, a dull sensation. She lay on her back, a thin pillow under her head, her arms atop a rough coverlet. From her elbows down was a mass of thick wraps and a tangle of IV tubes.

He touched her fingertips. "The doctor said you will be fine. Okay? You need to rest here at the hospital for a while. Tomorrow or the next day, I will take you home. Oh, honey, don't cry."

Tears seeped. He caught them against his thumb. She wanted to speak, to find out if it was all a dream, but the English words jumbled together incoherently in her mind.

He said, "I promise I'll stay with you until it's time to go. And then we'll return to the hacienda. It's your home, Tuyen. I am so sorry for not making you feel welcome there. I understand now that it's my responsibility to take your father's place, to love you like a daughter, to take care of you. I want to do that if you'll let me. Does any of this make sense to you?"

Again, understanding did not interpret all the words. But she saw her Uncle Max's face wrinkled in concern, his black hair messy, his jaw dark with stubble. And she heard the intent behind his many words.

A little smile danced on her lips. She started to nod her head, but it hurt too much. "It not dream." The effort to speak grated across her vocal cords.

"What's not a dream?"

"You and Nana talk. You want me home."

"Yes, we both want you home very much. You are our BJ's child. You are our family."

Her smile stretched. "I glad I not die."

"Me, too, honey." He brushed hair back from her forehead. "Me too."

She felt his gentle touch, saw his tender smile and the loving eyes that glistened as he looked at her. And for a fleeting moment she wondered if it was all a dream. Perhaps she had indeed awakened in that land of her ancestors where, according to her American grandmother, the Man-God called Jesus waited with welcoming arms.

Fifty-Five

Her eyes shut, Rosie savored a mouthful of the best tamale she had ever tasted in her entire life. She swallowed and looked at her dad across the patio table at the Casa del Gusto.

"Ah, Papi. Marry this woman quick before someone else does."

He only smiled in reply. Hands folded over his rotund midsection, he resembled a Buddha statue—one with Aztec features, wearing a white apron.

Next to him, Bobby chuckled. "At the very least, snag her recipes before she takes off and opens her own restaurant."

The enigmatic smile remained, sculpted from stone. Not even an eyelid twitched.

"Papi! You proposed!"

He shook his head slowly. "You are always playing the detective. All I am doing is enjoying this beautiful sight of you and Bobby no longer estranged."

"Esteban," Bobby said, not missing a beat, "I was going into taco withdrawal. I had no choice but to make up with her."

Rosie snorted, not buying that excuse. "Like there's no other place to get a decent taco?"

His face went deadpan. "No, actually, there isn't. And if we're estranged, I wouldn't be welcome here."

Her father roared. "Bobby, you are always welcome here, no matter what snit she's worked herself into."

"Snit?" Her voice rose. "Snit?" She would have said more but the men's laughter drowned her out.

Bobby rubbed his palms against his tearing eyes. "Rosie, your gulli-bility always takes me by surprise."

"Ha-ha. This one was no laughing matter. I almost killed an innocent man. I almost quit my job."

"But you didn't on either count." He leaned across the table, his face suddenly somber. "And just think." His eyebrows shot up. "You got a new boyfriend to boot!"

"Boyfriend!"

Again their guffaws cut off her protests. She sat back and gazed around the patio. In spite of the propane heaters warming the area, not many people braved the outdoor seating.

"Rosita," her dad said, "you started all this, you know."

"Started what?"

"This laughter. You are so happy tonight. You showed up here giggling. I haven't seen you like this since—well, since I don't know when."

Bobby nodded. "Mm-hmm. And curious how it's come on the heels of that Erik Beaumont business."

"Yes," her dad agreed. "Very curious. Why would she be delirious because this stranger, who she *arrested*, went into rehab? Explain that one."

"I have no clue, Esteban. We'll have to go on circumstantial evidence alone."

"I see it this way: she spends a night carting him around the county and then she's happy." Esteban smacked his hands together once and spread them open. Ta-da. One plus one equaled two. "It must be love."

"I agree."

Rosie huffed. "Are you two about finished?"

"Rosita." His tone admonished gently. "We're happy for you."

"You don't even like the guy."

"I cherish his sister Lexi. If his lovely mother were not married, I would invite her to dinner. He comes from good stock. There is hope."

"There's always hope when somebody checks in with Greg and Jillie."

"You talked with them, didn't you?" Esteban smiled broadly. "That's why you giggled."

She sighed to herself. Why fight these guys?

"Yes, I talked with Jillie today. He's only been there twenty-four hours, but he's embraced them. He's totally open to them praying with him. Totally open to God being real and working in him."

Her dad nodded. "Praise God."

Bobby's eyes leveled on her. "Ready for rehab is cause for, ahem, *giggling?*"

She positioned her mouth to speak, but a split second passed before the reply came. "Sure."

He smiled. In that momentary hesitation, he knew that she admitted what she'd been denying to herself.

She was falling in love with that pathetic waste of oxygen, aka Erik Beaumont.

Hey, Lexi." Rosie spoke into her cell phone, waiting next to the squad car in the restaurant's parking lot for Bobby, who still lingered inside with her dad.

"Hi." Lexi stammered through the lone syllable.

Rosie sighed to herself. She disliked that her new friend had reverted to her hesitant mode, no doubt pushed there with a shove from Rosie. At least she'd answered her phone, unlike the previous five attempts Rosie had made that day.

"Lexi, I apologize for yelling at you at Erik's the other night. For saying I might shoot him. I behaved despicably as a friend and about sixteen levels below professionally as a cop."

"We were both upset."

"No excuse. I'm sorry. I hope you can forgive me."

A beat passed. "I do." She didn't sound convinced.

Rosie remembered their conversation about forgiveness, about

Lexi's dad asking for it. "Don't let me off the hook. It might not seem like a big deal, but I was rude to you, Lexi, and it disrupted our friendship. It's not something we gloss over."

"Okay." Her voice gained strength. "Okay."

"Okay. I just needed to clear the air about that. So, how are you after your crazy Monday night spent playing hero? At last count you made two rescues, Erik and Tuyen."

"I, uh, I'm better than I was yesterday. Danny and my boss convinced me to take off work today. I've been painting."

"The giraffe?"

"Yeah."

"Great." She smiled. "I gotta see what you did with those eyelashes."

Lexi chuckled. "Give me a few weeks."

"A few weeks for eyelashes? That's a long time. I'd never have the patience. You know, if you get tired of painting or landscaping, you could go into rescue work. Seriously, you seem to have a knack for it. First your family and those firefighters. Then Erik, twice that I know of. And now Tuyen. You could be a medic or something. Be a heroine every day."

She groaned. "Not you too. I just got off the phone with this journalist who wants to include me in his article about heroes. Like I told him, during the fire I remembered a safe place before my eighty-year-old grandfather did. No big deal. And Erik? He's my brother. I'm worried sick about him so I try to help. Tuyen left a note that I pointed out was obviously suicidal, so then we searched for her. My dad's the one who saved her life. I am not a heroine!"

"A heroine pays attention and does what needs to be done, Lexi. That's you." She spotted Bobby walking across the parking lot toward her. "I've got to get to work. Let me know if you need a letter of recommendation for your EMT application."

"Yeah, right." At last there was a grin in her voice.

"Unless you want to be a cop."

Lexi giggled. "After that fiasco at the bar?"

Rosie laughed. "Probably not. See you."

"'Bye."

As she closed up her phone, Bobby reached her side. "You're laughing. Erik again?"

She wrinkled her nose. "Ha. I was talking to Lexi—ohmygosh!" *Fiasco at the bar. I just got off the phone with this journalist.*

She flipped the phone back open and hit the Send button.

"What is it?" Bobby asked.

She held up a finger. "Wait."

Lexi answered. "Hi—"

"What journalist? What were you talking about?"

"Huh?"

"You said this guy wants to include you in an article."

"Yes. He's writing about heroes. Gag me with a spoon."

"Lexi, who is he?"

"Nathan Warner. Some freelance reporter. Local. He talked to the firemen who were with us that night. They told him about me. I don't know why I said yes to an interview, but I did. Erik's call interrupted it."

"A stranger out of the blue contacts you."

"No, he contacted the fire department."

"What's the article about?"

"Heroes. A 'where they are now' sort of thing. He's a nice guy. Why are you asking all this?"

Rosie shut her eyes and examined what triggered her concern. It happened now and then, a vague feeling that reminded her of searching for a misplaced bowl. She could almost hear cupboard doors creak open and bang shut. It was there, but she wasn't sure exactly where.

She blew out a frustrated breath. "I don't know. Something doesn't jibe. Erik's a reporter. This guy's a reporter. That strikes me as odd. And out of the blue—"

"Not out of—"

"Close enough. Are you going to see him?"

"He's a nice guy."

"Lexi."

"Friday night. I'm meeting him at a restaurant downtown for dinner."

"I want to investigate him, and I'd rather you be close by. Meet him at the Casa instead, okay?" She met Bobby's gaze. "Tell him you have a craving for tacos."

Fifty-Six

Friday night, Lexi smiled at Nathan Warner. She hadn't heard from Rosie again and assumed the guy had passed inspection, which was great news to her. Not only was he cute in that boy-next-door way, he was as easy to talk to as Danny.

They sat on a back, covered patio she'd not seen before at the Casa del Gusto, a cozy area with walls high enough to block out the parking lot, lush plants, and plenty of heaters. Esteban personally waited on them and the few other patrons as if it were his private dining room.

Across the candlelit table, Nathan grinned. "Ahh. This is an amazing *mole.*"

"I helped Esteban create that sauce."

"No way."

"True."

"Wow. I'm impressed. The owner-chef seats us at his best table. He serves us complimentary appetizers and now, come to find out, you had a hand in this." He pointed his fork at the plate. "What other hidden gifts do you possess? Off the record, of course."

"You don't have to keep saying that, 'Off the record.'"

"It's to remind myself I'm not working."

"Are you a workaholic?"

"Not exactly. It's more like the nature of reporting. I mean, everyday life is 'copy.' There's always something to take notes on. Who knows? I might be able to use it in a piece some day."

"That's like art is for me. I see something and wish I had my camera to capture it so I could paint it later. A flower. A shaft of sunlight. A squirrel. The most commonplace stuff." She noticed the tilt of his head, the little smile. "What?"

"Nothing. Just you." The smile stretched. "You're creative *and* a heroine."

"I thought we already established that I'm not comfortable with that misnomer."

"But I believe the sooner you believe you are a heroine, the sooner you'll . . ." He pooched his lips together.

"The sooner I'll what?"

He hunched his shoulders and relaxed his mouth. "Armchair psychology. Sorry."

"The sooner I'll what?"

His shoulders straightened. His eyes, a mix of gold and bronze, locked with hers.

The intensity of his gaze created an almost physical response in her, not exactly unpleasant. There was no way she could turn from it.

He said, "The sooner you believe that you really did save lives, that you really did perform heroic deeds—no matter how inadvertently—the sooner you'll like yourself."

The truth of his words didn't nail her to the chair as much as did the compassionate tone. It propelled her to a level of intimacy she'd never felt with anyone. Suddenly she wanted to unleash all the hurts and fears that bound her to the belief she was unworthy of being called a heroine. Or, really, of being complimented at all about anything.

"I'm dyslexic. I barely made it through high school."

"That's a tough one."

"In middle school, the other kids called me 'Dyslexi Beaumont.'"

"Eww. You probably don't even like your name."

"Not much. I tried to go by 'Allie' for a while, short for Alexis, but it never stuck. And I . . ." Skidding to a halt, she closed her mouth.

He waited, tenderness written all over his face.

At last, in a hushed whisper, she voiced words she'd never spoken aloud. "I'm bulimic."

Nathan reached across the table, palm up, an invitation. A silent moment ticked by.

She unlaced her fingers from their tight clasp on her lap and laid a hand in his.

He squeezed gently. "I'm sorry for your pain."

An unfamiliar sensation trickled through her. She imagined a desert streambed receiving the first rain droplets after the dry season, drawing in the life-giving liquid.

Nathan smiled. "Allie."

They lingered over coffee and *empanadas*, easily moving onto other topics between bites of the yummy pastry with pineapple filling. To Lexi's relief, Nathan did not cast sideways glances at her as she ate. Nor did his demeanor change. He remained funny and attentive, curious but still repeating "Off the record."

"Nathan, don't you want to talk about anything on the record?"

"Next time." His brows rose up and went back down.

Hm. Next time.

"So what do you paint?"

Throughout the dinner she had touched on many topics concerning her family, things like the re-wedding event and the hacienda refurbishing. But as far as really personal issues went, she peaked at dyslexia and bulimia.

He winked. "Allie, you mentioned 'art' in the same tone you might say 'I just won a million bucks, tax free.'"

She smiled.

"So what do you paint?"

"It's not like my work hangs in a gallery."

"Tut, tut."

She laughed. "Did you just say 'tut, tut'?"

"I did." He had such a great smile. It curled his mouth, lifted his cheeks, and crinkled his eyes. "It means 'enough with the self-denigration.' Tell me about your art."

"Well." She fluttered her eyelashes. "If you insist. I work in oils. My current subject is Gigi, a stunning giraffe who lives at the Wild Animal Park."

"Are you any good?"

"Nathan! I can't answer—"

"Sure you can. It's easy. Do you dabble? Do you do paint-by-numbers? Is this some passing hobby?"

"No. I've been painting since I was two. It's like—it's like *breathing*."

Again with the intense gaze. "That would be better than winning a million bucks, tax free."

"Yes."

"My cousin owns La Rive Gauche."

"The gallery in La Jolla?"

"You know it?"

She nodded. "Who doesn't?"

"If you like, I'll introduce you to him. We have a good rapport. He'd love to see your work." Nathan smiled. "You look absolutely horrified."

"I've never shown—"

"Maybe it's time."

"But—"

"Think about it, okay? Meanwhile, I'll keep bugging you."

"That sounds like tons of fun." She rolled her eyes.

"It could be." He glanced over her shoulder. "Yikes! It's the cops."

Lexi turned and saw Rosie and her partner, in uniform, entering through the arched doorway onto the patio. She noticed then that the other tables had emptied. No waitstaff were around.

"Hi, Lexi." Rosie reached them, smiling, dragging a chair behind her.

"Hi." She heard the question in her tone.

"Mind if we join you for a few minutes?" She sat.

"Uh, no." Lexi looked at Nathan. "This is Esteban's daughter."

Rosie shook his hand. "Officer Delgado. My partner, Officer Grey. And you're Nathan Warner?"

"Yeah." The word stretched into two syllables. He shook Bobby's hand.

Bobby pulled out a notepad and sat down.

Rosie said, "I hope you enjoyed dinner?"

"It was great," Nathan replied, his tone still hesitant.

"Mind if we ask you some questions?"

"Do I need a lawyer?"

"You're not under arrest. If you admit to breaking a law, we may use that admission against you."

"Driving here tonight, I hit seventy-five in a sixty-five." He smiled, but his eyes didn't crinkle.

Rosie's fake smile showed a few teeth. "We just need a little information concerning my friend here."

"Okay." He looked at Lexi. "Interesting 'friends' you have."

"Rosie!" she cried. "What are you doing? You didn't say you were—"

"Mr. Warner." Rosie focused on Nathan. "Do you know Erik Beaumont?"

"The TV newscaster. Lexi's brother."

Lexi had told him as much, confirming what he already knew from reading old articles about the fire.

Rosie consulted a small pad in her hand. "Do you *know* him? Personally?"

Nathan hesitated. "We're acquainted."

"How?"

His face turned deadpan.

Lexi's stomach turned sour.

He cleared his throat. "We worked together. I was copy editor at Channel Three."

"Past tense?"

"I left to do freelance full time."

"When was that?"

"October fifteenth."

"Not long after the fire."

He tilted his head in assent.

Lexi's heartbeat raced. Nathan *knew* Erik? He *worked* with him and never mentioned that fact to her?

Rosie went on. "Were there problems at the station, problems specific to the fire story, around the time you left?"

"People were upset. Beaumont was sitting on the biggest story in years. In essence, by refusing to talk about his family's experience in the fire or allow them to be interviewed, he gave an exclusive to the other stations and the print media. He threatened to quit if anyone even attempted to contact his family."

Lexi remembered how Erik okayed the few interviews she did with newspapers and a local magazine. He was adamant, however, that his station would not benefit from his family's tragedy. He would not let them be exploited. Which was fine with Lexi. She'd used up all her courage talking to the print reporters. She had no desire to be on television and easily said no to requests from other stations.

Rosie said, "Are you saying Erik blackmailed Channel Three?"

"Not exactly. Things have gone south for him, I know, but before the fire he *was* Channel Three News. Nobody really thought he'd quit. They were angry, sure, but they respected his family's privacy. Felicia Matthews interviewed the firefighters who were there that night with the family." He glanced at Lexi. "No one, though, got close to the Beaumonts."

Rosie leaned forward. "Did you try?"

The patio swirled in Lexi's vision. She grasped the edge of the table.

"No, I did not try."

"Until now."

"Touché."

"Did anyone from the station attempt to contact a Beaumont family member right after the fire?"

"Yes."

Rosie clicked her pen. "Care to elaborate?"

Nathan took a deep breath. "He worked at the station. Sold advertising. A wannabe announcer. Erik didn't know him, but learned from his grandmother Indio that this guy had called her and set up an interview."

Lexi gasped. The incident had been ugly. Poor Nana. She'd practically lost everything she owned in the fire, but she was such a trooper that soon after she agreed to do a videotaped interview. She felt convinced her story would encourage other seniors. Erik had recognized the man's name and gone berserk. The interview never happened.

Nathan said, "His idea wasn't sanctioned by the station. He planned to sell it elsewhere. Erik insisted the guy be fired. His opinion carried a lot of weight. The guy lost his job."

Lexi twisted the napkin still on her lap. "Tall? Armani-suit type? Dumbo elephant ears?"

Nathan nodded once.

Rosie reached over and touched Lexi's shoulder, squeezing gently, never taking her eyes off Nathan. "Mr. Warner, have you been in contact with this man since he was fired?"

"Yes," he whispered.

"When?"

"Yesterday."

Nathan Warner knew not only Erik but the man in the bar too? The man who'd set Erik up? Who'd sent him on his merry way to find Felicia and Brett, armed with drugs and a toy gun? And he'd talked to that man *yesterday?*

Lexi was through the arched doorway as her chair clattered against the floor tiles.

Fifty-Seven

Bobby picked up the chair that fell when Lexi ejected herself from it.

Rosie chewed on the inside of her lip. There had been no time to warn Lexi. The pieces of the puzzle hadn't come together until thirty minutes earlier. As Papi was serving the empanadas, she and Bobby were learning that Warner had worked at Erik's TV station.

Knowing she couldn't have warned Lexi didn't help, though. The sight of her friend discomposing was enough to make Rosie cry.

"Delgado?" Bobby crooked his thumb toward the door, his way of asking if one of them ought to go after Lexi.

Rosie gave her head a slight shake. Lexi would have to take care of Lexi.

Bobby sat back down and Rosie narrowed her eyes at Warner. He appeared to be the nice guy Lexi had described—an open face, dressed for comfort, an easygoing manner. A likeable person.

She wanted to toss him in a holding tank with an assortment of repeat offenders.

He said, "I didn't mean to hurt her."

"Are you really doing an article about heroes?"

"I am now. I made it up. Then I met her and decided it's a good idea."

She huffed a noise of disgust.

"Mr. Warner." Bobby picked up his notepad. "What's this guy's name?"

"Reid Fletcher."

"Why don't you just start from the beginning and tell us what's going on?"

"He and I hung out together now and then. I was working toward going freelance with my writing, he was trying to break into radio or TV as a newscaster. After he lost his job, he had a hard time finding another one. He's at a small radio station up in Orange County, still in sales. He's pretty bitter about Erik. So much so that he vowed he would get vengeance."

Rosie clicked her pen in triple time. Lexi's story about the other guy was taking on substance.

Warner continued. "He came down one Friday night. I met him at a bar downtown."

Bobby said, "Date? Name of the place?"

Warner filled in details. Same date, same place in question.

"Beaumont walks in, pretty well lit already, doesn't recognize me. Reid acts like he just won the lottery. He grins and says, 'Payback time.' They get to conversing. I watched for a while, but I couldn't stomach much and left."

"What did you hear?"

"He egged Beaumont on, talking trash about his girlfriend. What a lowlife, hitting a guy while he's down. Next morning I read in the paper some cop shot . . ." He studied Rosie's face; his eyes grew wide. "You shot him."

Rosie ignored the comment. "What's the connection between you, Fletcher, and Lexi?"

He rubbed a hand across his mouth. "I noticed her that night, sort of hanging back, clearly with Beaumont, though. Clearly not in a date way. She was too wholesome and down-to-earth looking. I always got along with Erik, but he can be a real prig. When it comes to women, wholesome and down-to-earth are not on his radar."

Rosie held back a smile and caught sight of Bobby's smirk at her. Sheesh. Nothing got by him.

"Reid called me a few days later and admitted he might have pushed Beaumont too far, embellishing the gossip like he did about Matthews and the ballplayer."

"Did he say anything specific about the interchange with Beaumont, anything beyond a reference to gossip?"

"No. The guy's a magpie. He could talk his mother into disowning his brother."

Rosie didn't think Nathan Warner was lying. He appeared fairly wholesome and down-to-earth himself. Besides that, newspapers had reported the toy gun in Erik's hand, though not the drugs in his system. Apparently Warner had not overheard either being discussed between the other men at the bar. Apparently neither had Fletcher mentioned them to him in subsequent conversations.

"But," Warner went on, "he felt guilty about upsetting Beaumont. And he wondered if I'd seen the mousy chick with Erik." He shook his head as if in disbelief. "I told him there were a lot of mousey chicks present. He described Lexi to a tee and said he had learned she was Erik's sister. He said that after what happened, she might cause him grief. I pointed out that he wasn't responsible for Erik's choices. I mean, it wasn't like he drove the guy to Matthews' house and put a gun in his hand. What was the big deal?"

Rosie willed herself not to glance at Bobby. Not knowing yet how Erik got to Felicia's, they'd discussed that very possibility. His car had been found parked downtown. Taxi records had not revealed a trip that night between the bar and her place. A bus ride did not fit the scenario. It was too far for him to walk in such a short amount of time. Erik himself couldn't remember a thing.

Bobby said, "What'd Fletcher say to your point about him not being responsible?"

"He just said to trust him." Warner stopped talking.

Rosie clenched her hands into fists, not sure she could speak coherently.

"Mr. Warner, why did you trust him?"

He blinked a few times, as if he'd been elsewhere in his mind and needed to refocus on the surroundings. "He's my little brother."

Rosie bit the inside of her lip again, visions of Nathan Warner behind bars dancing in her head.

Fifty-Eight

Claire switched on the coffeemaker and settled into the chair she'd come to think of as her own in the hospital waiting area.

Max was in Tuyen's room. They'd hoped to have her at home by now, but although she was much stronger, the doctor did not want to release her just yet.

Max spent more time with her than Claire and Indio did combined. It was a marvel to behold her husband. His demeanor softened by the day. His heart was so evident she easily imagined a lush garden sprouting in his chest.

He'd laughed when she told him that. He said he preferred images of a sunny tennis court full of trophies engraved with his name.

She heard a buzz in her handbag. "Whoops." *Technology*, she thought wryly and rummaged for her cell phone. She'd grown used to the quiet at the hacienda. No traffic, no cellular signal, no people. Anymore it was an effort to remember to turn on the mobile phone when she drove down into the city. The mental note to turn it off while in the hospital most often escaped her.

She was the only one in the room, so she answered. "Hello?"

"Claire. This is Rosie Delgado."

"Hi!"

"I only have a moment. I wanted to alert you that Lexi is pretty upset."

Claire's stomach twisted.

"I thought you should know. Did she tell you about the reporter she met?"

"Yes. Nathan somebody?"

"Right. Evidently he's not exactly who she thought he was. We were talking here at my dad's restaurant when it all came to a head. She left on the verge of tears about twenty minutes ago."

"Why were you and Lexi—"

"I can't say just yet."

She recognized the all-business tone in Rosie's calm alto.

"Claire, I know Lexi has some emotional problems. I'm guessing she has an eating disorder. I just wanted you to be aware that she's going to have a rough go of it tonight." Her voice hushed. "I don't mean to intrude."

A curious sense of relief flooded through Claire. Someone understood her daughter. Someone who resembled a guardian angel assigned to her family.

"Oh, Rosie! You don't intrude in the least. Thank you for your concern. I'll check on her."

"Okay. How is Tuyen?"

"Still here in the hospital, but she's improving wonderfully."

"Glad to hear that. I have to go. Take care."

"You too."

Claire sat still, phone in her hand. The coffeemaker chugged through its final stages. The aroma smelled like Indio's best.

Claire smiled briefly and whispered, "God is good."

She shut her eyes and horrible images came of her baby being sick. By now her imagination had them down pretty good, very distinct and detailed.

As far as she knew, Lexi did not drink alcohol. At the moment, that was a major positive. Her body might be deteriorating at warp speed compared to the average young woman's, but things would not be compounded by her passing out and choking to death on . . .

Claire sat up straighter and dialed Lexi's cell number. No answer.

She punched in the apartment number. No answer, not even the machine. When her daughter painted, she sometimes turned off everything.

Would she be painting now though? From Rosie's description, Claire thought not.

"Claire?"

She looked up as Max strode across the room.

He sat in the chair catty-corner from hers. "I'm upset about Lexi. I just can't get her off my mind. It's a literal heaviness inside my chest."

She stared at him.

He hung his head, combing his fingers through his hair. The stubble on his chin was thick. Although he'd spent most of last night at home, he hadn't bothered to shave that morning before heading back to the hospital. "It's this business with Tuyen. I can't help but see Lexi in her. Neither of them really had a father growing up."

He raised his eyes to her. "Do you think it's too late? The forgiveness thing, when I confessed to her—that was a whole different entity. This is about the here and now. I want to—I don't know. Step alongside her? Somehow clue her in that I care? How do you and my mom do it? Phone calls, notes, cards, little gifts. A listening ear." His smile was sad. "Homemade chocolate-chip cookies. What's wrong?"

She wiped at the corners of her eyes. "Everything's right except for what Rosie just told me." After recounting their conversation, she said, "I think Lexi is either at home or heading to the hacienda."

"And I think I should be the one to check in on her."

"I agree." Claire nodded. "Which one first? We're halfway in between."

"Danny's backpacking who knows where. Let's call Mom and Jenna. If they haven't heard from her, I'll go to her apartment."

A moment passed in silent, palpable fear. Claire shoved aside the thought of the evening's mist and the curvy road up to Santa Reina.

"Claire, what would she do?"

"Cope with the pain." She winced. "She probably stopped at the market and loaded up on comfort food and videos. She'll turn off her phones and be watching a movie."

"And eating." He reached across the space between them and grasped her hand. "She's not so much like Tuyen she would . . . ?"

A cry of anguish tore at her lungs, its cut so deep there was no breath left to give it voice.

"Dear God." Max prayed with his eyes on her, his grip tight around her hand. "Protect Lexi. Give me words of life and love. Give her a heart to receive them."

"A . . ." Claire gulped for air and gave his hand one final squeeze. "Amen."

Fifty-Nine

After reining in her emotions and calling Claire, Rosie returned to the table with a large pitcher of water and three glasses.

As she poured, Bobby said, "Everything under control?"

"Yep. All set to hear exactly why it is this guy tricked Lexi into meeting him." She clunked a glass down in front of Nathan Warner. Water sloshed over its sides.

Bobby gave her one of his looks, then turned to a red-faced Warner. "Let me recap. You said Reid Fletcher is your half-brother. You have the same mom. And that's why you agreed to try to learn what Lexi knew about Fletcher's run-in with Erik."

"Right. Blood is thicker than water, no matter how flaky a relative is. He's younger. It was always my job to sort of look after him. It's carried over into adulthood."

Rosie sat. "Did he ever talk your mom into disowning you?"

"What?"

"You said it earlier, that he's such a magpie he could do that."

His complexion went from red to mottled crimson. "Officer, I don't think that's relevant to this conversation."

She leaned back in her chair. Maybe the guy had a bit of backbone after all, telling her to mind her own business. At least he was polite about it.

Bobby scratched his nose, almost hiding a smile from her but not quite. He cleared his throat. "Mr. Warner, I know we've already been through this, but one more time, please. You made up a story about wanting to interview Lexi in order to meet her. Then what?"

"We were interrupted that day at the coffee shop when she got a phone call. Reid hassled me to try again. He gets going on something and doesn't let go."

A bulldog and a magpie. More repulsive by the minute. Rosie kept her thoughts to herself.

"I told him yesterday that I was seeing her tonight, that I'd call him tomorrow. I met Lexi here. You two showed up. End of story."

Rosie said, "Didn't his behavior strike you as a little bizarre?"

"Not any more than usual. He's always been on the anxious side. Sometimes he gets overdone and misses work. I try to help him if I can."

"By bringing an innocent woman into this cockamamy bunk?"

Warner glanced down at the table and then met her eyes again. "The truth is—oh, never mind. I'll sound crazier than Reid and I know he's an A-1 goofball. Can I leave? Actually I think I will leave. If you're not arresting me." He pushed back his chair.

"Finish your sentence." Rosie softened her voice. "Please? Believe me, we hear nuttier things than you can imagine."

He worked his mouth around, as if weighing the consequences. "The truth is Lexi intrigued me from the get-go. When I saw her, I didn't see a mousy chick. I saw this paragon. This anachronism. Women her age in this city do not look like her. There was a vulnerability about her, but a mystique too. If I hadn't left that night, I would have talked to her. After we met at the coffee shop, man, I couldn't wait to see her again."

Rosie smiled. "Love at first sight isn't all that crazy, Mr. Warner."

He shrugged and stood. "Excuse me."

"Wait." Bobby rose and blocked his path. "How crazy is your brother? Crazy enough to hurt Erik? Crazy enough to harm Lexi?"

"N-no. No way. He's never been violent. What is going on? What is it you think Reid did? I told you. He lives up in Orange County.

He's got a decent job. Yeah, he holds a grudge and he got a kick out of tormenting Erik, but now he feels bad about that and hopes Lexi doesn't spread negative talk about him."

"Does he know where Lexi lives?"

"What is going on?"

Bobby was in his face. "Does he know where Lexi lives?"

Nathan Warner clamped his jaw shut.

Shaken by Bobby's fierce tone, Rosie got up. "Nathan, she's my friend."

He gazed at her, pain evident in his eyes. "Yes, Reid knows where she lives. Where she works. Where she buys her paints. He wanted me to be sure I could find her."

Racing behind Bobby, Rosie opened her cell phone, pulled up Lexi's number, and hit Send. It rang and rang and rang as they hurried through the kitchen and out the back door, then climbed into the squad car.

It rang and rang and rang as Bobby rammed the car through the wet, narrow streets of Old Town, up the freeway ramp, and smack-dab into five lanes of stopped traffic.

Sixty

Lexi swirled the paintbrush through a can of black enamel paint, thickly coating the hog-hair bristles.

Black: total absence of light. In all her years of painting she had never used unadulterated black. It was a personal quirk. To her there was no such thing as black in a painting that was meant to reflect the world. Not even during her phase of subjects on the verge of extinction had she used black.

She didn't even own a tube of it in an oil. She had to buy enamel in a can from the paint department at the discount store where she'd stopped for other essentials like cookies, cheese curls, ice cream, and two mindless comedy DVDs.

Now she turned toward the easel, the brush in hand full of paint on the verge of dripping. As was her habit, she stepped back to study the sixteen-by-twenty-inch canvas.

Gigi the giraffe gazed at her.

Lexi squinted and saw the graceful curves of the long slender neck, the play of light on her patterned coat.

The eyes drew her in, the sweep of lashes caught in half-blink.

Lexi did not often attempt such realistic delineations, but Gigi was different. Her eyes became the focal point, refusing to be merely hinted at in a blur of tones, light, and shade.

They stared back at Lexi now, reminders of the day she had photographed Gigi from the back of the truck. That day when she had begun to feel it was time for a fresh start.

A fresh start that had crashed all around her a short while ago when Nathan revealed his true colors.

Lexi stepped to the canvas and pressed the blackened brush into the lower left-hand corner, the best place to begin an arcing sixteen-by-twenty inch X.

Gigi's eyes luminesced. Light caught light and they shone.

And then Lexi Beaumont fell apart.

Sheer emotion had carried her from the restaurant to the store to her apartment. It unloaded the food in the kitchen and pried off the paint can lid. It now pushed her to her knees, the paintbrush forgotten against her khakis.

Was it rage? Grief? Fear? She didn't want to name it.

A great sob engulfed her.

"Oh, God! This creature is too beautiful. I don't want to destroy her. I am so tired of destroying. I am so tired of running. So tired of being filled with rage and grief and fear. I'm sorry! I'm sorry! I am so sorry! Help me! Oh, please help me!"

She shuddered. It felt like an earthquake rumbled inside of her. It ripped open caverns, long sealed shut and filled with years and years' worth of unshed tears and unspoken cries.

She pitched forward until her face rested against the floor, those tears and cries at last released.

"I quit! I quit! I quit!" She screamed the words, gasping for breath. "I want to do it Your way. I really do. I want what Nana always taught me. What Mom says. What Rosie says. Dear God, I want to know You like they do! Show me the black spots that Papa talks about, the black spots on my own heart."

A sudden blackness filled her vision. Black on black, darker than anything she could imagine. Shapes formed. Like in a painting, she saw shadows and she knew what they were. They weren't grief, rage, or fear. No, they went beyond, to a deeper level of darkness where no light could ever penetrate.

The shadows were hatred. Hatred of her father. Hatred of herself.

As she watched, long tendrils sprouted from them and grew. They coiled around something else, a fistlike shape that moved in a beating rhythm. The tendrils squeezed tightly and the beating slowed.

Lexi's chest ached.

"Jesus, I'm sorry. Forgive me. Help me to forgive Max. My dad. Please. I don't want to hate him."

The fistlike shape took on color. It faded to a raw umber, lightened to burnt sienna. Alizarin crimson took over. The black tendrils snapped and shriveled.

And then they disappeared altogether.

The heart beat in a large up-and-down movement. *Ka-boom. Ka-boom. Ka-boom.* With each beat it brightened until it became a splash of pink against a backdrop of yellow.

Lexi didn't stir from her bowed position. Eyes shut, she gazed at the image, lost in a sense of wonder and peace.

Tears flowed. It was as if all the junk she had bottled up inside herself liquefied and drained out through her tear ducts. After a time she felt emptied . . . except for a faint impression of something she guessed might be . . . maybe . . . could it be?

Yes, it could. Yes, it was.

Joy. Pure, sweet joy whispered in her heart.

"Pink?" She sat up, smiling. "Cobalt rose to be exact. And cadmium yellow lemon."

A feeling of euphoria whooshed aside the soft whisper. It gushed through her. In its wake came a thought, never before formed in her life, bursting like a new star being born in her mind.

God sees me like I see Gigi. He made me. He adores me. He thinks I'm gorgeous. When I hate myself, I obliterate His work. How can I receive good things from Him if I'm obliterated? No way.

Lexi sat up and chuckled. "Lord, this is Sunday school stuff. I should know it already. Obviously I don't, so I'm okay with it if You're okay with it."

Deep inside, from the center of that cobalt-rose beating heart, she believed He was totally okay with it.

Lexi surveyed the mess.

Sobbing with a paint-filled brush clutched in her hand was not a pretty thing. Black enamel smeared her khakis and ecru sweater and hands. It was probably on her face and in her hair. It was on the floor. At least it had hit the cheap rugs she used to protect the landlord's carpet.

All of it could wait. First came Gigi. That plop of black in the bottom left-hand corner would never do. Her giraffe was going to be all about light and life and digital photo-sharp eyes.

Lexi went to work, a wide-mouthed jar of turpentine in one hand and a rag in the other, the windows open to air out the fumes. Again and again she dipped the rag into the jar and rubbed it across the glob, wishing she had used an oil-based paint. Unlike the enamel, it would have easily wiped clean.

The enamel did not forgive like oils.

Hm.

"All right, God. I get it." She smiled, tickled at the conversation that had begun. Even if it was mostly a monologue, she knew He listened.

"As I was about to say, I'm like this enamel, right?" She scrubbed the rag against the canvas. "Not very forgiving. I keep things bottled up. Sticky and staining. Like ill feelings. I have a lot of ill feelings toward a lot of people."

The doorbell rang.

She chuckled. "Like Eileen."

Her neighbor was half-deaf and lived in the apartment next door. She was an amazing baker and excelled in the role of pest. Lexi usually ignored her bell ringing and Eileen would leave a plate of goodies on a tea tray in the hall for her.

It was probably time to mend that fence.

"Coming!" she called out, striding through the living room to the front door at the other end.

Rag still in her grimy hand, she twisted the dead bolt, moved to unlock the doorknob, and out of habit, paused. "Eileen?" She peered through the eyehole.

And saw part of a man's shoulder.

"It's Erik," came the voice the other side of the door.

Erik! Slurred muffled voice, leaning against her door for support, charming his way into the building!

"Oh, Erik!" She unlocked the knob and yanked the door open. "You—"

Her voice died.

In a swift glance she took in the man, his height, his dark hair, his svelte figure that would have looked better in an Armani suit than the Windbreaker and blue jeans. His Dumbo ears that disrupted a perfect flow of tall, dark, and handsome.

He wasn't Erik.

Sixty-One

Bobby swore through clenched teeth, flipped on the lights and siren, and slammed the gearshift into Reverse.

Normally Rosie took his testosterone-laden adrenaline rushes in stride. They had been through enough emergency situations together to build her confidence. She trusted his driving skills and his ability to make snap decisions.

But tonight was a different story.

Of course what made it different was the gnawing fact that the Beaumonts were her friends.

Not good. Not good at all.

She shouted above the siren's scream, "What are you doing?"

"What does it look like I'm doing?" he yelled, his arm on the back of the seat, his face toward the rear of the squad car.

"You're going backwards down the ramp against two lanes of oncoming traffic!"

"Sharp as ever—move it, bozo!" He bellowed as if the driver behind them could hear. "Move it!" He cursed again, not under his breath this time.

Conversation was wasted effort. She knew the freeway's shoulder ahead was blocked due to construction. The glimpse she caught of brake lights signified there must be an accident in the distance. It would tie things up for a long while. They'd have to take side streets all the way to Lexi's.

Rosie twisted around. Cars parted at a snail's pace, allowing Bobby to maneuver down the ramp also at a snail's pace. He was not a happy camper.

She radioed dispatch, explained the situation, asking for a unit nearer Lexi's place to go there ASAP.

There were problems with the request.

It was a busy night for the police. The department was short-handed. Was the woman even in an emergency situation?

Maybe not. The only verifiable info was that Reid Fletcher harassed her brother and knew where she lived.

Did Rosie?

She remembered the building address from when she'd driven Lexi there to pick up her car. The apartment number? Well, no, but she was at that moment searching databases on the squad car's computer—

The dispatcher said she'd see what she could do.

Rosie called Lexi's mom. "Claire—"

"Rosie! What is going on?"

"What's her apartment number?"

"Seven-C. Third floor. What—"

"Hold on." She passed the information on to dispatch. "Claire, have you talked to her?"

"No, she's not answering either of her phones. Her machine doesn't pick up. Indio hasn't seen her at the hacienda. Danny lives closest, but he's camping, out of reach. I talked with her boss and Jenna and a couple friends. Nothing. Max is on his way to her apartment."

Apartment! *Duh.* As in a *building*!

"Claire, what's the security like there? Does she have an outside entrance?"

"No. You have to call from the front and get buzzed inside. I have a key, though, and gave it to Max."

Rosie breathed more easily than she had in hours. Of course there were all sorts of ways to easily get inside such a building, the simplest being to walk in when someone walked out. But it could buy them some time.

"Claire, how soon will Max arrive?"

"Ten minutes, maybe? Depending on traffic."

Always. At least he was approaching from a different direction than they were. Once they got out of the current jam, it should take them less time. Depending on—

"Rosie—"

"Don't worry, Claire. I'll be in touch." She closed her phone, cutting Claire off in midprotest.

Sixty-Two

It was a nightmare.

Lexi could not speak.

She could not scream.

She could not move.

Time ceased to exist.

Before the first gasp had completed its heaving route through her lungs, the man was in her apartment, the door jerked out of her hand and shut.

He stood inches from her. "I can tell from the look on your face that you recognize me. That's too bad. I had hoped you wouldn't."

A heightened awareness commanded her senses.

She heard the click of the door latch . . . the clunk of the lock . . . ragged breath . . . the whistle of his through his nostrils . . . the fall of soft rain from the open windows in the back of the apartment . . . the hum of freeway traffic . . . the rattle of the refrigerator motor . . . the tick of the wall clock . . . the rustle of his jacket fabric.

She smelled the black coffee on his breath . . . the rain on his jacket . . . the pungent fumes of turpentine mounting in the corner where they stood.

She felt the soft cotton of the sweater against her skin . . . the pull of hoops on her pierced earlobes . . . the oiliness on her fingers and the rag they held . . . the cramp of her left hand stretched around the old mayonnaise jar.

She saw the tic at the corner of his right eye . . . the chicken pox scar on his temple . . . the cerulean rim around an iris of powder blue . . . the day's worth of blue-black stubble down his jaw . . . the full lips. An unnatural glint in overlarge black pupils.

"You have seen me, Lexi, haven't you?" His voice resembled Erik's, with silken tones fit for television.

Her heart pounded in her ears. She gasped for each breath, her vocal cords paralyzed from the effort.

"Cat got your tongue?" He smiled. "I don't want to hurt you, Miss Beaumont. I just want to make sure the cat has always got your tongue when it comes to, shall we say, certain topics. I think you know what I'm referring to. What is that awful smell?"

Up close, he wasn't as handsome as she had thought the night at the bar. As a matter of fact, he was nowhere near as good-looking as Erik. And a navy-blue Windbreaker? Not in a million years would Erik wear a navy-blue Windbreaker.

The man rubbed his nose and glanced at the jar. "Peuww. Turpentine. Oh, that's right. You're an artist. Well, well. Why don't you invite me in to see your etchings?" He grinned. "And we'll just chat for a bit. Once we get to know each other, I'm sure you'll understand why it's in your best interest to be quiet about a certain conversation you overheard."

He touched her right arm, a gentle caress, just above the elbow. He smiled.

A creepy-crawly sensation wormed up her arm.

His fingers gripped, pinching.

"Jesus! Help me!" Sheer terror burst the name from her. Outrage quickly followed. Righteous indignation crackled through every bit of her five-foot-two inch frame.

The man turned her from the door and pulled her forward a step.

With all her might, Lexi snapped her left arm across her chest, up and over her shoulder, flinging the contents of the jar out and upwards. The flammable, colorless liquid—an irritant to mucus membranes—splashed directly into the man's face, hitting his mouth, his nose, his eyes.

The guy had no business being in her home.

Sixty-Three

"Max, it's the gold one." Claire faced the back wall of Tuyen's room. She whispered and hunched her shoulders in an effort to hide the fact she was using a cell phone. Nurse Ratchet had already chewed her out once.

Max made a noise of exasperation. "They're all gold!"

"The really gold one. The super shiny one shaped like a beret."

She should have gone with him, but neither one of them had wanted to leave Tuyen alone. Although the nursing staff coddled their niece, and although she progressed physically, it was obvious she was not yet out of the woods emotionally.

Max was at Lexi's building, outside the main entrance. She heard her ring of keys clink as he fiddled with them.

"Max, you tried calling her again, right?"

"Yeah. Oh, good. Here comes a couple. I'll just go inside with them. Excuse me! Hold on, Claire."

He must have left the phone near his mouth. She could hear his side of the conversation. "What do you mean? Huh?" Pause. "But my daughter lives here. Seven-C. I just can't figure out which key—wait! You gotta be kidding me!"

"Max?"

"Unbelievable! They wouldn't let me go in with them. Said it's against the rules. Good grief, Claire, what are all these keys for?"

She ignored the rhetorical question and waited through a few moments of him huffing and puffing.

"Okay. Okay. This one fits. Got it. Yes, it turns! I'm in! Okay. Heading to the steps. Which one is her door key?"

Claire kneaded her forehead. "It has a dot of orchid nail polish on it."

"Orchid. That's purple, right? Ah, got it. Second-floor landing. Tuyen still asleep?"

"Yes."

"Okay, I'm on the third."

"Max?"

No answer.

"Max!"

"—noises. Call you back."

The line went dead.

Sixty-Four

A bellow exploded from the man and reverberated through the apartment. He let go of Lexi and clawed at his face. Losing his balance, he stumbled against the wall, blocking the door.

She dropped the jar and rag and sprinted for the kitchen, for the back entrance that led to a fire escape.

A heavy hand grabbed her shoulder. She fell against the sink and screamed, a small sound lost in the roar of his wordless, unending shrieks.

He let go of her again and crashed to the floor, whacking his arms against his head as if he wanted to tear it off. His legs flailed about, knocking over a chair and pushing the table askew.

Lexi couldn't get by him. She boosted herself up onto the countertop and scrambled along it. At the stove top, beyond the reach of his writhing legs, she hopped down. The teakettle clattered to the floor.

He screamed obscenities. "Help me! I can't see! I can't see!"

She bounded through the kitchen doorway back into the living room.

The man wailed an unearthly howl, the sound of an animal dying in the wilderness.

As she neared the front door, it burst open.

And Max rushed through it.

Max. Her dad.

"Daddy!"

"Lexi!" Her dad's arms tightened around her. "Are you hurt?"

Clinging to him, sobbing hysterically, she pushed until they moved through the doorway and out into the hall.

"Honey, are you hurt anywhere?"

She shook her head fiercely against his chest.

The man's howls were unbearable.

"Should I go in there?"

"Nooo!" *Don't leave me! Don't leave me!* The words screamed in her mind.

"I'm calling 911."

As he used his cell phone, she turned slightly and peered over her shoulder. They still stood near her open front door. She could see across the living room and into the kitchen. She could see the man thrashing about.

"What do you mean they're already here?" Her dad held her with one arm, his eyes watching the interior of the apartment. "I don't see any cops—what? Yes. Yes. Send an ambulance."

Lexi thought of how she and her mom had searched high and low for just the right building. Moving from her parents' house had been a major deal. While her friends went off to college and then into their own homes, she was content to stay put. Work, paint, socialize some, garden at the hacienda. For the most part, her daily life had not intersected with her mom or dad.

In time, though, she craved her own space, one where she could create a studio not attached to the garage. It took months to locate exactly what she wanted. Being near Danny was important, though she could not afford his beach-district rent. A spare bedroom with at least two windows for her studio was a nonnegotiable. And good security. No outside entrance directly to the apartment. At least three floors up.

She settled for a boxlike structure. The landscaping left much to be desired. The tiny balcony off the kitchen confined. But the apartment's cocoon environment worked for her. She felt secure.

Now, in the blink of an eye, that had been shattered.

She shut her eyes and tightened her grip around her dad. He

caressed her cheek, murmuring words she could not decipher. His tone soothed. Her sobs began to subside.

Footfalls thumped nearby. "Oh, thank God!"

"Rosie!" her dad said.

Lexi looked up and saw Bobby rush past, into the apartment. Rosie touched her shoulder and followed him inside. She immediately came back to them.

"What's on his face?"

Lexi inhaled a shaky breath. "Turpentine. You need—you need to flush his eyes."

She gave a quick nod. "Mr. Beaumont, get her out of here."

They sat in her dad's car in the parking lot, the heater running, dome light on, doors locked. Max clasped Lexi's hands between his on the console between the seats.

He phoned her mom, reassured her that she was safe, that he'd call back later.

Lexi's tears would not stop, but at least the hysteria had dissipated.

They watched an ambulance arrive and park near the door. Its siren wound down.

"Honey, drink some water." He handed her a bottle, keeping one hand around hers.

She swallowed a trickle and coughed.

"Did he hurt you?" Unmistakable rage filled his voice. His body vibrated with it.

"No." A new fear shot through her—that he would go back inside. "Daddy, don't leave me."

"Oh, honey. I won't leave you. Ever. I'll always be here for you."

She curled her legs beneath herself and leaned sideways into the soft leather, a sense of protection settling over her. "You are here. How? Why?"

"God told me first. I was sitting at the hospital and felt this overwhelming anxiety about you. I couldn't shake it. Then your mom told me Rosie had called and said you'd left the restaurant very upset. Mom gave me her keys and I came right here." He smiled. "Found the orchid dot."

She wiped a sleeve over her face.

"Here's Rosie." He popped open the locks and the policewoman slid into the backseat.

"Lexi, are you hurt?"

A fresh wave of tears erupted.

Max said, "She says no."

Rosie reached between the seats and squeezed her arm. "I'm sorry we didn't get here sooner."

Max said, "How did he find her? Why did he show up tonight?"

"All I can say at this point is he knew where she lived. My guess is that he was watching the restaurant and saw her leave alone. Then he followed."

"But why?"

"Later. Please, Mr. Beaumont. Let's get through our immediate concern." She cleared her throat. "Lexi, will you tell me what happened?"

"It was so awful!"

"I know."

"He's the guy, the one with Erik that night."

"I know." Rosie clicked on a penlight and opened her notepad.

After a few shaky breaths, Lexi began to relay the events, halting often to compose herself. Rosie took notes and did not interrupt, but Max fidgeted until he nearly bounced off the seat.

At last she said, "Daddy, it's okay."

He leaned over and kissed her forehead.

And then the tears flowed, this time from both of them.

Across the parking lot, the medics emerged from the building and rolled a stretcher toward the ambulance.

Rosie put her head between the seats. "They said he'll be all right. No permanent damage. Bet you knew that."

"Mm-hmm."

"Lexi." Now Rosie blinked back tears. "Please don't let this permanently damage you."

Lexi gazed at her friend and her dad, their faces close together, love for her pouring from them. She recalled God's love pouring into her as she cried out to Him just a short time ago, paint dripping from her brush.

She envisioned again the heart that was able to receive such love. It was clean and beating and pink. "Cobalt rose," she corrected herself.

The two foreheads furrowed.

"In a showcase of cad yellow lemon."

Four eyes blinked.

Lexi knew the damage would linger. She would not be able to live in her apartment at least for a very long time, maybe never. She knew she would relive the terror and bear the image of *victim* over and over. She would distrust and despise men, most especially Nathan Warner.

She also understood that she would measure life in Before and After categories again. Before The Fire. After The . . . What should she call this night's episode? The Horror? The Thrashing of the Bad Guy?

But there was now another Before and After. The one that released, the one that healed, the one that left no space for permanent fear and rage and grief.

She smiled at her dad and Rosie. "I'm going to be all right."

Sixty-Five

Sunday afternoon, when she should have been sleeping before her next shift, Rosie drove to the desert.

On the phone, Jillie Hennison had assured her Erik would be ready for a visit, even one that brought difficult family news. After briefly greeting her old friends, she went out to the backyard.

"Yard" was a loose term to describe the glorious desertscape. It stretched beneath cloudless blue until it disappeared in a distant shimmer. Vegetation was sparse, with the usual variety of cacti and mesquite. Patches of wildflowers sprouted between rocks.

Rosie walked past the pool to a covered patio, the only shady spot.

Erik rose, his arm in a sling. Shadows cast from the slatted patio cover danced across his face.

The hairs on Rosie's arms tingled. She decided then and there she may as well quit denying to herself that she liked the guy.

In that way.

"Rosie, it's good to see you."

"Thanks."

They looked at each other, and an awkward moment passed.

He held out his left arm. "Shaking hands doesn't quite get it."

Again with the tingles. She smiled and exchanged a quick hug with him.

"Have a seat," he said. "Iced tea?"

"Thanks." She sat across from him at the small resin table.

He poured, eyeing her above the pitcher. "Who are you and what have you done with Rosie Delgado?"

"Hm?"

"You seem a little short on words."

She felt nervousness in her smile. "How are you?" She heard hesitancy in her voice and coughed. "You look great."

"I feel . . ." He cocked his head to one side. "Like maybe I could feel great someday."

"Progress, then?"

"Definite." He nodded. "I'm all the way up to taking it one hour at a time. That's as opposed to five minutes. By this time next year, we could be talking one day at a time."

Despite his usual dry tone, there was a subdued air about him. His eyes were clear and a tan had lightly bronzed the indoor pasty skin. He wore shorts and a white polo shirt, clothes she had packed.

She said, "Are you—are you okay with me being here?"

"Greg asked me that very same thing. I have no doubt he would have told you not to come if I didn't want to see you. They certainly don't have a problem saying no, do they?"

She shook her head.

"I said"—He slapped a hand to his chest—"'Ohmygosh! You mean *Maria*? Yes, of course I want to see her!'"

More tingles. She smiled.

"Do you bring glad tidings from the inhabited world?"

Her smile faded. "Not exactly glad, but there is an adequately okay ending to it."

His eyes focused beyond her shoulder. After a second or two, he looked at her. "Okay, shoot."

Shoot. It was one of the first things he'd said to her. By the next evening she was praying for him. Within weeks she had indeed shot him. What an odd path.

"It's about Lexi," she said. "This will hurt, but we think you'll want to hear it now rather than later."

Rosie told the story as gently as possible, glossing over the ugliest of details like what Reid Fletcher had specifically said to Lexi.

Erik listened without comment. He lowered his head, an elbow on the table, and rubbed the back of his neck.

When she finished, he said softly, "It's all my fault, taking her to that bar, getting her involved in my cesspool of a life. Why did that creep have to go after her? Of all people?"

"It's over, Erik. She's okay."

"And Dad shows up late as usual. If he had gotten there sooner—"

"Erik."

He looked up at her.

"She told me she'd made her peace with your dad before Fletcher showed up. The way she sees it, if Max had come sooner, the guy could have hurt both of them. She said also she would not have known what it was to—and I quote—gather her wits and thrash the jerk who dared mess with her."

"Lexi said that?"

"Yes. She also said her dad was there just in time for the most important part: the hug."

Erik smiled, even as tears seeped from his eyes.

She waited as he cried quietly for a few minutes.

He wiped his face with napkins. "Greg and Jillie must spend a fortune on paper products." He sniffed and blew his nose. "Tissues or suitable substitutes everywhere you look."

"Mm-hmm."

"Rosie." He made eye contact. "Thank you for bringing me here. I think."

"You're welcome. I guess."

"It is the hardest thing . . . and the most amazing."

She nodded.

"The other day . . ." Tears welled in his eyes again. "I get extra credit for turning into a crybaby." After a moment he cleared his throat. "The other day we were talking. Which we do a lot of.

Anyway, I remembered an incident when I was twelve. Dad had coached my Little League team for years. One day he quit. More precisely, he abandoned the team mid-season. He just didn't show up for a game one night. Didn't even give the assistants a heads-up. I don't think he even came to watch a game after that. It was Beaumont Staffing. That was when it took off big-time. And that was when things got broken inside of me."

He pressed his lips together and didn't speak for a moment. "The team was in first place when he left. We ended up fifth. The guys blamed him." He jutted his chin and struck a teasing pose. "I admitted I've been a little annoyed over the incident for several years." He paused and flicked his eyes in her direction. "Maria, I swear you are the only person on earth I can say this to."

Already her heart sang. She resisted the urge to jump up and shout hallelujah. She knew what was coming.

"Greg prayed. I prayed. I asked God to fix the broken part. I imagined stuffing all the pain and hurts into a ball bag." He raised his good arm. "Then I handed the bag to Him." He lowered it. "I didn't see or hear anything, but I *knew*. Somewhere deep inside I knew it was done. I'd forgiven my dad."

She grinned.

Erik shook his forefinger at her. "And you knew that was going to happen."

She laughed. "Yeah, I did."

They meandered through the desert, the descending sun warm on their backs.

Erik said, "Don't tell Lexi, but I'm doing paint-by-numbers." He chuckled. "Actually, don't tell anybody. It sounds so pathetic."

"I won't be sharing this visit with others." Rosie glanced at him. "And it's not pathetic. Consider the process like you would surgery. A huge tumor was just cut out of you. You still feel pain from the incision. You need to rest. You do that by engaging your energies in simple activity."

"Like paint-by-numbers."

"Exactly."

"I'll give you one to stick on your fridge."

They walked in comfortable silence for a while. A turkey vulture flew overhead, looping gracefully through the air.

Erik stopped. "Speaking of the family."

She shaded her eyes with a hand and looked up at him.

"My parents are doing this thing in a few weeks, on the third. A wedding blessing."

"Lexi told me about it."

"When I first arrived here, I thought, *What a great excuse this will be. I can skip it.* But now." He shrugged. "Now I don't want to skip it. I want to embrace this hugely important event. I told Greg it'll probably kill me, but he says I'll survive and then I can come back here."

"That sounds like a good plan."

"I thought about inviting Maria to join me. But instead I'd like to ask Rosie."

She squinted. "What's the difference?"

"Maria is my savior, so to speak. Small *s.* Rosie is my good friend. I hope."

Tingles. "She is."

"So, will you go with me?"

"I, uh . . ." Go with him? Tingle overload.

"You have a boyfriend. Some big guy. Another cop. Forget I asked."

"No. No, it's not that. It's, well, I have some other news. Glad tidings."

"Glad tidings? You're withholding glad tidings?"

"Not exactly withholding. I just hadn't gotten to it yet." She bit her tongue. She really did not want to get to it. She could have spent the entire visit not getting to it. "Felicia missed her court date Friday."

"What court date?"

"The one in which a judge makes the temporary restraining order against you permanent."

"Which means what?"

"You're off the hook."

"Really? The order is no more?"

"Yes."

"Great. But what does that have to do with my inviting you to this wedding thing?"

"W-well, you can ask her. She was probably planning on going before, right? She must be a family friend since you two were together when—"

Erik burst out laughing. "Are you nuts?"

She bristled. "You called her from Santa Reina that night!"

"I called her to break the restraining order so the sheriff would have a reason to come and get me and then I would have a reason to call you. I already told you that."

"You're the one who's nuts."

"That makes two of us. The perfect couple."

Rosie raised her arms and dropped them at her sides, at a complete loss for words. She turned her back to him, put her hands on her hips, and kicked a rock. *Lord? I don't want to care for him in* that *way. He has more major issues than there are grains of sand in this desert! On top of which he is unemployed and too handsome for his own good—and talk about baggage! It would take—*

"Was it the word 'couple'?" he said. "Look, I know I don't have anything to offer except a really bad track record. It's just that you're probably the only true friend I've had in years, and I don't want to face that wedding without a good friend there to prop me up. That would be you. You know, I liked you better when you talked a lot."

"Rats." He was under her skin and he'd been there a long time. She spun back around. "I will not be your rebound girl."

His jaw dropped.

"You got that, Beaumont?"

A slow smile spread. His eyes crinkled. "Got it."

"You're not even my type."

"You think you're mine?"

"I just wouldn't want you to get the wrong impression."

"I won't. We go as friends."

"As friends."

"So, I take it you don't have a boyfriend?"

"That is none of your business."

He smiled again, warmly, his eyes intent on hers.

An easy silence unfolded between them again. She wondered if he read in her eyes what he conveyed with his own.

Tingles.

Big-time.

Sixty-Six

As Max left the room, Claire watched Lexi and Tuyen. Instantly they both tensed. If they'd been rabbits in a garden, their jaws would have stopped munching the lettuces. Ears and noses would be twitching.

Since Lexi's arrival at the hacienda Friday night and Tuyen's return on Saturday, Claire had noticed that same reaction time and again.

She set her paint roller in its pan. "Girls, let's take a break."

As one they nodded, laid down their paintbrushes, and joined her cross-legged on the drop cloth.

The four of them were painting one of the guest rooms. Now that it appeared their daughter and niece would be living with them at least for the time being, Max had declared the contractor's schedule null and void. They needed more refurbished space *yesterday*. Typical Max reaction.

At least it was a positive version of his inability to delegate tasks. They all jumped in to help. Besides getting walls painted, the project kept them all too busy to dwell on the past week's events.

But continuing to ignore the obvious might not be such a good thing.

She sighed. "He just went to the bathroom. He'll be right back."

"Who?" Lexi said.

Claire caught the twinkle in her eye, a hopeful sign that the horror of the attack had receded a tiny bit more.

For hours on end Friday night and most of Saturday, they had cried

324

and hugged. Refusing to leave her father's side, Lexi accompanied them to bring Tuyen home from the hospital. That night, both girls camped out in the sala on mattresses while Max slept on the couch.

"Mom, Tuyen and I are making up for lost time." Lexi reached over and patted her cousin's hand above its bandage. "Right, Tutu?" She used Erik's nickname. "We finally got a daddy. We are not letting him out of our sight."

Claire shut her eyes. Maybe she was the only one ignoring the obvious.

"Aunt Claire."

She looked at the blue eyes that always took her by surprise with their decidedly Asian lids.

"We be okay."

Lexi nodded. "Just not today."

Claire did not know where to begin with her thanks to God.

The girls were safe.

Lexi exhibited a new compassion for Tuyen, who responded with happy smiles and was talking more than ever.

Max was committed to pampering them with his presence rather than with gifts like he would have in bygone days.

A woman with the gentlest of voices called from the desert to say Erik was making progress.

Jenna and Danny were coming for dinner.

Indio was her old self, spry and full of praises, doting like—in Max's words—like a grandmother from the sappiest of flowery Hallmark cards.

And Ben was . . . Well, Ben had not gotten into the truck with his loaded rifle and driven down to the jail to shoot that man.

"Hey." Max appeared at the open doorway. "Who said it's break time?"

Lexi and Tuyen giggled, ecstatic five-year-olds who felt safe.

Thank You, Father.

Sixty-Seven

Lexi sat in the backseat of her dad's car. Tuyen was in front with Max. They were heading down from the hacienda to a mall in the city. It was time to choose the Little Black Dress for the wedding.

She and Tuyen were becoming fast friends, probably out of necessity since they spent so much time together. Although they had graduated from sleeping in the sala to their own rooms, they remained clingy with Max, not letting him out of sight for long.

Her cousin was naturally included in the mall outing. When Lexi said she didn't have the LBD yet, Tuyen shyly asked if she could exchange her dress for one with long sleeves.

Max was not into saying no to either one of them.

Surprisingly, the shopping trip had been Lexi's idea. She even invited Jenna to join them, but she couldn't miss school. Her sister's tenderness—she had visited nearly every day and even gone to Lexi's apartment to pick up her clothes—was another surprise.

In the ten days since The Episode, as Lexi had come to refer to it, life amazed her at every turn. Danny said it was her new eyes, the ones she saw with now that she'd forgiven their dad for not being perfect.

She couldn't even scoff at his spiritual explanation.

The Sunday after The Episode, still feeling like one giant exposed raw nerve, she fell apart all over again when Danny arrived at the hacienda. Camping in the mountains, he had been out of reach and didn't know what had happened until then.

Her twin emitted vibes almost as safe and solid as her dad, but not quite. Fear crept in whenever Max slipped out of her sight, and so she could go no farther than the corral for a long private talk with Danny.

She told him everything, from her struggle with bulimia to the black enamel paint to her prayers to the smell of that man's coffee breath. She held nothing back.

He cried so hard their dad had to come out and comfort him.

Now, she noticed the car slow. "Dad, where are we going?"

"To the lookout." He smiled in the rearview mirror at her.

"You never used to—" She stopped. Sentences containing the phrase "never used to" weren't making sense anymore.

"I know," he said. "I never used to stop here. But it's a new day."

He parked and they all got out of the car. The view embodied every cliché that had to do with breathtakingly beautiful. High above a canyon, it included a mountain range lost in purple haze.

Tuyen gasped. "It is magnificent. So grand."

"Isn't it?" Max pointed toward the left. "The hacienda is over that way, behind hills. Before the fire there were more trees. They'll grow back, though, and the whole vista will be as green as that part is." He gestured in the other direction. "Right, Lex?"

"Yep."

He gazed at her. His eyes glistened.

She remembered then that he had spent time on this very spot during The Fire.

"To think," he whispered, "I've almost lost you twice." He placed an arm around her shoulders and kissed her temple. "I love you, honey."

She could not count how many times he had hugged her and expressed his love in the past ten days.

Which explained, of course, why she could go shopping for the LBD and not even want to swing by a food market along the way.

She knew the journey wasn't over yet. Like Erik had said, the leopard's pattern couldn't change overnight. But for today, all the hungry corners of her heart were full.

As her dad searched for a place to park in the mall's lot, Lexi opened her cell phone, something she had avoided until now.

Five voice mails awaited. Because Erik, her boss, and Rosie had all called her several times at the hacienda's number, she figured the messages would not be from them.

She held her breath and began to listen.

"Lexi, this is Nathan Warner. I don't know where to begin. I am sorry. I am so sorry. I want to explain, although there is no explanation really. I-I—" His voice cracked. "Please call. Good-bye," he whispered.

Lexi closed her phone. She wasn't about to listen to four more similar messages from him. Rosie had come to the hacienda to tell her and her parents his story, about Reid Fletcher being his half brother, about him not knowing anything about what Fletcher had done. Rosie even seemed to like Nathan.

But still . . .

He was correct. There really was no explanation.

She caught her dad watching her in the rearview mirror.

"Everything okay?" he said.

She nodded.

"Want me to punch his lights out?"

She smiled and shook her head.

Ninety minutes later they were back in the car, two black evening dresses, two beaded bags, and two fancy pairs of heels tucked away in the trunk.

For the hundredth time, Tuyen grinned and said, "Uncle Max, thank you."

Lexi leaned forward from the backseat. "Dad, you're a better shopper than Jenna and Mom and Tandy all put together."

He laughed. "Okay, ladies, where to next? Danny's place?"

Tuyen nodded enthusiastically. "He teach me computer. Then I get job."

Lexi heard hope in her cousin's voice. Hope and a hint of future. A sudden longing flowed through her. She wanted that too. She hadn't worked or painted in ten days. She hadn't yet met with the pastor in Santa Reina for counsel—something even she agreed with her family was a good idea.

"Lex?" Her dad's tone conveyed that he figured something was up with her.

Weird how in tune he could be.

"I think." She paused, thought it over, and straightened her shoulders. "No. It's time. I *know* I want to get my art supplies."

"From the apartment."

She wrinkled her nose briefly. "Yes. Please."

"You got it." He turned around and started the engine.

They left Tuyen at Danny's beach house. Eager for computer lessons and evidently comfortable enough with him, she wanted to stay until evening, when he would take her home.

Lexi sat in the front seat. "Well, Dad, one down, one to go."

Braking at a red stoplight, he glanced at her. "What do you mean?"

"Don't you feel like you have a couple of leeches clinging to you?"

He chuckled. "No, it's not like that at all. You cling as long as you need to, honey. I'll miss you when you're ready to move on."

She had no response to that except another jolt of surprise.

"And you will move on." He drove through the intersection, his eyes on the road. "You are a beautiful, gifted woman. You're going to create many more paintings and landscapes and add beauty to the world."

She sniffed quietly.

"Besides that," he said, "I'm taking your mother on a honeymoon and you are not invited." He flashed a grin at her.

They parked in the lot behind her building.

Lexi made no move to get out of the car. She felt nauseated.

Her dad grasped her hand. "He's locked up."

She knew that. Someone had intervened and Reid Fletcher had gone from jail to a secure psych ward with stipulations, as she understood it, he would remain in one or the other for a very long time.

"Do you want to wait for Rosie to get here?"

Knowing Rosie wanted to walk through the scene with her, Lexi had called her to say they would be there. It helped hearing her in-charge, confident voice.

"Hm? Lex?"

She looked at her dad and saw those brown-black eyes gazing back at her. They resembled her grandmother's. The obsidian had softened to velvet. Amazing.

She smiled. "Who needs the police? I got my dad."

The scent of turpentine greeted them at the front door.

Max walked in ahead of her, slowly. She clutched a fistful of the back of his shirt.

Images bombarded. The man. His eyes. His smile. His breath.

His caress on her arm.

She wanted to throw up.

"Whew," Max said. "I bet you don't get back your security deposit. The owners will have to put in new carpet. You doing okay?"

"Mm-hmm." *Dear God.* "Yeah. No."

"Take it slow." He stopped, reached back, and drew her to his side, an arm around her shoulders. "Lord God, fill this place with Your presence, Your peace, and Your power."

The nausea dissipated some. She looked across the room into the kitchen. The chairs were upright, the table in place. No evidence of that night. The window above the sink was cracked open.

"Did Mom clean up?"

"Yeah. Jenna helped. You know, I didn't mean to imply you're moving out of here. Maybe after a time you'll be ready to come back."

Snuggled against him, in the confines of his arm, she wondered if she truly wanted to give up her home. She considered it for about three seconds.

"No," she said. "I don't want to live here. It's more than that night. This place is all old. My old life. It represents the way I don't want to live anymore."

He kissed the top of her head.

"Tuyen and I actually talked about being roommates. No clue when or where. You're going to need our rooms in August for guests."

"Yes, but I don't want you to feel pressured. Here's my idea, which dovetails with your roommate idea. We can take that tiny RV Nana and Papa lived in and trade it for a larger one. You and Tuyen could live in it for as long as you want. We'd have to figure out where you could put a studio, though."

She smiled. "Nana already offered their back bedroom."

He laughed.

"You may never get rid of me, Dad."

They were in the kitchen and his laughter was erasing the echo of shrieks.

Lexi introduced him to Gigi the giraffe. She still sat on the easel in the studio.

Max smiled. "She's beautiful."

"She's nowhere near finished, but I like her."

"I had no idea, honey." He shook his head as if in awe.

"It's not like I've shown you my work for a while."

"It's not like I've asked to see it." He glanced at her. "I'm sorry."

She stared at the bottom corner of the canvas, at the smudgy gray spot. "I almost destroyed her that night."

"Why?"

"I was starting to feel better. I was feeling comfortable with that Nathan guy. Then he told us he knew the man who was with Erik. I was so hurt. Ready to give up. But . . ." She shrugged. "Gigi looked at me and I couldn't do it. It was like God said, 'Hey, I'm here. Talk to Me.'"

She closed her eyes and pondered whether or not to continue.

Max rubbed her shoulder.

"Can I tell you something?" she said.

"Please."

"I remembered that time I fell off the balance beam when I was nine and broke my leg."

He nodded.

"You had come into the gym during my routine. I saw you and lost my concentration."

"I should have been there on time. I shouldn't have walked in late. I'm sorry, Lexi."

She winced, not wanting to push further but knowing she had to. "Mom rode in the ambulance, but you didn't. They said you could."

He grimaced. "And you remembered all these years how I abandoned you. Honey, I am so sorry."

"There's . . . there's more. After my leg healed, I was too scared to go back to gymnastics. I always blamed you for that."

He hung his head. "I wish there was another way to say I'm sorry."

"I know you are. I . . ." She held a deep breath. "I forgive you." She exhaled loudly. "The thing I realized is that even though I always loved art, it wasn't until I was laid up with a cast on my leg that I got serious about it. That's when all this started." She gestured to the room full of her art supplies and her work. "So, I forgive you and I thank God for bringing me through."

Max wrapped her in his arms.

Sixty-Eight

Anybody home?" Rosie called out as she entered Lexi's apartment through the door that had been left standing open. She imagined her friend wasn't quite ready to close herself up inside the place yet.

"Back here." It was Max's voice.

Rosie found them in the room Lexi used for her art studio. She noticed them both wiping at their eyes and thought, not for the first time, what an emotionally draining time it had been for the Beaumonts lately.

"Sorry." She greeted Lexi with a hug. "Am I interrupting?"

"No." Max brushed a hand across his cheek. "As Claire says, we seem to be living in the state of weepy these days."

"Understandable." She nodded. "Lexi, I have to confess, I already peeked at Gigi the other night when I was in here."

"She's not finished."

"I know, but she's incredible. I've started a savings fund for her. I get dibs on buying her. Bobby wants her too for his daughter, but you have to tell him no."

Lexi smiled.

Max said, "I'll go down to your storage bin and find some boxes."

"Thanks, Dad."

"I'll be right back."

"Okay."

Rosie watched the curious exchange. Max spoke in a reassuring tone. Lexi's eyes widened briefly as if in panic, and her voice went softer than usual. Her eyes followed every inch of Max's exit from the room and stayed on the doorway.

"You okay, Lexi?"

She waggled a hand.

"Yeah. I know you're not, but do you feel stronger?"

"I do. I can actually let him out of my sight now."

"Things going well between you then?"

She smiled and her eyes lit up. "Got my own papi."

Rosie chuckled. "I'd like to chat a minute before getting down to business. Let's sit on the floor."

Lexi settled onto the carpet with her, cross-legged. "What's up?"

To her surprise, Rosie hesitated. "It's kind of personal." She chose her words carefully. "I told you I went out to the desert and saw Erik. That he looks good. He's responding well to treatment."

"Blah, blah, blah. You told me all that. I've never seen this funny expression on your face."

Rosie picked at a thread in the rug. "He invited me to go to your parents' wedding. The blessing part and the reception." She looked up.

Lexi grinned. "That's great! Mom and Dad will be glad to have you there. Why don't you invite your dad and that woman he's dating to the reception? Bobby and his wife too. Mom's got half the city coming. And she uninvited Felicia, Brett, and Erik's producer and his wife. That leaves four openings."

"Really? Okay, thanks. I'll do that."

Lexi still grinned. "Is this like a date?"

"No! Uh-uh. We're going as friends. He needs . . . wants . . . uh, feels . . . my moral support would be helpful."

She giggled. "You like him."

Rosie sighed. "I seem to."

"He must like you too. He doesn't have female 'friends.'"

"That's what I'm afraid of."

"What do you mean?"

"He's a ladies' man. Look at me." She wiggled her fingers toward herself, pointing out her blue jeans, long-sleeve T-shirt, and pony-tail. "I mean, it ties your brain into knots trying to imagine him dating this, doesn't it?"

"Oh, Rosie. Why do you say that?"

"Lexi! The obvious. I'm not tall and blonde and blue-eyed."

"But he's sober now. He's bound to grow out of that cutesy phase."

"I don't know." She sighed again. "This is just between us, okay?"

Lexi laughed out loud. "I bet he already knows."

"Whatever." It was good to hear the laugh. She waited until it ended before going on. "Anyway, I bring this up for a reason. Nathan Warner."

"I don't want to talk about him."

"But you need to hear this. He really is a good guy."

"You told me that on the phone. But no way. After what he did?"

"There's a part I left out. That night you were at the bar with Erik, he noticed you. He wanted to talk to you, but he was too upset with Fletcher's behavior and left. Lexi, Nathan said you totally intrigued him."

"I didn't do anything."

"Nope. You were just being you."

Lexi drew her knees up and hugged them to herself. "He's that guy's half-brother."

"Bobby has the meanest brother in the world. Bobby doesn't have a hurtful bone in his body. And I've run every possible check on Nathan, read his work, talked to former employers. He's clean, Lexi. Smart and good-looking."

"He's left five voice mails on my phone."

"Persistent bugger too. I think it's only fair you give him a chance to grovel."

Lexi shrugged a shoulder.

"Your dad and I could come and stand guard."

"I don't think so!"

Rosie grinned. "Thatta girl. You can do it all by yourself."

Sixty-Nine

Ten days after Rosie suggested she give him the opportunity to grovel, Lexi met Nathan Warner at the same coffee shop they'd been in before.

She didn't quite go it alone. Although she had "unleeched" herself from her dad, she still didn't do much without some family member nearby. At the moment, Danny sat outside in his car parked next to hers, eyes on the shop's door.

Nathan stood when he saw her enter the shop. He pointed at a cup on the table and mouthed *Venti iced caramel macchiato, extra shot, extra whipped cream.*

A smile tugged at her mouth.

The problem with all the forgiveness business was she found herself wanting to believe the best of everyone. Well, everyone short of this man's brother.

She reached the small table and stood beside it.

"Hi, Lexi."

"Did you know he was going to hurt my brother?"

"I swear, I had no clue. Reid was angry. He blamed Erik for putting the kibosh on his one crack at breaking into the big time. That night when Erik walked in, Reid went after him. Verbally. I only heard his bitterness. I didn't hear any vengeful act in the making. I'm sorry. I should have."

"Did you tell him where I lived?"

"Good grief, no. He told me the night before you and I met for dinner." He glanced at a nearby table. "Lexi, let's sit down, please."

She noticed people were watching their exchange. She sat.

Nathan followed suit and slid the drink in front of her. "This may not help, but I'll say it anyway: he was never violent. I don't think he would have harmed you physically."

He was right. Hearing that didn't help.

"Lexi, I promise he will never hurt you again. I promise that I will never intentionally hurt you again. May I finish the story?"

She nodded, hands in her lap, head lowered.

"I began to wonder about Reid when he told me your address. And where you buy groceries."

Nausea churned her stomach.

"He said Erik seemed to have dropped off the face of the earth. So . . . he followed you. That's when I got worried. I told him to leave you alone. He said he just needed to know if you saw him arguing with Erik. I said I would find out."

She looked at him. His hands were gripped together on the table, his eyes down.

"I began to put two and two together. Why was it such a big deal to him? Did he have something to do with Erik getting to Felicia's? With the toy gun, even?" He shook his head. "Something was seriously wrong. I talked to our mom after that. I said Reid needed professional help. She agreed."

Lexi waited for him to continue.

"Then I met you for dinner." He raised his eyes to her. "You don't have to believe this, but I was going to tell you everything before our evening ended. I just didn't want to ruin our moment together." A sad smile crossed his lips. "It was a good moment. A connection. They don't happen often. At least not to me."

Warm fuzzies bubbled inside of her. There was no denying she'd felt the same, so much so she had opened up to him more than she ever had with anyone.

He said, "I guess that's the end. Except—Lexi, I am so sorry for what he did to you. I am so sorry I didn't run after you."

Like Rosie and Bobby would have let that happen.

"I should tell you the beginning of the story. I noticed you that first night and I said to myself *I really would like to know that woman.* When I figured out you were the one that might, according to Reid, ease his mind, I jumped at the chance to meet you."

"You went through Zak and made up a ruse about writing an article!"

"I'm sorry. I'm short on pickup lines. And I couldn't fake it, pretending I didn't know the first thing about you before we met. Lexi, short of a miracle, I know you can't forgive me. But I wish with all my heart that at some point we could pick up where we left off."

"I forgive you." The words sprang straight from her heart to her tongue.

His entire body visibly relaxed. The tense lines on his face softened. He took a deep breath, let it out, and whispered, "Thank you."

"Yeah, well." Her tone of absolution flip-flopped to harsh. Old reactions short-circuited the new attitude. "Danny says to forgive means to forget. And that part I'm not so sure about."

"I understand."

Lexi tried to avoid eye contact but the warmth of those tawny irises drew her back. She had told this guy everything. She was so gullible.

She said, "I just don't want to be gullible anymore. Are you even writing that stupid article?"

"I sold it. Two versions actually. One to a firefighting magazine. Another—the personal one about you—to a Sunday supplement. Only with your approval, of course. You are a heroine, Lexi. People will love reading about you."

"Don't flatter me."

"I'm not. I won't. I'm just groveling for a second chance to see you again."

A second chance. What if he trampled all over her trust again? Could she handle that?

She thought of her family, how their presence had become a

safety net. The knowledge that Danny sat right outside the door held her in a comfort zone she could not have found on her own. Maybe if she knew the family was nearby watching over her, then maybe another meeting with Nathan wasn't out of the question.

The wedding reception.

She stood up. "Saturday night. Hotel Del. Seven thirty. Black tie."

"I'll be there."

She hesitated. The black-tie part was optional. But . . . if she had to wear a little black dress, then Mr. Casual in his Birkis could wear a tux. Besides, his second chance should come with extremely high standards.

Lexi picked up her venti iced caramel macchiato, extra shot, extra whipped cream, swiveled on her heel, and made what she considered quite a nice exit.

Seventy

On a Friday afternoon in early June, the day before she planned to renew her marriage vows, Claire sat outdoors on the railroad tie steps that led down to the hacienda's parking area.

Only two cars sat on the new blacktop, hers and Max's. More would arrive soon. Danny and Jenna were driving together from the city. Indio and Ben would most likely ride in his truck up the hill from their house. Lexi and Tuyen planned to hike that same hill; they were checking out the newly delivered RV. Erik was on his way, driving himself after getting a ride in from the desert to his own car.

There was much unfinished business.

Jenna languished over Kevin, not due home until next spring.

Lexi and Tuyen, both still hurting but healing, faced the thousand and one household details of moving. The RV required some furnishings. Lexi wasn't crazy about the commute to work. Tuyen needed a job.

Ben talked to Tuyen, but not often and not directly and not with a smile.

And then there was Erik.

Which was the reason Claire waited alone on the steps for him.

The change in her eldest son was obvious when he parked his sporty car. No brakes squealed. No music blared. No gunned engine noise.

Erik climbed out, removing his sunglasses, a small smile on his lips, his right arm free from the sling. "Hey, Mom."

Claire met him with a fierce hug. "Welcome." She almost added "home," but swallowed the word. It wasn't his home.

"Thanks."

She kissed his cheek. "Let me look at you."

He twirled around for her, always the performer.

She smiled. "Seriously."

He leaned over and pressed his forehead against hers. "Twenty-five days sober."

Thank You, Lord. She whispered, "I don't want us to interfere, to undo anything."

He straightened. "Mom, how I react to people and situations is totally my choice. I'm in good shape. Trust me, this couple, Jillie and Greg, they would have strongly suggested I stay put if I weren't ready."

She stared at him. As always he was confident, but . . . where was the insolence? "Okay."

He watched her closely. "Go ahead. Tell me what's on your mind. I won't break, I promise."

"You've changed."

"I have."

"Your father has changed too."

He cocked his head to one side.

"Erik, let him change."

Slowly, understanding dawned in his eyes. His mouth curved into that signature half smile. "You mean not to react to the old Max. Not slip into my old way of relating to him. Like, um, snapping and barking like some rabid dog whenever he's in the vicinity?"

She spread her hands. "Does it make sense?"

He laughed. "Got it covered, Mom. I've forgiven him." He looked over her shoulder. "Speak of the devil."

Claire glanced back and saw Max approaching the top of the steps.

Erik touched her shoulder as he walked past her. "I hope you gave him the same talk."

Of course she had. Maybe it hadn't been necessary, but when Max said he was going to the office about the time Erik was due to arrive, she recognized anxiety signals. The remedy seemed so simple. *Let your son be changed.*

Erik's long legs quickly bridged the distance between him and his dad.

Too far to hear the brief words they exchanged, she understood them in her heart. The clues were easy to follow. Especially the big bear hug.

Late that afternoon, the family roamed through the hacienda, checking out the refurbished rooms. They observed what needed to be done and anticipated the first guests to visit the *Hacienda Hideaway - A Place of Retreat* in a few months.

At every turn Claire's heart overflowed with gratitude.

As a group, they sauntered into the sala. Lexi lingered behind in the courtyard.

Danny gestured at the walls. "I like what you've done in here with the lighter paneling, but it's still kind of stark."

"It is," Max said. "I asked Lexi if we could hang some of her paintings. She said she wants to work on a new series for this room."

"Yeah," Danny said, "you wouldn't want her last phase with all that on-the-verge-of-extinction. No offense, Lex—oh, I guess she's not in here. Man, talk about stark."

"I saw those," Max said. "I prefer Gigi the giraffe. She'd go perfect on that far wall."

Erik chuckled. "I do believe Gigi is spoken for by a certain policewoman."

Claire smiled. She'd been trying to suppress her delight ever since she heard Rosie was accompanying Erik to Saturday's festivities.

Ben stepped to a side wall and rapped his knuckles on it. "I miss the map. It went right here."

Danny said, "Your grandfather drew it, right?"

"Yep. Can't replace that one. It showed trees and hills and where the gold was." He shook his head, clearly disturbed at the loss.

"You know what, Papa?" Danny placed an arm around his shoulders and gazed with him toward the undecorated wall. "You can find just about anything on the 'Net these days."

"Can't find originals by your ancestors."

"That is true." Danny moved to a nearby chair, squatted down, and fished a hand beneath it. "But you can punch information to the right people and come up with a pretty good facsimile." He pulled out a long cardboard tube.

Claire stared in anticipation as he pulled a cap off one end. He reached inside, grinning the whole time, and slowly withdrew a rolled-up piece of what appeared to be parchment paper.

With a flourish he unrolled it. "Ta-da!"

They all gathered around him, Ben in the center.

"Not bad, huh, Papa? It's even got the different clumps of boulders and the oldest oak." He winced. "Which we think is growing back."

Ben clapped Danny's shoulder, clearly at a loss for words.

Indio wept. The rest of them oohed and aahed.

Erik said, "It's perfect, Dan. Great idea."

A high-pitched cry split the air. "Oh!" It was Lexi, from the courtyard.

Max was the first one through the door, Claire on his heels.

"Oh," she yelled again. "Come see this!"

"Lexi!" he shouted.

"Here!"

They rushed toward her voice at the far end. There she knelt, in the dirt, covered with it, surrounded by a pile of dried-up stems and leaves.

"Look at this!" She grinned, gently brushing her fingertips through the earth. "Here and here. And over there. Rosemary. Oregano. Jasmine. Honeysuckle. African daisy. Aloe and cholla. And more." She looked up, her eyes wide and glittery. "They didn't die!"

The courtyard was last on their to-do list. The fire had ravaged it. All the rooms of the U-shaped house opened onto it, and that was where junk had accumulated as the rooms were cleared. And Lexi had lost interest in it. No one else cared for the plants quite like she did.

"They didn't die!" Lexi exclaimed again. "There they were, sprouting under dead stuff and beneath the broken fountain pieces. Isn't this wonderful?"

Claire pressed a hand to her mouth.

Just like herself and her family. They had been sprouting under dead stuff, beneath broken pieces. Life hidden from view now emerged.

Yes, it was wonderful, indeed.

Seventy-One

Rosie slid from her SUV, grateful for the high vehicle. It made the balancing act atop three-inch heels much easier to perform than if she'd climbed up and out of a low car.

"Hi."

She spun on said heel, nose to Erik's chest, an expanse of stiff white shirt outlined with silky black lapels.

She looked above the bow tie. "Hi."

Nuts. How had she missed his approach? There were probably a number of reasons. Preoccupation with shoes. Skittishness about being Beaumont's "date" at the Hotel Del with San Diego's most elite. Admiration of the sweet little church before her, tucked back off a side road in the trees northeast of Santa Reina. Edginess over the plans, which included Erik riding with her back down into the city to the reception, about an hour's worth of alone time. Like a real date.

"You look beautiful."

Rosie let her immediate negative response fizzle away unspoken. Bobby and his wife had stopped by the house before she left, her own cheering squad. They said she was beautiful inside and out. Tall, blonde, and blue-eyed? No. But stunning in her own way. She should receive all like compliments with gracious dignity.

She smiled. "So do you." So much for gracious dignity.

He grinned. His not-so-subtle glance took it all in. Her hair, falling in waves to her shoulders. The new black dress, simple, straight, made

345

of some silky fabric with sequins. The heels, that vain concession to slimming linebacker calves.

"Did you bring your gun?"

"No." She smiled.

"Good." Erik dipped his head and kissed her cheek.

She laughed, pretending like her feet remained on the pavement. "Did you think I would you shoot you for that?"

"You never know." The setting sun glittered in his eyes behind his dark lashes. He smiled and crooked his elbow, holding it out for her to grasp.

It helped with the balancing act.

Rosie sat in a pew.

And waited for the heartbeat to slow, for the brain to focus on something besides the image of Erik. Tuxedos were designed for guys who looked like him. And that kiss? Friend to friend, sure. But still.

She sighed to herself and studied the church. It was much smaller than hers and of a different persuasion, yet similar with its crucifixes, stained glass windows, and incense. The program in her hand included traditional liturgy. Candles were lit on the altar. Flowers lined the altar rail.

Only a handful of people were in attendance for this private event of Claire and Max's special day. There was no organist, but off to one side a string quartet played soft classical music. She knew the musicians were close friends of Claire's.

Tuyen sat beside Rosie, lovely and happy. The haunted expression in her eyes had faded.

Ben and Indio occupied the same pew on Tuyen's other side. A thick bun at the nape of Indio's neck replaced her usual braid. Ben kept tugging at the collar of his formal shirt.

The priest walked in from a door behind the altar. Gentle faced, silver haired, dressed in white vestments, he was a large man. Rosie likened him to a teddy bear.

Max came next, followed by Erik and then Danny, all handsome in black tuxedos and white shirts.

The music changed to the familiar tune for brides, and everyone stood, turning to the back of the church. Lexi started first down the aisle, followed by Jenna. They carried small bouquets of purple and white blossoms and wore black dresses. Claire wore a magnificently beaded ivory dress that reflected every light ray in the church. She carried a bouquet full of whites and off-whites.

Rosie sighed to herself. Wedding, re-wedding, blessing, renewal of vows. Whatever. It was all beautiful beyond words.

Seventy-Two

All those months of dreadful anticipation had been such a colossal waste of energy!

As it turned out, the only difficult part of the church ceremony for Lexi had been resisting the urge to grab the photographer's camera. From her bridesmaid's perch up front, she had longed to record every nuance of the scene.

Unabashed tenderness shone in her father's eyes as he gazed at her mother. The back of her mother's hair glowed; the beads on her dress refracted candlelight into a thousand tiny rainbows. The pure white baby's breath in the bouquet her sister held contrasted with the black of her dress, a study in stark beauty. An otherworldly peace settled Erik's features. Danny stood statuelike, the rarest of rare sights.

Of course the tears in her own eyes might have botched her ability to focus the lens.

Now it was over. The ceremony part anyway. She stood with everyone outside the Hotel Del on Coronado Island. While the photographer snapped formal family shots, a new dread steadily chewed away at her earlier bliss. In just minutes she would have to go into the reception.

The unprecedented shindig held horrors for her.

It meant hundreds of strangers who would eye her as the youngest daughter, sister of the drop-dead gorgeous one.

It meant Nathan Warner. Or it didn't mean Nathan Warner. Would he show up or not? She wasn't sure which was worse.

It meant the countdown had started for her parents' departure. Their honeymoon, a cruise down the Mexican Riviera, was to last a week. Seven days could be an incredibly long, long time.

And the reception meant an abundance of food, an easy escape from the panic associated with the whole scene.

Now the camera flashed on the last official Beaumont clan photo. It was an outdoor shot, the hotel's exterior lights beaming on their faces, the sky and ocean invisible in the dark in the background.

Only Kevin was absent. She missed him. They all missed him. For one photo, they even posed around an empty area that Jenna would fill in with a picture of him. Jenna bawled, of course. She'd been doing a lot of that. Even Lexi was feeling sorry for her.

The photographer raised his head. "Lexi, you did not smile."

Everyone groaned. Behind the woman holding up a spotlight, Rosie chuckled.

"Sorry, sorry," Lexi said. "I'm ready now."

Forcing herself to pay attention, she clamped a smile into place and got through it.

It was time to join the party already in progress. As a group they entered the hotel and moved through the hallways. Lexi followed Erik and Rosie. Their heads were close together as they conversed.

Her brother had come home from rehab subdued and reflective, fragile around the edges, even. When he greeted her with a hug, he whispered that a leopard could change his spots with some help. She adored him. She adored Rosie. She hoped they adored each other.

Max sidestepped over to her and matched his stride with hers. "What are you giggling at?"

She nodded forward. "Curious couple."

"Indeed."

"I was just thinking I hope they adore each other."

He laughed. "I was just thinking, would you like me to hang out with you until we see if this Nathan character shows up?"

Lexi stopped and faced him. "Dad, this is your party."

"And you're my daughter."

With that simple sentence, Lexi's world stilled again. Her daddy loved her. Her heavenly Father loved her even better. Peace and joy chased away the hovering dread.

She smiled. "Thanks, but I'll be okay."

And to think she wanted to skip the whole re-wedding business.

Nathan was there. He stood inside, not far from the entrance, right in the center of an otherwise open path from the doors to the tables. He was the first person Lexi saw as she entered the ballroom.

She paused. Sights and sounds bombarded her. There were zillions, not hundreds, of people milling around. There were balloons and streamers and flowers. There was music from a string quartet. There was loud laughter and bubbling conversation.

Nathan smiled and walked over to her. The boy-next-door had morphed into something else. A tuxedo replaced the rumpled clothes, shiny black shoes the sandals, stylishly moussed copper sprigs the unkempt hair.

She liked the other look.

But she liked this one too. A lot.

"Hi, pretty lady."

The phrase swirled in her mind. *Pretty lady.* It was what Kevin always called Jenna. Secondhand, it turned her to slush. Firsthand, backed up with a gaze from the warmest eyes imaginable, it might melt her into a puddle right then and there.

Earlier that afternoon she had talked with her grandmother and poured out her confusion surrounding this guy. Nana prayed for her what she requested—that she would not be stupid and gullible. Then, like always, Nana added more. She asked God to give Lexi a trusting heart and the wisdom to know the balance between the two.

She probably shouldn't fall in love with him after the first three words out of his mouth. "I thought you were short on pickup lines."

"That wasn't a pickup line. I meant it." He smiled again. "And if you give me a second chance, I'll prove it to you."

"How will you do that?"

"I will escort you through this maze of people who are most likely scaring the bejeebers out of you. I will meet your parents and win your dad's approval. I will dance every dance with you. Then I will ask you out for tomorrow. Maybe a walk on the beach and dinner." He held out his hand, palm up. "Any or all of it will be an honor."

Okay, so maybe dreading the reception had been a colossal waste of energy too. Maybe the fumble queen of relationships had exited along with what's-his-name, the fireman. Maybe Erik was right— leopards could change their spots.

With some help.

Lexi smiled at Nathan and placed her hand in his.

Seventy-Three

Sunday afternoon Claire stood beside Max on the deck outside their cabin, on the cruise ship bound for Mexico. Leaning against the rail, they watched the California coastline shrink from view. Brilliant flecks of sunlight danced on the ocean's surface. Soft breezes carried a salty scent with promises of adventure.

Max kissed her. "I love you, sweetheart."

"I love you."

"They will be fine."

She laughed. "How did you know?"

"That you were thinking about the kids?" He grinned. "Probably the phone calls first thing this morning gave it away. I can't believe you invited them and my parents to breakfast. Our *honeymoon* breakfast, I might add."

She wrinkled her nose at him.

Part of the reception had been to treat the young people and Ben and Indio to a night at the Hotel Del before everyone went their separate ways. The plans called for Max and Claire to depart for the ship while the others enjoyed a leisurely morning however they chose. There was no talk of a group breakfast.

Still, Claire had harbored hopes. Their twenty-four hours of togetherness had been too sweet. Why not stretch it just a bit longer, savor the presence of everyone together? Her heart overflowed with the joy of being with all four of her children, her brand-new precious niece Tuyen, and her dear in-laws.

She phoned their rooms bright and early. Evidently the previous evening had been enough togetherness for the others because she received groggy "no thanks and good-bye already" from the girls, the guys, and even Indio.

Max bumped his shoulder playfully against hers. "They will be fine."

"Jenna's having such a hard time. She looked so sad all night. I don't know how—"

"Shh. God knows. All we can do is be there for her and pray. The others will watch over her this week. Okay? We can take a week off from anxiety."

"Okay."

"Way to be, Claire. I'm going to change the subject."

She sighed. She really had to relax and let go of the kids. "Go ahead."

"Wasn't last night just a great gift? And that Nathan was a surprise, huh? I like him."

"Me too. He had an obvious calming influence on Lexi."

"Yes. Speaking of calm, Erik is a new man."

"What an amazing transformation."

"Our God is an amazing God."

"Amen." Claire took his arm and nestled against him. "So is my husband. Thank you for giving me a wedding after all these years. It was an extraordinarily beautiful one."

"Thank you for marrying me again after all these years." He kissed the top of her head. "It has been a journey of sowing and reaping good and not-so-good."

"And gathering the kids close."

"But not for breakfast."

"Ha-ha. Max, I know it hasn't been easy working through the not-so-good stuff, but I'm grateful we did."

"It's made all the difference. We've learned to trust God and to trust each other."

"And find that safe place with each other. Do you think we can really create it now for others?"

"Claire, I'd say that's already begun within our family. The Hacienda Hideaway can only be an extension." He chuckled. "Did I mention I called the kids last night?"

She looked at him, puzzled.

"Told them if they dared show up for breakfast, they were in big trouble."

"You didn't!"

He laughed.

She leaned against him, hiding a smile, and basked in his love for her.

In silent wonder they watched as the horizon swallowed the coastline. Sky met sea in a blur of silvery blues.

"Claire, what do you think? Thirty-three more years?"

She kissed his cheek. "At least."

Author's Note

Although San Diego County is the setting for this series, I've taken liberty in fictionalizing several aspects of the area. In particular, Channel 3 News, Santa Reina, the Hacienda Hideaway, and the Rolando Bluff Fire exist only in my imagination.

Acknowledgments

M any people have come alongside during the writing of this story. They enriched the characters with their expertise and real-life experience. I claim responsibility for mistakes. My deep appreciation goes to:

Gary Smalley: for his definitive work in relationships, most especially in his books *I Promise* and *Change Your Heart, Change Your Life*.

Elizabeth, Tracy, and Patti John; Rhonda Cox, Trish Owens, Cheryl Paris, Janet Fyfe, and Carrie Younce: for all kinds of stuff.

Kaiya John: for helping Nonna with special words.

Karlie Garcia: for the Spanish.

Nancy Standard: for the art lessons.

Kelly Paige Standard: for technical information and an insider's view of the artist's life.

Katie Gesto: for her book *Hunger for Freedom*.

Ami McConnell, Leslie Peterson, Lee Hough, and the folks at Thomas Nelson: for being the professional "bookends" who brought it all together.

Tim: for everything else.

Reading Group Guide

1. Lexi and Erik are stuck in ruts in terms of their coping mechanisms. To a certain extent we all cope with life situations, we all need to protect ourselves from pain, we all need comfort. Can you identify ways in which you, too, might make use of coping mechanisms?

2. Why don't Lexi and Erik want to seek help early in the story? How did that affect them?

3. Lexi and Erik eventually see ways in which their dad, Max, unintentionally hurt them when they were children. It took many years for them to realize this and take steps toward healing. How did your parents unintentionally hurt you? What steps did you take—or what steps do you need to take—in order for healing to occur?

4. If you are a parent, how have you unintentionally hurt your children? Have you, like Claire and Max, asked for their forgiveness? What was the response?

5. What things have been sown in your heart? What has been reaped? Identify the flowers and weeds.

6. What do you think about forgiveness and forgetting? Is it hard for you? Easy? Why?

7. Do you believe God wants to heal our deep wounds? How has He healed yours?

8. In the first book in this series, *A Time to Mend,* Claire and Max had to overcome some deep personal issues in order to heal their marriage and relationship. What progress do you see in Claire since then? In Max?

9. Like the Beaumont family members, the Hacienda Hideaway is still under construction. What would your ideal retreat center be like?

Reader comments are always welcome.
Please write in care of Thomas Nelson
or send an e-mail to sallyjohnbook@aol.com.